"It's rare that a book can provide snickers and shivers at the same time, but Dorsey's gut-busting tenth novel about psychopathic vigilante Serge Storms, a man who can kill while dispensing trivia about the *Queen Mary*, delivers both. . . . Is *Lobster* cerebral? Not quite. But it's wickedly fun. Grade: A-"

Entertainment Weekly

"You can't help but love the sociopathic killer in Tim Dorsey's books. But Serge Storms murders the white-collar swindlers you would want dead anyway. And he does it so creatively."

Fort Myers News-Press

"The story drips with satire, overflows with Florida lore, and is so wacky and chaotic that the plot cannot be summarized. . . . Somehow, it all ends up making sense. Sort of. . . . Clearly, *Atomic Lobster* is not for everyone. But if you think The Three Stooges would have been funnier if Moe, Larry, and Curley used chainsaws and automatic weapons, Tim Dorsey is your kind of writer."

Associated Press

"Read *Atomic Lobster*. . . . Expect sex, violence, and slapstick as Dorsey spins a story that's both cringe-inducing and comedic."

Atlanta Journal-Constitution

"Fiercely funny. . . . Serge may be mellowing, but once he gets up to speed on Lobster Lane, he's as gonzo as ever. . . . Just relax, and let Serge drive."

Orlando Sentinel

Tim Dorsey [is] totally insane. . . . As a book critic, I have a habit of penciling a little 'ha' in the margin of comedic novels to keep track of how often an author makes me laugh. Let's just say there are plenty of scribbles in the margin of *Atomic Lobster,* and that translates to a good time for Dorsey fans. . . . It's a wild ride."

Florida Today

"Agreeably ridiculous. . . . If you prefer the Three Tenors to the Three Stooges, *Atomic Lobster* may not be your flagon of mojito. But if you think strippers, smugglers, gunrunners, duplicitous dowagers and one comely 'accidental virgin' all on the same tropical playground might be fun, Dorsey can hook you up."

Raleigh News & Observer

"Dorsey's tenth novel to feature Serge A. Storms . . . offers sex, violence, more violence, and Three Stooges–like action. . . . While Dorsey's brand of comedy isn't for the faint of heart, this fast-moving, raucous tale delivers its usual punch while gleefully skewering everyone and everything along the way."

Publishers Weekly

"My name is Arthur and I'm a Tim Dorsey addict. . . . Wonderfully ingenious."

San Diego Union-Tribune

"Truly a whale of a tale. . . . A fun, slapstick action adventure."

Montgomery Advertiser

By Tim Dorsey

ATOMIC LOBSTER
HURRICANE PUNCH
THE BIG BAMBOO
TORPEDO JUICE
CADILLAC BEACH
THE STINGRAY SHUFFLE
TRIGGERFISH TWIST
ORANGE CRUSH
HAMMERHEAD RANCH MOTEL
FLORIDA ROADKILL

Forthcoming in hardcover
NUCLEAR JELLYFISH

Atomic LOBSTER

TIM DORSEY

HARPER

An Imprint of HarperCollinsPublishers

This book is a work of fiction. The characters, incidents, and dialogue are drawn from the author's imagination and are not to be construed as real. Any resemblance to actual events or persons, living or dead, is entirely coincidental.

HARPER

An Imprint of HarperCollins*Publishers*
10 East 53rd Street
New York, New York 10022-5299

Visit Harper paperbacks on the World Wide Web at
www.harpercollins.com

10 9 8 7 6 5 4 3 2 1

For Janine

Make gentle the life of this world.

—ROBERT F. KENNEDY

Atomic
LOBSTER

PROLOGUE

My name is Edith Grabowski. I'm ninety-one years old, and don't you even *think* of asking me if I had sex last night. Okay, I'll tell you. Might as well since we're only going to have to answer another gazillion stupid questions about it in a few minutes when the camera lights come on.

Yeah, I did. Twice. And it was better than a poke in the eye with a sharp stick. Now go get your own.

We're backstage again. I don't understand backstage food. Tiny sandwich triangles with the crusts cut off, water that fizzes. They say it's more expensive. The world sure has changed since I was a girl. But our agent wants us to be polite, seeing as how the sex questions are why we get insane money to do these TV shows.

It's all because of the crazy cruise we took out of Tampa that went berserk. I'm just amazed at what people get hung up on. There's a bunch more interesting parts to our story. I mean, *everything* happened on that ship. People falling overboard, stampedes in the casino, fires, explosions, dead bodies, drunk tourists gouging eyes over life preservers, and the whole boat nearly sinking, not to mention the secret agent named Foxtrot. That's right, a spy! What *didn't* this story have? You probably already recognize everyone else involved. Even if you were buried in an avalanche and didn't hear about the cruise, I'm sure you remember that big fiasco on Triggerfish Lane ten years ago. There's me and my girl-friends, of course, and who could forget Serge, that lunatic back from God knows where? Then there's Jim Davenport, the super-nice family man. Poor Jim Davenport. How much can one person take? We ended with not one, but two collid-ing horror shows: those nine mystery deaths traced to the smugglers, and the just-released ex-con on a murderous ram-page of revenge! The only common denominator was Dav-enport, who ended up smack in the middle of the trainwreck. Make that shipwreck. But all the talk shows want to hear about is boinking.

What I said before about the sharp stick? I'm not com-plaining. Tons of women my age would kill for a man, but the ratio is like fifty to one with life expectancy. And a lot of the guys who *are* left have to bring medical equipment. Nothing breaks the mood like getting tangled in the oxygen lines. My own Ambrose went in his sleep a few years back. Very peacefully. So I should count my blessings. And yes, the sex, except there's so much more to life. Viagra had its role in the beginning. But after a while, you know, enough. The entire country snickers at every mention of the V-word like it's the most *hilarious* thing they ever heard. Let me give you the skinny from where the rubber meets the road: Whoever called them granny-abuse pills wins the cigar.

Granny. Something else that needles me. This attitude toward old people. We're either the objects of kind pity or cruel wisecracks. Our hearing isn't as bad as you think: Blue-hair, God's waiting room, all those remarks about our driving. You know what we talk about when you're not around? Getting in a Buick and plowing through a bunch of young people, then acting confused. So we lose our license. So what? Keep telling your little jokes.

They just gave us the signal backstage. We're on in three. And here we are again, me and my girlfriends. Who'd have thought we'd get a second fifteen minutes? It all started back with our retiree investment club that outperformed most mutual funds. The press got a big kick out of our names—Edith, Edna, Eunice, Ethel—dubbed us the E-Team without even asking. So this time around it's in our contracts, our new name. We're turning that "granny" slur on its head.

There's the ten-second signal. We can hear the applause. Showtime.

They just opened the curtains.

"Please welcome the G-Unit! . . . "

SIX MONTHS EARLIER, MIDDLE OF THE NIGHT

"Serge," said Coleman. "I don't think you should have any more coffee."

"Get off my case."

"But you know how you get—"

"Fuck it. If I feel like singing to the hostage, I'll sing. He wants me to sing. . . ." Serge looked down. "You want me to sing, don't you? . . . See, Coleman?"

"Serge, he's just screaming his head off."

"I take that as an enthusiastic yes. . . . Next song, with apologies to Johnny Cash. . . . A one, and a two . . .

I've been everywhere, man; the Keys without a care,
   man;
Spring Break on a tear, man; the Florida State Fair,
   man . . .

Hialeah, Fernandina, Boca Chita, Panacea
Tallahassee, Chocoloskee, Miccosukee, Weeki Wachee
New Smyrna, Deltona, Marianna, Ozona.
Homosassa, Buena Vista, Punta Rassa, Pasadena
Floritan, Tamarac, Manalapan, De Funiak

Cintronelle, Titusville, Carrabelle, Chapel Hill
Port Salerno, Pensacola, Hypoluxo, Sarasota
Caya Costa, Gasparilla, Opa-Locka, I'm a killa . . .

I've been everywhere, man! . . . "

"Okay," said Coleman, "I got the next verse."
"Rock on."

"I've been like everywhere
And we went to a bunch of different places and got
    really stoned
Then we went to another place and got stoned again
And we met these other stoners and went somewhere
    else and ate tacos
And I lost my keys and we couldn't go anywhere, so
    we just got stoned
Then we ran out of weed, but I remembered my keys
    were in the other pocket,
and we went somewhere to score, and got stoned . . ."

"Coleman . . ."

"And more people came over, and we found a bag of
    marshmallows and made s'mores . . ."

"Stop!"

". . . Then the liquor store opened—"

"Shut up!"
"But there's more."
"I know."
"Serge?"

"What?"

"He's getting heavy. I don't know how much longer I can hold his ankle."

"Only a few more minutes." Serge looked over the railing of the interstate overpass at the man dangling upside down. "How's it going?"

"Dear God! Don't drop me! I swear I won't do it again!"

"Serge," said Coleman. "My wrists are tired."

"Almost finished."

Coleman freed one hand and wiped a sweaty palm on the front of his shirt, then grabbed the leg again. "But this isn't like you. Dropping a guy doesn't seem as . . . what's the word I'm looking for?"

"Clever?"

"That's it."

"Oh, I'm not going to kill him."

"Then what are we doing out here?"

"This is Serge's Charm School. We're teaching manners."

A semi whizzed under the bridge. Whimpering below: *"Please . . . "*

"Coleman, what do you think? Give him a second chance?"

"He seems sincere."

"Okay, I guess we can hoist him back. Just let him hang one more minute for positive reinforcement. . . ."

Behind them on the isolated bridge sat their Key-lime '73 Mercury Comet with the doors open. Suddenly, loud cursing from the backseat.

"Uh-oh," said Serge. "Must have regained consciousness."

A six-foot-tall femme fatale leaped from the car. Breathing fire. And that's not all that was hot: she was a knee-buckling vision from every guy's deepest fantasy, innocently cute and sinfully sexual, all curves, freckles, wild blond hair flowing down over her black sports bra.

Rachael.

The kind of woman that makes men wake up dazed on the side of the road with mysterious welts and no wallet, and walk away happy. Serge had seen her type before. Very specifically, in fact, and he knew how to handle them. Like rattlesnakes. Never turn your back.

"Shit," said Serge. "I turned my back. Quick, pull him over the railing."

Rachael had legs that wouldn't quit, and now they were in full gallop.

"Motherfucker! You never slap me! You never put a fucking hand on me! . . . " She reached the edge of the bridge and elbowed Serge hard in the ribs.

"Ooooffff." Serge stumbled sideways, the wind knocked out.

She bent down and sunk her teeth into Coleman's left hand.

"Ow!" He reeled backward and cradled the bloody paw to his chest.

Serge regained his breath and ran to the railing. He looked down. "Whoops."

Coleman joined him and leaned over. "Where'd he go?"

"I don't know."

They spun and ran to the other side of the overpass. Still no sign. Serge sprinted to the end of the bridge and scampered down the embankment. Moments later, he returned at a casual pace.

"See him?" asked Coleman.

Serge shook his head. "Vanished into thin air." He turned to Rachael. "Jesus. Why'd you do that?"

"That motherfucker slapped me!"

"And you just kill him?"

"You never motherfuckin' hit a woman!"

"How could he have missed your dedication of feminine virtue, especially when you keep saying motherfucker?"

Coleman stared down over the rail at three dark lanes leading north from Bradenton. "What do we do now?"

"I'm hungry." Serge grabbed the car keys. "Let's hit Jack's."

TWENTY MILES AWAY

Johnny Vegas had an erection stronger than pestles pharmacists use to mash pills. He told himself he'd finally arrived at the gates of the Promised Land. Her name was Jasmine. Her pants were at half-mast.

They'd met an hour earlier at a Waffle House in Pinellas Park. The attraction was inevitable. Johnny had the thick black mane and sizzling Latin appeal of a hairstyling poster in Supercuts. Jasmine was a world-record nympho in her weight division. Her specialty, she told Johnny, was strategically positioning herself in public so she could "get banged silly" while talking to other people who had no idea what was going on below her waistline.

"But how is that possible?" asked Johnny.

She told him.

He coughed up diet Sprite and pounded his sternum with a fist.

Johnny had his own unique trait, which he judiciously omitted. The Promised Land business was no joke. You'd never guess it from his square-jawed *Playboy* features, but there had been much wandering in the sexual wilderness. An entire lifetime. It wasn't his come-ons or bedside manner. It was math. The equation between sales pitch and closing the deal. Somewhere out there, some guy in America had to fall at the bottom of the last percentile, cursed with absolutely the worst imaginable luck.

He was Johnny Vegas, the Accidental Virgin.

It was always something. Some kind of crazy, long-shot interruption at the precise moment of penetration that wrecked the delicate surface tension. And in Florida, the possibilities were endless: hurricanes, alligator attacks, brush fires, police manhunts, train derailments, roving bands of escaped monkeys, federal agents seizing Cuban children, and election recounts.

But, an hour after leaving the Waffle House, as Johnny wiggled Harley-Davidson panties down her legs, something told him this time would be different. She had just clocked in for work.

Jasmine's job required her to stand at a gate rising just above her navel, which required Johnny to lie on his back, contorted across two chairs. He fumbled in the dark and initiated clumsy foreplay. Jasmine moaned. Her eyes closed and head tilted back. A yellow light flashed across Johnny's face. Metal clanged. *"Yes. More to the right. That's it. Ooooh . . . "*

An unseen voice. "Ma'am, are you okay?"

Johnny froze. Jasmine opened her eyes. "Couldn't be better."

"Looked like you were about to faint."

"Just tired. Still not used to the night shift."

A car could be heard driving off. Another vehicle approached. Johnny froze again. The driver handed Jasmine a five. She made change and gave him a receipt. "Have a nice evening. . . ."

The car sped away from Jasmine's toll lane, the only one left open at this hour.

"Johnny, you can't keep stopping every time people come through. That misses the whole point."

"Sorry."

A late-model Cadillac Escalade headed north on Interstate 275. It reached the causeway near the mouth of Tampa Bay.

"You should have left earlier," said Martha.

"We'll be home soon," said Jim.

The Davenports. Good people. Jim and Martha. Martha was the consummate soccer mom whose emotional fuse matched her fiery red hair. Jim complemented her with an unflappable temperament, which made her madder. Everything about Jim screamed Mr. Average, except for one characteristic that distinguished him from almost everyone else. He was the most nonconfrontational resident of Tampa Bay, maybe the entire state.

"Isn't this route longer?" asked Martha.

"A little, but there's less traffic." Jim responsibly checked the speedometer. "And it's more scenic. We get to drive over the Skyway."

"Jim! We don't have time to sightsee!" said Martha. "It's after midnight!"

"Won't be much longer."

"Why didn't you leave earlier?"

"Honey, they're *your* parents."

"That's why I need you to say something. You know how I get with my mother."

"I know."

"What's that mean?"

"Baby, I'm agreeing."

Martha folded her arms. "This happens every time we go to Sarasota."

"Your mom's not that bad," said Jim.

"Are you trying to make me mad?"

"Okay, she is."

"I knew it. You've never liked her."

"What's the right answer?"

"So you're just telling me what I want to hear?"

Jim reached over and put a hand on his wife's. "I love you."

"I'm sorry. It's just every visit with my mom. Sticking her nose into how we raise our kids . . ."

"That's natural."

". . . All those supposedly idle comments. She rehearses them, you know."

"I know."

"Then her stall tactics when we're trying to leave. Why didn't you do something?"

"I did," said Jim. "I unlocked the car. You're the one who stood in the driveway talking to her for an hour."

"That's her Driveway Strategy. She compiles lists of important topics that are conveniently forgotten until we're out of the house. And now, here we are again, heading home at some ungodly hour with all the drunks."

"Maybe we should just stay over at her place if you don't like heading back so late."

"No! That's a worse nightmare! We can't just leave in the morning. She cooks a giant breakfast even though we tell her not to. Then we have to sit and talk a polite period afterward because she made breakfast. And *then* when it's time to leave, she springs the surprise guests."

"Surprise guests?"

"Jim, she does it every time: 'You can't leave now. The Jensens are on their way over.' 'Mom, you didn't tell us that.' 'They're on their way. You don't want to insult them.' 'We don't even know the Jensens.' 'You met once. They're dying to see you after all these years.' 'Mom, we really have to be going.' 'What am I supposed to tell the Jensens?' 'Who the hell are the Jensens?' . . ."

Jim drank in the calm view over the night water. "Look, there's a cruise ship. Maybe we should take a vacation."

"You're changing the subject."

"No, really. I'd love to go on another cruise. Remember the fun we had last time?"

"Jim!"

"It'll be better when we get home."

"It'll be the same when we get home. This whole state's driving me crazy."

"I thought you said you loved it here."

"I do. It's the most beautiful place I've ever lived."

"What's the problem?"

"It's the worst place I've ever lived. Just running around during the day doing chores, I see all these psychotics out on the street. We've had three burglaries this month in our neighborhood, they robbed the convenience store where I buy milk, that stockbroker got shot at the car wash I jog by every day, and some lawn-care guy was charged with those unsolved rapes. We're nuts not to leave."

"Honey, society's changed. It's like this everywhere."

"It's not like *this* everywhere. I always think I'm watching the local news when it's CNN or Fox. Half the stories are from down here. I saw one where this guy was dumped by his girlfriend, so he made copies of a sex tape they'd filmed of themselves, went to the department store where she worked, stuck them in all the VCRs in the electronics department and cranked up the volume on twenty TVs. The whole store ground to a halt. Except the ex-girlfriend, who ran screaming into the parking lot and got run over by the security cart."

"That's not dangerous, just weird."

"Jim, someone like that's capable of anything."

"But we live in one of the safest neighborhoods in town."

"Have you forgotten what happened ten years ago?"

"Right, it was *ten years ago*."

"It was a home invasion!"

"Honey, I know it was rough. That's why we saw those doctors. But it was just a freak thing."

"It can happen again."

"Anything can happen. We live in a big American city.

And you're right: lots of crazies out there. That's why it's important to avoid conflict with people we know nothing about. Then we'll be fine."

Martha took a deep breath and stared out the window. "Sometimes I think they won't give us that chance. I always have this creepy feeling, like, how many times a day am I brushing up against some time bomb and don't even know it? Could it be this guy in front of me in the checkout line, the people in that car passing us? . . ."

A '73 Mercury Comet flew by on the left.

Coleman was behind the wheel. Serge and Rachael were slap-fighting in the backseat. They had just finished fucking, which meant creative differences: After sex Rachael like to get wasted, and Serge like to drive over big bridges. They struck an unstable truce.

"Pilot change!" yelled Serge.

"Roger!" Coleman hit the brakes. Doors flew open. They raced around the car on the shoulder of the highway. The Comet slung gravel and took off again.

Coleman ended up in back with Rachael, instantly smoking joints, chugging a pint of sour mash and snorting stuff off their wrists. A large bridge appeared in the distance. Serge smacked the dashboard. "This is excellent! Isn't this excellent? Bridges are the best! This one has gobs of history! I know all about it! Want me to tell you? I'll tell you! It was twenty years ago today, Sergeant Pepper—"

"Shut the fuck up!" yelled Rachael.

"But he taught the band to play."

Rachael's head bent back down. "You're an asshole."

"I know you are, but what am I?" Serge rocked with childlike enthusiasm in the driver's seat, keeping rhythm with red beacons flashing atop suspension cables. "And look! There's a cruise ship! She's just about to pass under the

bridge! Isn't that great? We should take a cruise! You want
to take a cruise? Let's take a cruise! . . ."

"Shut up!"

"I absolutely must have photos!" Serge pulled over.

"You idiot!" yelled Rachael. "Keep driving." Her head
went back down.

Serge unloaded gear from the trunk and set up a tripod
on the west side of the causeway for time-lapse night pho-
tography. He held a shutter-release cable in his right hand
and pressed the plunger with his thumb. Tick, tick, tick, tick,
tick . . . Click. He advanced the frame.

Coleman walked over with his hands in his pockets.
"What'cha doin'?"

"Just gettin' my Serge on." He pressed the plunger again.
Tick, tick . . . "Look at all the beautiful twinkling deck
lights on that ship." Click. "Wonder what those people are
up to?"

A harbor pilot guided the SS *Serendipity* into the mouth of
Tampa Bay. A handful of passengers still awake at this hour
huddled on the chilly bow, admiring the majestic sight as
they passed under the Skyway.

At the opposite end of the ship, three isolated people
weren't paying attention to the massive overhead span
sweeping the moon's dim shadow over the deck.

"Chop, chop!" said Tommy Diaz. "We're almost into the
bay."

The other Diaz Brothers continued tossing weighted garbage bags of body parts over the fantail. The ship passed to
the other side of the bridge as the last evidence hit the dark,
foaming water of the propeller wake. Tommy Diaz finally
allowed himself to relax. He looked up at the Skyway and
an eight-ball-black '91 Buick Electra slowly cresting the
peak of the bridge.

The Buick crawled down the backside of the Skyway and finally eased into a toll lane, where a woman with eyes closed was banging the outside of her booth's metal door. *"Yes! . . . Yes! . . . Oh God yes! . . . Someone's coming! . . . Now! Put it in now! . . . "* Jasmine opened her eyes at the sound of the approaching vehicle.

She let out a heart-stopping scream.

Minutes later, no less than a dozen highway patrol cars surrounded a '91 Buick Electra parked on the side of the road just beyond the toll booth.

A hysterical Jasmine sat on a curb, consoled by a female officer.

Johnny Vegas leaned against a boulder on the other side of the causeway, staring out to sea.

A bulky state trooper in a Smokey the Bear hat stood in the toll plaza's office, questioning four short, white-haired women. He flipped a page in his notebook and pointed out the window at an ambulance crew gathered around two legs sprouting from the Buick's windshield. "And you have no recollection whatsoever of hitting him?"

"One minute he wasn't there," said Edith, "then he was."

"What did you think happened?"

"Maybe he fell from the sky."

Edna tugged the trooper's sleeve. "She always talked about plowing into people."

Another trooper entered the office. "Sir, we have witness reports of someone falling or jumping from an overpass near Bradenton."

The first trooper turned to Edith. "Did you come up through Bradenton tonight?"

She nodded.

"But that's over twenty miles. You just kept driving?"

"I'm confused."

The trooper looked back out the window as a Key-lime '73 Mercury Comet came off the bridge and pulled up to one of the booths.

Coleman gestured with a beer toward the side of the road. "There's a dude sticking through a windshield."

Serge threw change in the toll basket. "Florida happens."

THE DAY BEFORE THE INCIDENT AT THE
SUNSHINE SKYWAY BRIDGE

*T*en A.M. Soon, the regular afternoon sun showers would roll in from the east to cool things down. But for now, another sticky, cloudless morning in Tampa. Palm trees. Broken taillight glass. No wind. Minimum-wage people perspired under a covered bus stop at the southern end of the transit line. A '73 Mercury Comet entered the parking lot of a decaying shopping center and headed up a row of tightly packed cars.

Coleman twisted a fat one in his lips. "I'm bored."

"Just keep an eye out for cops." The Mercury reached the end of the row, made a U-turn and started up another. Serge assessed each empty vehicle, but nothing felt right.

"What about your first plan?" asked Coleman, flicking a Bic. "You said it would definitely work."

"It did." Serge glanced down at the Macy's sack atop the drivetrain hump on the floor between their feet. "Line the inside of a shopping bag by gluing ten layers of aluminum foil, then more strips along the seams. Guaranteed to defeat most stores' security detectors."

"What did you steal?"

"More foil. I ran out making my bag."

"Being broke sucks."

"Just watch for cops."

The Comet turned up another row.

"See anything?" asked Coleman.

"No."

"Then why are you smiling?"

"Because I *love* this shopping center. Britton Plaza." Serge pointed his camera out the windshield. "Note the giant, fifties-era arch over the sign. Not many left." Click. "And that movie theater. Sidewalks got jack-hammered in front of all the other stores for new ones, but they preserved the original marbleized pavement in front of the cinema with its metal inlays of happy-sad thespian masks, which I can never get enough of and—Hold everything!"

"What is it? Why are you slowing?"

"That old woman with the walker. Range, fifty yards." He reached under his seat for a crowbar.

"Serge! It's an old lady!"

"I'm not going to hit *her*." He rolled down his window and rested the steel shaft on the door frame. "Timing's absolutely crucial."

"What's happening?"

"Watch carefully. It'll all be over in a blink."

"I don't see anything. What am I supposed to be looking for? . . . Holy shit! That punk just nailed her in the face and snatched her purse!"

Serge didn't answer, his foot twitching on the gas pedal.

"He's running toward us!" yelled Coleman.

"Steady . . . steady . . . Now!" Serge hit the accelerator. Tires squealed. He swung the crowbar, clothes-lining the thief in the Adam's apple. Legs flew out. A body slammed to the pavement. The Comet stopped.

Serge opened the door and herded stray contents back into the purse. He returned to the car, driving a few seconds to a group of Good Samaritans who'd run to the woman's aid.

"Hey!" yelled Serge, hanging out the driver's window and twirling the handbag by its strap like a lasso. "Here's her purse. Catch . . ."

Serge slammed the gearshift in reverse. The Comet squiggled backward and screeched to a halt next to an unsteady man trying to get his footing.

Serge jumped out again. "Let me help you up." A knee to the crotch. "Coleman, the trunk."

"I'm on it."

A half minute later, the Comet skidded out of the parking lot and turned north on Dale Mabry Highway. "That *really* pissed me off."

"Me too," said Coleman. "I couldn't believe what I was seeing."

"It's the decline of the Florida shopping experience." Serge sped up to make a yellow light. "Old ladies getting mugged, no more S&H Green Stamps."

The Gulf of Mexico was typically serene, rippling with a leisurely wake behind the SS *Serendipity* on its return voyage from Cozumel. Three hundred miles to the mouth of Tampa Bay. A row of luxury suites on the port side faced the shimmering water. The second cabin from the end, number 6453, was registered to three Latin men in white linen suits. They were accompanied by a fourth occupant, decidedly against his will. Heels dragged across the carpet as the others muscled him into the bathroom.

"But I delivered the shipment just like you said! Didn't you get it?"

"We got it," said Tommy Diaz. He hung a trifold canvas case from the shower head and unsnapped it. The bag fell open to reveal a nineteen-piece kitchen cutlery set.

"W-w-what are those for?" asked the guest, now pinned to the bottom of the tub.

"Rafael, tape his mouth."

"Wait! Stop! Just hold on a second! . . . I don't understand. I did everything I was supposed to. You said you got the shipment."

Tommy pulled the largest carving knife from its sheath, touching the tip with his finger. "And don't think it's not appreciated."

"Then why are you doing this?"

"Because you know about the shipment."

Tape went over the mouth. The hostage's terrified eyes looked up at a trio of faces looking back down: the Diaz Brothers. Tommy, Rafael and Benito. Used to be the Diaz *Boys*, ten years ago when cousin Juan was involved. Juan was allowed in the gang because they swore to his mom that they'd treat him like a brother. Then Juan died in a tragic hurricane accident when they wouldn't let him into a cramped storm shelter because he was the cousin. That left them short with only two, so they let baby brother Benito into the gang like Andy Gibb.

"Rafael," said Tommy. "Turn up the stereo. This could get noisy."

" . . . *Send lawyers, guns and money . . .* "

"Hey, Tommy. It's the Z-man."

"Will you get back in here? He's a wiggler."

"Listen to all that racket he's making," said Rafael, "even with the mouth tape."

"This will quiet him down," said Tommy. "Hold those shoulders still."

" . . . *get me out of this! . . .* "

Tommy thrust with a firm crossing motion.

"Goddammit!" said Rafael. "Look at my new shirt!"

"Told you to hold him still," said Tommy. "It's like you've never worked with arterial spray before."

"I'll teach him to fuck up my threads!" Rafael reached for the cutlery set. "Bleed on me, motherfucker? . . . Take this! . . . And this! . . . And this! . . . And this! . . ."

"Rafael," Tommy said calmly. "What do you think you're doing?"

"What?" said Rafael, wiping red specks off his face with a cruise line bathrobe.

"What do you mean, 'What?'"

Rafael pointed at the tub with the knife. "The same thing you were doing."

"No," said Tommy. "What I did was business." He gestured with an upturned palm. "This is sick."

Benito tapped Tommy's shoulder from behind. "Is it my turn?"

"Turn?" said Tommy. "Are you blind? Look at this bloody mess. There's no 'turn' left to take." He twisted a faucet and washed his hands in the sink. "I can't believe we have the same parents."

"Why are you so sore?" asked Benito.

Tommy tapped his left temple with an index finger. "I try to teach you, but fuck it. You can chop him up yourselves this time."

TWO

THAT EVENING

𝒮erge worked efficiently in the dark with thick coils of rope. At this late hour he had the whole place to himself, just Coleman, the mugger and a steady drone of unseen traffic beyond the trees on Interstate 75. Serge finished the last knot and picked up a paper bag. Inside was a handkerchief gag and a tangelo orange.

"I swear!" said the punk. "I won't do it again!"

"I know." The gag went in the punk's mouth. The orange was for Serge. He began peeling. "Coleman, tighten the line to that post. . . . Coleman? . . . Where'd that idiot go?"

Something that sounded like a lawnmower engine chugged to life. Serge turned around; he stopped peeling the orange. "Unbelievable."

The noise grew louder as Serge approached a low rubber barrier. Coleman whizzed by: "Hcy, Serge. I hot-wired it! . . ."

Serge waited until his pal made another lap around the go-cart track. Red car number eight came through turn four. Serge reached back and fired his orange like a split-finger fastball.

"Ow!"

The cart spun out and crashed into a retaining wall of threadbare tires, ending up on its side. Coleman unbuckled his seat belt and spilled onto the track. He stood, rubbing his shoulder. "Dang it, Serge! Why'd you throw that at me?"

"Because I need your help. And you owe me an orange."

They began walking. Coleman picked between his teeth at a stubborn popcorn husk that he'd just remembered from the other day. "I'm still surprised at how you noticed the mugger. I never saw it coming."

"To survive down here, you have to think like an air-traffic controller, constantly tracking everyone around you at all times. I had my eye on that asshole ever since he walked onto the parking lot from the highway."

"Why?"

"Because if you're in a parking lot and shit's about to break, it's most likely coming on foot from the street. Now tighten the line on that post."

"It's already tight."

"Needs to be tighter."

"Why?"

"So he can't tip his chair over. Then my whole plan falls apart."

Coleman pulled hard on the knot. "This is why I got bored and went over to the go-cart track. It's taking way longer than your other projects."

Serge pulled on his own line. "Because I'm sending a strong message to his buddies."

"But he was by himself."

"It's a 'To whom it may concern.' " Serge fished a paper-wrapped cylinder from his pocket.

"You're using a whole roll of quarters?" asked Coleman.

"It's a detailed message."

Muted screams from under the hostage's gag.

"Shut up and like it," said Serge. "Mugging old ladies is the lowest."

"Yeah," said Coleman. "Good thing we were driving around looking for cars to break into."

Serge retrieved bolt-cutters from the Comet and ran off into the dark. He snipped the lock from a fuse box and threw breakers. Then he returned and stepped up to a chest-high metal control box and cracked open the quarters. Coins clanged through a slot at a steady pace. A finger pressed the start button.

Serge and Coleman sat cross-legged on the ground behind the safety net. The neon sign over their heads was dark:

FUN-O-RAMA.

In front of them, a machine cranked to life with rhythmic mechanical cadence. Behind them, the soothing hum of interstate traffic on the other side of a berm. Tractor-trailers, SUVs, sports cars, sedans, all racing around a '91 Buick Electra going thirty miles under the speed limit in the left lane.

"Why is it taking so long to get home?" asked Eunice.

"She's driving slow again," said Edna.

"Why are you driving so slow?" asked Eunice.

"I am not driving slow!" said Edith, her seat all the way up to reach the pedals.

"Everyone's passing us."

"Can you even see over the dashboard?"

"I'm taller than you, bee-ach."

"You've shrunk."

"Shut up! I'm trying to concentrate!"

"Are you going the right way?"

"I don't think she's going the right way."

"I know what I'm doing!"

"We're supposed to be going north," said Eunice.

"I think she's going south."

"You want to walk?" asked Edith. "I'll pull over right now."

"She had too many gins at dinner."

"I did not!"

"Is that why you're driving the wrong way with the blinker on?"

Edith looked around the side of the steering column. "Shoot." She hit a lever.

"We're still going south."

"I'm going north!"

Eunice pointed at the giant floating ball attached to the dashboard with a suction cup. "That's not what the compass says."

"Must be mounted backward," said Edith.

"The ball's floating," said Edna. "It doesn't matter how you mount it."

"Everyone shut up! I know where I'm going!"

"South."

LATER THAT EVENING

Coleman moaned through another five-star pass-out. Against long-shot odds, he had made it back to his bed. Bunk bed to be specific, bottom unit. The top mattress belonged to Serge. It was empty.

Another groan and eyes fluttered open. Serge's face was six inches away.

"Ahhhhhh!" Coleman pushed himself up. "You scared me."

"I can't sleep."

Coleman climbed out of bed and grabbed his bong. "How long were you staring at me?"

"Hour."

Coleman prepared to pack the pipe. He stopped and held the bowl to his eye. "What happened to the screen?" He began going through the carpet.

"Why can't I sleep?" said Serge.

"The dope will pull right through without a screen."

"Let's go do something."

"I know." Coleman snapped his fingers. "I'll get a screen off the sink faucet."

"Where should we go?" Serge walked over to the bookshelf and his collection of vintage *National Geographic*s with every issue since 1905 containing a feature on Florida.

"What the—?" Coleman stuck his pinkie up through the end of the faucet. "Someone already took the screen."

"I got it." Serge examined the magazines' spines. "We'll pick a place at random from one of the articles."

Coleman slumped in a chair. "What kind of loser would take a screen from a faucet?"

"Coke whore used to rent here."

"So?"

"A forensic team couldn't comb a place better for paraphernalia."

"I'll just use stems to block the hole."

Time passed. Serge turned pages. Water bubbled in a tube. A knock at the door. Coleman looked up. "You expecting anyone?"

"No," said Serge. "Unless it's that guy I've been waiting for my entire life."

"Which guy's that?"

"The one who knocks on the door and says, 'Your existence has just changed totally and for the better. Please come with me.'"

"Never heard of him."

"Neither have I," said Serge. "That's what separates me from the rest of society. A lot of people *say* they're into hope, but they aim too low."

Coleman repacked the bong. "I'm into hope."

"Like when you give yourself date-rape drugs?"

"I could get lucky." He held a lighter over the bowl. "I might have already, but that's the thing: Who knows?"

"Coleman, never mock hope. You might jinx it, and the Hope Guy will knock somewhere else."

Coleman flicked his lighter. "I hope some super-hot chick with low morals shows up for no reason and climbs into my bed."

Knock-knock-knock.

"Coming! . . . "

Serge opened the door. A potbellied redneck in a mesh-back camo cap swayed drunkenly under the naked-bulb porch light. Serge raised his eyebrows. "Are you the Hope Guy?"

"What?"

"To change my life. I'm ready to be taken away. Thought you'd look different, maybe have a name tag or a cape with lightning bolts."

The redneck squinted. "Who are you?"

"Serge. Next question."

The man looked past him into the room. "Is Sunshine here?"

"She moved out."

"I'm one of her regulars."

"She's gone."

From inside the room: "Is it that guy?"

"No. Someone looking for the hooker who used to live here. He's hopeless."

"See if he has my faucet screen."

The man continued wobbling on the porch, unfocused eyes begging Serge for something to cling to.

Serge shrugged. "Sorry. New management. This is now a think tank."

The man bit his lip, turned and weaved off across the dark dirt yard. The door closed. An exhaled cloud drifted along the ceiling. "Serge?"

"What?"

"Why are we living in this dump?"

"It's not a dump."

"A coke whore used to live here."

"Something else that separates me from society: Super-

Positive Perspective! Where normal people would whine about subpar accommodations, I choose to view it as upscale camping."

"Why are we in Sarasota?"

"Just temporary. Heat's on up north."

Coleman looked around their tight confines, the last of three units chopped up from a sixty-year-old clapboard house. Micro-fridge, hot plate, bunk bed, bookshelf, lawn chairs, five-inch black-and-white TV on a citrus crate. The single window faced a high-crime alley, but it was broken and boarded shut. "I've never seen such a tiny apartment."

Serge grabbed another magazine. "It's an efficiency."

"It's tiny."

"You know what rent is in Sarasota?"

"I thought you said this city was classy."

"It is—"

A rustling sound from the other side of the closed bathroom door. Serge reached under the sink for a plunger and fire extinguisher.

Coleman looked up from his bong. "What's that noise?"

"The rat's back."

"Rat?"

Serge spread his arms. "Huge motherfucker. Must have left the toilet seat up again. Drinks out of it like a Saint Bernard."

"If it's so big, how does he get in?"

"Wood's started to rot." Serge put on safety goggles. "You know in the corner where the floor is, like, gone? And you can see out into the yard?"

"What's the fire extinguisher for?"

"To blind him and make it a fair fight." Serge grabbed the doorknob, counted under his breath and burst into the bathroom. *"Unleash the dogs of war! . . . "*

The door slammed shut. Terrible crashing sounds. Coleman reached into his Baggie and picked apart a bud. Thuds against the walls. Something shattered. Banging sounds. Serge screamed. More pounding. Profanity. A crash.

Then it was eerily quiet. The door opened; Serge came out panting.

"What happened?" asked Coleman.

"I didn't want to do it, but he hated me for my freedom." Serge raised his right hand, dangling the trophy by its tail.

"Jesus!" said Coleman. "It's as big as my head!"

Serge walked toward the front door with the rodent. "What were we talking about?"

"How classy Sarasota is. Where are you going?"

"Dispose of the body."

"Wait for me. . . ." Coleman trotted out into the yard.

Serge slung the rat, and it landed on a big trash pile of dried leaves and other yard waste. He stood and stared.

"What are you waiting for?"

"Making sure he's dead. Don't want to fight this battle twice."

"I can make sure he's dead." Coleman pulled the lighter from his pocket. "Let's set him on fire. It'll be cool."

"No!" Serge threw out both arms in alarm. "Whatever you do!"

"But people are always burning yard waste."

"That's what the guy up in Hillsborough thought."

"What guy?"

"Made all the papers. True story: Some homeowner's burning a yard pile just like this one. And he goes inside for lemonade and opens the cabinet under the sink to toss something in the trash, and this rat's down in the bottom, gnawing a chicken bone. The rat had been driving the guy crazy for months, living in the walls and scampering through the attic at night like it had combat boots. So the guy grabs a rolling pin and beats it to death. Then he takes it outside and throws it on the burning pile."

"Good story," said Coleman. "What's the problem?"

"The rat's not dead. The heat wakes him up. It jumps off the pile and makes a beeline for the house. Except now its fur's on fire. The homeowner tries to intercept, but it zips between his legs, runs back inside and gets in the walls. Ignited the insulation. Whole place burned down."

 **THREE**

e're still going south."

"Will you shut up?"

"Edith, this is why you're not supposed to mix alcohol with prescriptions."

Edna twisted open a small plastic pill bottle in the backseat. "Makes mine work better."

"But you're not driving. . . . Gimme one."

"Here."

Eunice tossed it back. "Got something to chase?"

She passed a coffee mug. "Tanqueray."

"Oh, that reminds me!" said Eunice. "Heard the greatest dirt on Mildred. Guy at the liquor store told me."

"Which one?"

"Speedy Turtle Package."

"No, which Mildred?"

"Bingo Hall Mildred. Chuck who works the drive-through says she pulls up every morning with such regularity he can set his watch. Always has her order waiting in a bag—three Seagram's airline miniatures. She's got this travel mug on her console and starts pouring while driving away. Then she turns the corner and it's quiet. The package guys listen and there's three clangs in the Dumpster."

"That's terrible. Why do they keep selling to her?"

"Chuck said they'd go out of business. Apparently it's across the board: All day long, all our neighbors from the condo pull through on their way back from the pharmacy, Dumpster clanging nonstop until the early-bird special."

"Nothing happens?"

"Society's still in the dark about us. People think the bad driving is just poor reflexes, when half of us are completely gassed. . . ."

". . . Like our southbound driver."

"I'm not going to warn you again!"

"But Edith, what if the cops stop you and notice your breath?"

"They won't," said Eunice. "She just had a permanent."

"Ethel," said Edna. "You've been awfully quiet."

"Shhhh. I'm adding."

"Still with those numbers?"

Ethel continued jotting on a legal pad under a map light. Travel brochures cluttered the seat next to her. She finished the arithmetic. "Figures work out again. We should definitely try it."

"Let me see that." Edna grabbed the pad. "You're saying we can actually live cheaper on a cruise ship than in a retirement home?"

"I was skeptical, too, but the key is using the industry's business model against itself. They discount cabin rates as a loss leader and make a killing in the casinos and bars."

"But we drink."

"We'll smuggle bottles from the duty-free shops in port."

"Still sounds too good to be true."

Eunice pointed out the window. "There's the sign for Venice."

"Edith," said Edna. "You know where Venice is?"

No answer.

"Sixty miles south," said Eunice.

More silence.

"Edith? . . ."

"So I went a little south. Shoot me."

"Here's an exit coming up," said Ethel.

"You *are* going to take the exit?" said Eunice.

"Or she can just keep driving and at a theoretical point we'll start going north again."

Edith hit her blinker. "Cunts."

Three passengers in harmony: "Ooooooooooo."

The Buick curled down through a three-quarter-loop ramp.

"I'm telling you." Ethel tapped her notepad. "We could save a fortune."

They went under the overpass and back up a ramp.

"There's got to be a catch," said Edna. "It can't be this easy."

"Check the numbers yourself when we get back."

It became quiet in the car. Two red taillights faded into the night. A Fort Myers sign went by.

"Edith, what ramp did you take?"

"Why?"

"We're still going south . . . and headlights are coming at us."

Serge washed rat blood off his hands in the apartment sink.

Knock-knock-knock.

Coleman looked up from rolling papers. "Who now?"

Serge opened the door.

The potbellied redneck. "Know where she might have gone?"

"Yeah, away. If you hurry, you might catch her."

He closed the door.

Knock-knock-knock.

Serge opened. "You really have to stop knocking."

"But what if I don't find her?"

"Can't you just use your, you know . . ."

The man looked down in thought. "I forgot about that." He staggered away.

Serge waved. "Good luck."

Coleman became involved in a full-bong resin-scrape. "Why'd you have to pick the worst part of town?"

Serge reached for the bookshelf and gently removed a first-edition hardcover in a clear-plastic library-dust-jacket protector. He turned it toward Coleman.

"Midnight Pass?"

"Another Stuart Kaminsky masterstroke," said Serge. "Takes place right here in Sarasota."

"Who?"

"You know the Dairy Queen on the corner with U.S. 301?"

"I check their pay phone every day for change."

"Kaminsky's protagonist, Lew Fonesca, works in a building behind the Dairy Queen."

"So?"

"This house is also behind the D.Q. It's like we're living next door to a literary landmark." Serge carefully replaced the book on the shelf. "Can't believe the landlord isn't charging extra."

"How'd you find this pad to begin with?"

"Sharon used to live here."

Coleman stopped scraping. "You don't mean *the* Sharon."

Serge nodded. "Sometimes there'd be a little stink at the strip club in Tampa, like when she'd set up guys for us to rob, and we'd have to lay low down here with one of her friends who rented this joint."

"Where was I at the time?"

"You were here, too. I say that loosely." Serge opened another *National Geographic*. "Might want to start getting yourself together."

"For what?"

"The Night Launch. I can't sleep."

"Don't you mean Night *Tour*?"

"A direct offshoot of the Night Tour, but with critical distinctions."

"Man, if it's anything like a Night Tour, count me in! What happens?"

They grabbed chairs and took seats facing each other. Serge rubbed his palms together. "Okay, this is going to be so excellent. You know the concept of the Night Tour?"

"Intimately."

"Same idea except way more insane."

"But Serge! How is that even possible?"

"It starts when you're up in the middle of the night with insomnia. All societal conditioning says you must keep trying to get back to sleep because you have obligations in the morning. But the Night Launch says: Break the chains! Jump in your car and drive as far as you can! Watch the sun come up, then keep on truckin' into the next day, reality bent through the lens of sleep-deprived adventure! Never felt so alive! But you don't want to make a habit of it if you plan on owning a big house someday."

"What started the Night Launch?"

"Limits of the human brain. I'm perpetually contemplating life's mysteries, but God's put us on a no-fly list when it comes to all the big questions."

"Like, 'Why are we here?'"

"Please. I figured that out in third grade. I'm talking relativity, the daily transactions between mass and energy, when does inanimate matter make the jump to self-aware life? Got so frustrated one night I just jumped in the car and took off without knowing it was the first Night Launch. Three days later, I'm still awake in this state park, staring at a stone and a squirrel. What's the connection? Come on, concentrate. Looking back and forth: stone, squirrel, stone, squirrel . . . Blam! Hit me between the eyes! There *is* no jump. Life's already there, locked in the charges and orbits of subatomic particles, yearning to become more complex."

"Stones are alive?"

"Remember the Pet Rock? Everyone thought it was a joke. Except me. Bought mine at a Walgreen's. We were inseparable."

"Did it have a name?"

"Rocky. Went everywhere together. Finally he died. But since he was a rock, I didn't notice for a week. Of course a few days later, you know, it was just obvious."

"Were you taking your medication?"

"No. Anyway, I buried him on a warm summer afternoon. Terribly sad. I was going to get him a headstone, but then I'd have to bury that, and then bury that, and then that, and then I'm at the end of my life with a shovel and a long beard. So instead I bought a turtle. People laugh at turtles, but they're existentially unambiguous."

Coleman held a toke. "Where are we going on this launch?"

"Haven't decided yet. But check this out." He spread several magazines across the floor. "*National Geographic* is the best! Look at the progression of these articles: January 1940, 'South Florida's Amazing Everglades', October 1967, 'Threatened Glories of Everglades National Park'; January 1972, 'The Imperiled Everglades'; April 1994, 'The Everglades: Dying for Help.' Hello? Tallahassee? Anyone home?" Serge picked up an issue and began thumbing. He stopped. "What day is it?"

"I don't know. March twenty-something?"

"Coleman, it's the beginning of January."

"I was at the right end of the year."

Serge checked a bank calendar on the wall. "Can't believe it." He looked in his lap and slapped the photo on page 132. "This is a sign from God. He wants us to go here."

"Where?"

Serge answered by swinging into tactical mode, packing up anything of importance. He filled two duffel bags and gripped a rubber mouthpiece in his teeth, taking a test breath from a metal canister the size of a fist.

"What's that?" asked Coleman.

Serge pulled it from his mouth. "You were with me in the Keys when I bought it."

"I was?"

"The scuba shop. Remember asking that guy to modify your nitrous-oxide cylinder? Meanwhile, I found this. Diver's tiny emergency tank, ten minutes of reserve air. Another intensely cool gadget I had absolutely no use for, which meant it was as good as bought. And that brings us back to the Creator's hand of fate: Now I need it for the Night Launch."

A thud against the front door.

Serge and Coleman turned. Rustling sounds, then keys dropping. More fumbling. Keys dropping again.

"Should we grab a weapon?" asked Coleman.

Serge shook his head. "Whoever it is can do us no harm."

"How do you know?"

"Because those are the sounds you make when you're trying to get inside."

They walked across the room, and Serge opened the door.

Their jaws fell.

FOUR

MEANWHILE . . .

*C*ops quickly roped off the FUN-O-RAMA just over a berm from Interstate 75.

Two homicide detectives stood next to each other, sipping convenience-store coffee.

"What kind of demented bastard?"

"But you have to give him credit . . ."

The first detective looked warily at his partner.

". . . In a demented kind of way."

Industrious crime-scene technicians swarmed the batting cage. One dusted for prints around the pitching machine's coin-operated control box. Another filled evidence bags with dozens of bloody baseballs pooled at the feet of the sheet-covered body, still strapped into a chair over home plate.

Stunned silence filled the doorway of Serge and Coleman's apartment. They watched in awe as one of the most radioactively sexual women they'd ever seen pushed past them and stumbled bleary-eyed to the bunk beds: a statuesque hourglass with blond locks curling down the front of an ultra-tight T-shirt cut off midstomach and worn braless for so long that pert nipples had left permanent stretch marks. And those legs, racing up into denim shorts with a low, hip-riding waistband exposing panty lace and the top of a tramp-stamp tattoo. Serge had a weakness for that. This one was a unicorn.

The woman stopped next to the bunks. Clothes dropped to the floor. She yawned and arched her back in full bedtime stretch—the porch bulb out the still-open door silhouetting the kind of perfectly formed breasts found only in *Heavy Metal* magazine. Then she climbed into Coleman's bed.

"Serge! The hope thing really works!"

"There has to be another explanation."

"What else could it be?"

"Robert Downey Syndrome."

"You mean like when you get really, really fucked up, and your autopilot takes you back to someplace you *used* to live?"

Serge nodded. "This must be our hooker, Sunshine." He crouched down next to the bed. "Excuse me? Ma'am? . . ."—lightly tapping her cheek—". . . Yoo-hoo! Hate to interrupt your beauty rest! . . ."—tapping harder—". . . Hello! You don't live here anymore! . . ."—tugging her by the shoulders—". . . Shoo! Be off! You're late for Junior League! . . ."

Serge's shaking finally produced a moan. He sat her up. A woozy head sagged. "Let me lie down. I have to sleep. . . ."

"Sunshine!" yelled Serge. "You can't stay here!"

Eyes opened a slit: "Who's Sunshine?"

"You."

"I'm not Sunshine. I'm Rachael."

"You're not a hooker?"

"Fuck no. I just dance naked at the Red Snapper. Or hand jobs in the massage parlor, but only if they're threatening to turn off my electricity."

"Serge," Coleman said from behind. "I'm getting a weird feeling. . . . Doesn't she remind you of someone we knew?"

"Uncanny," said Serge. "Like they were separated at birth." Another hard shake. "Rachael, wake up!"

"Stop shaking me."

"No."

"Okay, okay . . ." Rachael straightened. "If you're not going to let me sleep, give me a sec. . . ." She grabbed her shorts off the floor, reached in a pocket and retrieved a folded rectangle of wax paper that contained what looked like Goody's Headache Powder. Her face went down for a long, noisy snort.

Rachael's head suddenly whipped back. "Whoa!" Eyes comically wide, a round white spot at the end of her nose. "God*damn,* I needed that!"

Serge tapped the end of his own nose. "You got something."

She licked a finger and wiped the spot, then rubbed it along her lower gums.

"That is so hot!" said Coleman.

Rachael reached in her other pocket and pulled out a crumpled pack of Marlboros. "Got a light?"

Coleman jumped forward and flicked his Bic.

"Coleman!" said Serge. "This is a clean indoor air state!"

"I can't help myself," said Coleman. "She's too much woman."

Rachael took a long drag and exhaled with malice out her nostrils. Her brain finished rebooting. She looked at her hosts. "What the fuck's going on? Who *are* you guys? Why'd you bring me here? And what did you do with my clothes?"

"Nobody brought you anywhere," said Serge. "You stumbled in yourself and took off your own clothes."

She looked around the room and began nodding. "Yeah . . . now I recognize this place."

"You must have lived here before."

"No, but I knew someone who did."

"Really?" said Serge. "Me too. But the landlord still insists we pay rent. So if you don't mind—"

"*Rachael! There you are!*"

They all turned toward the open apartment door. A muscular white Rastafarian stood on the threshold: "I want my money!"

Rachael scooted backward on the bed until she was against the wall: "Stay the fuck away from me!"

The man advanced: "You were supposed to sell the shit, not suck it all into your skull! I want my money, bitch!"

"Did you just call me a bitch?" She climbed from the bed.

Serge saw it coming and got in the middle. He was quickly sandwiched, the dealer and strung-out stripper clawing over his shoulders at each other. He turned sideways and thrust out both arms, giving each a hard shove in the chest that sent them tumbling in different directions. "If you can't play nice, I'm going to insist on a time-out." They charged and slammed back into Serge. The dealer got lucky and landed an open-handed wallop across Rachael's face.

Serge felt resistance slack off from her side. She stood in quiet shock. "You slapped me."

The dealer continued swatting the air over Serge's shoulders. "You're dead! . . ."

Rachael rubbed her cheek. "I can't believe you just fuckin' slapped me."

Serge's full attention was now on the man, seizing him by the front of his shirt. "I live here! I've never seen either of you before! Take this shit elsewhere!—"

"Serge!" yelled Coleman. "Watch out!"

FIVE

A FEW MILES AWAY

*T*he front door opened on a modestly landscaped ranch house just off Beneva Road in Sarasota. The Davenports walked out.

Martha turned around and kissed her mother on the cheek. "Thanks for the wonderful dinner."

"Yes," said Jim. "Great lamb chops."

"You're not going to stay over?"

"Mom, we have to get on the road."

"I thought you were staying over."

"No, we're *not* staying over. We talked about that on the phone. I made it very clear—"

"Oh, Martha, how could I have forgotten. Did you hear about your sister's son, Larry?"

"No."

"He got arrested!"

"Mom, we have to go."

"You don't care that your nephew is in jail?"

"I do, but it's almost midnight. I'll call my sister tomorrow."

"You haven't even asked what he did. Shoplifting! Women's underwear, and he doesn't even have a girlfriend. Makes no sense. We think he's being framed."

"He's not being framed," said Martha.

"How can you take sides against your own flesh and blood when you don't even know the facts?"

"Mom, it's Larry."

"What about Larry?"

"Too long to explain. We really have to be going."

"Did I tell you I had a new will drawn up?"

"No."

"I thought I did."

"Mom, you always do this!"

"Do what? Don't you want to know about the new will?"

"I'll call—"

"It gives you power of attorney in case something terrible happens to me, and I'm still alive but can't speak or signal you by blinking."

"Good idea."

"I've got it in the house. Let me go get it and we can read it right here in case you have any questions."

"Mail me a copy."

"You don't care if something terrible happens to me and I can't blink?"

"Mom!"

"Why don't I just die?"

Jim stood next to the Escalade, smiling painfully.

"Mom," said Martha. "We had a nice visit. Please don't end it again like the other times."

"What other times?"

"We seriously have to go." Martha walked briskly to the SUV. "Jim, hurry up and get in."

They simultaneously hopped through opposite doors. "What are you waiting for?" said Martha. "Start the engine."

"Your mom's still talking."

"Just go!"

Jim turned the ignition and threw the vehicle in reverse. Martha's mom cupped her hands around her mouth. "I really thought you were staying over. The Thompsons are coming in the morning."

Martha smiled and waved.

"What am I supposed to tell the Thompsons?"

They backed out of the driveway.

"I'll be dead soon."

Serge had ducked just in time.

Rachael stood fuming with a frying pan.

Coleman fitted the butt of a joint into locking hemostats and stared at the motionless body in the middle of the apartment floor. "Is he dead?"

"Not sure," said Serge, "but blood from the ears rarely precedes a big dance number." He squatted down and felt the dealer's wrist. "Weak but steady pulse." He looked up at Rachael. "Why'd you do that?"

"He slapped me."

"How could I forget?" said Serge. "Third Law of Stripper Thermodynamics."

Rachael got dressed, sat down next to Coleman and snatched the hemostats. She took a massive, double-clutch toke and handed it back, then unfolded the square of wax paper.

Coleman pointed. "Can I have some?"

She pulled it protectively around her far side. "No!"

Serge went through the dealer's pockets and stood up, riffling a fat wad of bills.

Coleman whistled. "Look at all that money!"

Serge crammed the roll into his hip pocket. "God's plan continues to reveal itself in all its glory. We needed cash for the Night Launch, and He delivered it to our door like a pizza."

"Plus the chick."

"The launch is in its final countdown. Internal sequence start." Serge reached for his keys. "Get your shit."

Coleman stood. "Yow." He grabbed a bedpost for balance. "Serge, give me a minute."

"Mission Control, we have a hold at T-minus ten."

"I'm okay. Just got up too fast."

"Coleman, you knew we had a Night Launch. Are you capable of not partying for eight seconds?"

Coleman grabbed a beer from the fridge. "I don't party *that* much. Do you think I party too much?"

"No, Coleman, you don't party too much. . . ."

"Didn't think so."

". . . Partying involves cake and ice cream and Chuckles the Clown. What you do is called getting outrageously trashed, falling down flights of stairs, bringing home drifters who piss in kitchen drawers, breaking furniture, chipping teeth, making holes in drywall, leaving your keys in the microwave, forgetting your wallet in the freezer, maintaining a channel-buoy physique, whispering to complete strangers in family environments if they know 'where there's any weed,' and keeping accomplishment at bay with a vengeance unseen since the Rape of Nanking."

Rachael licked her wax paper like a lollipop. "Will you two lame fucks shut the hell up?"

Serge stuck a pistol in his waistband and grabbed a duffel in each hand. "Ready!"

Coleman gathered rolling papers and a bag of herbs. "Ready!"

"Mission Control, we have a go. T-minus ten, nine—"

"Hey!" shouted Rachael. "Where are you going with all that money you took off Jimmy?"

"Is that his name?"

"That's *my* money!"

"I couldn't give it to you even if I wanted. It now belongs to the Night Launch." He headed for the door.

Rachael reached into her back pocket and lunged.

"Serge!" yelled Coleman. "Look out!"

He turned quickly, but it was too late. Rachael already had the knife under his chin. "I want my money!"

Serge dropped his bags and grinned.

Rachael pressed the knife tip, indenting Serge's skin. A single droplet of blood. "What's so funny?"

"Drugs. They have their own built-in satellite delay, like when CNN's interviewing a correspondent in Beirut. You're living three seconds behind me."

"What are you talking about?"

The knife suddenly appeared in Serge's right hand. He tossed it out the door, then grabbed her wrists, did a spin move and came around behind her, twisting both hands up against her back.

"Ow! You're breaking my arms!"

"This is yoga. You're way too tense."

"Let go of me!"

"You need to relax and get in tune with the Earth, like Native Americans who worship the Great Spirit."

"Let go of me!"

He twisted her arms higher. She screamed.

"Will you worship the Great Spirit?"

"What about my money?"

"Let me teach you about the Great Spirit, then you can come on the Night Launch. And if you behave, *maybe* I can arrange a little allowance."

"You fucker!"

He twisted more. A louder scream. "Okay, okay! Stop! I'll do it!"

"You gave me your word. I'm letting go now." Serge began loosening his grasp. "But one false move and I'll clobber you. I have three seconds."

He let go and jumped back.

Rachael spun around and steamed with fists clenched by her sides. But she didn't attack.

"Auspicious start," said Serge. "Now follow me and I'll teach you the ways. . . ."

Serge led her out the door and into the yard. "Sit right there in the dirt." She grudgingly complied. He picked up a long stick. "First you need to recognize that right angles symbolize the discord of the White Man. That's why I'm using this stick to draw a big circle around you, representing the spiritual cycles of peace and harmony that connect us all." He completed the circle. "Then you stay perfectly still in the middle and *shut the fuck up!*"

Serge went back inside, filling additional luggage with his books and *National Geographic*s.

"Taking all that with you?"

"Decided to blow this place," said Serge. "Anything of sentimental value, better grab it now."

"Shit." Coleman ran to the fridge and opened a beer. "How do you know so much about women?"

Serge hoisted a strap over his shoulder. "You just have to remember that inside they're all still little girls. See? Isn't she adorable?" They looked out the door: Rachael sitting in the dirt, cursing, lighting a Marlboro and wiping drug mucus off her upper lip.

Coleman looked toward a moaning sound near their feet. "I think he's coming to."

"We'll just have to bring him along." Serge pulled the pistol from his belt, gripped it by the barrel and cracked the top of Jimmy's dome. Moaning stopped. "But that's it. Membership's now closed. This Night Launch is getting too popular."

Rachael stood when she saw Serge and Coleman approach, dragging Jimmy by the ankles. "What about my money?"

"After the Night Launch clears the tower," said Serge. "You can come out of the circle now."

She grumbled and followed.

Serge glanced at her hand. "And no smoking in the car."

"Bite me!"

"Guess you don't want your money."

"Dammit. . . . Wait up!" She took a quick series of drags and ran after them, flicking the butt into a pile of yard waste. A lifeless rat began to stir.

SIX

SOUTH TAMPA

Whoop! Whoop! Whoop!

Martha Davenport sprang up in bed. "What's that?"

"Our burglar alarm." Jim rolled over and squinted at a digital clock. Four-thirty.

"Think someone's downstairs?"

He squinted again, this time across the room at the most advanced alarm keypad on the market. "Says it's the garage."

"Jim! Do something!"

He climbed from the sheets, walked across the room and locked the bedroom door.

"That's it?"

"Okay . . ." He reached up in the closet and climbed back into bed with something.

"Jim, are you going to show him you won third place?"

Jim set the bowling trophy between their pillows and snuggled under the sheets.

"Jim!"

The phone rang. He grabbed it.

"This is Proton Security. We show a motion sensor in the garage."

"So does our keypad."

"I've already called the police. Are you in a safe place?"

"I think so." Jim got out of bed and peeked through curtains. "I'm looking down at the garage."

"Anyone there?"

"No. He's already at the end of the street with my lawnmower."

The police response was efficient and polite. A young officer filled out the report. "Anything missing besides the lawnmower?"

"The motion sensors."

The officer finished and handed Jim a yellow copy. "For the insurance company. Make sure all your doors are locked." He tipped his hat.

It was quiet again in the Davenport bedroom. Jim turned his head on the pillow. Martha was staring back.

"What?"

"You know."

"Where are we going to move?"

"Anywhere."

"Martha, we can't sell the place every time something happens in the world. First Triggerfish Lane, then Manatee Drive and now here."

"Jim! A dangerous criminal was in our house!"

"The garage."

"Next time it *will* be the house. But you don't care."

"Honey, petty theft happens everywhere. It's okay—"

"Don't start with that!"

"With what?"

"Being calm."

"You want me to get excited?"

"I want you to do something!"

Jim grabbed the remote and turned on the TV.

"Are you deliberately trying to start a fight?"

"I'm checking the news. Maybe there's something on that guy in the windshield at the Skyway."

"Exactly what I'm talking about. It was the most disgusting thing I've ever seen."

"They were just old people who couldn't drive."

"But if it's not one thing . . ."

Jim clicked over to the Channel 7 Action First Eyewitness Report. Flashing police lights at one of their neighborhood convenience stores. Little plastic flags on the ground marked bullet casings. Martha opened a book. "You can stay. I'm moving."

"We can't move now." He clicked the remote. A major house fire behind a Dairy Queen in Sarasota.

"Why can't we move?"

"We're renovating. We'll never get our price with the place torn up."

"What will it matter if we're murdered?"

"You're overreacting."

The bedroom briefly brightened.

Martha sat up. "What was that?"

"Police helicopter."

"And I thought she was crazy."

"Who?"

"Our old neighbor," said Martha. "She warned us about the grid streets: When everything's laid out straight, it's easier for criminals to dart in and out from the main arteries and elude cops. Puts every psychopath on the west coast within striking distance."

"Honey—"

"Heard she just moved into a serpentine neighborhood."

"How about this? Let 'em finish the work on the house. Then, if you still feel the way you do, we'll move to a street that curves. Why don't you try getting some sleep?"

"Can't."

"Thought you were over that."

"You've just been out like a light. But I'll be up at some

crazy hour looking down from the window, and there are all these people there."

"Where? Our front yard?"

"No. A block over on that main drag that cuts through our neighborhood. Just walking up and down the sidewalks all night. What can they be doing?"

Jim shrugged.

She threw the covers off her legs and went over to the window. "It's like this entirely different species crawls out after we go to sleep at night."

Jim got up and walked up behind his wife. He wrapped his arms around her. "I promise it'll be okay."

Martha rested her head back on his shoulder. "You know what's really underneath it all?"

"I do."

"And you're not worried?"

"Baby, the home invasion was ten years ago."

"But there's one McGraw left—and he swore he'd get even with you for killing his cousins."

"That was self-defense."

"Jim, you did what you had to. It doesn't change the threat."

"But he's still in prison."

"For how long?"

"A *long* time. Besides, there's a law requiring authorities to inform victims before a prisoner's release."

Martha took a deep breath. "Maybe I should make another appointment with the doctor."

"That's a good idea."

They held hands again and stood in front of the window. Jim looked up. "The moon's beautiful tonight."

Martha looked down. A man wheeled a gas grill up the sidewalk. "The Fergusons just bought that."

* * *

MIDDLE OF NOWHERE

North Florida might as well be south Georgia. It actually is, at least where the St. Mary's River carves a tongue of land almost down to I-10 between Baker and Nassau counties. Undiscovered territory. Oaks, moss, national forests, a couple of speed traps between the flea markets in Lawtey and Waldo where U.S. 301 slices down the state from Jacksonville. God's country. Only a single industry to speak of. But they never closed.

The lights burned bright at one of the franchises. It was just before sunrise, though still quite dark from a blanket of anvil thunderheads drifting across the rolling farmland. No rain yet. One of those violent, nervous skies that just waited.

The lights, more specifically, were floodlights, perched on tall poles around the perimeter, pointing down inside the property like a backwoods high school football field. Sometimes they even played a little sports at this place, except right now all the athletes were locked in their cells. Union Correctional maximum-security prison. But everyone called it Raiford.

The stillness broke. Motion in the yard. A tight formation of guards moved toward the front gate. They entered a narrow walkway of Cyclone fence and razor wire. In the middle, one head stood above the others. Ankle chains shuffled. The prisoner wore a fresh, cheap suit with too-short pants; the jacket creased from where wrist manacles attached to the waist restraint. A hockey mask covered the face because of his classification as a biter.

Normally an inmate wasn't restrained upon being released. And there weren't half as many guards. But this was Tex McGraw, the biggest, meanest, nastiest in a long, tainted bloodline of infamous McGraws. Tex hadn't seen freedom since the early nineties, wrapping up a stretch for extremely aggravated battery. Much had happened in the meantime, including the notorious McGraw Brothers home invasion in Tampa, foiled by an unassuming family man on Triggerfish Lane. Tex was helpless in his cell when he learned of his cousins' demise. Now, approaching the prison's front gate, there was but one all-consuming thought on his mind. The guards continued anxiously. The one in back carried a cardboard box of the prisoner's meager possessions.

It began to rain.

Correctional work was the unimaginable. Getting hit with feces, blood, urine; at any turn, the chance of your arm being yanked through metal bars and sliced sixty stitches wide with the melted point of a toothbrush. The guards coped by mentally compartmentalizing the nightmare and leaving it at the gate on the way home. But this was one day they were glad to be locked inside. Someone out there was going to end up dead.

Florida had no choice. New laws required inmates to serve a minimum 85 percent of their sentence. McGraw had just completed 130, including time added for bad behavior. Every last day gone. Not even the possibility of supervised parole.

The guards reached the front of the yard. The tower opened the gate. Rain became a deluge. Half the team held Tex's limbs fast; the rest quickly undid locks and buckles. They finished the last cuff and shoved him out of the prison. Tex turned around.

"Boo."

The guards jumped and slammed the gate shut. The safest place in the state was now inside Raiford. The officer with Tex's belongings heaved the box over the top of the fence. It broke open in the mud, scattering toiletries, amphetamine-laced candy bars, a Bible with a shank in the spine and dozens of ten-year-old newspaper articles about a reluctant hero named Jim Davenport.

Tex left it all in the puddles and began trudging south.

The guards watched intently as the ex-prisoner's outline faded into the driving rain. They began to untense. Suddenly, a maniacal roar echoed across the open field. Lightning crashed, momentarily illuminating a distant, hulking figure with fists and face raised straight up at the storm.

And he was gone.

The guards went back inside. They passed the thick, shatterproof glass of the processing office, where other personnel handled paperwork on inmates, both coming and going. One officer tapped a keyboard, dispatching release reports for local law enforcement to notify victims.

Tap, tap, tap. "Uh-oh . . . Hey, Stan, my computer froze again. What was that thing you said to hit?"

"Control, alt, delete."

"Hit delete?"

"No. Control, alt—"

"Oops. Already did it. Where'd that file go?"

SEVEN

THE NEXT MORNING

*S*erge considered breakfast the most important meal of the day. It had to be celebrated when the fishermen and crab-trappers ate: before first light. Hence his initial Night Launch stop after the Bradenton overpass. They were just beyond the mouth of the bay on St. Petersburg's transitional Thirty-fourth Street. Pawnbrokers and car-title-loan hustlers had crawled in like hermit crabs, filling the exquisite architectural shells of landmark restaurants, gas stations and motels. Predawn derelicts wandered through traffic, froze in headlights and raced back to the curb in a game of Homeless Frogger. Serge could have spit.

But the drive was more than worth it for the surviving jewel. Serge turned off the road and parked in front of a concrete chicken. He ran for the front door and pulled up short. Coleman crashed into him. "Why'd you stop?"

"I absolutely love the moment I first enter Skyway Jack's. Smoky aroma from the grill, din of a community coming to life, dockmen, construction workers, fiduciaries, reading the sports section, debating the direction of our republic." He threw open the door and spread his arms. *"Good mornnnnnnnning, Florida!"*

Silence and stares. Serge lowered his arms. "Probably

not fully awake yet. I was hoping for a bunch of high-fives running down the aisle."

Conversation resumed. A waitress led them to a back booth. Serge ordered his "usual": steak, bacon, toast, hash browns, grits, southern biscuits and sausage gravy, sliced grapefruit, pancakes, whipped butter, orange juice, tomato juice, coffee and three eggs, sunny-side up, which he seasoned with heavy salt, heavy pepper, heavy Tabasco sauce. "Shoot. Ruined them again. Excuse me? Can I get different eggs? And more coffee . . ."

"Serge," said Coleman. "All the waitresses' T-shirts have fried eggs over their boobs."

"It's Skyway Jack's. Used to be next to the bridge before they lost an eminent-domain fight when the state widened lanes."

Replacement eggs arrived. Serge grabbed toast for yolk dipping. "Coleman, don't you see what's happening?"

"Breakfast?"

"The magic of life On the Road! Kerouac, *Easy Rider,* Oklahoma Sooners! God bless America! And it's not even light out yet. Nothing more invigorating than getting a jump on the sun! The three of us family-bonding like Norman Rockwell: me with the maximum-excellent breakfast and *two* newspapers, you spiking your OJ with Smirnoff, Rachael ordering nothing, smoking outside and offering truckers reacharounds."

"What's the plan?"

"Not in my hands anymore. The launch rules all."

Serge worked through food with exclusivity, entirely finishing each item before moving to the next. He left a big tip along with a handwritten note of local travel advice, then paid at the cash register and finished his morning tradition with toothpick and mint. They collected Rachael from behind a Dumpster, got back in the Comet and headed west to pick up the route along the coast.

"Quiet back there!" Serge fiddled with the radio. "Want me to have an accident?"

"She won't get back on her side!"

"I *am* on my side!"

"Stop touching me!"

"You spilled my drink!"

"Serge, will you make Rachael—"

"Knock it off!" yelled Serge. "If I have to pull over!"

"Look," said Rachael. "On the floor."

"What is it?"

"I think I found some dope."

"Let me see."

"What do you think?"

"Doesn't look like dope."

Serge banged his head on the steering wheel.

"What could it be?"

"Maybe a clump of weeds that fell off my shoe or something."

"Shit." Rachael threw the dope out the window.

A brief spell of quiet, except for the mild rumble of an old brick street beneath the tires.

Something slammed the back of Serge's seat, pitching him forward. He checked the rearview, Rachael and Coleman wrestling and pulling hair.

"That's it!"

Two minutes later, Coleman and Rachael stood silent and respectful beside the car.

"You two going to behave?" said Serge, aiming his gun.

They nodded.

"Okay then . . ."

Whisper: "You started it."

"You did."

"Enough!" Serge tucked the pistol away. "But if I hear another word."

The sky gave up traces of light. Serge reached through

the front window of the parked Comet and found Eric
Burden on the radio.

" . . . *There is . . . a house . . .* "

The Mercury sat along a sandy shore. The lapping, incoming tide chased tiny crabs. A smile spread as Serge slowly
scanned the tranquil panorama: coal-black western sky, growing brighter to the south over a fleet of outgoing fishing skiffs,
brighter still toward the pier and a large, pastel-green wooden
building arched like a Quonset hut.

Coleman came around the car in a nippy breeze and
rubbed his arms. "Where are we?"

"Gulfport." Serge watched a seasonal white pelican hover
off the flats. "Bottom of the Pinellas peninsula at the northern lip of the bay."

"Place looks old."

"We're in one of those isolated geographical anomalies
that's below the radar of devil-worshipping developers. But
not for long. That ancient green building to our left is the
sacred ballroom called the Casino."

Coleman's hair flopped in the beach wind. "I've been
meaning to ask, why do you love Florida so much? I've
never seen anyone so obsessed with something, and *you're*
obsessed with everything."

"If I had to put my finger on one aspect, it's visual intoxi-
cation," said Serge. "Like here. This neighborhood is one of
my favorites, a collage of beauty from around the state: Key
West color, West Palm architecture, Miami Beach accents,
Coconut Grove landscaping. Look! . . ." He pointed toward
a ribbon of orange light on the eastern horizon. "Here comes
the day. Coleman, let's observe this miracle in the reverence
God intended."

" . . . *They call . . . the rising sun . . .* "

The melody changed, volume increased. A sonic calam-
ity. Serge turned: "What happened to God's sound track?"

Back at the Comet, Rachael leaned through the driver's

window, bent sharply at the waist, ass cocked, cutoffs riding high. She twisted a radio dial.

"What the hell are you doing?" yelled Serge.

"This music sucks." She came back out of the window. A driving bass beat shattered the peace.

" . . . *I just wanna live!* . . . "

"That's the last straw!" Serge took an angry step forward.

Coleman yanked him back by the shirt.

"Coleman, what are you doing?"

"Check it out. . . ."

He did. Rachael had begun gyrating, slowly at first, her eyes closed, full lips parted. One hand ran through blond locks and over her chest; the other raised a pint bottle that she chugged straight.

Coleman jumped. "My vodka!"

"It's being put to better use."

Rachael accelerated her hip-grind, flinging the empty bottle over the car and sliding palms down the inside of her thighs as she turned in an erotic circle, the effect enhanced by a black leather jacket with purple, goth lettering: GOOD CHARLOTTE.

Coleman placed a hand over his heart.

"You okay?"

"Almost swallowed my tongue. I've never seen a woman . . . dance like that."

"She's professionally trained, probably at a magnet school," said Serge. "And I could use the workout. Guess I'll just have to do her."

"What do you mean, 'do her'?"

"Is that unclear?"

"No. But I'm always thinking I want to do some chick, and it never makes it so."

"Need a three-day weekend to explain. Involves everything from chromosomes to dental floss."

" . . . Don't . . . care . . . what happens to me! . . . "

"Also, what's with your taste in women?" said Coleman. "Usually it's the older, brainy chicks. But in between there are these complete opposites."

"I'm a connoisseur. This is cleansing the palate for the next '59 Bordeaux." Serge walked toward the car. "Get in the fuckin' backseat!"

Rachael continued dancing. "What?"

"Time to pay the piper." He twisted an arm behind her back again.

"Let go of me!"

"You're welcome."

FBI FIELD HEADQUARTERS, TAMPA DISTRICT

Typical attire. Dark slacks, white shirts, thin black ties. Conference room. At least two hours before their shifts normally started. Dozen agents in all, watching the same video on the large-screen TV: other agents in spaceman biohazard suits, going back and forth from a van (Universal Pest Control) and a modest, single-family home draped in a termite tent.

The conference room door opened. An agent from Washington entered. His name was Washington. He looked toward the screen. "What site's this?"

"Nine," said the Tampa case agent, Nick Moody.

"Then we have a cluster."

"Yes and no."

"How's that?"

"They're grouped on the timeline, but with no pattern. Victims literally all over the map." He pointed at the map: Colored pushpins decorated the wall like a shotgun with the choke open. Tampa Bay, Polk and Pasco counties, Crystal River, Arcadia and one way over by Okeechobee.

"Profiles?" asked Washington.

"Auto mechanic, banker, college student, priest, cocktail

waitress. Same as the geography, no pattern whatsoever. Quantico turn up anything?"

"Still analyzing the data," said Washington. "So random it looks deliberate."

"At least it's stopped," said Moody.

"That's what worries me."

"You want *more* victims?"

"Nine cases in barely a week," said Washington. "Then a month, nothing."

"That's a good thing," said Moody.

"Not if it was a test run," said Washington.

"We have no way of knowing that."

"We do. NSA's heard chatter. Can't talk about it."

"Wonderful. Listen, I know how you feel about this," said Moody. "But now would be a really good time to activate Foxtrot."

Washington shook his head. "Can't risk exposing that kind of asset unless we absolutely have to. There's still a price on Foxtrot's head. . . . Get me Wicks on the line."

The Davenports had been up before dawn. Uncharacteristic activity beneath the sheets.

"Come on," said Martha. "We still have time."

"What's gotten into you?" asked Jim.

"Family life. We're always too tired at night. It's been . . . a while."

"Ow! You got me in the eye with your finger."

"Sorry."

"It's okay. I'll use the other."

"Talk to me."

"I am."

"No, I mean, you know . . ."

"I don't."

"Dirty."

"What?"

"Don't make me feel more self-conscious than I already am."

Jim fumbled below the sheets to get things going. "Where'd this new you come from?"

"I read a magazine in line at the supermarket. I think we should try something different. . . . Need help down there?"

"No, I think I got it."

"Couldn't believe what that article said. So I asked my girlfriends. . . ."

"Martha."

"What?"

"I need some help."

"Okay, hold on." She reached down. "Start talking."

"What do I say?"

"I can't tell you what to say. That'll ruin it."

"I don't know—"

"Make something up."

"What if it's stupid?"

"I promise it won't be. Please? I really think it'll get me excited."

"How do you know?"

"That magazine article. I started getting wet at the cash register."

"Martha!"

"Jim! This is hard enough for me to express as it is. Now hurry, start talking."

"Okay, let me think. . . ."

The sun peeked over the horizon at a waterfront park. Then it dipped back down below window level. It bobbed up again. Then down again. Then up, then down, up, down . . .

The Comet sat beneath a group of palms next to the Gulfport Casino. Coleman stood a few feet away by a swing set, furtively cupping a roach.

"Coleman! . . ."

He turned and looked back at the car: Serge's face bobbing up and down in the backseat window, Rachael's legs in the air.

"What is it, Serge?"

He bobbed up. "The sunrise . . ." He bobbed down. He bobbed up again. "It's beautiful. . . ."

Rachael growled and cursed in a sultry voice below window level. "Fuck your stupid sunrise!"

"Stupid sunrise?" Serge thrust violently. "Take *that*!"

"Owwww! Damn you! . . . Again."

The Davenports' master bedroom was hushed. Sheets began rising and falling. "Jim, what are you waiting for?"

"I feel awkward."

"Please talk to me. I really want you to."

"Okay . . . uh . . . *take my hot, throbbing love-missile.* . . ."

"Jim?"

"What?"

"Shhhh. Don't talk."

"Yes! . . . Yes! . . . Faster! . . . Faster!" yelled Rachael. *"Hurt me with your hot cock! . . . "*

Serge bobbed up. "Coleman . . ." He bobbed down.

"What?"

Serge bobbed up again. "Could you move a little to your left? . . . You're blocking my view. . . ."

EIGHT

ALTERNATE U.S. HIGHWAY 19

A '73 Mercury Comet sped north from St. Petersburg, up through Clearwater and Dunedin, respective ethnic strongholds of Scientologists and Scotsmen. The January 1947 issue of *National Geographic* lay open to page 132 in Serge's lap.

"Six minutes," said Coleman. "Five minutes, fifty-five seconds . . . Five minutes, fifty . . ."

Serge gritted his teeth, blue knuckles on the steering wheel.

". . . Five minutes, thirty-five seconds . . . Five minutes . . ."

Serge screamed and attacked the sun visor. "You're driving me insane!"

Rachael crumpled an empty cigarette pack. "What's the stupid counting about?"

"He does this every time," said Serge, unbending the visor. "Seven A.M. . . ."

". . . When they start selling alcohol again," said Coleman. "Four minutes, thirty-five seconds . . . Four minutes, thirty seconds . . . Start looking for a convenience store. . . . Four minutes . . ."

Later in the countdown: Coleman stood with a beer

suitcase in a Grab 'N Dash. There were two lines at the registers. One that moved, and a much longer, stationary one that stared at a wall clock and chanted. ". . . One minute, fifteen . . . One minute, ten . . ."

Serge paced the sidewalk. "Come onnnnnnn!" He waved a *National Geographic* at the store window. "This only happens once a year!" Rachael tore the cellophane off a fresh, untaxed pack of Marlboro Lights meant for export that had been sold on the black market by a Honduran gang working the port.

Coleman finally climbed back into the car, and he and Rachael ripped open the twelve-pack like wild dingos. Serge threw the Comet in gear and floored it up Alternate 19. Eagles on the radio.

" . . . *The Greeks don't want no freaks* . . . "

It was a short, ten-block drag race. Serge skidded into the first available parking slot, jumped out and popped the trunk. He grabbed something from a duffel bag and slammed the hood. "We have to hurry!"

Coleman and Rachael remained glued in the backseat, cracking more beers.

"No! No! No!" yelled Serge, snatching for cans that they pulled out of range. "You're going to make me late for my special day!"

"It's cool," said Coleman. "We can take 'em with us." He reached under his seat for a pair of small, flexible magnetic sheets.

"What are those?" asked Serge.

"Watch." Coleman wrapped one of the rectangular magnets around his beer. It had a Coca-Cola design. "This way you can drink on the street." He handed the other to Rachael.

She curled a Pepsi magnet around her own can. "Where'd you get these?"

"They sell them wherever there's a college nearby." Coleman reached under the seat again and held up a plastic funnel attached to a long, clear tube. "Same place I got my beer bong."

Serge pounded fists on the roof. "Can we go now?"

They headed up the sidewalk: ancient buildings, ancient boats, ancient storefronts with bolts of cloth, ancient family bakeries that let the aroma of fresh Mediterranean bread do their advertising. The cool morning street reverberated with the tin echo of low-fidelity radios all tuned to the same lyrical foreign language. Fourth-generation locals had arrived first, for morning coffee from the homeland, and now tourists, who filled the sponge docks, sponge museum, sponge souvenir stands, getting their pictures taken with the statue of a sponger in an antique brass diving helmet.

"Serge," said Coleman. "What's the deal with all the sponges?"

"Shhhh!" snapped Serge. "Keep your voice down. You always culturally embarrass me."

"How?"

"Like on Calle Ocho when you asked the lunch-counter lady what a Cuban sandwich was."

"Didn't want to eat strange shit."

"You're in Tarpon Springs, sponge capital of America. Or was, until they started making artificial ones in factories."

Rachael finished her beer and tossed the can in the street.

Serge screamed.

"I'm on it!" said Coleman. He trotted off the curb. A station wagon hit the brakes and honked. Coleman peeled the Pepsi wrapper from the can and stuck it in his pocket. Then he threw the can back in the street.

Serge yelled again. He dashed over and grabbed it.

"What's wrong with you guys? Littering is like taking a big dump on the community." He looked around. "Where's a designated garbage receptacle?"

"Up there," said Coleman. "End of the block."

A thunder of footsteps went by, high school boys wearing the same white shorts and shirts, all clearly athletic except the last one, a scrawny youth a foot shorter than the rest, panting hard. *"Hey guys! Wait up!"*

The group stopped. *"Nikolai wants us to wait up."*

Nikolai reached the gang. They shoved him in the bushes and took off. The boy crawled out. *"Wait up!"*

Serge approached the garbage can. "Hate bullies . . ."

A deep voice from behind. "Hold it right there, fella!"

Serge turned around. A police officer marched toward him. "You're under arrest for open container."

"What?" Serge looked at the can in his hand, then stared daggers at Coleman and Rachael. "You!—Why!—I'm gonna!—" He clenched his eyes shut, the slide show of a grim future flickering inside his skull: handcuffs, photos, fingerprints, fifty positive hits in a computer network's unsolved-crime database, and, finally, death row. Of all the jams he'd squeezed out of just for this! He had to think of something fast. He opened his eyes. . . .

ALACHUA COUNTY

Inland Florida is like another state, especially toward the north end of the peninsula. More Dixie than South Beach. Horse ranches, church steeples.

The prominent feature is population. Not much. But on this January morning, the country roads were unusually busy, all in one direction, toward Gainesville. The nature of the traffic was another departure: newer vehicles, expensive, sporty. With Christmas break over, nearly fifty thousand students were returning to the University of Florida.

State Road 24 ran particularly slow, a tiny, two-lane highway, the end of the only southbound route down from Jacksonville. Just inside the county line, a large farmhouse appeared atop a hill. Hanging plants and a cedar swing on the front porch. A birdhouse made from hollowed-out gourds. No farm activity. Because this type of outskirts residence was increasingly favored by tenured professors who needed sanity.

Sunlight streamed through the kitchen, where a coffeepot perked beneath a window overlooking a feeding station and an arriving hummingbird. A fresh cup was poured. A man tested the temperature with a tiny sip. He took careful steps across the varnished floor slick with blood. Red hand streaks ran down cabinet doors and the refrigerator, more splatter by the sink, which held a carving knife, tip snapped off. The man casually walked around a woman's body and into the living room, searching for anything else of value. An open suitcase on the dining room table was almost full. He strolled past the fireplace and went through the pockets of a man's body slumped in another spreading pool. He finished enjoying his coffee.

A noise outside.

A black Camaro drove up the dirt road to the house. Gators license plate and fraternity bumper sticker. A young man in a polo shirt bounded up the steps. He was about to knock when the door opened. His expression changed.

"Who are you?"

"Handyman."

The youth peeked around the husky frame. "Where are my parents?"

"Not here."

"Car's in the driveway."

"Maybe someone gave them a ride."

Their eyes remained locked for the longest time. The man in the doorway smiled. The youth slid a foot backward. "I-I-I think I'll drop by again later."

"Why don't you wait? They said they'd just be a few minutes."

"No, I'm really in a hurry." The young man took another step back and pointed at his Camaro. "Have to be somewhere." He took off running.

NINE

TARPON SPRINGS

*S*erge pleaded desperately with the cop. ". . . Honest, I found this beer can in the street. The garbage bin's right there. I was just tidying up civilization."

"Sure you were, buddy"—reaching for the cuffs.

"Wait. Officer, I know how this looks. A guy's carrying a decapitated head down the sidewalk, he's probably not a mortician. But I'm always on trash patrol. Ask around. Littering's a crime, too, right? So I'm like police auxiliary, and we take care of each other. The Blue Wall of Silence"—wink—"smell my breath . . ." Serge blew a hot gust in the officer's face.

The officer fanned it away, but he had to admit: no alcohol.

"Officer!" Coleman stepped forward. "This man's innocent. I can prove it!"

"Wonderful," said Serge. "My lawyer's here."

"It was my can," continued Coleman. "I mean, I drank it legally, but then forgot and littered. Luckily my friend Serge was there. He hates litterbugs. You should have seen what he did to this one guy. He'll never litter with his right hand again—"

"Stay where you are!" ordered the officer. He sniffed the

air. Even at a range of three paces, Coleman smelled like a brewery. The cop turned to Serge. "Let me see that can."

Serge gave it to him. The officer turned it over. Nothing came out. Street discretion time. Drunk guy with no beer can; sober guy with empty one. The whole situation was highly weird and utterly routine. "Okay, I actually believe you." He returned the cuffs to their leather holster and snapped it shut.

"You're kidding," said Coleman. "You're just going to let him go? Because cops can be real pricks."

The officer handed the can back to Serge. "Throw it away first chance you get. And you might want to take care of your friend. He's dangerously close to disorderly conduct. . . . Have a nice day."

The trio resumed walking. A small boy crawled from shrubbery. *"Guys! Wait up!"*

Serge's face reddened. "Can't tell you how much I hate bullies! People think you just grow up and forget about it. But you don't. See what's already happening to that kid?"

"No."

"The syndrome of seeking approval from your tormentors, who only continue sapping self-esteem in a vicious circle that leads to a colorful menu of emotional disturbance in later years. Luckily I caught mine in time. Probably never guessed I was picked on."

"You were?"

"Well, once. Nobody could prove anything, and the bully was too freaked to rat me out, but after they cut him down from the radio tower even the guidance counselors avoided me." Serge looked up the sidewalk. "I wish I was *that* kid's guidance counselor."

"What would you say?"

"Find a radio tower."

They took a few more steps. Serge stopped. "Where are they going?"

"Who?"

"Those kids turned up that street. They're heading the wrong way. They'll miss the big event." Serge ran to the end of the block and looked around the corner. "Shoot! Of course! *We're* going the wrong way! I just naturally assumed it was Dodecanese Bayou at the sponge boats, but it's the other by the war memorial."

GAINESVILLE

A black Camaro raced down a dirt driveway and joined traffic on Route 24. From the road, it was difficult to make out the third body on the farmhouse steps.

Tex McGraw worked his way across campus and passed the stadium. He reached Interstate 75 and sped south. On the other side of the highway, a late-model Cadillac Escalade headed north.

"I think this is our exit," said Martha.

Jim hit the blinker and began getting over, but a Mustang saw the flashing taillight and sped up to close the gap. Jim jerked the wheel back to avoid a collision. "Where'd that guy come from?"

"He did it on purpose!" said Martha. "What's with people who accelerate as soon as they see your turn signal?"

"Martha, please stop giving people the finger in traffic."

"He made us miss our exit!"

"There's another in two miles. We'll double back." Jim broke into a smile. "Can't believe Melvin's already halfway through his freshman year. Seems like only three seconds ago he was in Little League."

Martha looked out her window at higher learning. Traffic snarls, flirting between cars, low-speed fender benders, and thousands of empty vehicles left at crazy angles across lawns, curbs and sidewalks like they'd just held the Rapture. "I don't know why he wanted to ride with his friends instead of us."

"It's natural."

"But he doesn't mind using our car to lug all his stuff."

Jim took the next exit. Slow going across town. Massive, chaotic foot-traffic in all directions, a designer-brand refugee movement of students pack-muling stereo systems, plasma TVs, computers, golf clubs, wet bars, no books.

"This really brings back memories."

"I don't remember all the kegs."

"Martha, we were exactly the same when we went to school. . . . Here's his apartment building."

"There he is!"

Jim turned into a crowded parking lot. "Where?"

"Waving to us from the balcony."

TEN

DOWN ON THE BAYOU

*T*he church could withstand any hurricane.

Built from huge quarried slabs, it stood proudly as it had for over a century at the corner of Tarpon and Pinellas avenues. The architecture was exotic even for Florida.

For the last hour, a throbbing crowd had gathered on the sidewalk. The front doors finally opened. Cheers went up. A bearded man appeared in an immaculate robe and tall bejeweled hat. He waved with dignity during his short walk to a waiting car, which drove him another brief distance.

A second, larger crowd at Spring Bayou erupted when the vehicle's doors opened. The adulation grew louder as they followed the bishop down to the gently curving seawall. A small fleet of wooden dinghies was already anchored in the water, each containing several boys in white swim trunks, sixteen to eighteen years of age.

On the opposite side of the bayou, Serge tapped page 132 of *National Geographic*. "The kids in the boats. Looks exactly the same sixty-one years later. These people are all about tradition. Like St. Nicholas Church we passed earlier. One of the state's greatest landmarks that nobody even knows exists. The Mediterranean dome and spire were patterned after Aya Sophia in Istanbul. . . ."

"Can we go now?" asked Coleman.

"But we haven't seen it yet."

"Seen what?"

"It's January sixth. I've been waiting for this my whole life. The ultimate Greek tradition."

"But you're not Greek."

"But I love Greek Orthodox," said Serge. "I'm down with any faith that's into bitchin' pastry."

"Wait a minute," said Coleman. "These aren't the people who drink ouzo. . . ."

"The same."

"Those cats rock!"

"That's what I've been trying to tell you."

"Can we stay?"

"Sure."

"Catch me up on what's happening," said Coleman.

"Okay, billions of years ago primitive nuclei began forming on the ocean floor and evolved into one of the earliest multicellular organisms in the phylum Porifera. . . ."

"You have to go back that far?"

"I don't do half-ass history."

"When's the ouzo part?"

"Not for billions of years. These creatures developed tiny pores called *ostia*, which filtered nutrients from the water, becoming the first sponges. . . ."

The religious ceremony on the other side of the bayou continued. Time passed. ". . . Ten thousand years ago, migratory peoples began settling along the Aegean coast. . . ." Serge woke Coleman with a nudge. ". . . Frescoes appeared in Crete depicting the sponge's role in hygiene. . . ."

Rachael's half-conscious head peeked over the sill of the Comet's back window and tried focusing on Serge and Coleman at the edge of the water.

". . . Next, the Bronze Age . . ."

She reached for another Valium but passed out again first.

The bishop bestowed blessings. The crowd brimmed with building anticipation.

". . . Non-Greeks triggered the Key West sponging boom of the nineteenth century. But sponges aren't known for their fleetness and greedy divers soon wiped out their own harvest. Meanwhile, savvy Athenians overtook them by expertly managing the warm Gulf waters of Tarpon Springs. . . ." Serge poked Coleman again. ". . . Where they remain to this day. The high school team is the Fighting Spongers."

"Must have dozed. Did I miss anything?"

"Just the terrible spicule fungus of 1938." Serge grabbed the tote bag at his feet. "Looks like they're starting."

The crowd's roar increased as the bishop approached the water's edge, his vestments sparkling in the winter sun. Children waved small American and Greek flags. Suddenly, the bishop raised a white cross over his head, and the mob went berserk. He rotated in a semicircle, displaying the religious treasure for all to see. The cheering seemed like it would go on forever. Then, abruptly, quiet. Nobody had to tell them. The moment was here. The bishop pulled the cross back over his shoulder. The youths in the boats crouched like swimmers on starting platforms of a hundred-meter freestyle.

One final pause for drama . . . and the cross was flung.

All eyes followed the brilliant white icon, soaring higher and higher before reaching its apex, flashing briefly in the light and arcing over into the water. The boys leaped from their boats; the bayou erupted in a splashing froth to the deafening encouragement from shore.

The 102nd Epiphany dive for the cross was under way.

* * *

UNIVERSITY OF FLORIDA

Melvin ran down the stairs and hugged his parents.

They unloaded the back of the Escalade, carrying boxes past open doors of other rooms furnished with stolen milk crates and cinder-block shelves. The Davenports made the top of the stairs. Blaring music and snatches of conversation.

"... *Then you scrape the inside of the banana peel and smoke it.*"

"*That's a myth.*"

At the end of the balcony, three students were steadying a fourth, whose head hung over the rail. "*You'll feel much better if you just throw up the toxin and ease into a mellow trip.*"

Melvin stopped in front of the last unit and shifted the cardboard box he was holding for a better grip. "Here we are."

Martha pointed behind her. "What's that about?"

"Just my roommate." Melvin pushed the ajar door open with his foot.

Two more trips and the SUV was empty. They sat around and had a nice visit until Martha grew concerned.

"What is it?" asked Jim.

"He doesn't have enough cleaning products."

"You brought two full boxes."

"We have to go to the store."

"All right." They headed downstairs.

Coleman stood in chest-deep water under a boat lift. He peeked out from behind the concealment of an oyster-encrusted pier, straining to see what was happening on the other side of the bayou. Some kind of confusion around the dinghies. Kids diving over and over. The crowd on the seawall exchanged puzzled glances.

Coleman ventured from behind the pylon for a closer look. "What the hell's taking so long?"

Behind him, a loud splash as something broke the surface.

Coleman turned and grabbed his chest. "Jesus, don't *do* that!"

Serge pulled the emergency air canister from his mouth. "Hurry up. We don't have much time."

Coleman raised the disposable, underwater camera attached to his arm with a rubber wrist strap. He aimed it at his pal.

Serge grinned and held a white cross next to his face.

Click.

Coleman lowered the camera. "Can we go now?"

"Professionals never just take one picture. What if my eyes were closed? Then we'll have to come back next year."

Coleman advanced the film with his thumb. Click.

"Again!"

Click.

"One with me kissing the cross."

Click.

Dozens of baffled teens dog-paddled in the background. Now and then, one would take another deep breath, dive back down and come up empty.

Click.

"A profile shot. Which is my good side? Screw it. Shoot both."

Click. Click.

"Underwater action sequence."

They submerged. Click, click, click . . .

Coleman came up breathing hard. "I'm out of film. *Now* can we go?"

"Absolutely not. I have to return this thing."

"You got to be shittin' me. We spent all this time getting that, and you're just going to give it back?"

"Coleman, I *have* to give it back." Serge rinsed spit from the air canister's mouthpiece. "This is a sacred religious event. It would be grossly disrespectful to interfere."

"But I want to party. I only agreed to all this because I thought the ouzo part was coming up."

"It is. Just a little longer."

"So I'm going to be stuck here waiting again?"

"No. Here's what I want you to do. . . ."

Coleman listened until Serge finished. He furrowed his brow. "That'll never work."

"Just do it!"

Serge stuck the mini-tank back in his mouth and disappeared beneath the water.

ELEVEN

GAINESVILLE

$\mathcal{T}$ he Davenports were on a cleaning-product run. For five seconds. Less than fifty feet from his son's apartment door, Jim stopped behind a Jeep with homemade plywood speakers built into the rear bay.

"What the hell's he doing?" said Martha. "The road's clear."

"I think he's talking to that girl in a bikini leaning against his door."

"I *know* what he's doing," said Martha. "That's no place to talk. He's blocking the parking lot's exit."

"I'm sure he'll just be another moment."

"If you're not going to do something, I will!"

"Martha, please."

She rolled down her window. "Hey! You in the Jeep! Move it!"

"He couldn't hear," said Jim. "Stereo's too loud."

Martha reached across her husband and leaned on the horn.

"Martha—"

A tanned, muscle-bound man got out of the Jeep and walked back to Jim's door. A meaty fist pounded the window. "You just fuckin' honk at me?"

Jim lowered his window a slit. "Actually my wife—Yes, I honked at you."

"What's your fuckin' problem?"

"No problem." Jim grinned.

"You just honk at me for fun?"

"Jim!" yelled Martha. "Don't take that from this creep!"

"Martha, please. Let me handle this." He turned back to the window. "You're blocking the exit."

"Out of the car! I'm going to seriously fuck you up!"

Jim hit the electric button closing his window. He faced forward.

"Jim!" said Martha. "What's wrong with you? You're twice his age!"

"Martha, that only works if I'm twenty and he's ten."

More banging on the window.

"So we just take it?"

"He'll eventually go away."

The bishop took off his hat and scratched his head.

The kids from the dinghies were milling around back on land now, everyone staring perplexed into the dark water. Murmurs rippled through the crowd.

Coleman strolled along the seawall and came up behind the audience. One of the people in back was much smaller than the rest, hopping on tiptoes for a view. Coleman tapped his shoulder.

Nikolai turned. Coleman bent and whispered. He stood back up and smiled.

The boy was suspicious. "Who are you?"

"A friend of a friend," said Coleman. "What have you got to lose?"

Nikolai shrugged and began worming his way through the crowd. Without notice, the small boy stepped up to the seawall, took a deep breath and dove in.

"What the heck's he doing?"

Nikolai reached the bayou's silty floor and felt his way through typical Florida bottom debris. Gun, gun, knife, gun, human femur, brass knuckles, gun . . . He was just about to surface when something seized his ankle. He panicked and thrashed, trying to reach air, but the hand's grip was too strong and pulled him back down. Another hand pressed something into the youth's right palm and curled his fingers tightly around it. The ankle was released.

Nikolai broke the water's surface, gasping for breath.

The crowd exploded.

The youth was so unnerved he didn't realize what was going on until he noticed they were all pointing at his hand.

The cross.

On the other side of the bayou, Serge surfaced and climbed over the seawall. He joined Coleman beside the Comet and watched Nikolai being carried away on shoulders toward the promise of another daylong street celebration. Serge opened the trunk and tossed his spent air canister in a tote bag.

"Sorry about complaining earlier," said Coleman. "That was an awfully nice thing to do."

"Community service is underrated." Serge zipped the bag closed. "I think my karma just got ten thousand frequent-flier miles."

"Are we finally to the part about the ouzo?"

"Yes," said Serge, grabbing a newspaper out of the trunk. "Here's the part about the ouzo: It's illegal in this country."

"Serge!"

"Makes people crazy." He flipped through the paper. "Glad I saved this thing from breakfast. I'm clipping the Epiphany article for my scrapbook."

"Okay," said Coleman. "Then can we at least go to that dive?"

Serge flipped another page. "Which one?"

"The Bridge Lounge."

"Just over the Anclote River. Good choice. Excellent vintage sign with martini glass." Serge tossed the newspaper back in the trunk; it randomly fell open to a small article about a notorious inmate named McGraw being released from Raiford.

The trunk slammed shut.

INTERSTATE 75

A champagne Cadillac Escalade drove south. It passed the Ocala exit and a faded billboard for Silver Springs. A snapped-off sideview mirror dangled by its electrical control cord outside Jim's window.

Silence.

"Martha, please say something."

"We just bought this car."

"I'll get it fixed."

"But why should we have to pay? It's not fair."

"Honey, life's not fair. We need to focus on our blessings."

"And we just let these jerks walk all over us every day?"

"Not every day."

"Yes, every day!"

"I know it's frustrating, but we made the smart move."

Martha folded her arms tightly and stared out the window.

"Baby, if we're getting defrauded by a big company and a lot of money's involved, then we complain. But this is Florida. We can't allow ourselves to be provoked into fights with every idiot we meet on the street. You have no idea what baggage they're bringing to the table."

"So we have no pride?"

"Pride's irrelevant," said Jim. "We have a family. Never entangle your life with a stranger when the only thing to gain is the last word."

"If I'm insulted, I have a right to the last word!"

"Forget insults. At this very moment there's at least five hundred people in our city who, if they could get away with it, would slit our throats for the possessions in our house."

Jim was wrong. There were 762.

"You're paranoid," said Martha. "You need therapy."

"I know you're upset."

"I'm completely serious."

"About what?"

"Therapy."

"I thought you were joking."

"There's this new support group I heard about."

"What kind?"

She told him.

"I don't need to go to that."

Martha folded her arms tighter.

"Okay," said Jim. "Make you a deal. I'll go, but only if you do, too."

"What? With you?"

"No, to your own group . . ." He told her what kind.

"I don't need to go there."

"It's only fair," said Jim. "You're the one who's always harping on that."

Martha gritted her teeth. "Okay, it's a deal."

TWELVE

PORT OF TAMPA

A ship's horn made a deep, deafening blast.

Balloons, streamers, people cheering and uncorking champagne.

Rachael was on the third deck of the cruise terminal's parking garage, hiding in the Comet's backseat with third-day psychosis. She raised her sweat-drenched, wild-eyed face to peek out the window. The horn sounded again, and Rachael curled up in quaking fear on the floorboards. She loved partying!

Down on the docks, a mass of people waved at the about-to-depart ship.

"Safe journey!" shouted Serge. *"Take lots of pictures!"*

Coleman drank from a "Pepsi" can. "Who are you yelling at?"

"Everybody," said Serge, cupping his hands around his mouth again. *"Pay attention to the lifeboat instructions! Did you know sharks can actually leap six feet out of the water? . . . "*

"You know people on the ship?"

"Nope. . . . *Ever seen a body recovered at sea? . . . Pleasant trip!*"

"Then what are we doing here?"

"I love to come to the port and pretend I know someone on a ship," said Serge. "Another of life's overlooked little pleasures—plus a free pass to go ape-shit in public. . . . *Bon voyage, Joe, you crazy bastard! . . .*"

"Look at all those people up there," said Coleman.

". . . *Willy, you forgot your heart medication! Willy? Oh, my God, he's turning blue! . . .* Wonder what's going on in their lives? It always perks me up to speculate. . . ." He began pointing. ". . . That woman's cheating with the dude who cleans her air ducts, that guy spends all his time upset about Mexicans, that man's in perfect health but will suddenly projectile-cough impressive clots of blood during the big client dinner, that couple will lose everything answering an e-mail from Nigeria by the widow of the foreign minister trying to transfer twenty million dollars out of the country. . . . *Mary! Don't give anyone herpes this time! . . .*"

Coleman giggled. "You just fucked the cruise for everyone named Mary."

"See the fun you can have?" Serge beamed proudly and thumped his chest. "I'm a seafarin' man! Ain't this ship a beauty?"

Coleman stared almost straight up at the majestic bow with aqua-and-orange trim. Staterooms, towering green-glass atrium, obsessive people already running laps around the smokestack on the exercise track, many more celebrating on balconies.

"SS *Serendipity*," said Serge. "Flagship of Caribbean Crown Line registered in Liberia. Three thousand passengers. A hundred-gross tonnage of enabler for people with eating, drinking and gambling disorders."

"What are you talking about?"

"You've taken a cruise, right?"

Coleman shook his head.

"You're kidding. I thought of all people."

"I haven't been on one, okay?"

"Familiar with Las Vegas?"

"Of course."

"Add a rudder and subtract government. The whole country's into excess, even when *fighting* excess, and cruises are the nation's bad habits on steroids. All the things you're not supposed to do on land you're *supposed* to do on a cruise because it's one of America's official responsibility-free zones, like Mardi Gras, New Year's Eve or Courtney Love. Twenty-four-hour free buffets all over the place, raunchy stage shows, countless bars that won't cut you off as long as you can knee-walk into a casino and blow the mortgage—"

"Whoa! When can we go?"

"Easy, Gilligan. We're broke again, remember?" Serge looked up at the Titillation Deck, where four elderly women waved over the railing and blew noisemakers.

Eunice clutched a party horn in her teeth. "Who are we waving at?"

"Everybody," said Edna. *"Woo-hoo! . . ."*

"Do we know anybody down there?"

"Not a soul," said Edith. "This is one of life's free little pleasures. . . . *Susan, Chuck, see you next week! . . .*"

"Let's pick out some people," said Ethel.

"Why?"

"For fun. See if we can confuse them. Like how we get a big kick waving at people we don't know in Morrison's cafeteria, and they halfheartedly wave back in social awkwardness."

"What about those two guys?"

"Wave!" said Edna.

"Serge," said Coleman. "Are those old ladies waving at us?"

"I think you're right. But they must have us confused with someone else. Let's wave back."

"What for?"

"Confuse them. It's lots of fun. . . . *Happy Trails! . . .*"

The celebratory waving of the old women became unsure. Edith lowered her hand. "Do we know those guys?"

"I don't think so."

"They seem to know us."

"Now *I* feel awkward."

"Maybe it's a double-reverse sting," said Edna.

"What's that?"

"What we were doing to them except vice versa," said Edith.

"They're fucking with us?" said Eunice.

"The sons of bitches!"

"Serge," said Coleman. "Those old ladies are shooting birds at us. Except the one on the end who's doing the Italian thing under her chin."

"This is bullshit," said Serge. "Just because they're old they think they can act any way they want. . . . *Fuck you! . . .*"

A balcony one floor below the Titillation Deck: "Check out those guys on the dock."

"Which ones?"

"The two jumping around shooting birds with both hands."

"Are they shooting them at us?"

"I think they are! . . . *You motherfuckers! . . .*"

Down on the dock, people pointed: "Look at those guys on the fourth deck!"

"They're flipping us off, the cocksuckers. . . . *Eat me! . . .*"

Someone landside grabbed a bottle by the neck. He winged it at the ship; glass shattered against the hull and rained into the water. Rotten food flew back from the Tranquillity Deck. More gestures and profanity. People on the pier rummaged trash cans for ammo. Ship's passengers flung debris that splatted on the dock.

"Ow." Coleman grabbed a bloody spot above his left eyebrow. "What the fuck was that?"

"The country coming apart." Trash exploded around them as Serge headed for the exit. "Let's go greet planes at the airport."

TEN P.M., THE DAVENPORTS' MASTER BEDROOM

Jim and Martha lay side-by-side in unflattering pajamas.

"I don't know what you mean," said Jim. "What's wrong with our sex life?"

"Just quantity and quality."

"I thought everything was fine."

"Don't take it personally."

"How can I not take *that* personally?"

"Jim, it's normal. Most people married this long fall in a rut. I was talking to my girlfriends about us at lunch."

"You discussed our sex life?"

"You wouldn't believe the feedback about you. Remember Susan?"

"I'm not sure I want to hear."

"They have these manuals. Susan said she recalls meeting you at a dinner, so she insisted on letting me borrow this book with pictures: all these positions and accessories I never would have dreamed, like this string of metal balls that you pull really slow—"

"Martha, why can't we just keep going the way we are?"

"We can. I'm just talking about a little variety."

"What kind of variety?"

"Role-playing. Susan told me this one game where she and Phil wear each other's clothes."

Jim covered his eyes. "I play tennis with Phil."

"We should discuss our fantasies."

"I don't have any fantasies."

"*Everybody* has fantasies."

"Do you?"

"Of course," said Martha.

"I had no idea."

"Because we never talk about it."

"You know I love you," said Jim. "If it'll make you happy . . ."

"You too. Tell me what you want. I'll do anything."

"This is just such a surprise. I'll have to think about it. Do you know what you want?"

Martha nodded. "Several things."

"Name one."

"I want you to be a bad man."

"What? You want me to act like a jerk?"

"Not a jerk, a desperado. You know how certain women are always fatally attracted to the *wrong* guys? I married you because you're so nice. But it would be a change of pace—just fantasy, you understand."

"How am I supposed to be a bad man?"

"I can't tell you. The surprise is part of the excitement. Tomorrow night?"

THIRTEEN

TAMPA

A tastefully restored 1923 bungalow sat a couple blocks south of Azeele Avenue. Daisy yellow. Sprawling porch with hip roof and restored supports. To either side were long lines of similarly rehabbed homes in a historic section of Tampa that was bouncing back after police got the memo to chase winos north of Kennedy Boulevard. But the area remained a buffer zone, still too sketchy for family life, and the homes had been converted into a variety of light-impact professional offices with top-shelf alarm systems. Signs in brass and carved wood for accountants, law firms, M.D.s.

The sign in front of the 1923 home indicated psychiatry. Through the front window, a man and a woman could be seen sitting across from each other in a pair of antique English chairs.

"Love your new digs!" said Serge. "Didn't want to mention anything, but that last place was a shit hole."

"Serge, maybe you can change the subject with other people—"

"Did you see where that thirteen-foot Burmese python escaped into the Everglades? Swallowed an alligator! . . ."

"Serge, you disappeared for a year," said the psychiatrist.

"Then you just show up on my doorstep and expect everything to be peachy?"

". . . Ruptured his stomach."

"What?"

"Huh?"

The doctor sighed and looked down at an old patient folder. "We were last talking about faulty rage control."

"You can click your little pen open and check that off the list!"

The pen remained unclicked.

"What's the matter?" asked Serge, head hanging straight back, admiring crown molding.

"Your knuckles are all skinned up."

"They are?" He held out both hands and turned them over. "Oh *that*. No, it wasn't rage; it was sex."

"What possible kind of sex?—"

"Rachael. She fucks like a hurricane! I'm more of a typhoon, sometimes a dust devil, but every once in a while a quick-forming Midwestern squall with hail, but not golf-ball size; you know those cute little popcorn pieces that hop around your lawn? . . ."

"Serge . . ."

". . . We were humping our brains out just this morning, and right before I came, I started flashing on Andrew Jackson, the Sanibel Lighthouse, Warm Mineral Springs, my View-Master collection. Okay, that last one was because I was actually looking at View-Masters at the time. . . ."

"Serge!"

"What?"

"How do you explain the bump on your forehead? Are you still head-butting people?"

Serge felt the top of his head. "Oh, that was sex, too. She caught me looking at View-Masters."

The doctor maintained poise and jotted in her file. "Despite the protracted absence, I'm glad you came back. Indicates at least a minimal desire to address your problems."

"Problems? I don't have any problems."

She put her pen down. "Then what are we doing sitting here?"

"You're a great conversationalist. Coleman's got a good heart, but you can only use words from books that come with crayons, and the rest of the guys in my circle don't even know what a newspaper is."

"So if you're not here to explore the truth about yourself, what were you expecting to talk about?"

"The *Miami Vice* movie. I loved it, with an asterisk for lack of character background. Did you know it was based on episode fifteen of the first season, 'Smuggler's Blues,' originally aired February 1, 1985, with Glen Frey? What did you think of the casting?"

"Serge . . ."

"Or if you're more of an art-house type, we can critique Jim Jarmusch's *Stranger Than Paradise*. I even tracked down the Surfcaster Motel in Melbourne. The staff was polite for the first few hours I interrogated them, but in the end I got the feeling they weren't art house. . . ."

"Serge—"

He reached in his pocket. ". . . Got excellent photos of the room where the main characters holed up before Eddie wigged and hopped a direct flight to Budapest. Right, I know what you're thinking: Budapest. The *Melbourne* airport. But you have to suspend disbelief if you ever want to enjoy another movie or watch the president for more than fifteen seconds without running into the street demanding a new constitutional convention."

"Serge, I didn't go to school all those years to discuss Florida movies."

"Then you got gypped."

"Serge!"

"Okay, okay. Here's what's bothering me. You want the truth? I don't have a legacy."

"Legacy?"

"Well, I have one, but it's the wrong kind. Think of all the great creative legacies from history. Either a defining moment, like the photo of Mount Suribachi, or a fertile period, from *Beggars' Banquet* to *Exile on Main Street*. I need to leave a universally respected mark in this world or what's the point?"

"What brought this on?"

"I Googled myself. People have no idea how words can hurt."

The doctor sat up rigid, for authority. "I can't treat you anymore if your heart isn't into it, which I'm beginning to seriously doubt. I want you to prove me wrong."

"How?"

She wrote on a piece of paper and gave it to Serge.

"What's this?"

"The support group I want you to attend."

"But I don't do good in groups. I'm a lone wolf. You know the song 'Desperado'? I hate that song because it's for dorks who keep getting dumped and say, 'I'm just not meant for one woman.' Correct: You're meant for zero."

"Serge. This is an ultimatum. Go to the group."

"But these people are messed up."

"I'm afraid I'm going to have to be firm." The doctor stood. "You need to attend at least one meeting before I'll agree to see you again."

"Okay." Serge slipped the note into his wallet. "But I'm telling you it's a mistake."

GULF OF MEXICO

The water was pleasant and calm. The SS *Serendipity* reached the midpoint of its return leg from Cozumel.

The G-Unit made its way to the aft promenade and grabbed four hot, moist cafeteria trays just out of the washer. They slid them along aluminum rails. The front tray stopped.

"What's the matter?" asked Edna.

"Where's my lasagna?" said Edith.

"What lasagna?"

"The one I like."

The trays began moving again. And stopped again. "Where's my salad dressing?"

"And the crumbled hard-boiled eggs?"

"What happened to the tapioca?"

All around them, scores of other retirees with empty trays, wandered the cafeteria at random angles in a fog of confusion.

The casual observer would have blamed senility.

It wasn't.

A ten-year, double-blind study from the Mayo Clinic concluded that even in late stages of dementia, the last to go is the lobe of the brain in charge of cafeteria layout.

The G-Unit was on its first cruise, but the others were veterans. "Where's the creamed corn?" "My veal?"

In the beginning, cruise executives were delighted by the growing trend of repeat bookings among retirees. Past experience had shown them to be among the most coveted customers: suckers for "senior discounts" who spent ten times the savings on slots and early-dinner-seating cocktails.

The industry aggressively catered to this clientele by hiring suave, relatively young ballroom dancers to offset the widows-to-widowers ratio. There were extra chocolates on the pillows, and the turn-down crew was schooled in the ancient Oriental art of towel folding. Each evening, guests would be greeted upon returning to their cabins by Godiva and cute terry cloth swans or ponies or kitty cats in the middle of their beds.

Then, new numbers started coming in. There had to be some kind of mistake. The latest groups were barely spending at all. That's when the main offices noticed something even more alarming from Florida ports: Waves of retirees were booking so many consecutive cruises that they were actually *living* on the ships. Quite inventively, too. They chipped in for tiny communal apartments near the port, where they kept keepsakes. Some had relatives deliver prescriptions and exchange laundry during turnarounds in port; others hailed taxis for biweekly errand runs. And if there were any medical problems at sea, it fell to the ships' doctors: free health care!

The cruise lines' very survival depended upon people who were bad at arithmetic. And retirees on fixed incomes are the nation's math elite. The seniors crunched the numbers. As long as they stayed away from the casinos and bars, it was a no-brainer:

God's waiting room was going to sea.

The thrifty new breed of customer displaced free-spenders. Profits plunged. Something had to give. Cruise companies tried to summarily cancel reservations on shaky grounds, but one of the widows' sons was an attorney. A good one. The reservations had to be honored, so they drafted a new battle plan.

The first beachhead was the cafeteria.

Edna waved from behind a bank of ferns. "Found the lasagna."

Another hidden voice: ". . . Tapioca."

People changed direction in a slow-motion Easter-egg hunt. "They've rearranged everything."

"But they did that yesterday, too."

"Weird."

After lunch, it was nappy time. The G-Unit took an elevator to their deck. Edith opened the stateroom door. In the middle of her bed was a bath towel folded into a coiled cobra.

THE NEXT DAY

Serge walked down the hall of a utilitarian building just east of the Hillsborough River in the social services part of town. He stopped at a room, rechecking the piece of paper the psychiatrist had given him. He opened the door and stuck his head inside. "Excuse me. Is this Anger Management?"

"Suck my dick, motherfucker!"

"Thank you." He took a seat in a grade-school desk, folded his hands smartly and grinned.

The meeting's moderator smiled back. "Would you mind standing and telling us your name?"

He got up. "My name's Serge."

"Hello, asshole!"

"Sorry," said Serge. "I didn't quite catch that. . . ."

FOURTEEN

SATURDAY MORNING

*T*he dawn was unusually crisp. Two people sat at the end of a driveway in the kind of folding cloth chairs with beverage holders that parents bring to soccer games.

Tied to the street sign at the corner: a balloon and a homemade sign in the shape of an arrow. YARD SALE. The balloon was key.

Early birds had been arriving since first light, sorting through a clothesline of frayed corduroys and bell bottoms. Others browsed tables of housewares and bric-a-brac that traced decades of fierce consumerism. The Davenports themselves were amazed when they set up an hour earlier. Chinese checkers, lava lamp, Ouija board, tabletop Eiffel Tower cigarette lighter.

Jim laid out paisley potholders. "Look at all this junk."

Martha held something up. "What were you thinking?"

"What is it?"

"A stuffed beaver."

"I don't remember buying that."

Their curiosity shifted to customers. Martha made change for someone buying a golf club for fifty cents. "We'll sell you the whole set for two dollars."

"I don't play golf."

"Why are you buying that?"

"It's only fifty cents."

Martha made change and looked at Jim. "I'm glad we're moving."

"We still have to find a house."

A man walked away with a sand wedge over his shoulder.

"Our real estate agent says it's a buyer's market."

"At least we're getting rid of all this junk. This should have been done years ago."

"'At least'?" said Martha. "You're not changing your mind about moving?"

"No, I just meant—"

A new voice. "Excuse me?"

The Davenports looked up: a short, fireplug of a man in a too-tight T-shirt that said VAGITARIAN. He held a spherical black-and-white TV from the seventies.

Jim smiled. "How can I help you?"

"Does the TV work?"

"I don't know. It's a dollar."

Martha: "She's already got four houses to show us, and two are on Davis Islands."

"Can we afford Davis Islands?—"

"Excuse me?"

Jim turned. "What?"

"I don't want it if it doesn't work."

"Okay."

Martha: "It'll be nice to have a bigger place."

"Bigger?" said Jim. "Prices are crazy right now. I just assumed we were getting something smaller."

"Why would you think that?" Martha collected seventy-five cents for three Tijuana Brass albums.

"Because our second child just left for college," said Jim. "Families need more room when growing, not shrinking."

"Excuse me?"

Jim turned. "Yes?"

"What if I get the TV home and it doesn't work?"

Jim shrugged. "It's a dollar."

"I'll think about it." He walked away with a round TV under his arm.

Jim whispered sideways, "Who would wear a T-shirt that says something like that?"

"I'm glad we're moving."

Another voice, this one hostile out of the gate: "Excuse me!"

"Yes?"

"What's this thing?"

"A stuffed beaver."

"What's the deal?"

"It's a dollar," said Jim.

"No, I mean I don't understand."

"Understand what?"

"A stuffed beaver. Who would want to buy such a thing?"

Martha leaned and whispered. "A vagitarian."

Jim chuckled.

"Are you laughing at me?"

"No," said Jim. "Another customer."

"What the hell kind of yard sale are you running?"

Coleman dropped a head of lettuce and chased it under a table. He came back out. "Finding anything?"

"No." Serge inspected a tomato with a magnifying glass. "Just keep looking."

Coleman replaced the lettuce in the produce cooler and picked up another head. "Being broke sucks."

"That's why we're here." Serge slowly rotated a bell pepper.

"I still don't see how this is going to make any money."

"Oh, it'll make money all right. You see those articles

about what idiots are paying in Internet auctions for vegetables that look like Elvis and the Virgin Mary?"

"No. How much?"

"A lot. But word's out, and the market's glutted. So I'm carving my own niche: eBayers with at least four years of college education." He nodded at the tomato in his hand—"Cervantes"—and dropped it in his sack.

Coleman moved to another shelf. "I found something." He held up a potato. "What do you think?"

"Who's it supposed to be?"

"Mr. Potato Head."

"You're having trouble with the concept. Look at this."

"An onion?"

"Che Guevara." Into Serge's bag.

Coleman looked around. "Where's Rachael?"

"The medication aisle." He grabbed a zucchini. "That should keep her out of our hair."

Behind them: "Excuse me? Sir?"

Serge turned.

A smiling manager. "May I be of assistance?"

"You know what Copernicus looks like?"

"Sir, our employees couldn't help but notice: You're handling every fruit and vegetable in the produce department."

"Not yet," said Serge.

"Sir, don't get me wrong. We want you to be a satisfied customer—"

"That's why I picked this store," said Serge. " 'Where shopping is a pleasure.' "

"Check it out," said Coleman. "A turnip that looks like Merv Griffin."

"Sir." The manager's smile was gone. "You're welcome to purchase what you already have in the bags, but I'm afraid I'm going to have to ask you to—"

An assistant manager ran up. "We've got a problem."

"What is it?" asked the manager.

"Some woman's trying to buy forty boxes of sinus capsules. She's acting crazy."

"Probably a meth-head," said Serge. "And you thought groceries would be a quiet job. . . . Oooooo! Marcel Proust acorn squash . . ."

The manager turned to his assistant. "Tell her the limit's two. Any more problems, call the police." Then back to customers fondling carrots . . .

Moments later, Serge was being rung up at register three. "This is a first. Eighty-sixed from the produce section." He finished paying and grabbed his bags.

"Look," said Coleman, "at Customer Service. It's Rachael."

"Gimme my fucking Sinutabs!"

"Keep walking," said Serge. "Life's too short."

Jim opened his mouth, but the angry yard-sale customer was already stomping away. *"Stuffed beaver for Christ sake!"*

Martha threw up her arms. "Where are these nut jobs coming from?"

Jim pointed at the corner. "Our balloon. They're powerless in its presence."

"I can't wait to move."

Jim glanced around. "Where'd that other guy go?"

"Who?"

Jim accepted a roll of pennies for a wooden tennis racket with broken strings. "The one who took the TV without paying."

The morning wore on. Dollar for fondu skewers. Fifty cents for a lazy Susan. They got haggled down to a dime for a Baggie of nonmatching poker chips.

Martha shook Jim's arm. "I don't believe it."

A man walked up the driveway. VAGITARIAN.

"Maybe he remembered he didn't pay for the TV," said Jim.

"I seriously doubt it."

"Excuse me?"

Jim smiled. "Yes?"

"You said it worked."

"I said I didn't know."

"I took it home and tried it." The man handed the round television to Jim. "It doesn't work."

"Sorry."

The man stared at Jim. Jim smiled.

"So?" said the man.

"So what?"

"I want my dollar back."

"You never paid."

"Yes I did."

"I'm quite sure," said Jim.

"Fine!" The man grabbed the TV back and walked away again.

"Jim!" said Martha. "Stop him!"

"It's only a dollar."

"I can't wait to move."

The man with the TV continued down the street and reached the corner.

Martha turned to her husband. "Did he just pop our balloon?"

Serge sat in front of a computer terminal in the downtown public library. He stared at the screen. "I don't get it. There must be something wrong with the Internet."

"What's the matter?" asked Coleman, lurking over his shoulder.

"Haven't gotten a single hit on any of my vegetables, and I even set the starting price at ninety-nine cents."

"I don't think anything's wrong with the Internet," said Coleman. "Look . . ."

They turned to Rachael, tapping the next keyboard.

"Who would have guessed she'd even know how to turn on a computer," said Serge. "It's only two o'clock and she's already made seven hundred dollars selling naked pictures of herself. How is that possible?"

"Because twin-headed dildo action is big!"

"I have to get my mind off this, or a major funk is brewing."

"What are you going to do?"

"Might as well get started on my legacy." Serge headed for the elevators.

"How do you do a legacy?"

"By being a pioneer whose groundbreaking advancements will revolutionize all aspects of modern life as we know it." He looked at his watch. "Fifteen minutes should do."

They got out on the first floor and passed a rack of newspapers on wooden poles. Serge marched purposefully for the information desk. A woman looked up.

"Can I help you?"

"Yes!" said Serge. "Give me The New Thing!"

"The what?"

"Make it a surprise. Hit me!"

"I'm . . . not sure I understand—"

Serge pointed down. "Your sign says Information?"

"Yes?"

"Fire away! And make it big. Anything special stashed behind the counter?"

Serge reminded the librarian of something. She glanced over at a communal lunatic reading area where the regular cast of homeless talked to themselves, played invisible card games, started unzipping their pants. . . .

The librarian jumped up. "Henry!"

"Whoops. Forgot."

She sat back down and opened her desk drawer for aspirin. "I'm sorry. Where were we?"

"The New Thing!"

"Not sure what you want, but we have a large display in fiction for *The Da Vinci Code*. That's supposed to be big."

Serge gnashed his teeth. "I hate the fucking *Da Vinci Code*." He quickly covered his mouth. "Pardon my French. Actually it's Anglo-Saxon. More hypocrisy! People use gutter language, then try to weasel out by lying that they're talking French and being sophisticated, like *menage à trois*, endless possibilities! 669, 696, 969, 966, 694—that's when the last person's legs are crossed . . ."

"Sir . . ."

". . . I love life! Always trying to stay on top of human endeavor, eager for the future: What marvelous breakthroughs are just around the corner for mankind? Will this finally be the epoch of lasting peace and disease eradication? Crap, it's *The Da Vinci Code* Century."

"You just said you wanted something new."

"That I did. Fair enough. *The Da Vinci Code* it is. Maybe I can find a way to stop it." He grabbed Coleman by the arm. "We're off!"

The librarian jumped up again: "Henry!"

"My bad."

They arrived in fiction and stared at the immense wall display.

"Wow!" said Coleman. "Look at all these books! *The Da Vinci Code Proven at Last, The Da Vinci Code Debunked, The Da Vinci Code Diet, The Da Vinci Code for Cats, Break Free from Da Vinci Code Companion Books . . .* "

Serge grabbed his stomach. "I may be ill."

Coleman picked at something on his arm. "So whose code is the *Da Vinci Code*?"

"Is this a trick question like, 'Who's buried in Grant's Tomb?' "

"No, I—"

"Coleman! You're a genius!"

"I am?"

"Da Vinci was a renaissance man."

"What's that?"

"Someone who can't keep his mind on any one thing. That's me! I'll leave my mark by not concentrating on leaving my mark."

"How are you going to do that?"

Serge hurried for the door. "I'm starting a new collection."

FIFTEEN

THAT NIGHT

*J*im Davenport's muffled voice came through the closed bathroom door of the master bedroom. "Ready?"

Martha lay tucked under the covers. "You're not supposed to ask if I'm ready."

"Okay, but you are ready?"

"Jim."

"You don't want to mess with me. I'm capable of anything. I'm a *baaaaaad man*!"

"Come on."

"Okay."

The bathroom door opened. "Don't ask for mercy."

Martha sat up in bed. "Jim, what's going on?"

"You wanted a bad man."

"You're wearing a pirate costume."

"I'm a pirate."

"Are you serious?"

"From everything I've read, they were bad." He crawled into bed and began stroking Martha's hair.

She put a hand over her mouth. "Jim, I'm sorry. I can't make love tonight."

"What do you mean? You're the one who scheduled this."

"It's the costume."

"I'll take it off."

"The pirate image is already stuck in my head. You know how I have to be able to keep a straight face."

Jim fell back on his own pillow and stared at the ceiling fan. "I'm sorry. I'm new to this."

"Please don't feel bad." Martha reached over and reassuringly held Jim's hand that was covered by the plastic hook. "Maybe we should see a sex coach."

"Martha, are we pandas?"

She reached for a book on the nightstand. "Have to get up early tomorrow anyway. Our real estate agent's got all those houses."

"So you definitely want to move?"

Faint cursing from street level. Martha opened her book. "Yes."

Jim got out of bed and walked to the window. Down on the corner, three shadowy people struggled at a bus stop. More swearing. A woman in a halter top had a pudgy guy in a headlock. The third person tried to break it up. They tumbled over the bus bench and rolled across a lawn. A motion sensor tripped.

Martha turned a page. "What's happening out there?"

"Three people were fighting, but they ran away when the Johnsons' security lights came on. . . . Now they've stopped in front of the strip mall for a meeting."

"Meeting?"

Jim stepped closer to the window. "Wonder what they could be talking about? . . ."

"What the hell's wrong with you two?" said Serge. "Families are trying to sleep around here."

Rachael shoved Coleman in the chest. "Fuckhead here can't read a fuel gauge."

"Hey," said Coleman. "It's not my fault we ran out of gas."

"You moron!" She grabbed him by the hair and yanked his head side to side.

"Ow! Ow! Ow!"

"Knock it off!" said Serge. "What's done is done. We'll just walk to that gas station and get a spare can. Besides, there's a silver lining." He pointed back up the street. "We got to see Plant High School, the first stop on my new renaissance collection tour. Coleman gave me the idea."

Rachael threw down a clump of hair. "The retards leading the retards."

"You're welcome to leave anytime you want," said Serge. "But you'll miss the tour."

Rachael poked a finger in an empty cigarette pack and threw it aside. "Tour?"

"Tap into the spiritual undercurrent of genius. Total spectrum of disciplines, from science to politics to art, that have graced our fair state. Like the high school back there where Stephen Stills graduated . . ." He reached in his pocket and produced a clear plastic tube of dirt.

"What's that?" asked Coleman.

"Soil sample from the high school. My legacy needs a dirt collection." He held the tube to Coleman's ear. "Listen."

"I don't hear anything."

Serge placed the tube next to his own ear. " 'Suite: Judy Blue Eyes.' Just imagine, Buffalo Springfield, CSN&Y, Woodstock . . ." He held the tube inches from his eyes. ". . . And it all started here. . . ."

"You said we were going to make some money!" said Rachael. "And score!" Her left hand flashed out and smacked the plastic tube from Serge's hand. It broke on the ground.

Serge gasped. "Stephen!" He fell to his knees. "Coleman, Stephen needs us!"

"What do I do?"

"Grab Rachael's cigarette pack from the weeds."

"Got it. . . . Here you are."

Serge uncrumpled the empty pack and gently scooped dirt inside. He stood and wiped his forehead. "Crisis averted."

"That's it," said Rachael. "I'm done with you boobs." She ran across the street and accosted a random night wanderer. A negotiation. The man handed her something.

Coleman looked down at the cigarette pack in Serge's hand. "That's the collection you were talking about at the library?"

"Actually it wasn't my first choice. I was originally going to start a sperm bank."

"Sperm?"

"I figured if you're going to collect, *collect*. You know how there are those institutes in Sweden with samples from internationally famous geniuses? But then I started running the logistics through my head: ordering watermarked stationery, composing the request letters, which have to be very delicately worded. And nobody would reply anyway. All those places in Sweden are well connected through Nobel Prize cocktail receptions. That's the thing about starting a jiz farm: It's all who you know. Plus the special freezers cost a fortune. Dirt's less maintenance."

"Where'd you get the idea?"

"Had it bouncing around my head several years ago. But I'd never heard of anyone else doing it, so I figured it must be stupid."

"What changed your mind?"

"*Saving Private Ryan*. That scene after the D-day invasion where this sergeant collects a little tin of sand and adds it to a canvas bag full of tins marked with names of other battles. I said, 'Hey, that's *my* idea! He stole my fucking idea!' Then they made me leave the theater—"

Rachael came screaming back across the street with something under her arm. "Get him the fuck away from me!"

The man in chase: "Give it!"

She hid behind Serge and peeked over his shoulder. "Protect me."

The porky pursuer finished a rapid wobble across the road and reached the curb. "She ripped me off!"

Serge stared at the man's T-shirt. VAGITARIAN.

"I didn't rip you off!" yelled Rachael. "You gave it to me!"

"I want my television!"

GULF OF MEXICO

The G-Unit's empty stomachs growled on the way out of the restaurant. They normally wouldn't have conceded cafeteria arrangement to the cruise company, but they were on deadline. The real priority was ballroom dancing. They never missed it.

Like tonight. The quartet moved quickly up the Fantasy Deck. The carpet was movie-premiere red. Everything else shiny: faux-gold doorways and banisters reflecting harsh rows of cabaret lightbulbs.

"There's the ballroom," said Edna.

"Where'd all those people come from?" asked Eunice.

"Told you we should have gotten an earlier start," said Edith. "It's getting more popular."

They stood in the back of a large, anxious mob. The doors opened. Everyone charged inside, a trail of bent canes and walkers lost in the stampede.

The sound system struck up Guy Lombardo. A disco ball spun. The G-Unit made its move. Flecks of light swirled over the hardwood floor. They zeroed in on a pair of men by the punch bowl who looked like David Niven and Don Ameche, but a rival gang from the Catskills had the angle and executed a flying wedge.

"Over there!" yelled Eunice.

James Mason and Cary Grant in later years. The women

took off. More trouble, this time a rolling screen block from Boca Raton.

"Damn," said Edna.

They made a sweep of the room. Everyone worth taking was taken.

"I guess it's the Brimleys," said Edith.

"Not the Brimleys."

They looked across the ballroom at a gathering of stocky gentlemen leaning over the bar. Curiously, every last one of them bore a striking resemblance to each other, like they had all been contestants in a Wilford Brimley look-alike contest.

Unbeknownst to the women, the Brimleys' similarity of appearance was no accident. The men had, in fact, been participants in a number of look-alike events, all veterans of the annual Hemingway contest in Key West. But as time and barroom falls took their toll, those Hemingways who could no longer make the grade were put out to stud on cruise ships. They could be counted on for two and only two things: always available, and always completely hammered.

"Okay," Edith sighed. "I guess it's the Brimleys." Since there had never been any competition for these men, the G-Unit was in no hurry. Just then, a championship quilting team from Vermont blitzed their left flank and snagged the leftover dancers.

"What just happened?" said Eunice.

"I don't get it," said Edna. "They were always available before."

"This is no accident," said Edith.

"What do you mean?"

"The cruise line's ratcheting back the gender ratio."

One of the Brimleys took a nasty spill, pulling the lead quilter down with him.

"Let's watch TV in the room."

They arrived back in their cabin. Edith grabbed the remote control and swatted a towel-scorpion off the bed.

SOUTH TAMPA

Jim stood at his upstairs bedroom window. "I'm starting to appreciate you talking me into moving."

"Why?" Martha looked up from her book. "What's going on out there?"

Rachael clutched a small TV to her chest. "It's mine!"

"No it's not!" said VAGITARIAN. "I only let you have it because you promised to—"

Serge held up a hand for the man to stop. "I have a pretty good idea what she promised, and I don't care. *Caveat emptor.*"

"What's that mean?"

"Never trust a stripper."

"I'm not leaving until I get my TV!"

Serge raised the front of his tropical shirt, revealing the butt of a chrome automatic pistol tucked in the waistband. "There's nothing more to see here. Please disperse."

The startled man stumbled backward into the street and was nearly clipped by a drunk driver in a Dodge Dart.

Serge turned around. "What the hell do you want with that stupid TV?"

"Hock it. Good for a dime bag." She set it on the ground and began going through her pockets for cigarette money. "What's this?" She retrieved a small, forgotten square of paper, unfolded it and snorted hard, then licked residue. The paper floated to the ground.

Serge bent down for the piece of trash. "Will you stop doing drugs and littering?"

"I'll do any fucking thing I want!"

"And lower your voice! You're disturbing the community."

"I talk as loud as I want! *Ahhhhhh! Ahhhhhh! . . .*"

Two people walked by on the sidewalk lugging a patio table—"Good evening"—then two more with the matching chairs.

" *. . . Ahhhhhh! Ahhhhhh! Ahhhhhh! . . .* "

"That's it!" Serge twisted a hand up behind her back again and wrapped his right forearm across her neck, compressing the larynx. "Are you going to be quiet?"

She gasped for breath like a grouper on a boat deck.

Serge suddenly felt a sharp pain where she'd stomped on his instep. "Yowwwww!" He released his grip and hopped on one foot.

Rachael picked up a rock and hurled it with surprising accuracy. Serge ducked, and the stone skipped across the street, clanging off the hubcap on a passing Sunbird.

Brakes screeched. The driver jumped out with a baseball bat that is factory equipment on most cars in Tampa after midnight. "What the fuck?"

Serge whipped out his pistol. "Something I can help you with?"

The driver jumped back in. The Sunbird screeched away. A smaller rock hit Serge in the back of the head. "Ouch!"

Rachael reached to the ground for more ammo. She stopped halfway. Her left eye began twiching. Then her other eye. She scratched her arms and chest, then began ripping at her hair with both hands. *"Ahhhhhh! Ahhhhhh—! . . . "*

Serge cocked his pistol. "What did I tell you about that yelling?"

" *. . . Ahhhhhh! Ahhhhhh! I'm not trying to yell this time. . . . "* Rachael ran in terrified figure eights, clawing the top of her head. *"Help! Help! For the love of God! . . . "*

"What's going on?" asked Serge.

"Too much crank," said Coleman.

Rachael ran past them at full gallop. *"Get rid of them! . . . "*

"Get rid of what?"

"Snakes! My hair is full of snakes! Ahhhhhh! . . . " Rachael sprinted down the street. *"Ahhhhhh! . . . "*

Serge cupped his hands around his mouth. "Watch out for that oak—"

" . . . Ahhhhhh!" Smack.

"—tree."

Rachael bounced off the trunk and grabbed the bloody wound on her forehead. *"Ahhhhhh! . . . "* She turned around and ran back the other way.

Serge and Coleman simultaneously sat on the ground. Their heads swiveled left to right as Rachael went screaming by. *" . . . Snakes! . . . "*

She crashed over a garbage can at the corner, got up and reversed direction again. *" . . . Somebody! Help! . . . "*

Coleman's head rotated as she went by. "This is better than *Bum Fight* videos."

A half block away, Martha Davenport looked up from her book. "What's all that racket out there?"

"I don't know." Jim tried to get a better look out the window. "Sounds like some woman's being attacked by snakes."

"Snakes?"

"That's what she says." He watched as Rachael hit the ground, rolling furiously back and forth. Dirt covered her face, mixing with the blood pouring down from her forehead and getting in her nose and mouth. *"Ahhhhhh! Ahhhhhh! There's motherfuckin' snakes in my motherfuckin' hair! . . . "*

"That's odd," said Coleman. "A little bit ago I thought she was the hottest chick I'd ever seen, but for some reason I'm not that turned on anymore."

"It's the same with all women," said Serge. "Sexiness depends on what part of the day you catch them."

Coleman grabbed the spherical TV from where Rachael had left it. "Wonder if this thing works."

Up in the window, Jim had a nagging sensation that he

recognized the wiry man down on the street. Must be mistaken.

Rachael finally stopped rolling around and walked back to Serge and Coleman.

"Hope you're happy," said Serge. "You disturbed a citizen."

"Where?" asked Rachael.

Serge indicated by raising his chin toward a second-story silhouette backlit by his wife's reading lamp. "That guy on the next block. Probably just trying to sleep in peace."

Rachael shook a fist at the distant window. "What are you looking at, motherfucker?"

Jim then noticed the outline of Coleman's nonwarrior constitution and it all snapped into place.

"Oh, no."

SIXTEEN

THE NEXT DAY

*T*hrough the front window of a 1923 bungalow, two people sat facing each other in frosty silence.

"I don't understand why you're so upset," said Serge.

"*You* don't understand why I'm upset?"

"I went to the meeting just like you said."

"I've been getting calls for three days. The moderator never wants to see you again."

"I said I'd pay for the broken desks."

"What a mistake!"

"Didn't I warn you?"

"And yet you still claim you have no problems."

"Right. They started it. Never seen so much hostility in one room."

"So you just beat everyone up?"

"No, I didn't *just* beat everyone up. At first I was consummately polite, but what do I get in return? You should have heard those potty mouths. Everything was 'blow me,' 'bite me' . . ."

"Serge . . ."

". . . Eat shit and die—"

"Serge!"

"What?"

"Now you're just repeating yourself."

"No, they each said something different. Suck my asshole. Lick my balls . . ."

"Serge!"

"What?"

"I've got the theme."

"So you see I'm in the right?"

"Your anger's far worse than I ever imagined."

"*My* anger? I was the happiest person in the room. At least when I arrived."

She got out a piece of notepaper and began writing. "I don't know why I'm still bothering with you."

Serge pumped his eyebrows. "We have that magic."

"I'm going to try something. Very experimental. And risky. But you're an extreme case. That's why you have to make me a promise."

"Name it."

"No more fighting at meetings, especially this one."

He didn't answer.

"Well?"

"I didn't realize it would be *that* promise."

"Promise!"

"Okay, I promise. What kind of meeting?"

She handed him the slip of paper. He read it and looked up. "You've got to be joking."

"I couldn't be more serious. It seems counter-intuitive, but empathizing with these people might be a constructive experience. If you feel you're about to lose control, just get up and leave."

"Fair enough."

TAMPA

The real estate agent was so cheerful you wanted to beat her to death.

"Jim! Martha! Wonderful to finally meet!"

"Me too," said Jim. "Listen, I tried getting the price from you on the phone. . . ."

The agent was also a hugger. Big squeezes for both Davenports. She had a ruby-red blazer with an azalea scarf. A gold metal name tag on the right breast pocket: STEPHANIE. Beneath: TEN-MILLION-DOLLAR ASSOCIATE.

Jim looked up the driveway. "How much?"

"Martha, I absolutely adore what you're wearing!"

Martha glanced down at her warm-up suit from the gym.

Stephanie walked ambitiously toward the Spanish Mission house. "You're going to just love living on Royal Palm Island."

"I thought this was Davis Islands," said Jim.

"Technicality," said Steph. "We have a motion before the city council."

"Why?"

"Money," said the agent. "Like when they changed spider crab to Alaskan king crab. Plus the plural Davis *Islands* confuses everyone. Looks like a single key from the air, but a tiny, more exclusive islet was carved into the side when they dug the sailboat canal. That's where we are now."

"What about whoever this Davis guy was?"

"Dead. You need to get in before the name change," said Steph. "Make a killing."

"We just started looking," said Jim. "We're not even sure we can afford—"

"And the neighbors!" said Stephanie, arms springing out in both directions up the street. "You can't put a price!"

"Speaking of price . . ." said Jim.

Stephanie solemnly raised a hand. "You can't put one." She turned toward the front door. "Shall we peek inside?"

Martha took a single step into the foyer and gasped. Sunlight streamed through two-story-high vertical glass windows. "Oh, Jim! . . ."

"It's got to be too much."

"But what if it isn't?"

"How will we ever know?"

"Why are you whispering?"

"Because I don't want her to hear me."

"Maybe she *should* hear you."

"I don't want her getting upset with me."

"Jim, this is what I keep talking about. You have to act more assertive."

"But she's working for us," Jim whispered. "I shouldn't be put through this kind of discomfort."

"That's why you need to say something."

"Can we talk about this later?"

They resumed walking. Martha crossed the living room and lovingly ran her hand along the mantel. "This would be a great spot to display my antiquities."

"You collect antiquities?" said Steph. "Me too!"

"They're not much," said Martha. "I just dabble."

Steph pointed at the mantel. "That's the perfect place."

"Jim, it's the perfect place. . . . Where'd Steph go?"

"Over here!" echoed the Realtor's voice. "You're going to be knocked out!"

Martha followed the agent across glazed terra-cotta tiles with cerulean-blue diamond accents. "Stephanie, what are they asking?"

"And the kitchen! . . ."

Martha turned the corner. Her hand went over her heart. "Jim! The kitchen!"

"Honey, the countertops are worth more than my car."

Steph gestured at the glistening Corian surface. "Countertops are the second most important consideration in real estate, right after location." She turned to Jim. "Whatever's spent on them, you get back triple in resale value."

"So we'll be paying for three countertops?"

"Think resale."

"We haven't bought it yet."

"It's never too soon," said Steph. "You want to sell this place?"

"This isn't our house."

"I see you need to discuss it with Martha. But don't take too long: It's a red-hot seller's market!"

"I thought you said it was a buyer's market."

"It is."

"I don't understand."

Steph winked. "I'll play with the numbers."

"Speaking of numbers . . ."

Steph walked over to the jumbo, brushed-steel refrigerator and changed channels.

"The fridge has a TV?"

"Liquid crystal," said Steph. "It can also be programmed to run a slide show of children's drawings."

"I used to just tape 'em to the front," said Jim.

Steph shook her head.

"That's not good?"

"And this stove comes Internet-ready."

"Why?"

"To control it from your cell phone."

"I don't mean to be rude," Jim told the agent. "But we might be wasting your time. We really need to know the price."

Since the kitchen had already put the hooks in Martha, it was okay. She told them.

Jim's turn to gasp. "That's everything we have! More!"

"Honey," said Martha. "I think we can do it."

"But we'll be stretched," said Jim. "What if the market goes south? All the financial shows say existing homes are getting bubbly."

"You know what kind of shows those are?" said Steph.

"Stock market shows. They want the money to come back." She led them into the master bedroom. "The market's a shell game. Real estate, on the other hand, never goes down."

"When did they develop this island?" asked Jim.

"Just before the 1925 Florida land bust. Here's your bathroom. . . ."

"Jim!" said Martha. "His and hers sinks!"

"Saved many a marriage," said Steph. She pointed at a wall-mounted TV aimed at the toilet. "Jim, you like sports?"

Martha gazed into the romantic, two-person Jacuzzi. "It's everything we've ever wanted."

"Know who else lives on this side of the island?" said Steph, leading them to the rear of the house. "One of the Bucs, a hockey player, and a local TV anchor." She invaded personal space and lowered her voice. "Plus two city councilmen, which is why we get extra police patrols, but you didn't hear it from me."

"Jim . . ."

"Martha . . ."

"Your backyard . . ." Steph opened the curtains and slid a glass door.

Sailboats, sun, seagulls.

Martha's heart skipped. The patio featured the ceramic mosaic of a loggerhead turtle made from colorful broken pottery. The swimming pool was the kind that perpetually spilled over the top and into a recirculation trough, creating the illusion that it extended into the bay.

"I've always wanted a pool like that," said Martha. "Ever since I saw it in an architecture magazine."

"This is the house," said Steph.

"What house?"

"In the magazine. The photographer was standing right where you are." Steph dipped a hand into the cool, azure water and ran it along her neck. "Makes you want to dive right in!"

A splash off the seawall.

"What was that?"

"Pod of dolphins lives along this side of the island," said Steph. "You could sit out here at sunset and watch them for hours."

"Jim, I've never felt so sure of anything in my life."

"Martha, we discussed our maximum price on the way over."

"But we didn't know it would be like *this*."

"I shouldn't be telling you," said Steph. "It's a divorce sale. That's why we have to move quickly before others swoop."

"Jim!" said Martha. "We have to swoop!"

"No offense," Jim told Steph. "But I don't like to be rushed into big decisions."

"You have no choice," said the agent. "It's going to hit the papers Monday."

"What is?"

"Indictments. That's why the divorce."

"It's going to hit the papers!" said Martha.

"What are we dealing with?" said Jim. "A drug kingpin?"

"No," said Steph. "Big cheese at the zoning department. Got lots of the work on this place comped for favorable rulings. Like that incredible barrel-tile roof!"

"Jim, the roof!"

"Let's start the paperwork!"

They walked through the house and out the front door. Jim pointed back over his shoulder. "I thought we were going to do paperwork."

Steph closed the front door and secured the lock box. "In the car."

"Are we going somewhere?"

"No."

"Why not sign at the dining room table?"

"It's better in the car."

They headed for the curb. A '73 Mercury Comet sped by.

Serge looked out his driver's window at mailbox numbers. "Coleman, you sure those apartments are over here?"

"That's what this map says."

"You idiot! You're holding it upside down. The apartments are on the other side of the island."

The Davenports turned quickly at the sound of screeching tires. The Comet made a left and disappeared at the end of the block.

"What the heck was that?" asked Jim.

"Probably someone's kids," said Steph. "They tend to be a little spoiled around here. Nothing to worry about."

The '73 Comet reached the east side of the island, made a left on Danube and pulled into the parking lot of a dingy apartment building. Serge got out and stood perfectly still.

Coleman walked around the car and popped a Pabst. "What is it?"

"Shhhh!" Serge stared up the street. "I'm having a moment. It hasn't changed a bit after all these years. An oasis of old Florida revivalist architecture and generous public green spaces. Most of the streets are named for bodies of water. Fuckers tore down the coliseum."

"Didn't you used to have an apartment here?"

"How could I not? It's venerable Davis Islands, created by the visionary D. P. Davis, who seawalled and dredged this eight-hundred-acre paradise atop Big and Little Grassy Keys at the mouth of the Hillsborough River. Of course I'd murder anyone who raped an ecosystem like that today. But this was eighty years ago, so it was a historic rape."

"Is this Davis dude still around?"

"Fell overboard during a cruise in 1926."

"I thought they only started doing that lately."

"He was a visionary." Serge turned slowly. "I remember this place from the movie."

"Movie?"

"The FBI Murders: In the Line of Duty." He stepped to the side of the road. "Climactic scene was filmed right under my feet." He took a plastic tube from his pocket and bent down for a soil sample.

"Must have missed it," said Coleman

"Made-for-TV docudrama on the biggest shootout in the history of the Bureau. Happened during Florida's Wild West cocaine-cowboy eighties."

"Now I remember," said Coleman. "But wasn't that Miami?"

Serge nodded. "Cheaper to film in Tampa. Here's the cool part: If you were watching closely, which was me, the real-life firefight followed a stakeout on South Dixie Highway. But in the movie, they're actually driving on Armenia Avenue in West Tampa, then they make a right turn and suddenly they're ten miles away on this island. The cars crashed into that Dumpster, where David Soul and Michael Gross got shot to pieces. This is a happy place."

From the Comet: "Give me my fucking money!"

They turned around. Rachael. Her head dropped below window level, then reappeared with frosted upper lip. "You stole it while I was sleeping!"

"I didn't steal anything. It's a short-term loan."

"Gimme my money!" Head back down.

"We need it for first month's rent," said Serge. "And the new computer for my big plan."

Head came up. "I worked hard on those Internet photos! You didn't sell a single vegetable, and now you're just playing with stupid dirt."

Serge looked sideways at Coleman. "I knew that was coming. There's often tension in a relationship when the woman's career is going better."

They walked toward the apartment building. Coleman climbed over a broken box spring in the breezeway. "What a dump."

"But it's quiet. The landlord said four old ladies live next door, and they're almost never home."

An hour later, Serge and Coleman were locked in the bathroom.

Banging on the door. "My money!"

"You're just making it take longer," Serge yelled back, hands in thin latex gloves.

The regular lightbulb over the sink had been replaced by a red one. A small table stood in the bathtub. It held four photographic developing pans. A clothesline stretched from the towel bar to the showerhead, where Coleman had mounted his beer bong. Twenty small, white rectangular pieces of paper hung from clothespins. More white rectangles sat in the developing pans. Serge fed a handful of one-dollar bills into the empty fourth tray.

Coleman took a plastic tube out of his mouth. "You're using photo fluid?"

"No, bleach." Serge checked some of the blank rectangles on the clothesline. Dry. He took them down.

"I thought the red lightbulb was for photo fluid," said Coleman. "Why do you need it with bleach?"

"I don't. For some reason I want to be in Amsterdam." Serge removed the gloves and turned to his new laser printer atop the toilet tank. He began feeding rectangles.

"Where'd you get this idea?"

"Three weeks ago when I was paying for gas, the clerk hit my fifty-dollar bill with one of those yellow markers." Serge inserted more plain rectangles. "The nerve of her thinking I'd try to pass counterfeit money."

The printer began spitting out hundred-dollar bills. Serge examined one of the notes with a magnifying loop. "In addition to solving our cash flow, I'm also fighting crime."

"Looks like you're committing crime."

"It's the new reverse values. Ask any Republican." He examined another bill. "You're now allowed to do whatever you want in the name of homeland security."

Coleman poured another cold one into his funnel. Serge pulled more paper down from the clothesline. "Safety ultimately depends on the economy, which our Treasury protects with high-tech security features on currency. I'm troubleshooting their performance."

"How are they doing?"

"Not so good." Another batch went into the printer. "They overthought. The extra safeguards are excellent, but it all still comes down to the reliability of the clerk behind the register with that yellow marker."

"But Serge, I always see them use the marker. You'll get caught the first time you try."

Serge pulled a yellow marker from his own pocket and held it to Coleman's face, then hit one of the new hundreds.

Coleman ran a hand through his hair. "Looks like when I pass a real bill."

"The best way to defeat high-tech is by going low-tech." Serge began stuffing his wallet with cash. "The markers don't check denomination, just government paper, which I used."

Bang! Bang! Bang! "My money."

Serge opened the door and gave Rachael two grand.

"Oh . . . thanks."

The door closed.

"But Serge, I still don't get the part about how this helps the government."

"Counterfeit dough is like a game of hot potato. Whoever's holding the money last gets burned. Like stores that use yellow markers."

"So?"

"Some companies have started using ultraviolet scanners

that are needed to detect the new security features. Cost around a hundred dollars. But others are still trying to get by on the cheap with markers, which are about a buck." Serge fed more blanks into the printer, removing fresh C-notes and flapping them in the air. "I've just raised the price of those markers to a hundred dollars."

SEVENTEEN

DAVIS ISLANDS

*G*et your signing hands limber!" Steph led the Davenports down the walkway of their future house.

They climbed into a black Expedition with magnetic realty signs on the doors. Jim and Martha were in the backseat. They began driving across the island. Steph was a verbal machine gun on the cell phone, handing forms over her shoulder. The Davenports autographed next to little "Sign Here" stickers and passed pages back up to Steph, who fed them into a wireless fax machine on the front passenger seat. She hung up the phone, speed-dialed another number, handed Jim a page, took one back from Martha, slid it into the fax, rolled down her window and snapped a photo of a new home that had just been listed with her agency.

Jim scribbled his name again. "Who's driving?"

"Shhhh," said Martha

Steph hung up and fed another page. "That's the last. Now we wait."

A ring tone. The Pet Shop Boys. *Let's make lots of money.* "Steph here. I'll tell them right now." She hung up. "They accepted your offer."

"So soon?" said Jim.

"Congratulations." She pulled up in front of a French

café in the strolling district. A young couple in boating attire waited at the curb. Steph moved the fax for the man to sit up front, and the Davenports scooted over to make room for the woman in back.

"Tom, Jane, have I got some great homes to show you. . . ." She looked in the rearview. "Want me to show them yours?"

"What?"

"Perfect opportunity. Don't wait too long."

The Expedition sped back across the island and stopped in front of the new Davenport place. They got out. Jim turned to wave, but Steph was already pulling away. *"No, you can't put a price . . . "*

Martha threw her arms around her husband's neck. "I love you!"

Jim stared over her shoulder in a trance.

From behind: "Jim! Martha!"

They turned.

A pyramid-shaped woman jogged toward them, checking the cardio-monitor on her wrist. She had plastic, trash bag–like running pants to trap perspiration and a pink T-shirt with sequins: DIVA IN TRAINING. She waved cheerfully as she reached the driveway and continued jogging in place.

Martha blinked. "Gladys? Gladys Plant? Is that you? . . . Jim, look, it's our old neighbor."

Gladys checked her wrist again. "Hope you don't mind if I keep running while we talk. Heart rate . . ."

"But what are you doing over here?" asked Martha. "I thought you moved to a serpentine neighborhood. Grid streets were too dangerous."

"That's right." Gladys bobbed. "But the dirtballs finally figured out serpentine streets."

"Streets that curve aren't good anymore?"

"They're out," said Gladys. "Now you have to move completely offshore. Luckily there's this great little island right here in the bay. Criminals don't know about it yet."

"That just sounds like we're retreating."

"We are."

"Hear that, Jim?" said Martha. "We made the right move."

"You're in paradise," said Gladys.

A delivery van pulled up. A man in shorts hopped out and checked the house number against his packing slip. Eight-eighty-eight. He handed Jim a cellophane-wrapped welcome basket of cheese and wine. The van left.

"Must be Steph," said Gladys. "Treats her clients right . . ."

"How thoughtful," said Martha.

". . . Treated Mr. Simmons a little too right, if you know what I mean. Wife found an earring under the bed. She never learned who, but still a messy divorce. Steph picked up the sale." Gladys pointed up the street. "Now it's *my* house. Steph said that earring knocked ten grand off the purchase price. Excellent agent."

Jim opened the gift card.

"Steph?" asked Martha.

"Wants to know if we're ready to sell."

"Don't," said Gladys. "You can't find another place like this in the whole state. It's a quirk of geography, like a tiny village in New Hampshire. Families safely walk these quiet streets at any hour, and yet . . ."—she gestured up at the top of the Tampa skyline towering over date palms—". . . we're in the shadow of downtown. The professionals who work those top floors love it over here. We're only five minutes away, but it's like a million miles."

"Why?" asked Jim.

"Remember the pair of tiny bridges at the tip of the island? They're the only way on and off. This whole place is one big dead end. That's kryptonite to scumbags."

"You don't have *any* crime over here?" asked Jim.

"We got a few old apartments, and the renters tend to get a little rambunctious from time to time, but that's all on the east side of the island; they never get over this way." Gladys pressed a button on her wrist and stopped bobbing. "Nope, it's like the fifties over here. If anything happens, the police just roadblock those bridges. So nothing happens. Even stupid criminals aren't that stupid."

A '73 Mercury Comet sped by.

"Coleman! You've got the map upside down again!"

The Davenports turned at the sound of screeching tires. The Comet made a skidding left and disappeared around the end of the block.

"Probably someone's kids," said Gladys. "Speaking of your new neighbors, bet you're dying to know . . ."

"Actually," said Jim, "we've had a pretty busy—"

She began pointing at expensive houses. "That's Tyler Ratznick's place. State senator. He should own a taxi company the way they're always bringing him home after midnight when he's blotto. Next is Skip Hismith, local TV anchor. Don't know how they're still married. Fight constantly. Loud, too. She's always locking him out of the house, and he keeps whispering through the door to let him back in. Finally, he buried a key outside, then he had to bury a whole bunch of keys because while he was on the air she started going around the yard with a metal detector. Next, Vinny Carbello. He's in the witness-protection program."

"How do you know that?" asked Martha.

"Tells everyone. Used to be a big deal in Jersey. Guess he misses the attention. Same with his friend in that house on the other side, Franky Four-Fingers."

"Jesus," said Jim. "We've got a neighbor whose finger was cut off by the mob?"

"No," said Gladys. "Happened last week. Lawnmower. All the protected witnesses who hang out at Island Pizza are still giving him grief. The giant Victorian spread is the Wagners. Launched a coupon-swap site on the Internet and sold it for a mint back before anyone knew it was stupid. And the Yorks, funeral home that switches prices on the caskets because who's going to argue once Aunt Gerty's in the box; the Babbits, hardware store chain, nothing fishy; Doctor Gamboru, who fled a genocide and has liposuctioned half the island; Bill and Fred, who are gay and have the best parties; the Flemings, who obviously *aren't* gay because of that atrocious largemouth-bass mailbox. Then we come to all the silk flags hanging from porches. Guess the idea just caught on at that end of the street like trophy wives at the other. Indian arrowhead flag is the Moultries, big Florida State alumni; the golf-ball flag, retired commodities broker Gaylord Wainscotting, absolutely obsessed with the game; the Birminghams and their millionth-degree Masons flag like anyone gives a damn; restoration-award flag is the Sikorskys, architecture firm; the flying-stork-and-bundle-of-joy flag almost never comes down at the O'Malleys, who have eight or nine now; the butterfly flag . . . the Gronquists just like butterflies; the Longshank-Scones, who overdo their accents and work into every conversation that they're Welsh royalty, but most of the neighborhood doesn't even know where Wales is, so they hang an extra-large flag of their family crest with that Gaelic lion on its hindlegs, wearing a crown and juggling chess pieces or some bullshit. . . ." Gladys finished turning all the way around, pointing at the house she was in front of. ". . . Now you." She pressed a button on her wrist and began jogging away. "Welcome to Lobster Lane!"

THAT AFTERNOON

The new support group had better accommodations: the bingo room of a Catholic church in south Tampa that also doubled as the local voting precinct.

This time Serge was early. Quite early in fact. He and Coleman sat alone in a room full of empty Samsonite chairs. Best seats in the house, front row, middle.

Others began trickling in, grabbing their usual spots in the back row. Those arriving later took the penultimate row and so forth, until the latest arrivals timidly shuffled toward the front.

The moderator arrived and opened a briefcase at the podium. He had a gray ponytail and a faded NO NUKES T-shirt. He noticed the newest members in the front row and gave them a welcoming smile. Serge smiled back, flashing him a wildly enthusiastic thumbs-up.

The moderator was perfect for the job, possessing equal part cheer, empathy and naive optimism. He had three graduate degrees in liberal arts from some of the nation's most prestigious universities, which meant he drove an embarrassing car. As is often the case with such groups, the moderator was also a recovering member. He tapped the microphone. "Good evening. Hope everyone had a great week. . . . You might not have noticed, but we have some new friends with us tonight. . . . Sir, would you mind standing and introducing yourself?"

Serge popped out of his chair and twirled to face the room. Over his head, the group's name was written in the tiniest of unsure letters on the blackboard: NON-CONFRONTATIONALISTS ANONYMOUS.

"Howdy! I'm Serge!"

"Hello, Serge."

"Is that a breath of fresh air or what?" said Serge. "Can't tell you how nice a little hello is after that other group. 'Douche bag,' 'fuck face' . . ."

"Serge . . ."

He turned around. "What?"

The moderator smiled. "Pleasure to have you with us. Would you like to introduce your friend?"

"You mean Coleman?"

A man in the back row became woozy and crashed into the chair in front of him.

"Jim Davenport?" said Serge. "Is that you, Jim? . . . It is!" He ran to the rear of the room and pulled his old buddy up for a big hug.

"Serge," the moderator called after him. "We're not supposed to use last names in here. Confidentiality . . ."

"It's okay," said Serge. "Me and Davenport go way back—I mean Jim, whose last name is something other than Davenport. We were neighbors ten years ago on Triggerfish Lane. He was like my big hero: law-abiding family man, pillar of the community, impulse control. Which meant society pissed all over him. Luckily I was there to offer protection. Then guess what happened! *He* ended up protecting *me*! Remember the big home invasion a decade ago during that Fourth of July party? The infamous McGraw Brothers? I was the one in the buffalo costume. Anyway, I didn't know Jim had it in him. Never fired a weapon in his life. But he was a crack shot that day. Saved my life, so I owed him unending loyalty. Swore I'd never leave his side. Then I got a little distracted for ten years. But now I'm reunited with Jim, and this time I promise to be like glue!" Serge held Jim out by the shoulders. "How've you been, big guy? I need to come by your place after this and say hi to Martha—"

Jim's legs buckled, but Serge caught him on the way down. "Everyone, back up! Give him some air!"

The moderator rushed over. "What happened? Should I call nine-one-one?"

"Just fainted." Serge fanned Jim's face. "Probably thrilled to see me after all these years."

Jim finally came to. He found himself sitting in the middle of the front row, wedged between Serge and Coleman.

"Excellent! You're awake!" Serge said loudly. "Was worried you were going to miss all the good stuff. This moderator knows his job! Quite unorthodox, because it looks like he used to be a weirdo in college . . ."

"Excuse me?" the moderator said meekly.

". . . We're about to leave on a field trip!" Serge told Jim. "Didn't know the group took field trips or I'd have fixed a snack. Remember those little cheese and crackers in separate compartments with a plastic spreader? Mom always packed those when my kindergarten class was visiting a planetarium or the Jupiter Inlet Lighthouse. Always ended up with more cheese . . ."

"Excuse me?"

". . . Jim, guess where we're going? You'll never guess. That means you're supposed to guess. Okay, I'll just tell you. The zoo! Our moderator is going to lead us in this crazy experiment with the animals. That's the unorthodox part I mentioned. So what if they laugh at him—"

"Excuse me!"

Serge looked up. "What?"

"I'm sorry. I didn't mean to yell at you."

"No, I was rudely talking when you were," said Serge. "Yell away. I might kick the crap out of you, but that's just involuntary reflex. Doesn't mean I'm right."

Silence.

"What are you waiting for?" asked Serge. "Proceed."

"Thank you." The moderator addressed the rest of the room. "Now if you'll all follow me to the parking lot . . ."

Minutes later, a white church van drove north on Mac-Dill Avenue.

"This is just like my field trips in kindergarten!" said Serge. "We should all sing! Everybody, after me: *'If you're happy and you know it . . .'*"

The van passed through the entrance of Lowry Park Zoo, passengers clapping and stomping their feet. They got a group discount at the ticket booth, and the moderator assembled them inside the turnstiles.

"Okay, I'll go over the exercise one more time. We're heading to the cages with the big cats. What I want you to do is wait until one of the lions or tigers looks your way. Then I want you to stand your ground and stare back. Under no circumstance do you break eye contact."

"Serge," whispered Coleman. "This guy did too much acid."

One of the members raised his hand. "I'm scared."

"Me too," said another. "What if we make them mad?"

"They're in cages," said the moderator. "And they aren't going to get mad. They won't even know what's going on. That's the whole point: a perfectly safe and controlled assertiveness exercise."

"Come on, guys!" said Serge, extending an arm outward, palm down. "Form a circle and put all our hands together like a championship football team! No fuckin' animal comes in *our* house and stares us down!"

"Excuse me?" said the moderator.

"What?" asked Serge, standing alone with the only outstretched arm.

"Please."

He lowered his arm. "Okay, we'll do the circle thing later. Plus I have a few of my own field-trip ideas. Nothing builds confidence like live ammo."

The moderator led the jelly-kneed group through the park and lined them along the rail in a viewing area. "Now don't look away . . ."

One hour later:

The van arrived back at the church. Members jumped out and ran for their cars.

"Serge," said the moderator. "Could I have a word?"

"What's up?"

"I don't want to sound critical. . . ."

"You mean getting kicked out of the zoo? Go ahead and be critical. They completely overreacted."

"Serge, I said to just stare."

"No, you didn't say '*just* stare.' You said 'stare.' I added the other stuff for extra credit."

"All those end-zone dances?"

"Don't forget loud roaring and pawing the air like I had sharp claws."

"What were you thinking?"

"Needed to establish myself as the alpha male."

"You got in a shoving match with the zoo's staff."

Serge grinned and slapped the moderator's shoulder. "Alpha male."

The moderator looked at his shoes. "We've never been thrown out of anything."

"Congratulations. Huge progress."

"Progress?"

" 'Thank you' would be sufficient."

"Thank you?"

"You're welcome."

"Hope you don't mind me asking, but are you sure you have the right support group?"

Serge nodded and fished a scrap of paper from his pocket. "See? That's the note from my psychiatrist."

INSOMNIA

Serge couldn't sleep again. Same as every night. He grabbed his leather journal and pen:

Captain Florida's Log, Star Date 4830.395. My legacy grows. Another excellent day of dirt collecting! Started at the University of Tampa because it's housed in the landmark nineteenth-century Tampa Bay Hotel. Before hitting it big with The Doors, Jim Morrison lived around here with his grandparents and filled notebooks with lyrical observations. The song "Soul Kitchen" refers to the hotel's Moorish architecture, *"Your fingers weave quick minarets."* But here's the thing I learned about dirt collecting: You can't just stand in front of a historic building and go six feet down with a post-hole digger. Guards make you run with your dirt sack. Then I'm driving over the bay on the Courtney Campbell Bridge, and you know how crazy they drive in Florida? Some idiot almost made me have a giant wreck! Coleman said maybe I should spend more time steering than writing in my notebook, but I said, It's okay, Jim did this all the time. Then we cruised to 314 North Osceola Avenue in Clearwater, where the Lizard King's old house had been torn down for a condo. Practically in tears as I dug my hole and ran away again. The Pinellas Park Library was around the corner, so I dropped in to go through old phone books for the address where Jack Kerouac spent his final years, and one of the directories spelled his name KEROWAC. What a footnote find! Now I'm happy again, standing in Kerouac's front yard, minding my own business, working on my tenth hole, when this nosy neighbor yells, What are you doing with that shovel? I say, Taking a core sample. Then I hit some kind of water line and he became completely unreasonable. Next stop: the venerable Beaux Arts Coffee House, where both Jack and Jim used to read poetry. We pull up to 7711 Sixtieth Street. You guessed it: Torn down. It got pretty emotional as I read a verse I'd composed for the moment. Simply called "Jim":

St. Pete poetry
Miami penis arrest
Dead in Paris tub

Coleman asked why it was so short. I said it was haiku. He said, What's that? I said, Japanese poetry, seventeen syllables. Small country, so space is at a premium. Then I bent down and scooped soil into a Baggie by hand because a shovel might attract attention from the next-door police canine academy, but an officer came over anyway and asked what the hell I was doing. I said, Reading poetry, collecting dirt. And you? Then Rachael and Coleman started wailing on each other in the car again, and I had to excuse myself. Almost forgot, Rachael was with us the whole time, constantly fouling the mood. She's fast becoming the most obnoxious and morally reprehensible person I've ever met. Don't know how much longer we can continue having sex. But who am I to argue with God's plan? He wanted alpha males to populate the planet by impregnating multiple partners, so he gave females the gift of irrationality, able to morph the least little thing that happens anywhere in the world into being your fault, especially if it's your fault. Watch any nature show. The top lion is perfectly happy with a lioness, but then he inexplicably moves on. Why? She was trying to change him. . . . Getting sleepy now, but excitement over tomorrow is keeping me up. It's going to be the crowning moment of my Jim Morrison scavenger hunt. That's right, the Clearwater Library. Bet they'll be thrilled to see me again!

EIGHTEEN

MOVING DAY

*T*he big truck all but blocked traffic in front of the Davenports' soon-to-be-former home. Ramps out the side and back. Large mats to protect furniture. Hand trucks for all occasions.

Since it was only a crosstown move, the Davenports hired three men by the hour. To save additional cost, Jim and Martha had spent the previous week carefully packing and sealing everything, then piling the boxes in efficient stacks in the middle of each room. They segregated the most fragile belongings, which would be transported in their SUV.

The movers possessed immense physiques in both respects, the contradictory breed that simultaneously looks incredibly strong and terribly out of shape. Spine-snapping forearms and medicine-ball beer guts. Two of them carried an antique dresser toward the front door.

"Nice day," said Jim.

"If we didn't have to fuckin' work." The dresser cracked into the doorframe.

Not a lot of buddy talk after that. Jim picked up splinters and walked out to the driveway. Martha loaded a box of china in the back of the Escalade. "Jim, come here."

"What is it?"

"That guy over there by the truck. What's he doing?"

"I don't know."

"He's not doing anything."

"I'm sure he's doing something," said Jim. "He's holding a clipboard."

Martha set the carton of dishes behind the backseat. "He's not doing shit. I've been watching for a half hour."

"What do you want me to do?"

"Go make him work."

"What?"

"We're paying for three guys to lift. We're getting two."

"Honey—"

"If you won't go, I will."

"No, stay here. I'll be right back."

The man standing next to the truck made a checkmark. He felt a presence. He looked up. "Can I help you?"

Jim smiled cordially. "Mind if I ask what you're doing?"

The man looked back at his clipboard. "Working."

"What's the clipboard for?"

"Have to inventory box contents in case you make a claim."

Jim leaned and read the clipboard upside down. "All the contents spaces on the form are blank. You're just writing 'box, box, box.' "

"You sealed all the boxes before we got here."

"What's that mean?"

"I can't take inventory." He made another checkmark.

"Will we still be able to file a claim if the contents spaces are blank?"

"No."

"Can you help the other guys carry stuff?"

"No."

Jim walked back to the SUV. Martha loaded a bubble-wrapped vase. She looked back at the moving truck. "He's still not working."

"He's taking inventory."

"But the boxes are sealed."

"That's why he can't take inventory."

"Jim, what's wrong with you? Why are you letting them screw us?"

"Because they're really, really big."

"Jim! Make him work!" She stacked another box in the back of the SUV. "I'll be damned if *I'm* going to carry stuff all day and pay him to stand around doing nothing."

"Martha, those are prison tattoos."

"So?"

"They're handling everything we own. If I make them mad, they could do something to get back at us."

"They're not allowed to!"

"I don't think permission is part of it."

"Jim!"

Two movers wheeled a dolly to the curb. The third wrote on a clipboard. He looked up.

Jim smiled. "Me again. Listen, I was just talking with my wife, and there's really nothing of value, so we'll take our chances with the claim thing." Another smile.

The mover looked down and wrote "box."

"Please don't think I'm trying to tell you your moving job," said Jim. "But we'd prefer you did some moving."

The man angrily flipped a page on his clipboard. "You'll have to sign this waiver."

"That's all? You didn't say that last time."

The mover answered by lifting a box off the dolly and heaving it deep into the belly of the truck with an echoing crash.

CLEARWATER

The public library filled with street people taking shelter from another routine afternoon rain shower.

A pair of men approached the reference desk.

The head researcher was on the phone. She held up a finger. "Just a sec." All the nearby history had gotten Serge aroused. He mentally took off her glasses and let down the silky black hair that was up in a professional bun. Then he put her in a skimpy streetwalker skirt and high heels. No, not right. Cheerleader? Naughty nurse? Nope, nope. One-piece beauty-contestant bathing suit with silk sash: 1966 ORANGE BLOSSOM QUEEN? Nope. Rodeo clown? Maybe. She got off the phone. Serge put her library clothes back on.

"How can I help you?"

Serge smiled his widest. "We're here to see The Door!"

"I'm sorry. Door?"

"Yes! And I'll bet you're glad we're here!" He looked around curiously. "Where is it?"

"What?"

"The Door! I read when they demolished Jim's house, one of the doors was donated to the library for permanent exhibition." He rubbed his palms together with high friction. "Can't wait to touch it."

"Oh, you're a *Doors* fan. Yeah, we've gotten a few calls about that. Don't have the exhibit up yet. It's still in storage."

"Where?"

"Not sure."

Serge winked. "Of course you're not sure. Good thinking. Lots of kooks just drooling to steal it. Not me, obviously, because heritage belongs to everyone. So you can tell me. Where's The Door?"

"Really, I . . ." She stopped and caught herself in the gaze of Serge's penetrating ice-blue eyes. And that smile of his. Not your typical hunk, which is why she hadn't noticed it earlier, but there was something intangible about this guy. She never went for men at first meet, and couldn't understand the melting feeling inside.

He put out his hand. "Serge."

She shook it. "Liz. Pleasure to meet you."

"Pleasure's all mine. I'm Serge."

"You just said that."

"Thinking about The Door."

For the next fifteen minutes, Coleman fidgeted through a scene that had unfolded so many times before: Serge leaning against the corner of a reference desk, making time with another library science grad.

Liz finally stood and called over to the circulation desk. "Rob, looks like it's slowing down." She picked up her purse. "Thought I'd take an early lunch."

NINETEEN

DAVIS ISLANDS

*T*he moving van choked traffic on another narrow residential street. Lobster Lane. The truck was almost empty. Two men came through the front door with a mattress and went upstairs. The piles of boxes in every room made it like a maze. A third mover entered the house, lifted a box high in his arms and dropped it.

"That's the last. Sign here."

Jim took the pen. "What am I signing?"

"That you got everything."

"But I don't know yet. We haven't unpacked."

"You didn't want an inventory."

"Then does it make any difference whether I sign or not?"

"No."

"What if I don't sign?"

"You have to."

Jim signed. They handed him a yellow copy.

"Do I need to keep this?"

"Not really."

They left.

It was quiet. Jim took the moment to finally relax and enjoy new home ownership.

Atomic LOBSTER **147**

Loud footsteps. Martha ran down the stairs. "My gold necklace is missing."

"I'm sure it's somewhere. We haven't unpacked yet."

"That's the first box I opened! I set my little jewelry cabinet on the dresser. Then I left to get another box from the car."

"You think they stole it?"

"I *know* they stole it! I'd put the necklace in the top left drawer, and when I went to get it out and hang it on the knob like I always do, it was gone."

"I'm sure there's an explanation."

"They were alone in the bedroom with the mattress just a minute ago."

Jim hurried up the stairs. "Maybe you just got confused with all the packing. It's probably in my jewelry box." Jim opened it. "Where's my watch?"

"Which one?"

"My favorite."

Another charge down the stairs. The front door flew open, and Martha ran into the street. "Come back!"

But the van was already at the end of the block.

Jim walked out and joined her.

"I'm going to report them!"

"Baby, we're starting a new chapter in our lives with this beautiful house. Let's just move on."

"No! We shouldn't have to take it!" She grabbed the yellow receipt from Jim's hand. "Here's the phone number."

"Honey, this is how it always starts on those Court TV shows when they find the couple axed to death in the basement."

"You have an overactive imagination."

"They're out of our lives. Let's not drag 'em back in."

"Okay, but I'm only not going to complain because I have so much work to do with the new place. And because you're going to your meeting tomorrow."

"I thought I'd skip this meeting because of the move."

"No, you're definitely not going to miss the meeting after what you let those guys get away with."

"But honey—"

"These meetings are important. I'm holding up my end with the anger-management sessions, even though I hardly need them."

"You don't understand. There's someone else at the meetings I have to tell you about."

"Stop!" said Martha. "Don't say a word! That was part of our deal: We have to completely commit to the programs. And one of the first rules is confidentiality."

"This is different," said Jim. "I have to tell you. He's—"

Heavy footsteps came toward them on the sidewalk. "Martha! Jim!"

"Gladys!" Martha looked at her husband. "It's Gladys."

Gladys stopped and bobbed in place. "How'd the move go?"

"They stole from us!"

"Who'd you use?"

Martha held up the yellow sheet. A logo of a cartoon truck with a toothy grin. "Moving Dudes."

"Geez, you *never* use Moving Dudes. Should have checked with me first."

"We didn't know."

"I'm still surprised they stole from you," said Gladys. "If you absolutely have to use them, everyone knows to just pay the protection and it'll be fine."

"Protection?" said Martha.

"The extra guy who stands around doing nothing. What did they get from you?"

"I don't want to talk about it."

Jim turned toward the house. "Martha and I were just saying how great it is to be out here."

"Jim," said Martha. "I know what you're trying to do."

"No, really. You were pretty sharp picking out this place. Have to admit I was against it at first because we're extended on the mortgage. But now I'm so glad you convinced me. As long as we don't have any major unforeseen expenses. What are the odds?"

A cell phone rang. Martha reached in her pocket. "Hello? . . . Oh, hi Debbie . . ." She lowered the phone. "It's our daughter."

"I remember."

The cell went back to her head. "Where are you? . . . Great, you'll have to come over. . . . What? . . . No, I can't guess. . . . Yeah, I'm ready. . . ."

Martha screamed.

Jim grabbed her arm. "What's happened to Debbie?"

Martha waved him off. "That's fantastic! I'm so happy for you! . . . I'll tell him right now. . . . Love you too!" She hung up.

"What is it?"

"Our baby's getting married! Isn't that great news?"

CLEARWATER

"You sure you're watching?" said Liz. "I could lose my job."

"Don't worry." Serge glanced up and down the hall. "I do this all the time."

She wiggled an old key into a brass knob. "You can't tell anyone. You gave me your word."

Serge put up two fingers. "Scout's honor."

Liz opened the storage closet. "I should have my head examined."

"Coleman, wait out here. If you see anyone coming, knock three times. You got it?"

"Of course."

"Don't fuck up."

"I told you, I got it."

Serge went inside the closet and closed the door.

"I can't see," said Liz.

"Here's a switch." A light came on. Serge froze. "Oh my God! It's . . . The Door!"

Three knocks.

"Shit!" Serge killed the light. He crept to the door and opened it a crack. Coleman's face was inches away.

"Pssst, Serge. What if someone comes?"

"Knock! Three times!"

"*Ohhhh.* That's what that was about."

"Yes!" The door slammed. The light came back on. The unhinged Morrison door leaned against the far wall. Serge could almost see a glowing aura.

"You know," said Liz. "I used to be a huge Doors fan. I mean, to look at me now—"

"I never judge a book's cover," said Serge.

"The other girls were crazy about Jim because he was a *Tiger Beat* heartthrob."

"But you got into him because of literary allusions. *The Doors of Perception.*"

"I *love* Aldous," said Liz.

"Me too. *Naked Lunch*?"

"Without saying."

"Kesey?"

"Oh my God, yes! . . . Wait. You can see all that in me? Most of my friends are so conservative. I feel like I have to hide—"

"That you did psychedelics?"

"I wasn't going to say that. But, yeah." She blushed. "How'd you guess?"

"I sense your inner freak flag."

"But that was a long time ago. And you have to understand, back then it was about love and higher consciousness. These new drugs today turn people into armed robbers and strippers."

"I wouldn't know."

Liz looked around. "What's that music?"

"The portable speaker for my iPod."

" . . . *Come on baby light my fire* . . . "

"One of my favorites!"

"Mine too."

"What are you doing?"

"Stroking your hair . . ."

"Please. Stop . . ."

Serge slowly slipped his other hand around her back. "That means 'don't stop.'"

Liz felt their mouths growing closer. "No . . ."

"That means 'yes.'" He suddenly grabbed her by the back of the head for a deep, hard kiss. Their lips finally parted an inch. Liz's eyes stayed closed. *"Ohhhh, Serge! . . ."*

Serge jumped back. "Okay. Help me lift the door."

Her eyes sprang open. "What?"

"I can't raise it by myself."

"You're stealing it?"

"Of course not."

"Then what are you doing?"

"Big surprise. But we don't have much time. Come on, grab the other side."

Everything in the last two decades screamed for Liz to get the hell out of that closet. But something about this guy made her feel like junior year at the university. Had she really become so stuffy? Next thing she knew, her hands had a grip on the left side of the door. "What do you want me to do?"

"Turn it horizontal and carry it to the middle of the room."

They shuffled sideways in the tight space and lowered it to the floor.

"I'll kill the light," said Serge.

"What for? . . ."

The hallway outside was quiet. Too quiet. And no pot.

Coleman picked his nails. He looked at the ceiling. He looked at his shoes. This sucked. He looked at the doorknob.

It was jet black inside the closet. Just heavy breathing, clipped conversation and creaking wood.

The knob turned. A sliver of light from the hallway entered the room. The sliver grew wider as Coleman opened it farther. The edge of the light finally reached Serge's bobbing derriere.

"Oh, yes!" said Liz. "Fuck me on The Door!"

"That's what I'm doing," said Serge.

A sudden jump in volume as Liz neared her peak. " . . . *The Door!*"

"Wait . . . Where's that light coming from?" Serge looked over his shoulder. "Coleman! What the hell are you doing?"

"Are you going to be much longer?"

"Fuck me on The Door!"

"I don't know, Coleman. These things take time."

Liz abruptly pushed Serge off, and flipped onto her stomach. "Quick. The *other* way."

"What?"

"Hurry or I'll lose it!"

"You're the boss," said Serge. "Man, when you let your hair down . . ."

Creak-creak, creak-creak, creak-creak . . . Liz's right fist pounded on the wood in rhythm with Serge's efforts. . . . Bang . . . *"Yes!"* . . . Bang . . . *"Yes!"* . . . Bang . . . *"Yes!"* . . . Bang . . . *"The Door!"* . . . Bang . . . *"Don't stop!"* . . . Bang . . . *"I'm almost there! . . . "*

"Serge, can I wait out by the car?"

"No! Watch the door!"

Creak-creak, creak-creak . . . Bang . . . *"Yes!"* . . . Bang . . . *"God!"* . . . Bang . . . *"This is it! . . . "*

"Coleman, why are you still standing there?"

"I'm doing what you said."

"Not *this* door, you idiot!"

"Oh." He went back in the hall.

Ten minutes later, the closet opened. Serge stepped outside buttoning his shirt.

"*Now* can we go?" asked Coleman.

"Can you try to be more annoying?"

"But I'm standing around while you're having all the fun."

Serge pointed back at the closet. "What? In there? That wasn't fun. That was research." Serge slipped a hand into his hip pocket and produced a clear plastic tube containing small flakes. "Had to distract her while I took a paint sample."

Liz stumbled into the hall. Serge spun around and whipped the tube behind his back. "There you are!"

She collapsed against the doorframe. "Wow! That was the best I ever . . . I mean, I never . . . How was I? Did you enjoy yourself? I thought you were because I heard your fingernails scraping the wood."

Serge secretly slid the plastic tube into a back pocket. "You're the greatest." He looked at his watch. "Yikes, is it this late?" He pointed up the hall. "Listen, thanks for the tour, but we gotta be—"

"Oh my God!" She was staring down. "You were so good I peed myself!"

"I always feel if a job's worth doing . . ."

Liz checked her own watch. "I have to rush home and change. I can't go back to the reference desk like this!"

"Actually, you can," said Serge. "But your idea's better. . . . Well, see ya!" He and Coleman took off.

Liz yelled after them: "You'll call like you promised?"

"Definitely."

"Remember my number?"

"Of course."

"What is it?"

"The one you gave me." They disappeared into a stairwell.

TWENTY MILES EAST OF TAMPA

Flames licked high into the night sky.

It was one of those empty parts of inland Florida that would soon become a sprawling planned community sold to Michigan retirees before they became bitter at how incredibly far they were from the beaches pictured in the sales brochure.

But right now, it remained a remote piece of scrubland only accessed by dirt logging roads. The flames rose from a bonfire in the middle of a clearing. A chorus line of animated silhouettes danced with abandon in front of the fire, throwing arms in the air and howling at the moon, evoking some ancient ritual from Stonehenge or Easter Island. Except in ancient times, they wouldn't have all been wearing matching T-shirts: 21st ANNUAL MCGRAW FAMILY JAMBOREE.

The bonfire was surrounded by a circle of pickup trucks and honky-tonk domestic sports cars with racing detail. One had its trunk open to increase stereo volume on Molly Hatchet. Later and deeper into the George Dickel, *Flirtin' with Disaster* would acquire a backbeat of lever-action rifles fired into the air.

This year's family gathering was even bigger than usual, thanks to the recent prison release of the clan's biggest member. They gathered around Tex, shaking hands, slapping his back, then got down to vittles. The reunions always featured a fish fry, and the McGraws did it right. A charred, fifty-five-gallon barrel sat atop a welded metal frame and its own robust fire. Inside the drum: boiling vegetable oil and succulent freshwater catfish fillets. The drum was presided over by a stubby, four-hundred-pound man in bib overalls and no T-shirt. "Ham-Bone" McGraw. His nose more closely resembled a hog snout. Because he had a novelty plastic hog snout strapped around his head with a rubber band. He was the wit of the family.

An extended chow line of kissin' cousins stretched before him. Their paper plates already held beans and fried
okra as Ham-Bone tonged sizzling seafood.

The roar of a bored-out engine came down one of the
dark logging roads. A double-cab pickup bounded into the
clearing. Tex's three most trusted kin hopped out, Lyle,
Cooter and Spanky McGraw. They had difficulty dragging
the fourth person from the truck because his arms were
wrapped around one of the headrests.

"No! Stop! Please! . . ."

A last, hard tug, and the reluctant guest was jerked from
the truck and flung to the ground at Tex's feet. He looked out
of place at the jamboree in his shredded business suit.

Tex yanked him up. "You're one useless defense attorney."

"I did everything I could! I swear! But they had too much
evidence, plus they found you at the scene covered in blood."

"Well then it's perfectly reasonable," said Tex.

"It is?"

"Except I'm not a reasonable person. Remember? You
argued that at trial. Insane." Tex slid his hands inside thick
protective rubber gloves that reached to the elbow.

"I'm begging! Whatever you're thinking . . ."

"Okay, I'll give you a chance." He slapped the attorney
lightly on the cheek. "We'll let you go if you win a little
game we play around here."

"Sure, anything. What is it?"

Tex grabbed him by the back of the collar. "Bobbing for
catfish." He slammed the lawyer's face down into the boiling oil. Arms flailed, the barrel filled with bubbles. Tex
pulled him up. "Got a fish yet? Nope." Back down into the
barrel. Back up. "Fish? Nope." Down. This time, the attorney's arms fell limp. Tex casually released him, and he
flipped backward into the dirt, face still fizzing. Even the
most hardened McGraws had trouble keeping food down.

Tex walked back over to the trusted trio. He pulled a piece of paper from his pocket and crossed a name off the top.

"What do you want us to do now?" asked Cooter.

"Keep working down the list."

TWENTY

TAMPA

*T*he bingo room's air conditioner hummed loudly amid the conspicuous absence of conversation. A few people grabbed last-second Styrofoam cups of coffee and returned to their seats. The wall clock hit seven. Non-Confrontationalists Anonymous was back in session.

"Good evening," said the moderator.

A hyper-enthusiastic hand waved from the middle of the front row. "Ooooh! Ooooh! Me! Me! Pick me!"

"Serge? What is it?"

Serge smiled and leaned back in his chair. "Good evening to you, too!"

The moderator took a deep breath. "Thank you." He looked up at the rest of the members. "Since last week has anyone had a relevant experience they'd like to share?"

Front row, same hand. "Ooooh! Ooooh! Me! . . ."

"Serge," said the moderator. "How about letting someone else in the group have a chance to talk?"

"Sure, no problem. Except they never say anything because of, well, the creepy way they are."

The moderator pointed toward the last row. "Jim, what about you? I understand there was a problem with some movers?"

"Where'd you hear that?"

"Serge mentioned it to me before the meeting."

Serge turned around in his chair. "Jim, tell 'em. It's a great story!" He winked back at the moderator. "Even Jesus would have opened a can of money-changers-in-the-temple-whup-ass if they were His movers!"

"Serge, please," said the moderator. "Allow Jim to speak."

"I don't want to," said Jim.

"Can I?" asked Serge. He jumped up and faced the group. "These three movers were big and mean and smelly! Horrible scars, flaming skull tattoos, and the biggest had this milky eye that always seemed like it was looking at you. . . ."

The moderator placed a hand on Serge's shoulder. "I think Jim should tell his own story."

"You sure?" said Serge. "I'm great at stories. Like that part about the eye? I made it up."

"Please?"

"Okay." Serge sat down, and Jim forced himself to stand. He demurely described events of the move.

Before the moderator could respond, Serge was back on his feet. "Let's get some fuckin' spiked clubs and chains and shit! . . . Who's with me? . . . Wait, let me rephrase that: Who's *against* me? . . ." Serge turned to the moderator. "It's unanimous."

"Violence never solves anything," said the moderator.

Serge's head jerked back. "It solves *everything*. Didn't you study history at all in those universities? How are we ever going to learn to deal with confrontation?"

"Serge, for some reason I get the feeling that you don't have a problem with confrontation."

"Bullshit!"

"I stand corrected."

"Serge," Jim begged. "I don't want any trouble."

"Too late," said Serge. "I swore my undying loyalty to you. We must respond in overwhelming numbers!"

The moderator glared at Serge.

"What?"

"If you continue to talk about violence, I'm afraid I'll have to ask you—"

"I was just joking before," said Serge, fingers crossed behind his back. "I'm suggesting Jim makes an appointment to see the moving company's manager, and the whole group goes down to the office, and we talk it over calmly like mature adults. It'll be an excellent field-trip exercise. They won't let us back in the zoo."

"I'm shocked."

"You don't like it?"

"No, it sounds so . . . reasonable."

HEADQUARTERS, MOVING DUDES

Serge and Jim sat in a pair of chairs across the desk from the manager. The manager was confused by all the self-conscious people several rows deep along the back wall of his office.

"Who are those guys?"

"We're on a field trip," said Serge. "Thanks for having us. Community support goes a long way toward recovery."

The manager looked down at his phone message. "I thought this was about a claim."

"It is," said Serge. "Wristwatch, gold necklace."

The manager checked Jim's customer file. "But he signed a waiver. And refused inventory."

"That's right," said Serge. "The thefts were retaliation for not wanting the inventory."

"Are you insinuating these things were stolen?"

"No," replied Serge. "I'm saying it outright."

Jim placed a hand on Serge's arm. "Please. It's not that important. Let's leave."

Serge pushed the hand away. "I know what I'm doing."

The manager rubbed his chin. "I think Bodine's in the lot stowing an overnight load."

"Bodine?" Serge jotted on a scrap of paper. "I didn't catch his last name."

"Biffle." The manager leaned toward his intercom. "Sally, send Bodine in." He sat back. "We'll get to the bottom of this."

"In ways you never dreamed," said Serge.

The door opened. A giant entered. The support group shuffled to a far corner.

"You wanted to see me?"

"They say a watch and necklace were stolen from the Davenport move."

"Who did?"

Silence. Serge elbowed Jim. Jim was paralyzed. Serge elbowed him again.

Bodine faced them and clenched his fists. "Well?"

Serge sighed. He reached over and grabbed Jim's slack jaw, moving it up and down as he spoke out the corner of his mouth. "I say you stole."

"I didn't take a thing!"

Serge worked Jim's jaw again: "Yes, you did."

"You calling me a liar?"

"A big fat ugly liar."

"Why you little worm!"

The manager jumped up. "That's enough. Bodine, you can go."

Serge called after the departing mover: "I'd expect as much from someone who lives in Lutz."

"Lutz?" said Bodine, stopping in the doorway. "What are you talking about? I'm from Gibsonton."

"My mistake." Serge wrote on the scrap of paper. "This

has all been a big misunderstanding. Jim must have lost the stuff in his house."

They shook hands with the manager, and the group left. The moderator stopped Serge in the parking lot. "I'm shocked!"

"What did I do now?"

"No, that went very well. I thought you were slipping with the fat liar part, but it turned out nicely in the end."

"Jim didn't get his stuff back."

"But we won an even bigger victory," said the moderator. "I think the group really benefited from this."

"Never helps to get excited." Serge slipped the scrap of paper into his wallet.

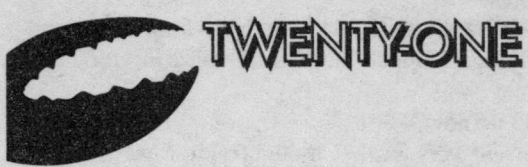

TWENTY-ONE

THE GULF OF MEXICO

*F*our white-haired women stood alone outside the locked ballroom doors.

Eunice checked her watch. "We're a half hour early."

Edith stared resolutely at the doors. "If this is what it takes."

"Hunk alert," said Edna. "Three o'clock."

Coming down the promenade was a tall, physically sculpted man. Muscles filled out his white, smartly pressed officer's uniform. Four gold bars on each shoulder.

Except for comedians and magicians in the nightly stage show, the ship's crew was almost entirely foreign. With rigid demarcation: bartenders, waiters and blackjack dealers from the Baltics; cooks and cleaning staff, Pacific Rim; officer corps, Mediterranean.

That accounted for the steamy Latin magnetism of the man approaching the G-Unit. Clinging adoringly to his right arm was a vivacious sophomore from the University of Wisconsin. The man smiled politely and tipped his cap as they passed.

He suddenly jumped and grabbed his bottom.

"What is it?" asked the student.

"Someone pinched me."

Edith stared off and whistled.

The pair continued up the hall, the student clutching his arm even tighter. "You're really the captain? . . ."

The G-Unit watched them depart.

"I'd let him eat crackers in *my* bed," said Eunice.

"Why don't any of the dancers look like him?" said Edna.

Five minutes later and one deck below, the man in the white uniform unlocked a door with a magnetic card. The student in a Bucky Badger jersey walked through the middle of the giant cabin and twirled around. "I didn't realize officers' staterooms were so luxurious!"

They weren't. This was a penthouse suite.

Since the cruise line wasn't an official navy, there was no law against impersonating an officer, and the crisp, mail-order captain's uniform rarely failed with the women.

TAMPA

Back in their apartment, Coleman and Rachael burned up joints. Serge burned up the phone lines.

". . . That's right, Roger . . . because it's a last-minute thing. . . . See you there. . . ." ". . . Bob, Serge here, something's come up. . . ." ". . . Stan, it's me, Serge. . . . Yes, I know what time it is. I wouldn't be calling if it wasn't important. . . ." ". . . Jim, Serge . . . impromptu meeting. . . . Of course the moderator knows about it. . . ."

A half hour later, Serge and Coleman stood beside a '73 Mercury Comet. Rachael was down in the backseat, going through the carpet with problem-gambler optimism. Other cars began pulling into the church parking lot.

"What's going on?" asked Jim.

"I'll tell you when everyone's here," said Serge.

More cars arrived until it was a full set. Puzzled

support-group members got out and whispered to each other.

"Pipe down!" said Serge. His eyebrows went up. "Wow. I've never had people pipe down that fast." He began pacing. "First I'd like to say thanks for coming on such short notice. I had to be intentionally vague because my phone might be tapped. . . ."

The group took a step back.

". . . We're going on another field trip. I can't tell you the final location for your own safety. Just stay close to my car and we'll caravan over."

"But it's the middle of the night."

"Precisely," said Serge. "The perfect time to resolve conflict."

"Where's the moderator?"

"Meeting us there." Serge climbed into his Comet. "Everyone follow me."

They didn't want to go, but they didn't want to disagree with Serge even more. Cars began rolling out of the parking lot. Coleman produced a fat one and pressed the Comet's cigarette lighter. Serge pulled out his favorite Colt .45 automatic and set it in his lap. "I love field trips."

"Me too," said Coleman.

"Let's play a road game."

"Okay," said Coleman. "I got a good one."

"How's it work?"

"Everyone searches around the car for—"

Rachael sprang up in back and excitedly hung over the seat between them. "Look! I found some kind of pill!" She popped it in her mouth.

"Shit," said Coleman. "Rachael already won."

The dysfunctional motorcade turned south on Interstate 75. Tall lightpoles went by at distant but even intervals, sweeping the hood and windshield with a yellow glow. Bright, dark, bright, dark. "Let's sing," said Serge.

"Okay."

The Mercury got off the interstate at Big Bend Road, and a long line of cars slowly curved down the exit ramp. They turned east, leaving development behind.

Serge: *"That cat Shaft is a bad mother—"*

Coleman: *"Shut yo mouth!"*

Serge: *"Just talkin' 'bout Shaft . . . "*

The Comet drove deeper into the sticks. They entered the kind of neighborhood with drainage ditches instead of sidewalks. Serge pulled a scrap of paper from his wallet. It had the name and town that he'd scribbled in the movers' office and, now, an address from the phone book. He cut his headlights and pulled onto the shoulder. "There's the place. Last house on the left."

"Then why are we stopping way back here?"

"Stealth is everything." He got out and popped the Mercury's trunk. People from the other cars collected around him. Serge removed a cardboard box.

"Where's the moderator?"

"Must be running late," said Serge. "We'll just have to start without him." He opened the box. "Everyone take one."

The first member's hand came out of the carton. "Halloween masks?"

"Sorry. They only had the Seven Dwarfs."

"So why do you get to be Batman?"

"Last one left." He slipped the disguise over his face. "Move out!"

They tiptoed down the street and behind a mobile home. The rear door was child's play. Serge's hand found a switch. A lamp went on, but the person in bed continued snoring.

Serge shook a shoulder. "Wake up."

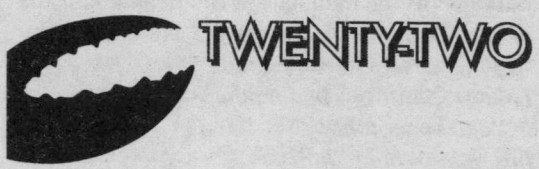

TWENTY-TWO

GULF OF MEXICO

*T*he line outside the ballroom was halfway down the hall. The double doors opened. Another stampede.

The G-Unit saw them right away: fresh meat. Three new guys sampling trays of mini-quiche. Most debonair in the whole room. Latin spice, too, just like the "captain" in the hallway, except a bit older. But nowhere near as ancient as the rest of the guys. So what were these hot new dancers doing here? Who cared? The race was on!

The quilting team soon pulled even, but the G-Unit boxed them on the inside rail and shot past at the finish line.

Edith staked her claim. "Hi! . . ."—panting hard.

She'd caught him midbite. "Mmmm . . ." He finished chewing and dabbed his mouth corners.

"Let's dance. . . ." She jerked him onto the floor. A napkin fluttered.

The rest of the G-Unit dragged his pals from the steam trays in quick succession.

The men's chiseled handsomeness would have been enough, but then another pleasant surprise: They could cut a rug with the best. The ladies were swept away. The tango, the rhumba, the watusi.

The rest of the women simply gave up and formed a large, good-natured circle, clapping in unison as the couples strutted to "Tequila."

The Brimleys were out of demand again, which was more than fine. Extra drinking time over at the bar. Behind them, the tempo swung to surf music. The G-Unit pinched their noses and did the swim, then mid-dance introductions: ". . . Ethel and Eunice on the end there . . ."

"I'm Steve. This is Miguel and Richie."

A loud crash. A Brimley was down. But nothing could stop the dance-floor magic. Edith made a pair of Vs with the first two fingers of each hand and pulled them across her face. "I saw this in *Pulp Fiction*. . . ."

One deck below, Johnny Vegas's captain's uniform inflated with hope. The Wisconsin gal just *had* to be the one: There was no possible way he could fail this time! Except she was driving him crazy by stretching out the preliminaries, like asking him his name. "Mine's Danielle. . . ." Just talk, talk, talk. She strolled over to the stereo. Wonderful, he thought, now she wants to snuggle to "soft sound of the seventies."

A thud from the ceiling. A Brimley.

To Johnny's utter astonishment, the sophomore began a sexy little solo dance with the expertise of a ten-year pole dancer. She swiveled her hips and ran hands through silky brown hair. "Tell me what you like."

Johnny pushed his tongue back in his mouth. "There is one thing."

"Name it."

"Wear my captain's hat?"

She fit it on her head and saluted. "Aye-aye . . ."

MEANWHILE, OUTSIDE TAMPA

Snoring continued. The mobile home's bedroom looked like it had been ransacked by its own occupant. There was an open suitcase with dirty laundry and souvenirs. Someone had just gotten back from vacation.

More travel junk on the dresser. Swizzle sticks, matchbooks, postcards, paper cocktail umbrellas, shot glasses, loose pesos, rumrunner tumblers, drink-till-you-drop wristbands, native onyx hash pipe crafted the old way by new peasants, deck of cruise-line playing cards.

Serge shook him again. "Yo! Wake up!"

The man rolled onto his back with even louder snoring. Serge seized both shoulders hard. "Awaken!"

Nothing.

"Serge," said Jim. "I want to go."

"But we haven't even started." Serge peeled a sticky note off the nightstand. In poor handwriting: "Get Davenport." He turned back to the bed and produced a chrome .45 automatic from his waistband, gripped it by the barrel—*"Good day . . . Sunshine! . . . "*—and cracked the sleeping man's noggin like he was opening a walnut.

The man shot up into a sitting position and grabbed his forehead. "Ow! Fuck!"

"Bodine," said Serge. "We need to talk."

Sleep cleared fast. Bodine saw Serge's gun and the room full of Halloween masks. He scooted in retreat until the backboard stopped him. "Don't! Please! Tell Tommy I was going to call him. I swear. We got delayed in port. You have to believe me!"

"I believe you," said Serge.

"You do?"

"Sure," said Serge. "Except I don't know who the hell Tommy is." He extended his shooting arm.

Bodine covered his face. "Don't kill me!"

"Then cooperate."

He peeked between fingers. "Cooperate? How?"

"What's this sticky note, 'Get Davenport'?"

"Oh, that's something else. Doesn't concern you."

"Humor me."

"Some asshole filed a complaint where I work. I wanted to remember his name so I could get even."

Serge nudged Jim. "You're on."

"What do you mean, 'I'm on'?"

"I've got your back."

"This is crazy."

"Make you a deal," said Serge. "Just tell him what you told the rest of us at the meeting, and we leave. Nothing will happen."

"That's it? Swear?"

"My word of honor. I'm just going to stand in the back of the room and observe. You have the floor." Then, waving the gun at the rest of the group: "Get up there and give your friend moral support."

The gang tentatively surrounded the bed. Serge began going through a dresser on the other side of the room. Jim adjusted his Bashful mask so the eyeholes lined up. "Uh, I kind of want you to, you know, give back the stuff you stole."

"I didn't steal from anybody!"

"That didn't come out right," said Jim. "I'm not accusing. Maybe you were confused. It's just that my wife's necklace—"

"Wait a second. Now I know you!" The man jumped out of bed. "You're that wimp who reported me at work! . . ."

Serge removed a necklace and watch from the dresser.

". . . You almost got me fired with that bullshit!" He stepped forward and poked Jim hard in the chest. Jim and the rest of the group backed up in unison. "You think missing jewelry is bad? Wait till you see what I do to you for breaking into my trailer! . . ." He poked Jim again. The group retreated another step.

In the background, Serge leaned against the wall, shaking his head.

". . . You're going to regret ever setting eyes on me!" The poke became a shove. Then another. "I know where you live! I'll burn down your fucking house with your whole fucking family!"

The members had backed up all the way to the door. Serge pushed his way through the group. "Okay, this isn't going exactly how I'd imagined. Study my technique." The butt of his pistol smacked the skull much harder this time, opening a spurting gash. Serge grabbed the dazed man under the armpits and dragged him into the bathroom. "Guys, I'll just be a minute." The door closed.

A violent symphony: Porcelain smashed, then a mirror. Horrible screams. *"You're killing me! . . . "* Gurgling from the toilet.

"You don't go near Jim or his tenth cousin!" yelled Serge. "You've already forgotten where he lives!"

"Who's Jim?"

More toilet splashing, followed by desperate gasps for breath.

"Have I made myself clear?"

"Yes! Yes! Anything! Please! . . ."

The door opened. The gang recoiled at the ghastly sight of Bodine.

Serge jabbed him in the back with the gun. "Now apologize!"

"Where is he? I can't see with all the blood in my eyes!"

"Three steps forward."

"I'm really sorry about stealing your stuff. You'll never see me again. Just keep that lunatic away from me!"

Serge began pulling him back toward the bathroom.

"What are you doing?" said Bodine. "I told him what you wanted."

"Remedial instruction in case you begin to forget later on."

"No, I'm begging." The man went limp. "I'll make you a deal."

"You can't make a big enough deal."

"Yes I can. Just give me a chance to show you. I'm begging!"

Serge turned to Jim. "What do you think?"

"I want to go home."

"He's trying to make amends," said Serge. "Let's at least hear his offer."

Bodine nodded hard. "It's a great offer!" He rushed to his suitcase and reached under some clothes.

"Freeze!" said Serge. "How do I know you don't have a weapon in there?"

He backed away. "Check for yourself."

Serge kept his gun on Bodine as he walked sideways and reached into the luggage. He pulled out a heavy clay object. "Statue?"

"Pre-Colombian," said Bodine. "Priceless."

"How'd you end up with it?"

"Smuggled. There's a huge black market with all these artifact collectors. The guys in Cozumel said I'd increase my investment tenfold when I sold it to these dealers coming over tonight. That's who I thought you were at first."

Serge tossed the statue up and down in his palm. "They lied."

"What do you mean?"

"It's Chac-Mool."

"What's that?"

"The most common souvenir in all the Yucatán. Every street corner has 'em. It's like coming back from New York with a plastic Statue of Liberty."

Coleman reached for the reclining clay figure. Serge slapped his hand. "You'll drop it. You're drunk."

"But you said it was worthless."

"Still a tacky souvenir, which to me is invaluable."

"The statue guy looks stoned," said Coleman. "What's with the bowl in his lap?"

"It's a replica of the famous figure atop that pyramid in Chichén Itzá. The bowl is where they put still-beating hearts of human sacrifices. . . . Hey, Jim, how'd you like a cool statue?"

"I want to go home."

"But we're having fun."

"You're insane!" Jim gestured around the bloody room. "How is *any* of this fun?"

"Someone crossed one of my friends, so I got to pistol-whip him senseless, destroy his bathroom, give toilet-snorkeling lessons and leave with a cheesy souvenir. Everything I love in life. Want the statue or not?"

Jim buried his hands in his pockets.

"This is your revenge," said Serge. "Take it or we'd don't leave. Cops might be on the way."

"Darn it!" Jim grabbed the statue from Serge. "Now can we go?"

Dwarf masks filed out the front door. Bodine waited until it closed. Then he ran around the trailer in a panic meltdown, flinging clothes at his suitcase. "What have I done? I lost the statue. They'll kill me for sure!"

Bodine zipped the luggage shut, ran to his front door and opened it.

He froze. "Wait! No!—"

TWENTY-THREE

GULF OF MEXICO

*D*anielle shook Johnny Vegas's shoulder. "You okay?"

"M-m-m-m-m- . . ."—pointing up at the captain's hat.

She reached for the top of his shirt. "Now I undress you. . . ."

"B-b-b-b-b- . . ."

Danielle finished the last button and licked his stomach down to the belt buckle. Then the zipper.

"Whoa! Guess you *do* like the hat." Johnny moaned and involuntarily arched his back. A rousing dance beat pounded down from the ballroom directly over them.

She saluted again. "Captain, permission to come aboard."

Finally! The day he'd been waiting for his entire life! Lucy wasn't going to pull the football away from Charlie Brown this time!

The sophomore squealed as she prepared to wiggle on down. Something blurred at the edge of her vision. Danielle's head snapped toward the balcony. "What the hell was that?"

"I didn't see anything. Go back to what you were doing."

"What do you mean you didn't see anything? Something huge flew past the window."

"Oh, *that*," said Johnny. "Just one of the Brimleys."

"Someone fell overboard?"

"The ship's barely moving."

"You're the captain!"

"I'm off duty."

Danielle ran naked onto the balcony and leaned over the railing. "He's screaming for help."

"I'm sure someone else will hear him."

She jerked a life ring off the outside wall and slung it with accuracy.

Johnny joined her at the railing and watched the bobbing man hook his arm through the float. "Problem solved. Now where were we?"

"You're a pig!" She ran back into the suite and practically jumped into her clothes. "I'm out of here!"

The door slammed.

A deep, long horn sounded. A powerful spotlight pierced the fog. A mile ahead, flashing red warning signs. Two more loud blasts as the train clacked toward another rural intersection without crossing-guard arms.

The engineers peered out the diesel's windshield, looking for another fool driver trying to beat the odds. The frequency still amazed them.

But no idiots this time. The engineers relaxed as they sailed through the crossing and back into the empty night. Conversation returned to sports.

"They'll never trade him because of the salary cap."

"His knee goes out every year like a clock."

These were the cliché milk runs. Another empty cargo backhaul. The rest of the state had its share of rail traffic, but nothing like the central Gulf coast, stuck in the golden age of the iron horse. The reason was phosphate, an essential fertilizer ingredient, and this particular part of Florida was the world capital. Giant cranes called draglines quarried vast tracks across Hillsborough and Polk counties. The industry was so weight-intensive that trains were the only viable method to get it to port. They also found a ton of prehistoric fossils down in those pits. They called it Bone Valley.

The diesel's horn blew through another intersection.

"At least we get to play Green Bay at home in December."

Taped below the instrument panel was a faxed bulletin from Miami. Central Florida may still be in the golden age, but Miami had just revived the era of the Great Train Robbery.

Another ungated crossing. The crew concentrated. Safely through again.

A rookie engineer pointed at the bulletin. "Should we be worried? I mean, we don't have weapons or anything to defend us."

The others laughed. "You new to Florida?"

He nodded.

"Whole 'nother world down Miami way," said an older engineer. "They can't even keep utility lines from getting dug up for copper and aluminum, and now junction boxes are disappearing from street corners. These morons don't know anything about those boxes except they fetch fifty bucks in South America."

The rookie peeled the bulletin off the control panel and read it again: Bandits hanging concrete blocks from overpasses at windshield level. Engineers saw them and stopped, or didn't and shattered the safety glass and *then* stopped. Either way, thieves hopped aboard and robbed the crew.

Another crossing. Flashing red. Doppler effect: *Ding-ding-ding-ding-ding* . . .

The rookie taped the bulletin back on the panel. "I'd still feel better if we had a gun."

"I told you: That's just Miami. Before concrete blocks it was voodoo chickens."

"Chickens?"

"Few years back, we started noticing unidentifiable debris on the tracks. Turned out to be a bunch of smelly voodoo shit: chickens and goat heads and little dolls. The iron rails represented some kind of connection to dead relatives. The low guy on the train's totem pole had to clear the mess off the tracks. Until they realized the ceremonies involved stuffing valuable jewels in the chickens. Then the top guy got the shovel. . . ."

The train was on a long, dark stretch of track near the county line, far between crossings. Nothing to worry about.

"If it's just Miami," said the rookie, "why'd they send us the bulletin?"

"Insurance. The whole state got them—"

"Holy Jesus!" The rookie pointed out the windshield.

"What the hell's that doing out here?"

"Hit the brakes!"

Screeeechhhhhhhhhhhhhhhhh.

"Oh my God!"

The train continued grinding and sparking down the rails. Hearts pounded. No time to stop before hitting the convertible Trans Am parked across the tracks.

"Grab something!" Everyone braced. At the last second, the car scooted out of their path and down into a ditch.

Everyone exhaled with relief.

Crash.

Windshield impact. They ducked after the fact, but the

safety glass had held. They slowly stood back up as the train squeaked to a halt.

"What on earth?"

They all leaned for a closer view of the blood splatter. "Is that an eyeball?"

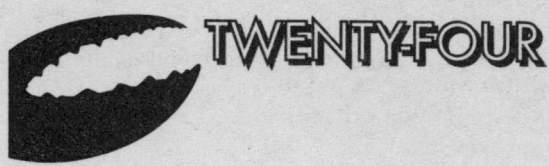

TWENTY-FOUR

BEFORE SUNRISE

*T*he fifty-car phosphate train would not be on time this morning. Nor would all the others stacked up for miles behind the crime scene.

A detective's face glowed in the flickering string of railroad flares. His name was Sadler. "Let's go over it one more time."

"What's to go over?" The engineer sat on a pile of spare wooden ties next to the tracks. "We saw the car. Then, out of nowhere, splat."

They looked back. An evidence team on ladders tediously scraped the locomotive's front glass. More investigators down in a ditch, swarming the Trans Am.

The engineer wiped his forehead with a bandanna. "Any idea what happened?"

Sadler jotted in a notebook. "Still trying to figure that." He stopped writing when he noticed a familiar FBI agent standing off to the side. "Bureau taking over the case?"

"Just observing."

"This wouldn't have anything to do with those other nine unsolved deaths. . . ."

The FBI agent gave him a look that said the subject was off limits.

Sadler's partner, Detective Mayfield, was down at the sports car. He climbed back up the embankment and walked along the edge of the tracks between the train and the flares.

"Anything?" yelled Sadler.

"Yeah," said Mayfield, looking back at the Trans Am. "Sickest thing I ever seen."

FOUR HOURS EARLIER

Three men in spotless linen suits walked across a dark yard of weeds and dirt.

The last one gestured with his Uzi toward the driveway. "Bodine's car's gone."

"For his sake, he better not be in it."

They reached the front of a rotting mobile home in southern Hillsborough County. The leader was about to knock when he noticed the door ajar. He pushed it open. "Bodine? . . ."

The three split up.

"He's not in here. . . ."

"Not in here either. . . ."

They regrouped in the bedroom.

"What a mess."

"Where'd all this blood come from?"

One picked up a deck of playing cards. "Here's his crap from the cruise ship."

"Statue?"

"Nope."

"Damn," said the leader. "Find that statue. Tear the place apart!"

The leader circulated through the trailer in deep thought. Around him: dresser drawers and ceiling tiles in flight, cabinets cracking off walls, pillows sliced, mattress disemboweled.

The leader worked his way back to the bedroom. He swatted floating feathers away from his face. "Stop."

The destruction was too loud.

"I said *stop*!"

The others became still. "What's the matter?"

"It's not here. Either Bodine's gone into business for himself, or someone beat us to him."

"What do we do now?"

"Find Bodine. Or whoever took the statue."

"Hold it." One of them reached down next to the dresser. "Look what I just found."

"What is it?"

"A sticky note. Says, 'Get Davenport.' "

"Think it has anything to do with the statue?"

EIGHT MILES AWAY

Coleman drove through the empty countryside on an unmaintained dirt road. At least he *thought* it was still a road, but the passage through the woods had grown narrower and bumpier. He'd long since lost orientation, except for the taillights of the car Serge was driving up ahead.

They were another ten minutes deeper into nowhere when Coleman saw the Trans Am's brake lights come on. He watched the Firebird angle up a steep incline before easing to a stop.

Serge leaped out of the car. "Make it snappy!"

Coleman walked up with coils of rope over his shoulder. "Serge, you're parked on railroad tracks."

"Just hand me the rope."

"I forgot where I left it."

"On your shoulder."

Serge took the line and walked to the front of the car.

Coleman pulled a joint from behind his ear. "How'd you know about this road?"

Serge stared straight up. "I poke around a lot. Been planning this one for years, and there couldn't be a more perfect spot." He heaved the rope into the air. It fell back without results. "Just never found the right transgressor. Didn't want to be unfair and have the punishment not fit the crime." He gathered the rope and threw it hard again.

Coleman flicked his lighter. "How's this the perfect spot?"

The rope fell impotently at Serge's feet. "That sturdy tree branch. Usually they cut 'em back over the tracks but this is too remote. . . . Maybe if I stand up here."

Serge climbed onto the hood. He heaved again. This time the rope made it over the branch. "There we go." He caught the other end as it came back down, and fashioned an intricate knot.

Coleman exhaled toward the stars. "Choo-choos ever come this way?"

"All the time. That's why we have to hurry." Serge finished his knot and removed the Trans Am's smoked T-top. He darted to the back of the car, gun in one hand, key in the other.

The trunk lid popped and hands instantly went up in surrender. "Please! Don't! Whatever you're thinking—"

"Get out of the fucking trunk!"

A leg went over the side. "What are you going to do to me?"

"Oh, you don't want to miss this."

Fifteen minutes later, Serge was in the zone.

"I'm begging you!" said Bodine, bound in the driver's seat. "There's still time to stop!"

"Should have considered that before you threatened Jim's family."

"But I thought we settled it with the statue."

"That was just for Jim's sake. His stomach isn't built for this."

"I'll never go near him!"

"You're just saying that because I'm here, and you're sitting there, like . . . what's the technical term? Oh, yeah, completely fucked. But I can't always be around Jim in case you change your mind."

"I take it all back! I swear!"

"Sorry," answered Serge. "You said burn up his whole family. That threat's out there forever. It's a bell you can't unring."

"I'll leave the state! I'll leave the *country*!"

Serge shook his head. "Threats must be dealt with according to severity, and a decent, law-abiding family is near the top of my NATO strategic defense protocol."

The man whimpered.

"Time for the safety checklist!" Serge leaned over the driver's seat and examined the tautness of two straps. "Seat belt and shoulder harness fastened—check!" He tested cuffs locking the man's wrists to the steering wheel. "Hands at the approved ten-o'clock, two-o'clock driving position—check!" He hit the horn and turned on the lights. Nothing. "Fuses pulled—check!" He inspected his knot and slid it tighter. "Noose around neck—check!" Serge reached into the car and turned the ignition key, then grabbed the stick shift. "I'd strongly advise you to put your foot on the brake."

Bodine did.

Serge threw the car into drive.

"Give me one more chance!"

"One more chance? Sure, I'll give you one more chance."

"Thank you! You won't be sorry!"

"Here's your chance: I'm going to leave now. If you can figure a way out, you're free to go. Let's see. Handcuffs prevent you from getting at the noose, seat belt or gearshift. So you better keep that foot on the brake. But then you'll get hit by the train, which can't see or hear you because I pulled those fuses, so you better step on the gas. But then the seat belt and shoulder strap will hold you in the car and your head will pop off. Therein lies the dilemma. When you hear that train a-comin' round the bend, what will you do? Brake? Or gas? Deal, no deal?" Serge scratched his head. "Shit, you're in a real jam. But I'm sure you'll figure something. I got the impression you thought you were a lot smarter than me. . . ." Serge walked back to his own car, starting to sing.

Bodine struggled vainly against the cuffs. "Don't leave!"

Coleman climbed in the Comet's passenger side, and Serge got behind the wheel. " . . . *Let the Midnight Special . . . shine its ever-lovin' light on me . . .* "

The man watched over his shoulder as the Mercury's taillights disappeared back into the woods. Completely quiet and dark again. Actually quite peaceful.

Then a rumble. Bodine turned. A blinding white beam hit his eyes.

TWENTY-FIVE

DAVIS ISLANDS

*J*im hadn't slept so late since college. He'd climbed into bed just before daybreak and was out before getting the second shoe off. His final thought before nodding: Bury that damn statue in a ten-foot hole or throw it in the sea before the police find out about the mobile home invasion.

Martha had awoken when her husband arrived all sweaty, and she was conflicted. What kind of support group meets in the middle of the night? On the other hand, it showed Jim's commitment. Questions would be saved for the morning, which became afternoon. . . .

Jim finally raised his head and shielded his eyes against sunlight. The bedside alarm said one o'clock. He yawned and entered the dining room to the steaming aroma of blueberries. Martha came out of the kitchen with potholders. "I made you muffins."

"Thanks, hon." He grabbed one. "Ow."

"They're still hot."

He juggled. "I haven't slept like that in I don't know."

"How do you feel?"

"Like a million. Maybe I just need more rest."

"Oh!" said Martha. "Almost forgot! Let me show you where I put it."

"Put what?"

"Can't believe you were so thoughtful." She waved him over and pointed at the mantel.

Jim became dizzy.

"I set the statue right between that mask from Puerto Rico and those Guatemalan fertility dolls." Martha gave him a big, neck-wringing hug. "Of course it's just a replica—there's no way you could afford the real thing—but still so sweet of you!"

The doorbell.

Jim jumped.

Martha walked toward the front of the house, glancing back. "You okay?" She opened the door.

Gladys Plant jogged on the mat. "Did you see the noon newscast?"

"I was baking."

"Oh my God! This dirtball got decapitated at the railroad tracks! The bloody head smashed into this train's windshield, and an eyeball got squished on the glass. Do I smell muffins?"

Martha led her neighbor over to the table. "That's terrible. . . . Careful, those are still hot."

"I haven't even told you the best part." Gladys blew on a muffin. "The victim worked for Moving Dudes. Wouldn't it be ironic if it was the same guy who ripped you off?"

"Jim, you're white as a sheet," said Martha.

"Get him a chair!" said Gladys.

They slipped it under him just before he went down.

"Want us to call a doctor?"

He shook his head and slapped his chest. "Gas."

"TV talked to a witness," said Gladys. "Bunch of guys in dwarf masks—"

The doorbell again.

Jim jumped again. "What the hell was that?"

"You sure you're okay?" Martha answered.

"Who is it?" asked Gladys.

"Just the police."

Jim grabbed the edge of the table. The room began to spin.

"Honey, come over here," said Martha. "The officer wants to talk to you."

Jim pushed himself up and walked to the gallows.

"We're handing out these flyers," said the patrolman. "Seen anything suspicious lately?"

"No!" said Jim. "Why? Anything look suspicious?"

Gladys arrived and stuck her head between the couple. "What's going on? Did I miss anything good?"

Martha read the pamphlet. "Three recent burglaries on this side of the island."

"Thought the island didn't have that kind of problem," said Jim.

"You don't," said the officer. "That's what's so odd. They got sloppy at one house and tripped the alarm. We road-blocked the bridge, but nothing."

"You mean it's one of our neighbors?" said Gladys. "I have some ideas."

The officer shook his head. "We thought that at first, but the common denominator was a bunch of puddles in kitchens. Sent samples to the lab. Came back *salt* water."

"I'm not following," said Martha.

"Scuba divers. They're coming and going over the seawall."

"I knew it," said Gladys. "It's a *straight* seawall."

"I'm still confused," said Jim.

The officer began walking away. "Apparently there's enough to steal over here to justify the effort."

"So what are we supposed to do?"

"I was just told to hand out pamphlets."

THAT AFTERNOON

A newspaper lay on the dashboard of a '73 Mercury Comet. It was folded to the article Serge had just discovered about McGraw's prison release. The Comet sat next to a phone booth outside a convenience store in downtown Tampa. Serge examined the frayed end of a metal cable where the phone book used to be. "Trotskyists." He went inside the convenience store. He ran out.

"Hey, you! Come back here with my phone book!"

Serge sped off in the Comet, flipping through yellow pages. Rachael lay in the backseat, taking self-portraits with Serge's digital camera. Coleman was up front rolling numbers. "What are you looking for?"

Serge clicked a pen and made a circle. "If McGraw makes a move on Jim, our apartment's too far away to respond in time. I picked up something about his street."

They stopped at a red light. People in other cars stared.

"How's the phone book fit in?" asked Coleman.

Two bare legs cocked up in the Comet's backseat, feet out the window. A camera flashed. The light turned green. Cars followed.

"You have to read social classes," said Serge. "The more expensive the homes, the more likely the owners have *other* homes."

Ten minutes later, the Comet was parked in the section of south Tampa called Palma Ceia. The car's occupants sat in a row of three chairs in front of a desk. The desk was in a small office of a faux-Mediterranean strip mall featuring four-dollar coffee and five-dollar ice cream cones.

Serge studied a six-page list of addresses. The person behind the desk studied the trio. Not a good vibe. He would have already shown them the door, but he wanted to leer at Rachael a little longer.

Serge turned another page. At the top: TAMPA BAY HOUSE SITTERS.

"Do you have references?" asked the man behind the desk.

"No," said Serge. "Asking someone for references is demeaning. I *give* references."

"Then I'm sorry," the man said distractedly. "Afraid we won't be able—"

"What the fuck are you looking at?" yelled Rachael, rubbing her gums. Heads in the lobby turned.

The man made an urgent, pushing-down motion with his hands. "Please lower your voice."

"Hey, everybody!" Rachael shouted. "Perv-man here was checking out my tits." She faced the desk again. "You look, you pay!" She grabbed a pen and wrote something on the edge of the man's calendar. "That's my website. You look like a gag-ball fiend."

The trio left. The man copied the website onto a scrap of paper and slipped it into his wallet. Then: Where'd my address list go?

TWENTY-SIX

DAVIS ISLANDS

*M*artha Davenport hummed merrily as she dusted the living room mantel around her favorite statue.

Jim stood in the background. How was he going to pull this off? Maybe wait till she was out of the house and say he broke it. No, he'd get in trouble. Maybe say scuba divers stole it. No, she'd file a police report. Maybe—

"Jim, what are you doing over there staring at me?"

"Nothing."

"You're up to something."

"No, I'm not." He ran out the door.

The weekend street was alive. Skateboards, pruning shears, cars getting Turtle-Waxed, the air heavy with that great Saturday morning Florida smell of freshly cut St. Augustine grass.

Jim grabbed a garden hose and began watering so he wouldn't look like he was up to something. Across the street, a riding lawnmower made circles around a date palm. The driver wore a gold silk warm-up suit and matching gold chains. He waved at Jim. Jim returned the greeting timidly, at stomach level. It was the only riding mower Jim had ever seen with a sun umbrella, cocktail holder and TV set. His neighbor's bottom spilled over the sides of the seat, and the mower appeared to labor under the weight like a swaybacked donkey.

The mower stopped. Uh-oh. He was coming over. Jim froze. No-man's-land. Too far to sprint to the house without looking obvious.

"Yo!"

"Hi."

"Jim, right? My name's Vinny. Or Vinny No-Neck. But not Masturbating Vinny. That's another guy, even if they say he looks exactly like me."

They shook hands.

"Nice lawn you got there. I'm in the witness-protection program."

Jim went over to turn off the hose. Vinny followed and pointed at a dry patch. "You missed a spot."

"I wasn't really watering."

"So Moving Dudes stole some stuff." Vinny leaned closer and covered his mouth in case lip-readers were watching with binoculars. "I can take care of that thing."

"No! . . . I mean, no, I'm sure we just misplaced it."

"Next time, let them know you're with me." Vinny deliberately fiddled with his pinkie ring. "Nothing will disappear. In fact, extra stuff will show up."

"Listen . . ." Jim turned toward his house. "I have to—"

"What are you doing right now?"

"My wife and I—"

"Got an idea!" Vinny pointed up the street. "I was just about to go up to——'s place. Watch the big game. Why don't you join us?"

"Can't. We have to . . . Wait, did you say——?"

Vinny nodded. "Played for the Bucs. At least at the end, after he was washed up with the Steelers. Tampa grabbed him off waivers, but he only lasted half a season. Liked the climate so much he kept the second home here."

Jim became a child. "This is incredible. I heard a player lived on the street, but I didn't know it was——. Growing up in Indiana, we didn't have the Colts yet, so Pittsburgh was my team! And he was my favorite player!"

Vinny slapped him on the shoulder. "Let's go have a couple of pops."

"You mean I can actually meet him?"

"Meet him, shmeet him. If he has a few too many, you might even wrestle on the floor."

"I can't believe this! I'll have to tell my wife!"

"Jesus, Jim, you're bouncing all over the place. You really must be a fan."

"You have no idea!"

"Bring a camera. I'll get a picture of you two."

Jim burst through the front door, his voice echoing across the tiles: "Honey! I have someone I'd like you to meet."

A disembodied voice from the kitchen: "Who is it?"

"Just come out here."

Martha entered the living room, drying hands with a towel. She stutter-stepped when she recognized the neighbor, then regained composure. She set the towel down and manufactured a smile. "You must be Mr. Carbello." She extended a hand.

"Vinny." He leaned and kissed it.

Martha gave her husband a non-idle look.

Jim jerked a thumb sideways. "Me and Vinny were going to go watch a game. . . . There's my camera!" He grabbed it from the top of an opened moving box.

"But we have those plans," said Martha.

"What plans?"

Her eyes transmitted gamma rays. "Jim!"

"What?"

Another false smile at Vinny. "Would you excuse us a moment? . . . Jim, I'd like to talk to you in the kitchen."

Jim followed. "What is it?"

Vinny worked his way around the living room, studying family photos.

Martha was using one of those angry whispers that is louder than actual talking.

"Have you lost your mind?"

"Honey—"

"He's a gangster!"

"Shhhh! He'll hear you."

"The guy's a hood! You're not going!"

"But honey, he knows——."

"Who's that? Another killer?"

"No, one of my favorite sports heroes of all time. I must have mentioned him a hundred times."

"You're not going, and that's it!"

Jim's head popped out of the kitchen. "Vinny, just be a second."

Vinny nodded. Jim's head disappeared.

"Honey, he said I might be able to get my picture taken."

"Listen to yourself. You want to hang out with the mob?"

"He's retired."

"Jim!"

Vinny moved to another photo. Jim, nine, holding a fish. Dang, the kid was skinny.

"But—"

"That's final!"

Jim reappeared from the kitchen, camera hanging sadly from his shoulder. "I'm awfully sorry, but something's come up."

"Forget about it," said Vinny. "But mind if I ask you a question?"

"No."

"Who wears the pants?"

"What?"

Vinny angled his head toward the kitchen. "Couldn't help but overhear."

"Sorry about that. She doesn't mean it."

"Not worried about me. Worried about *you*."

"What do you mean?"

"Dames will be dames. That's why they make aspirin. But there's a certain point when a guy's got to do what he's got to do."

"What are you saying?"

"You just want to watch a little game on TV, not to mention meet a Hall of Famer. Where's the sin in that? It's not like you're going over there to bang some broad, although I can set you up."

"Vinny!"

"Say no more. Some guys are faithful. I got respect for that. But *you* also deserve respect. Am I not right?"

"No, I mean yes, I mean what was the question?"

"I kept this floozy in Brooklyn. Regular tiger in the sack. Toilet got so clogged with Coney Island whitefish we had the plumber on speed-dial. But she also had a mouth on her. Nothing a little rap in the teeth couldn't fix."

Jim jumped back. "I'd never hit Martha! I think you better leave."

"You got me all wrong."

"I do?"

Vinny nodded hard. "I can tell you're not the hitting type. She should be grateful. Compared to getting smacked around, you watching a game with the guys is practically romantic." He grabbed Jim by the arm. "Let's go."

"Shouldn't I tell Martha?"

"Definitely not. I know women. She'll respect you much more for standing up to her. Probably let you cum on her face tonight."

"My wife . . ."

"We're missing kickoff."

They left and headed up the sidewalk. A Comet passed them the other way.

"We're in luck." Serge tapped a circled address on the last page. "They have a house on Jim's street."

The Comet stopped in front of a place near the end of Lobster Lane. Serge gasped. "Oh, baby! Will you look at her!"

Rising before them: a three-story contemporary waterfront manse. All white, vertical wall of translucent glass blocks illuminating the foyer and a collection of oversized, abstract art spiraling up behind a staircase that poked through the roof and onto a widow's walk of curved, tubular steel rails. In the yard, sea grapes, bird-of-paradise, azaleas and the centerpiece: a manicured twenty-foot traveler's palm fanning out across the gleaming facade.

Serge placed the back of a hand to his forehead. "It's everything I've always wanted. Did you know there was a strict rule on *Miami Vice*? All bad guys had to live in postmodern homes. True. Watch the reruns."

Yelling erupted from the front steps. A stocky, bald man with boardroom suspenders berated undocumented yard help.

The Comet sped away.

"Serge," said Coleman. "If that's the house, where are you going?"

"Can't let him see this car. Or you two, no offense." He parked at the end of the block. "Stay here with the car. I'll be right back."

Yelling grew louder as Serge neared on the sidewalk.

". . . What am I paying you people for? All you do is take water breaks. . . ." The man sipped a frosty mint julep.

Serge reached the front of the house and turned up the walkway toward the porch. He fashioned his most convincing smile. "Beautiful place you have here!"

"Thanks. Who the hell are you?"

"Serge Storms."

The man warily shook his hand. "Gaylord Wainscotting. What do you want?"

"The same thing you do. House-sitting."

"*You're* the house-sitter? Agency didn't say you were coming."

"Agency didn't send me. I'm in business for myself."

Gaylord looked Serge over. "I'll need references."

"References? Sure." Serge pointed up the street. "Jim."

"Jim?"

"Your new neighbor. Three houses up."

"Oh, the Davenports." He nodded. "Nice people. Only talked a couple times. Jim's a little on the quiet side, but Martha seems like a wonderful woman."

"She is."

"Where do you know Jim from?"

"Uh . . . we meet each week. We're in the same *club*."

"You and Jim belong to the club?" said Wainscotting. "*I* belong to the club. Living on this side of the island, I should have known Jim was a member. Wonder why he didn't tell me?"

"Are you serious?" said Serge. "It's not exactly the kind of thing you talk about."

"Couldn't agree more," said Wainscotting. "Can't stand this new wealth that puts on the dog."

"Those fuckers!"

Gaylord laughed. "No shit . . . Say, I like you. If they accepted you in the club, no need for any background checks. Their membership committee's worse than the FBI." He finished his plantation drink and smacked Serge on the shoulder. "Let's go inside."

They entered through a front door with a giant heron etched into the glass. "What are you drinking?"

"White grapefruit," said Serge. "Chilled, not iced."

"Loosen up. I got Chivas, Stoli, Johnny Walker Blue."

"I drink *after* business."

"Good for you. Luckily I'm finished with business for life." Gaylord poured himself a generous Belvedere vodka martini. "Made most of mine in the stock market. Good broker, if you know what I mean."

"A little Martha Stewart birdie in your ear?"

Gaylord winked. "How'd you make yours?"

"Currency conversion."

"Now you *really* got my respect. I don't have the stones for that kind of action. The least little fluctuation in the dollar and you're ruined."

"That's why I only work with great big fluctuations."

"Bet you made a lot of money."

"Literally."

Gaylord finished his first martini and began fixing another. "We're a lot alike—have to do the club together sometime."

"Just say the word."

Gaylord dumped ice in a sterling cylinder, capped it and began shaking. "I *love* the club. Why haven't I seen you there? Or Jim?"

"We go Tuesdays."

"You should try Wednesdays. The most tender prime rib in town."

"We just get stale coffee and doughnuts."

"But they're supposed to have stone crab on Tuesday."

"You sure we're talking about the same club?"

"I know, I know. But last year was an exception." Gaylord uncapped the shaker. "With all the staff turnover, you never knew which club you were going to get. Guess they still have some kinks to iron out. I'll talk to Remington. Meantime, switch to Wednesdays. Nothing like a big steak after a round of golf."

"Golf?" said Serge. "I hate the fucking game!"

"What?"

"You'd have to be a complete idiot to play that stupid shit."

"Tell me about it," said Gaylord. "I could murder the guy

who invented the elevated green. But it's an addiction worse than any drug. What are you going to do?"

"Feed the monkey."

Gaylord speared an olive. "Why'd *you* join the club?"

"Deal with aggression."

"Feels like I'm talking to a mirror." Gaylord refilled his martini glass to the brim. "That's why I joined. It's like therapy."

"What do you mean *like*? It *is* therapy."

"No shit. Eighteen holes and I'm a new man." He took a large sip. "Just one question. If you belong to the club and all, why do you need to house-sit?"

"Sold my place on Bayshore a few days ago. Broke my heart, but local prices were beginning to bubble. Rule number one . . ."

". . . Never get emotionally attached to an asset."

"Now I just have the Hamptons spread."

"Cape Cod here."

"But I couldn't give up the club," said Serge. "Figured I'd house-sit until my Realtor finds something else."

Gaylord raised his glass. "To the club."

"The club."

A horn honked.

They looked through the glass front door. Another honk. A rust-eaten Comet at the curb. Rachael behind the wheel. Then she really laid into it for one of those ten-second blasts that got every dog barking for five blocks. Serge slapped himself on the forehead. Gaylord pointed with his cocktail. "Who the hell are those jackasses?"

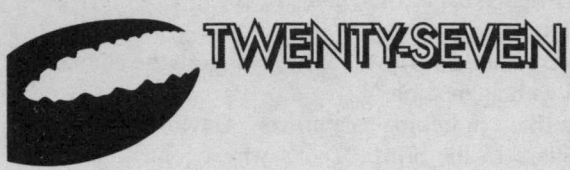

TWENTY-SEVEN

848 LOBSTER LANE

*D*ing-dong!

Two men stood on a welcome mat.

Jim looked up in awe at the building. "I can't believe this is his *second* home."

Vinny pressed the bell again. "You should see the Pennsylvania compound."

The door opened. Jim's mouth fell. A steamy blonde with black roots in a thong.

"Vinny!"

"Mandy!"

Big hug.

Vinny turned. "I'd like you to meet my friend, Jim. He's faithful, so don't blow him."

Mandy smiled and shook his hand. "Pay no attention to Vin. He's always joking. Nice to meet you."

Jim opened his mouth, but nothing came out.

She looked at Vinny. "Cat got his tongue?"

"The strong silent type." Vinny stepped through the door without invitation. "Is——here?"

"Game room. You know the way."

Jim followed Vinny through the living room, another hot

babe on the couch. She looked up from a mirror and offered Jim a straw. "Booger sugar?"

"What?"

They turned the corner. A long, dark-paneled hallway led to the inner sanctum. Jim checked out the rows of framed *Sports Illustrated* covers that seemed to go on forever. Finally they were standing right in front of it. The Door.

"Here we are," said Vinny. "Holy of Holies."

"——is on the other side?" said Jim.

Vinny knocked hard.

Through the wood: "Shit, who the hell is it?"

"Me, Vinny."

The still-closed door: "Jesus, you scared the hell out of me! Anyone with you?"

"My friend, Jim."

"Who the fuck's Jim?"

"My friend," Vinny whispered sideways: "Don't make any sudden moves until he gets used to you. I think he's been basing."

"What?"

Vinny pounded the door again. "Open up. I'm getting old out here."

The door: "Vinny? . . ."

"What?"

"Is that you?"

"Open the fuckin' door!"

Jim heard fumbling with a variety of locks, bolts and chains. The door opened a slit. A single eyeball scanned back and forth. "You sure it's cool?"

"Let us in, you cocksucker!"

The door opened the rest of the way.

"Vinny!"

"——!"

Hugging time again.

"Got the stuff?"

Vinny reached in the hip pocket of his warm-up suit and tossed a Baggie of light-blue tablets. "Those should bring you down."

The player tossed back a handful of pills and headed for the liquor cabinet.

Vinny gave Jim the all-clear wink. Jim was only two steps inside when his legs stopped working, the same reaction for every first-time visitor to Guy Heaven. The game room was bigger than most banquet halls. Pool table, card table, slot machine in one corner, pinball in another. Full-service bar. Refrigerator with keg tap through the door. Overpadded black leather sofas and La-Z-Boys aimed variously at nine TVs, including the centerpiece eighty-four-inch high-def, currently showing a replay of the '79 Super Bowl, Pittsburgh driving in the red zone. The eighteen speaker surround-sound with subwoofer and ceiling flush-mounts made Jim feel like he was in the middle of the tackle. The smaller televisions featured pornography and live satellite feeds from Vegas sports books.

Then Jim saw it. Vinny could tell his new pal was stricken. "Go ahead and look. Just don't break anything."

Jim walked across an Astroturf putting green until he was standing in front of the trophy wall: built-in shelves and soft recessed spotlights, one for each of the hundred-odd gold statues and plaques and old footballs on tees, dated with stats. Jim could recall every game represented by each of the balls, and even the games represented by little brass plates where football tees were curiously empty. He reached the next wall, the one with sliding glass doors overlooking the football-shaped pool. Thick vertical blinds were drawn tight, keeping the room grotto dark.

Jim peeked outside. His eyes went first to the exquisite sight of Mandy sunning herself next to the diving board. Then he noticed more people. They were on the other side of the seawall, down in the bay, dozens of 'em: canoes and kayaks and rafts and some just treading water in life vests, all quietly staring at the house. They seemed to be waiting for something to happen. Jim slowly pulled a cord for a better look. . . .

"Close those fucking blinds!"

Jim jumped. Vinny rushed over and made the room dark again. "Sudden light overstimulates him."

Serge gritted his teeth and glared out the glass front door at Coleman and Rachael. "Those are my . . . business associates."

Gaylord stared dubiously at the beaten-up vehicle and, for the first time, gave Serge a disappointed look.

"I'm into vintage cars," said Serge. "Haven't had a chance to restore that one yet."

"*Ohhh,*" said Gaylord. "Read an article. Lot of money in that. Why don't you invite your associates in?"

"We're on a tight schedule."

"I insist." He went to the front door and made a big inviting wave. "Don't be strangers."

Two minutes later, Coleman was lining up shot glasses, and Gaylord couldn't pull his eyes off the chick.

"Take a picture," said Rachael. "It'll last longer."

Coleman snapped his fingers. "Over here, moneybags. We're on the clock. Those eight shots are yours; these are mine. One every sixty seconds or until we lose somebody. Go!"

Serge covered his face. "This can't be happening."

Two empty shot glasses slammed on the wet bar. "So, Coleman, what do you do?"

"What do you mean, 'What do I do?'" He grabbed Gaylord's wrist, monitoring the Rolex's second hand. "I hang with Serge."

"Business loyalty. I respect that."

"Now!" said Coleman. Shots went back. Gaylord turned to Rachael. "And what do you do?"

She looked at Serge. "What's with this fuckin' guy? What do I *do*?"

"Gaylord," said Serge. "She runs a profitable website."

"Really? I'd like to see it. We can pull it up in my study."

Serge's arms flew out in alarm. "No! You can't! It's down for repairs!"

"Fuck you!" Rachael shoved Serge in the chest. "Don't ever interfere with my business. . . . Come on, Gayboy."

"Gaylord."

"Whatever." She led him around the corner.

"Hey!" Coleman yelled after him. "You'll lose the game. I'll get your shots."

A door closed.

Coleman grabbed a glass for each hand. "Serge, what a sweet deal! I checked when he wasn't looking. There's all kinds of bottles back here."

Serge pounded a fist on the bar. "Don't you dare screw this up on me!"

"Relax," said Coleman. "The dude parties! Plus he digs Rachael. He may be rich, but he still likes to get his freak on."

A half hour later, shot glasses lay scattered everywhere. Coleman was passed out in the middle of the floor, limbs bent unnaturally like he'd fallen from a balcony. Serge sat on the edge of the sofa, rocking nervously. Rachael came back into the living room, thumbing a thick wad of currency.

Serge stood quickly. "You killed him?"

"Hell no," said Rachael. "He paid me in cash. Didn't want a credit card trail."

Gaylord emerged. "Have to be somewhere. Why don't you familiarize yourself with the place?" He jingled something. "Here are the keys. We leave next Monday."

Before Serge could respond, Gaylord stepped over Coleman and was out the door. A Jag sped off.

The ex-Steelers player was on the main couch, working with a glass bulb. He finished his business and slid the paraphernalia tray under the sofa. "Vinny, let's throw it around."

"You got it, big guy."

The player went to The Wall and grabbed a game ball off a tee.

Jim raced over to Vinny. "Oh my God! We're actually going to play catch?"

"Don't cream your pants."

They exited the sliding doors and walked past the diving board. Vinny nudged Jim. "Mandy's a dish, eh?"

"Who is she?"

"His girlfriend."

"Thought he was married."

"Divorced."

Jim looked back at the house. "Who was that other woman with the cocaine?"

"There's always a million chicks hanging around. But Mandy's his girl."

"Vinny!" yelled the player, smacking the football in his throwing hand. "Go long!"

Vinny began trotting around the far side of the pool. Not a pretty sight. Then he turned and ran backward, waving an arm. "I'm open! I'm open!"

The ball sailed through the air . . . and over the seawall. Pandemonium in the water. Someone floating on a swim noodle raised his prize. "I got it!" The others grumbled, paddling canoes and kayaks back into position.

The player jogged toward the sliding glass door. "I'll get another."

He came back out with a ball from an overtime divisional playoff.

Then Jim couldn't believe his eyes. The player patted the ball and pointed at *him*. "Post route!"

Jim ran along the near side of the pool and watched the ball take flight. It was a timing pattern. Jim kept his eyes skyward as he curled around the shallow end. It seemed to hang forever. Perfect spiral, laces, Wilson. Jim heard heavenly music. Then he saw the ball land in his hands. Unbelievable. He'd just caught a pass from——! He could now die in peace.

But other business first. Jim found himself teetering on the edge of the seawall, twirling his free arm for balance, hopeful eyes below in the water. Then he found equilibrium. The canoe people sagged. Jim strolled back and casually tossed the ball to his hero like he did this every day.

"Nice catch, sport."

Jim fought the urge to weep: *He called me "sport"*!

Vinny's turn again. He ran like a sack of tomatoes. Another ball splashed into the bay, another trip back inside to the trophy shelf.

Jim's turn. Buttonhook pattern, another circus catch. Growing discontent in the water. "Who *is* that guy?"

On it went. For five minutes. Vinny and the player got bored and wanted to call their bookies. They headed toward the house.

For the last hour, Jim had been rehearsing how he would, with the utmost dignity, broach the topic of his interest in the player's career. Not like all the other idiots who claimed to be his number one fan. Jim dashed up to the player. "I'm your number one fan! . . ." He became verbally incontinent, babbling statistics and big games.

Vinny grabbed his shoulder. "Down, puppy."

"No, it's okay." The player's ego inflated. "What's your name, sport?"

He called me "sport" again! "Uh . . ."

The player smiled at Vinny. "He forget his own name?"

"It's Jim," said Vinny. "Hey, Jim. Go get your camera, and I'll take a picture of you two."

"I'll be right back! Don't go anywhere!"

Jim returned with his Pentax and handed it to Vinny. Click, click, click.

Mandy rose from the lounger. "Why don't I get a shot of the three of you?"

Click, click, click. The whole time, Jim: ". . . Remember the Cowboys blizzard game at Three Rivers, when you played the second half with two broken ribs? . . . Or the famous 'drive' against the Dolphins? Ninety-six yards from scrimmage with two to go? . . ."

The player beamed. "Ninety-seven."

". . . The next year you led the league in all-purpose yards. . . ."

"Jim," said Vinny. "Settle down."

"He's fine," said the player, postponing that call to his bookie and grabbing a patio lounger. He slapped the one next to him. "Jim, have a seat. . . . Mandy, baby, can you get some drinks out here?"

It was the beginning of a beautiful friendship: Jim, intricately reciting an entire career and taking more photos; the player, staring up from behind Bulgari sunglasses, envisioning Jim's play-by-plays in the sky and knocking back cocktails strong enough to strip furniture.

". . . You practically invented the press conference no-show! . . ."

The player was in excellent spirits. "Let's barbecue!"

Vinny took over the grill and flipped rib eyes. He insisted on wearing the chef's hat. Jim's inner child grew younger. He followed the player around like a pet, taking copious photos of his every mundane action.

They ended up back on the porch.

Jim advanced his film. "Let me get a picture of you and Mandy."

"Sure."

They posed together. Click. Then the player suddenly threw her over his shoulder. She giggled and kicked her feet. He spanked her bikini bottom. Then he went to set her down on the poolside lounger, but it was more of a fall as they collapsed together and nuzzled. Click, click, click.

Jim went over to the smoking grill.

"Jimbo!" said Vinny, brushing mesquite. "Bet you're glad you came, eh?"

"I . . . I . . . Vinny, this is—Can I call you Vinny?"

"You need a pill?"

"No, it's just . . . This is the best day of my entire life. I mean outside of marriage and births." Jim snapped his fingers. "I know what I'm going to do. I'll enlarge one of the photos and mail it to him as a present. I'll have it professionally matted, with a big, expensive frame. Think I got a good one of him and Mandy—"

"Jim, you have to be cool. If you're going to hang out, you can't act like some fruitcake fan. How do you want your steak?"

"Medium. That's the thing. He's got a million insane fans all over the country. . . ." Jim popped the exposed film canister out of the camera and stuck it in his pocket. ". . . He'll never remember me."

"Of course he'll remember you."

Jim shook his head. "But he might if he likes the photo. Then if I ever get to come back over, it would be neat if he recognized me."

Vinny hung steak tongs on the side of the grill, turned and squatted in a boxer's crouch. He playfully punched Jim in the stomach. "You're a crazy fuck, you know that? Wouldn't last five seconds in Jersey, but that's why I like you."

"Vinny . . ."

"No, really. You're one of the genuine good guys."

"Vinny . . ."

"It's so refreshing. I don't know any good guys, except Good Guy Moe. Saw him once take this meat hook—"

"Vinny . . ."

"What?"

"Fire."

Vinny turned. "Shit." He hit the grill with a glass of Bacardi 151. Bigger flames.

"Mandy, would you be a dear and grab some more steaks from the fridge."

"Sure, Vin."

She hopped up pertly and scampered inside. Seconds later Mandy slowly walked backward out of the house like she was at gunpoint. Her voice cracked as she called to the player: "Baby?"

"What is it?"

"Someone's here to see you."

The guys turned.

"What have you done with my husband!"

"Martha," said Jim. "What are you doing here?"

She marched around the pool and gave Vinny the toxic eye. He stared down at shoes he couldn't see. Then she stomped right up to——. "I don't care how famous you are! Stay away from Jim with your drugs and bimbos and mob buddies!"

The player shrank back on his lounger. ". . . Sorry."

Martha yanked her husband by the arm. "Let's go!"

The other two guys leaned and watched until they were sure she was gone, then the player looked at Vinny. "What the fuck was that about?"

"He's happily married."

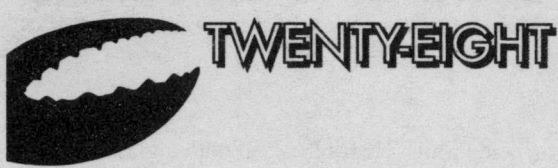

TWENTY-EIGHT

GULF OF MEXICO

*T*he G-Unit arrived at the ballroom doors earlier than ever before, but the line was already around the corner.

"What's going on?" asked Edna.

"Those new dancers are what's going on."

This far back, it was over before it had begun. The doors finally opened, and the women resigned themselves to an evening of punch and cookies. They stared across the room at the flock of women swarming around the new guys.

"Why aren't they dancing?" asked Edna.

That's when she noticed Steve enthusiastically waving them over.

"What do you think he wants?"

Five minutes later, the G-Unit and the rest of the room couldn't believe the reversal of fortune: These new guys had fought off all comers, waiting for Edith and her friends, whom they now spun and waltzed around the floor.

Edith was beside herself. "Steve, you're a marvelous dancer!"

"Just following your lead."

"And such a gentleman . . . But why'd you wait for us?"

A charming smile. "You and your friends are special."

Edith's own blushing smile: "Oh, please . . ."

It went like that all night, every night, from Tampa to Cozumel and back again. The other women finally gave up, and the Brimleys were back in play.

CIA HEADQUARTERS, LANGLEY, VIRGINIA

Two agents returned to a dim room. One sat down at a computer; the other watched over her shoulder.

"Where's the ship now?"

"On its way back to Tampa," said Special Agent Denise Wicks.

"Any more on that chatter we picked up?"

"Nope. Just the name of the ship."

"Not even a time range?"

"We don't even know if they're planning anything."

"Agent Foxtrot now lives in Tampa. When they hit port, it would be easy to activate—"

"Still too risky."

"When did you first meet Foxtrot?"

"I don't know," said Wicks. "Sixteen, seventeen years ago? . . ."

KUWAIT CITY, 1991

Operation Desert Shield was still a week away. Iraqi soldiers roamed streets at will, tanks at both ends of a wide thoroughfare through the center of the previously thriving financial district. Now, broken glass and charred BMWs, every building pocked with machine-gun fire.

The street was normally jammed, but no traffic or pedestrians these days. The few Kuwaitis who hadn't been able to flee now hid in whatever cubbyholes the soldiers hadn't been able to detect when they'd swept the city. Troops milled in front of sacked storefronts. An Iraqi colonel walked down the middle of the road with his enlisted assistant. He had a thick, jet-black mustache, and he was laughing.

The assistant listened attentively as they continued up the street. The colonel stopped mid-sentence. The assistant looked sideways, then down. The officer lay in a spreading purple-red puddle from a silent forehead bullet. The assistant stood bolt straight, threw his hands up in surrender and didn't move. Nearby soldiers ran in directionless confusion; others rushed up the stairs of the biggest building at the end of the street, the one with the giant, ornate tower. Obvious sniper nest. That's why the shooter was down on street level, technically a few inches below, camouflaged in a dirt depression dug twelve hours earlier under cover of night.

By the time they reached the top of the spire, the sniper was gone like a ghost. The colonel's assistant remained motionless in the middle of the street, arms still up, and didn't move for the next three hours until sunset.

It went like that each day, all over the city, without pattern or clue. Psychological warfare. Top-ranking officers picked off by an invisible enemy. Five more colonels and a general. Regular soldiers left untouched, except cramped muscles from standing till dark.

The agent was the stuff of mythology, a proverbial lone wolf who could survive and inflict havoc for weeks behind enemy lines with no trace of ever having been there. It was years of training, but it was more. Logic dictated some fierce, bulging warrior appearance, but if you ran into the agent in a supermarket back home . . . well, the last person you'd expect. Because the most invaluable trait was that one-in-a-million mental makeup you can't teach. Even at the moment of the killshot, the agent's pulse never budged.

Code name: Foxtrot.

Desert Shield was launched. Kuwait liberated. They called Foxtrot in for new orders. The "Shield" became "Storm." The invasion of Iraq. First business: Control the skies. Ill-trained Iraqi pilots were no issue. The real danger came from anti-aircraft ground radar directing surface-to-air missiles. Stationary sites were bombed to molecules. The problem was a handful of mobile radar trucks. By the time allied planes could trace the active ping, off they'd zipped.

Intelligence arrived. General headquarters location of a mobile squadron west of Mosul, trucks darting around at night, then returning to the concealment of a building or overhead netting, where they were protected by platoons of elite commandos.

Foxtrot's mission: forward recon thirty miles beyond the nearest other American. Locate the radar trucks using any technique available, then break radio silence with the airbase. When the F-16s were in range, Foxtrot would laser-paint the target. Only one problem. Once radio silence was broken, Foxtrot would also be a target. The plan had no escape clause.

The first moonless night, a two-seat special-ops dune buggy dropped the agent in a sea of sand. It took most of the evening for Foxtrot to avoid Iraqi patrols and cover the remaining ground on foot until the first lights of Mosul danced along the flat horizon. Then two more hours flanking quickly in the cool night desert, following the sounds of the returning radar trucks and confirming the base with a night-vision scope.

Time got tight. A hole was quickly dug as the sky began to lighten. Camouflaged cover fashioned. Foxtrot burrowed in with the radio and laser. The plan was rolling smoothly.

Then the wheels came off.

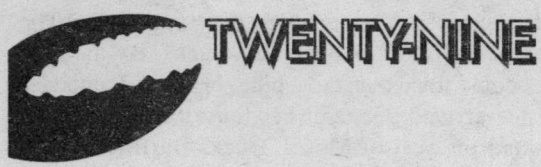

TWENTY-NINE

FOXTROT

angley, Virginia: one year after the mission in Iraq.

Brown, leafless trees. Scattered crusts of snow dotted the shoulders of the parkway as spring began its thaw. A sign at the heavily guarded entrance: CENTRAL INTELLIGENCE AGENCY.

The low building sprawled. Somewhere deep inside, another black-box debriefing. This one had the tone of unofficial reprimand that would never see ink. Foxtrot sat respectfully and listened to the long table of superiors.

"You violated protocol."

"The mission was in your hands."

"You've never hesitated before."

"Why didn't you shoot the civilian?"

The questions weren't intended to be answered. Foxtrot's pulse was like a day at the beach.

"The directive is more than clear."

The purpose of the directive was to eliminate tough calls by making them ahead of time. The tougher the call, the greater the need for an advance decision. Then, all that remained was reflex.

This was one of the toughest calls of all, but that's why

they call it war. Foxtrot was too good to be detected in desert surveillance, except by accident: Always a slim chance that some peasant or farmer with world-class bad luck might stumble upon the one-person bunker and become curious about its camouflaged cover. The directive: If he lifts the cover, shoot him with a silencer-equipped sidearm, and pull the body inside with you. They'd gone over it dozens of times.

"What the hell happened?"

They expected an answer this time.

"Everything was going by the book," said Foxtrot. "Then the sun rose . . ."

. . . The sun rose out of the eastern sand with wavering lines. *Lawrence of Arabia.* The Anvil. Foxtrot switched to regular binoculars. Substantial Republican Guard presence but none the wiser. American planes already in the air. Just waiting for the word. A laser dot hit the side of a building; a hand reached for the radio.

A nearby sound. Right flank, five o'clock. Foxtrot turned toward a slit in the camouflaged lid. Vision was obscured, but one thing was certain: not military. Dammit. Foxtrot switched off the laser and slowly rolled over, bracing the pistol for a mandatory head shot if the unfortunate civilian raised the cover. Perfectly still. Seemed like forever. Sandy footsteps. *No, please, don't . . .*

Dusty hands raised the camouflage. Foxtrot's pistol aimed right between the eyes. For the first time ever, a skipped heartbeat. The trigger finger wouldn't respond. The civilian ran off sounding the alarm.

"Son of a bitch!" Foxtrot leaped from the hole and looped an arm through the laser backpack, then raced straight for the radar compound, radio mike in hand: " . . . *Bravo, Foxtrot. Deliver package . . .* " The radio was flung aside. The screaming civilian had troops scrambling out of buildings. Foxtrot ran straight for them. One of the Iraqis saw the apparition sprinting out of the desert. He began shooting, and the others joined in.

Bullets raked the ground at Foxtrot's feet. In the distance, an approaching roar of F-16 Falcons, pilots on the radio. "Where's that laser?"

The radar compound deployed two jeeps with .50-caliber mounts. The desert became alive with bursts of sand exploding all around Foxtrot, who never broke stride toward the trucks. Straight at death.

The direction and sound of the jets said they were five or six seconds out. Foxtrot dove belly down onto the sand and aimed the laser. The .50-calibers had been erratic from bounding over the dunes, but now the jeeps hit a flat stretch, and one of the gunners drew a bead. The strafing started sixty yards ahead and ripped through the sand on a direct line that would cut Foxtrot in half headfirst. The bullets reached fifty yards, forty, thirty—Foxtrot's right eye stayed glued to the laser sight—twenty, ten . . . the first guided bunker bomb hit. The concussion blew the gunners into the air and upended both the jeeps. Debris rained.

Back at the base, a bird colonel inspected videos from the F-16s' onboard cameras. Total success. But where was Foxtrot?

"Presumed killed in action," said the classified report.

Three days later, a security detail of U.S. soldiers chatted at a checkpoint on the Kuwaiti border.

Someone suddenly appeared right beside them.

"Shit!" They fumbled for M-16s before recognizing U.S. gear under all the filth. "Where the hell did you come from?"

"Can't tell you that," said Foxtrot.

LANGLEY, VIRGINIA

The story ended. People at the table shook their heads.

"Jesus," said Special Agent Denise Wicks. "I don't know

if I'm more pissed off by your insubordination or because the mission succeeded despite it."

Foxtrot didn't speak.

"Stand."

The agent did.

Wicks walked over. "I can't believe I'm doing this." She pinned a medal for valor on Foxtrot. "Congratulations."

"Thank you."

Then she unpinned it and put it back in her pocket, because the mission never existed.

They sat back down. Officialness over. Time for smiles.

"So, you're really leaving the service?" said Wicks.

"Doing the same thing too long. Thought I'd try something else."

"Like what?"

"Don't know yet," said Foxtrot, thinking back to the unforgettable face of that civilian in the desert who'd stumbled upon the camouflaged nest. A five-year-old girl.

"Where do you think you'll go?"

"Guess back home to Tampa."

THIRTY

*T*he sun waned on the grimy part of town past the old railroad depot. Two dozen men fidgeted in an alley of broken glass and blowing newspapers.

Serge had called another wildcat team meeting of Non-Confrontationalists Anonymous. He had his new video camera, and he was pumped!

If only they could get started. Serge had never met people with so many questions. Why did they have to wear costumes? And makeup?

"Because they'll give you the anonymity to role-play like you couldn't otherwise. Plus the comic relief of the outfits I picked—Well, if my hunch is right, I may just strike a previously undiscovered chord with the rest of the country, make a killing on the Internet and leave my legacy."

"Where's the moderator?"

"He'll be here any minute," said Serge. "Please, take your places. . . . Coleman, you ready with the camcorder?"

"Ready!"

Serge took a seat in a director's chair, raising a homemade cardboard megaphone. "And . . . *action*!"

Two of the group's members squared off like a pair of

kids on the playground who've never fought before. Lots of dancing around, then the occasional, awkward punch that only swishes air.

"Come on!" Serge yelled into the cardboard tube. "Fight!"

Five more minutes of passive jockeying until one of the timid swings accidentally found a cheekbone.

"Ow! Bastard! You hit me!"

"I didn't mean to! Are you okay?"

Wham.

"You hit me back! You fuck!"

"Sorry, don't know what got into me."

Wham.

"Perfect!" shouted Serge. "You're getting the hang of it." He turned to the rest of the group waiting against a brick wall plastered with rave-club flyers. "Okay, everyone else in!"

"But . . ."

"Get over there!"

They reluctantly joined the first pair. Another slow start. But the alley's close quarters precipitated more accidental punches, leading to deliberate ones. It grew nasty, the way only amateur hour can. Kicking, biting, hair-pulling. Then they went off Serge's script, picking up garbage cans, pipes and bottles.

"Coleman! This is incredible! You getting it?"

"Every second."

An Escalade drove up.

"Jim," said Serge. "You're late."

"They're killing each other! What the heck's going on?"

"I'm curing them."

"Serge!"

"There's still time for you to get in there—"

"We have to talk." Jim stepped aside. Someone flew by into a pile of boxes. "I can't take this anymore."

"Take what?"

"I saw on TV about that business at the railroad tracks. Why did you do that?"

"Me?"

"You're saying you didn't do it?"

"Jim, Jim, Jim, you must have more trust." He reached in his pocket. "Here."

"What's this?"

"Free tickets."

"Serge! Enough's enough!"

"I know you're upset right now. But think of Martha. Those tickets were expensive. You'll have a great evening."

Jim pushed them back. "If you want to do a favor, just leave us alone."

"But those tickets are guaranteed to help with your bedroom problems."

"I—You can tell?" A bottle smashed against the brick wall next to his head. "How'd you know?"

"Just use the tickets."

Jim took them and began reading. "What's this special service about?"

"I can't spell *everything* out for you. . . ." Serge raised the megaphone. "Phil! No cement blocks!"

GULF OF MEXICO

The G-Unit used to stay on board when the ship reached port. Didn't need the hassle of those insane Cozumel crowds. But then something changed, thanks to Steve and his footloose friends. A reawakened zest for life. They bought stylish sunglasses, purses and bright floral dresses from the ship's galleria. Laughter filled their stateroom. Hurricane glasses clinked, quarters tumbled into slot machines. Edna became a regular at the waterslide.

Then the ship hit port, and the G-Unit was first in line, casing security procedures.

"I see a crack," said Edna. "Everything goes through the X-ray for safety, but they only spot-check at the declarations table."

"We'll exploit it with our age."

They raced slow-motion down the gangway, hitting Mexico like spring-breakers. Bustling outdoor markets, cafés, snorkeling lessons, nightclubs. Then they returned to the ship and smuggled duty-free Kahlúa past security without question.

The gals locked the door to their cabin, and the room filled with giddiness.

Knock-knock-knock.

"Hide the liquor!"

Another knock.

". . . Just a minute." Edith eventually opened the door a slit. "What do you want?"

A steward smiled and cradled a bottle in a towel.

"What's that?"

"Champagne."

"We didn't order any."

"It came with a card," said the steward.

Edith grabbed the bottle and envelope.

The steward smiled with tip-ready hand. The door closed.

"What is it?" asked Eunice.

"I don't know." She set the bottle on a table and tore at the envelope.

"What's it say?"

"Will you wait?" Edith opened the card: FROM YOUR SECRET ADMIRERS.

"Who do you think?"

"I have a strong suspicion." Edith twisted the wire harness off the cap, stuck the bottle between her legs and grunted.

Pop.

"Ow!"

"Put ice on it."

TAMPA

The headless body at the railroad tracks wouldn't go away, thanks to the press.

Politics rolled downhill from the mayor to the police chief to the unfortunate agents in charge of the case. That would be Sadler and Mayfield. Both excellent homicide veterans, both overweight. In their spare time, Sadler liked to build scale model planes from scratch, and Mayfield didn't. It never came up.

The detectives had started the investigation with two desks, a shared phone and the distracting noise of a busy police office.

"What kind of a sick place are we living?" said Sadler. "This mess with the train, plus those nine deaths the FBI still hasn't solved."

"We're not supposed to talk about that," said Mayfield. "The press can't find out."

"They've already reported it."

"They reported the individual deaths. But they're just not supposed to know they're connected."

"Think *this* is connected?"

"Who knows?"

The TV affiliates wouldn't connect the nine deaths for some time, if ever, because it involved reading documents. The decapitation, on the other hand, was made to order for sweeps week. The mayor felt the heat, and otherwise austere resources flowed.

A task force was tasked. Fifteen top investigators reported to Sadler and Mayfield. They got a conference room and a water cooler. Phone company people installed new lines. Handcarts arrived with stacks of cardboard boxes: the victim's court records and his mobile home contents. Agents began unloading. Others cleared bulletin boards of thumb-tacked suspect photos from the last task force. A rookie dumped a handful of RICO mug shots in the trash.

Sadler walked seriously toward the front of the room. "Listen up everyone. We got a nightmare and no leads. Just a partial fingerprint from a pillow in the victim's mobile home. The lab guys are working on it. Meanwhile, we're starting from the beginning." He waved a thick stack of pages. "This is Bodine Biffle's record. We're going to track every codefendant, known associate, girlfriend, relatives, neighbor, and anyone who worked with him at Moving Dudes. I want to know if his dry cleaner had a parking ticket. . . ."

The room grumbled.

"Quiet down," said Mayfield. "If the answer's here, we're going to find it."

Into the afternoon: tedium, coffee, sandwiches, guys standing to stretch. Bulletin boards filled with fresh index cards. Investigators opened more boxes; others called out hundreds of potential cross-references to the rest of the room. No matches.

One agent peeled through recent receipts. ". . . Luck Pawn, Payday Check Advance, Caribbean Crown Line, Hubcap Emporium—"

"Back up," called an agent on the other side of the room. "Did you say, 'Caribbean Crown'?"

"Right."

"What is it?" asked Sadler.

"Sir," said the second agent. "We had someone go missing a few weeks back on a cruise out of here."

"Thousands sail from Tampa every week," said Sadler.

"This one had a rap sheet," said the agent. "And his body parts washed up in the mangroves at Terra Ceia."

"What ship?"

"Serendipity."

The other agent looked up from his cruise receipt. *"Serendipity."*

An hour later, everyone at the bulletin boards. The life history of the missing cruise passenger took shape: crime jacket, phone records, stolen Diner's Club—each shard of his existence assigned to a separate index card.

Someone pulled a card off the board. "Think we might have something. The motel where he stayed before boarding the cruise." The agent called a name across the room.

Another agent at another bulletin board: "It's a match."

"Excellent work," said Sadler. "Still a long shot. Travel agencies often bundle the same motels with the same ships. But worth checking."

Mayfield came up and grabbed one of the index cards. "More than worth checking."

"Why do you say that?" asked Sadler.

"I know this place. It's a shit hole."

"So?"

"You won't believe who owns it."

"Who?"

Mayfield had just told him when a breathless detective with a computer printout ran into the room. "Sir, database got a hit on that partial fingerprint."

THIRTY-ONE

DAVENPORT RESIDENCE

*J*im buttoned a freshly pressed shirt. "Martha? You almost ready?"

"Give me a minute. . . ."

"The reservations are for six."

The bathroom: "You've told me eight times."

"But for this we can't be a minute late. You know how long you always take to get ready—"

The door opened. "How do I look?"

Her racy new scarlet evening dress hit Jim in the stomach. Especially the strapless part.

Martha began to frown. "What's the matter?"

"Wow."

Her smile rebounded. "Was afraid you wouldn't like it."

"You kidding?"

She leaned over the dresser. "Just let me make sure I have all my stuff." Such a dress normally would have been accessorized with an elegant clutch purse. Instead, Martha rummaged through an oversized canvas Siesta Key beach bag, then hoisted it over her shoulder. "Think I got everything."

The Davenports headed out of the house. Jim held the passenger door.

"You're such a gentleman."

They drove a short five minutes to the south end of Davis Islands. The islands had a tail: this long, thick sand spit that curled in a crescent around a broad lagoon. A road ran atop the spit and ended at the exclusive Davis Islands Yacht Club. Along the way, the shore formed one of the hundred-odd Florida bathing areas nicknamed Beer Can Beach, where off-islanders created an economic pressure drop at the yacht club's gates. The lagoon inside the crescent was a squatters' community of houseboats and live-aboard schooners anchored in what was originally a 1920s seaplane basin. But the seaplanes were long gone. Today, wealthy locals landed their Cessnas and Piper Cubs just over the seawall on modest runways of the adjacent Peter O. Knight Airport.

Jim pulled into a parking slot at the airport's cozy terminal with retro parasol overhangs. "This is so exciting," said Martha. "I can't believe you actually planned this."

"Plus it's free."

"You remember the tickets?"

Jim flapped his hand. "Right here."

They went inside and took seats in a space the size of a doctor's waiting room. Martha practically bounced with anticipation. "I didn't even realize a service like this existed."

"Neither did I, but my friend knew all about it."

"The one from your support group who gave you the tickets?"

A booming horn blasted.

"What the heck was that?" said Martha.

Jim pointed out the window behind them. "Cruise ship."

Martha stared up at four tiny old ladies waving at the world from one of the towering top decks. "Holy cow! Looks like it's going to crash into the island!"

"There's a deep ship channel that runs along the east seawall," said Jim

"But it's so close."

"It's a narrow channel."

Martha stood and followed the ship around to the other windows. She watched it grow small in the bay. She looked at the western sky and watched something else grow large.

A blue-and-white twin-engine Beechcraft made its final approach, coming in low across the water. It cleared the fence at the end of the runway for an expert three-point landing.

"Is that ours?" asked Martha.

"I think so."

The eight-seater taxied past a row of private planes tethered to the side of the runway. The propellers spun to a stop. A glowing couple exited the plane, squeezing each other's arms and laughing. Then the pilot. He opened the terminal's back door and stuck his head inside. Red, sound-suppressing headphones hung around his neck. "Davenports?"

"Over here," said Jim.

"This way."

The trio walked across the tarmac.

"I've never done anything like this before," said Martha.

"Most people haven't," said the pilot. "Just relax and have fun. . . . Watch your step."

Martha climbed aboard. Jim was right behind with the tickets: TAMPA BAY MILE-HIGH CLUB.

The interior reminded Martha of a John Denver song. Shag carpet, dim lights, love bed. She pointed back at the midsection. "What's that?"

"Privacy partition," said the pilot, standing on the runway at the passenger hatch. "Just like the one I have behind my seat."

"Another couple's back there?"

"They were on the last flight and wanted to go around again."

"But—"

"Don't worry," said the pilot. "The engines are so loud it'll be like you're all alone." He closed the hatch.

"Jim," whispered Martha. "There's another couple."

"I'm sure they have better things than to worry about us."

"I don't know if I can go through with this now."

"Martha," said Jim. "I was happy the way things were. *You're* the one who wanted to spice things up with weird stuff."

"Not weird. Variety. There's a difference."

"You got variety here."

"On the other hand, it might help."

"What might?"

"Article in this women's magazine. Some people get turned on by having others in earshot. The whole risk of discovery. I could be one of those people."

"Could be?"

"I don't know. I've never tried. We've never tried *anything*."

"Thanks."

"You know what I mean."

The pilot started the engines. Left prop jerked first and began spinning, then the right, faster and faster. He turned around in his seat and shouted over the growing noise. "Before I close the partition, I need to mention a few things. . . ."

"You have to give a safety talk on a flight like this?" asked Martha.

The pilot shook his head. "Been hassled by the police. They say I fall under the new adult-use ordinance. So when we reach international waters I'll ring this." He held up a small brass bell. "I'm supposed to tell you no fooling around until then, but that's your business. Also, when we hit 5,280 feet . . ."

"That's a mile," Jim whispered.

"I'm not an idiot," said Martha.

". . . I'll ring the bell again."

"Why?"

"Customers have asked."

"One question," said Jim. "How'd you get into this business?"

"Back in the day, people joined the mile-high club with quickies in lavatories of major airlines. Usually half-empty red-eyes from the Coast. But heightened security after nine-eleven created all kinds of new jobs like this." He closed the partition.

The Beechcraft raced down the runway. The sun had just set. A red beacon flashed on the plane's roof as wheels lifted off.

Martha reached in her tote bag and pulled out a giant, gleaming, state-of-the-art vibrator.

"Martha!"

"I know it's embarrassing. But it's *all* embarrassing to me. The magazines said I have to work through it if I'm ever going to discover my needs."

"You need that?"

"We'll find out. The articles said these things make some women have orgasms like earthquakes."

"I just can't picture you going up to a register and buying that thing."

"I wore sunglasses. And a hat and big coat."

"No mustache?"

"All the women were dressed like me."

"An adult store full of women?"

"It was the Todd, up at Fletcher and Nebraska. They market to women."

"How?"

"Cute curtains." She loaded four D batteries and screwed the back shut. Then she pulled a polishing rag from her bag and began buffing the sleek rocket.

"That thing looks expensive," said Jim.

"Most expensive they had," said Martha, rubbing extra hard on a particular spot. "If anything's going in me, it's got to be classy." She finishing buffing and hit a button. It roared to life like a leaf blower.

"Holy cripes," said Jim. "Did they have anything with more horsepower?"

"No."

"Martha, I want you to be happy, but—"

A bell rang.

"Here . . ." She handed it over and hiked up her dress.

"What do I do?"

"Surprise me." Martha lay back on the love bed and closed her eyes. "Just don't drop it."

Crash. The sound of batteries rolling across the cabin floor.

Martha opened her eyes. "Please tell me you didn't break it."

"No, the cap just popped off." Jim reloaded the batteries and screwed the end shut again. He hit the switch. Quiet. "Martha?"

"What?"

"It's broken."

"I can't have anything nice."

"Honey, this is our special night. Let's enjoy it."

The Davenports sat on the bed and held hands as they looked out the window at the darkening Gulf of Mexico. They exchanged mischievous looks and began giggling.

The bell rang again.

Martha pushed Jim down onto the sheets. She knelt and pulled the dress off over her head, revealing recent purchases from Victoria's Secret. Lace panties and pushups, both black.

"Good God!—"

She grabbed Jim's shirt collar with both hands. Buttons flew.

"Martha! What's gotten into you?"

"I don't know. This plane thing's a super turn-on. That's

why we have to try new stuff." She opened his belt but hit a snag. "What the fuck's wrong with your zipper?"

"Martha! Your mouth!"

"Goddamn this thing!"

"Let me get it. You'll rip skin."

"Just hurry!"

Jim pulled his pants down. "There."

Bam. She shoved him back down, climbed aboard and rode like a rodeo star.

"Who *are* you?" panted Jim.

"I don't know," said Martha. "But whatever you do, don't stop!"

BACK ON SHORE

A convoy of white government sedans raced north at the edge of the Gulf. All along the shore: towering new luxury condos that obliterated the strip's personality and stacked assholes thirty stories high.

The old roadside funk was gone: breakfast diners, beach bars, neon. All, that is, except for a few defiant hangers-on. One joint postponing a date with the wrecking ball was the kind of run-down, off-brand motel seen along the side of the highway with a swimming pool full of brown leaves and a single car in front of room 17 that makes passing motorists wonder, What's *his* problem?

A dozen sets of blackwall tires made the same screeching left turn and sped up the driveway under a crackling, half-burned-out sign:

HAMMERHEAD RANCH.

The people in the motel office heard squealing brakes.

Rafael Diaz looked out the window. "It's a raid! Run!" He and Benito hid in a closet.

Tommy Diaz casually arose from behind the registration desk. "Calm down. You look guilty." He walked to the office door, opened it with a jingle of bells and got a badge in the face.

"Detective Mayfield. This is Detective Sadler."

"To what do I owe the pleasure?"

"The two guys you murdered on my watch," said Sadler.

"Murders?" said Tommy. "That's terrible!"

"Cut the bullshit."

"Why? Am I a suspect?" said Tommy. "Do I need to call my attorney?"

"You're not charged with anything," said Mayfield. "Yet."

"We're legitimate businessmen. Why do you think we had anything to do with these tragedies?"

"Because both victims stayed here before taking cruises," said Sadler.

"And we matched your fingerprint to a pillow in one of the victim's homes," said Mayfield. "How do you explain that?"

"You just said he stayed here."

"So?"

"Must have stolen the pillow from his room," said Tommy. "My fingerprints are all over my own motel. Is that now a crime?"

Sadler held up a signed court document. "Search warrant." In the background, a battering ram came out of a trunk.

Tommy opened a desk drawer and handed Mayfield a large metal ring of brass room keys. "Use these. Wouldn't want the department to have to pay for accidental damage."

Mayfield tossed the ring to someone behind him. Then he stepped forward with an accusing finger. "You're going down."

"Is that kind of talk really necessary?" said Tommy. "I'm a big supporter of law enforcement."

A closet door creaked open. Rafael and Benito peeked out, heads stacked vertically.

"You messed up this time," said Mayfield. "We know what you're into."

"Please, enlighten me."

"Cocaine got too risky and expensive. . . ."

"Cocaine? You mean like on the TV?"

". . . That's where Bodine Biffle and Dale Crisp came in," said Sadler.

"Who?"

"The guys you killed," said Mayfield. "And we know why."

Sadler slapped the warrant on the front desk. "They were smuggling antiquities for you."

"Antiques?" said Tommy.

"*Antiquities,*" said Sadler. "Pre-Colombian. From the Yucatán. Tulum, Chichén Itzá."

"Fascinating story," said Tommy. "Quite an imagination. Are you writing a book?"

"We refreshed ourselves with your criminal record. Big-time smugglers. Just changed rackets."

"Detectives . . ." Tommy shook his head with a dismissive smile. "Those other matters are part of the distant past. We're respectable innkeepers now."

"What happened?" asked Sadler. "Figured it would be more profitable to whack your mules instead of paying them?"

Tommy's smile was unflappable. A diamond glistened in a gold front tooth.

"Just before coming over here, we reinterviewed witnesses," said Mayfield.

"Educated Biffle's girlfriend about accessory after the fact . . ." said Sadler.

". . . And she spilled everything. The cruises, black-market artifact trade. Moving Dudes didn't pay too good, so he did a little moonlighting for you bringing statues in."

"What's that word they use in court?" Tommy tapped his chin. "Oh, yes. *Hearsay.*"

The two detectives began walking out. Sadler turned at the door. "Your days are numbered!"

Tommy laughed. "If I didn't know better, I'd say that sounds like police harassment."

"It is."

Tommy maintained the sparkling smile until they were out of sight, then dropped it. "Will you idiots get out here?"

His brothers crept from the closet. "Are they gone?"

"No, they're tossing the place."

"We're going to jail!" said Benito.

"They don't have squat or we'd already be wearing bracelets." Tommy grabbed a pointy paper cup from a wall dispenser and stuck it under a water tap. "You're reacting exactly how they want."

"What are we going to do?"

Tommy glanced toward a wall calendar from the Mexican Board of Tourism.

THIRTY-TWO

EXACTLY ONE MILE HIGH OVER
THE GULF OF MEXICO

*I*t was the best sex they could remember since the kids were old enough to talk.

"Oh, Martha!"

"Oh, Jim!"

"Let's buy a plane!"

"Okay!"

Other side of the privacy partition: *"Jim? Jim Davenport? Is that you?"* The partition unsnapped. Serge poked his head through, wearing a Batman mask. "Thought I recognized your voice."

"Jesus!" Martha covered her breasts and rolled off her husband.

Jim stared in speechless horror.

Serge stared back. "This a bad time?"

"Jim!" said Martha, grabbing the dress to cover herself further. "Who the hell is that?"

"Martha," Jim said in a trembling voice. "This is my friend from the support group who gave us the tickets. Remember how you said I couldn't reveal his name?"

Martha made an angry motion with her eyes for Jim to get rid of him.

"Listen," Jim told Serge. "Don't you think you need to get back to whoever you're with—"

"Her name's Rachael."

". . . back to Rachael."

"It's okay," said Serge. "I'm just getting a B.J. now. I can talk."

"What?"

"In fact, it makes me *want* to talk. Hard to believe, but Peter O. Knight used to be Tampa's main airport. I can see it all now, silver DC-3s, alligator suitcases. . . . Rachael, watch the teeth . . . the terminal decorated with the 1930s art deco murals of George Snow depicting the history of flight, Daedalus to the Wright Brothers and Tony Janus, restored and on display at Tampa International's Airside E, for those keeping score at home . . ."

"Jim!" yelled Martha.

"Where are my manners?" said Serge. "Rachael, get up here. There are some people I want you to meet."

Catwoman stuck her head through the partition. "Meowwww!"

"What a coincidence!" said Serge. "Can't believe you used your tickets the same night! We'll have to go out like this more often."

Catwoman's tongue went in Serge's ear. "Well, that's the old Bat Signal. Later . . ." The partition closed.

Martha reclined on the bed and folded her arms rigidly.

Jim went to touch her. "Honey . . ." She flinched away.

Jim fell back and stared at the plane's ceiling. They lay in frosty silence.

Not totally silent. Despite the engines' drone, conversation began filtering through the partition.

". . . You remember the Davenports," said Serge. "I've mentioned them a dozen times."

"Oh, that's right," said Rachael. "The dorky couple."

"They are *not* dorky," said Serge. "Just haven't been around the block like you and me. That's why I got them the tickets."

"You wasted your money," said Rachael. "They wouldn't know what to do if they had diagrams."

"They're just having a difficult time sexually."

"He told you about it?"

"Every detail. His wife's trying to get him into all this kinky shit, but so far nobody's come."

Martha covered her face in mortification.

"Why do you have such lame friends?" said Rachael.

"They are not lame."

"Yes they are!"

"I'm warning you!"

"What are you going to do, hurt me?"

"You'll beg for mercy."

"You wouldn't dare!"

"Oh yeah? How about this. Does that hurt?"

"Oh, God it hurts! It hurts, you fucker!"

"And this?"

"That hurts, too! Stop! Please! Owww! . . ."

"And this!"

"That does it!" snarled Rachael. "Your cock's going to get it now!"

"Owww!" yelled Serge.

"And this!"

"Yowwwwwwww!"

On the other side of the curtain: Jim felt his shoulder poked. He turned.

"Jim," said Martha. "You're absolutely not going to believe what I'm going to say next. *I* don't even believe it."

"What?"

She glanced toward the partition. "They're getting me incredibly aroused."

"You're right. I don't believe it."

She threw her dress aside and climbed on top of Jim. "Have you been listening to them?"

"Not trying to."

"Think you remember most of it?"

"Martha, what are you asking?"

She found the right position, slid down onto him and gritted her teeth. Her voice changed to something Jim hadn't heard before: "You wouldn't dare hurt me!"

"What?"

"You're hurting me! You're hurting me!"

"I'm not doing anything! I swear!"

"Your cock's going to get it now!"

"Martha, you're scaring me!"

On the other side of the partition:

"I'll fucking kill you!" shouted Rachael. "Take that, you no-good motherfucker!"

"Why you mangy cunt!" yelled Serge.

"Wait, stop."

"What's the matter?"

"Our sex life is in a rut," said Rachael. "Fantasy role-playing."

"What about it?" asked Serge.

"We should try it," said Rachael. "We're always just being ourselves."

"Who do you want to play?"

She glanced toward the partition.

"You're joking."

"Who can explain sex? Their clumsiness is making me hot."

Other side of the partition: Martha was bucking so wildly that Jim had to grab her hips to keep her from being thrown clear. Screaming her head off: "Oh yes! Oh yes! Oh yes!" Just about to explode, when . . .

"Martha," said Jim. "Why'd you stop?"

She looked toward the partition. "Listen . . ."

From the other side:

"Oh, Martha!"

"Oh, Jim!"

"I don't know how to fuck!"

"Me neither!"

"How do we do it?"

"Give me that tiny needle-dick of yours."

"Is this the right hole?"

"Oh, Martha!"

"Oh, Jim!"

Martha rolled onto her back again. "How can this possibly get any more embarrassing?"

The partition opened. Batman pointed at the floor next to their bed. "You using that?"

Silence.

"Thanks." Serge grabbed the broken vibrator.

The partition closed.

THIRTY-THREE

918 LOBSTER LANE

*F*irst thing the next morning, a rusty Comet pulled up the driveway.

The home's front door was already open. Gaylord Wainscotting wheeled a last piece of luggage down to the curb, where Mrs. Wainscotting and ten other suitcases were already assembled in descending order of height, including Mrs. Wainscotting.

A limo arrived. The driver loaded bags.

Gaylord shook Serge's hand. "Thanks for doing this."

"Enjoy Cape Cod."

"Enjoy the club."

The chauffeur placed the final item in the trunk and slammed the hood. Wainscotting climbed into the backseat. The window rolled down. "Treat the place like your own, unwind a little."

"I'm slammed," said Serge. "Work . . ."

"You can work anytime. Have some fun."

Serge shook his head. "Way behind deadline. We'll be quiet as mice. In fact the neighbors probably won't even know anyone's home."

"Glad I hooked up with you," said Gaylord. "All kinds of

cautionary tales about hiring the wrong house-sitters. One guy from the club had his place burned to the ground."

"She couldn't be in better hands," said Serge.

"Just don't work too hard."

"No other way."

Gaylord laughed. The limo drove off.

Serge whistled a blissful tune and strolled toward the house. He opened the front door. Stereo blasting, Coleman filling shot glasses, Rachael . . . Where was Rachael? A drum-roll of shattering glass from the kitchen. *"Goddammit!"*

Coleman cradled a phone receiver against his shoulder and knocked back bourbon. " . . . *Sure you don't need directions? . . . Yeah, it's going kick out the motherfuckin' jams. Later . . . "* He hung up and dialed again. "Hey, Serge . . ."

"What are you doing?"

"Shots."

"No, the phone."

Coleman put up a finger for Serge to hold a sec. *"Thumper? Coleman . . . No, I don't have the money. Listen, what are you doing Saturday? . . . "*

Coleman hung up and dialed again.

"I'm waiting," said Serge.

"Calling people for my party . . ." Coleman placed his spherical black-and-white TV on the counter and slapped the side. " . . . *Psycho Sal? Coleman . . . You still have to wear the ankle monitor? . . . "*

"Party?"

"Going to be killer!"

"Have you lost your mind? We can't throw a party!"

Coleman hung up again. "Serge, it's the ultimate party pad." He slapped the TV.

"We've been entrusted with the care of this house," said Serge. "The guy's only been gone a minute, and you're already sowing the seeds of destruction."

"Relax. Just a few of my closest friends." He dialed the phone and slapped the TV. "Serge, you know how to fix this thing?"

"Just keep slapping."

Rachael came into the room with a giant sterling service tray. She set it on the dining table, dumped a generous pile of white powder and began cutting rails with a razor blade.

Serge stood in amazement. "And just what do you think you're doing?"

Rachael leaned with a straw. "What the fuck's it look like?"

"You're scratching their tray all to hell!"

"Eat me!" Diver down.

" . . . *Slasher? Coleman . . .* " Slap.

Rachael pinched her nose. "Coleman, crank the stereo!"

"It's already up the whole way."

" . . . *We won't get fooled again! . . .* "

Coleman was about to make another call when he saw what Rachael was doing and dashed over to the table. "Can I have some?"

She shielded the tray like a protective mama bear. "Mine!"

"But you got plenty."

"Get away!"

"Give me some!"

"Let go of me!"

"Just a little bump! . . . Ow! . . . Serge! She's going for my balls!"

"They're trained to do that. Directive Seven."

The wrestling match was inelegant and vicious. They rolled across the floor and slammed into a table leg. A silver tray crashed to the ground.

They stood and stared down in mute horror. Rachael punched Coleman in the stomach. "Now look what you did!"

"Shit. Okay, we can salvage this," said Coleman. "I've

been here before. Stay perfectly still. Don't create any air currents until the haze settles."

Serge witnessed unprecedented discipline from his stationary companions.

Finally: "Now!" said Coleman. They dropped to their knees, herding dust with their hands and licking.

Serge headed up the stairs. "I wash my hands of this fiasco."

The widow's walks of Tampa's waterfront mansions were perfect for telescopes and binoculars. People watching big ships or sunsets or stars at night.

Serge's binoculars were aimed in a different direction, down the street. Jim Davenport's head filled the twenty-magnification view field.

Coleman came up the stairs with a bottle of Rémy Martin by the neck. "What are you doing?"

Serge adjusted the focus as Jim walked across his lawn with a ladder. "Protecting our friend. So far, so good. No sign of McGraw."

Coleman looked toward Serge's feet. "What's the rifle for?"

"In case McGraw slips under my perimeter and I can't get down there fast enough."

Coleman turned toward the bay. "There's a bunch of people in kayaks and canoes behind that other house. . . ."

"Hold it! Trouble! Oh my God!"

"What is it?"

"Jim's replacing a floodlight, but he's a step too high on the ladder. The one with the yellow warning label of a stick figure falling off a ladder."

"Serge, who's that over there walking toward him?"

"Where? . . . Oh, no!" Serge grabbed the rifle and chambered a round. Crosshairs tracked a stranger heading toward the house. He began pulling the trigger. He stopped.

Coleman took a swig. "Why aren't you shooting?"

Serge set the rifle down. "Just the UPS guy." He picked up the binoculars. "Sure wish Jim would get off the top step. Doesn't he know that's insane?"

"The kayaks and canoes are now behind our house."

Serge swung the binoculars toward their backyard. "Rachael's just sunning herself naked." The binoculars panned back the other way. "Picked up a second bogie."

"Bogie?"

"Martha. Heading for their car . . . Jim's calling to her, but she's ignoring him. Now he's waving for her to stop backing out of the driveway and . . . He fell off the ladder! Jim's down! Jim's down! . . . He's up! Martha patches out! Jim's running down the street after her! She's gone."

"What was that about?"

"They had a monster fight. Poor Jim. I know I'm being tough on myself, but I can't help think I'm almost responsible."

"Why's that?"

"Martha was crying inconsolably when our plane landed last night, even though I fixed the vibrator for free. I chased her out the passenger hatch, waving it in the air to give it back, but she just wailed louder and nearly went into one of the propellers."

"That would have sucked."

"I need to make it up to Jim." Serge lowered the binoculars and started downstairs.

Jim Davenport had moved his ladder to the northeast corner of his home. Just a few more twists on the floodlight.

The bushes below: "Psssst! Jim! You're one step too high!—"

Jim looked down.

"It's me, Serge. . . ."

Thud.

"Jim!" Serge leaped from the shrubs and bent over his

fallen neighbor. "You okay?" He tapped his cheeks. "Wake up! Come on, big boy! . . ."

He slowly came around. "What happened?"

"Everything's all right. You just took a spill from the ladder. Luckily . . . actually, there isn't a lucky part—"

"Holy God!" Vinny waddled across the street in silk warm-ups. "I saw what happened. Is he okay?"

Coleman brought up the rear. "Anything broken?"

Jim, tiny voice: "Please leave me alone."

"Understand perfectly," said Serge. "You're having marriage issues and can't think straight about ladder safety."

"What kind of issues?" asked Vinny.

"She bought a vibrator," said Serge.

"Martha?" Vinny's head snapped back. "Doesn't look the type. How big?"

"Like a Polaris," said Serge.

"Jim, Jim, Jim," said Vinny, shaking his head. "You gotta jump on top of that. Broad gets a taste for electricity, and suddenly you're spending entire weeks by yourself with the curtains closed and a stack of *Hustler*."

"Yeah," said Coleman. "It's great."

Serge reached for his wallet. "I need to make amends for the other night." He handed Jim a folded-over wad of cash. "Take Martha out this evening. Great bistro on the other side of the island."

"No. This has to stop." Jim pushed the money back; Serge pushed harder the other way. "I insist."

"Jim?" asked Vinny.

"What?"

Vinny was staring up the street. A brown truck at the curb. "Remember you said you were going to frame one of the pictures you took of——by the pool and mail it to him?"

"I sent it two days ago."

"Was Mandy in the photo?"

"Yeah."

"How'd you send it?"

"UPS."

"Holy shit!" said Vinny.

"What's the matter?" asked Serge.

"That's his wife's car in the driveway."

"*Wife,*" said Jim. "You told me he was divorced."

"She's not supposed to arrive for another month," said Vinny.

"Wife?" said Jim.

"Is that her?" asked Serge.

"Where?"

"The woman at the door signing for a package . . . Jesus, Vinny, you're white as a sheet."

"You don't understand. His wife's fuckin' crazy. She frightens *me*." He dabbed perspiration off his forehead. "I wouldn't be surprised if she also came after Jim for this."

"Me?"

"Then we'll just have to get the package back," said Serge.

"But how?" asked Vinny.

"Go as a group," said Serge. "There's four of us. We can easily create a diversion and grab the box."

They began walking up the street.

"I'm not kidding about his wife," said Vinny.

"You're worrying in advance about what's never going to happen," said Serge. "This'll be child's play."

They reached the house and stopped at the end of the walkway.

"You're right," said Vinny. "I think it might work."

"Of course it'll work," said Serge.

"In a few minutes we'll all be laughing about this," said Vinny. "I mean, how fast can she open that package?"

Bang, bang, bang.

They looked at each other. "Gunfire?"

Bang, bang, bang. Splinters exploded from the front door.

"Run!"

They scattered in various panicked directions. Except Jim, who ran in a circle in the street until Serge grabbed him by the shoulders and lined him up with his house. "Straight ahead. You can't miss it." Then he and Coleman dashed back to their own pad.

Coleman reached under the bar for a bottle. "I must have heard eight gunshots."

"If it's like my relationships, they're already in the middle of make-up sex." Something on the counter caught his eye. Serge picked up a flyer.

Coleman came over with a tumbler of rum. "What is it?"

"A pamphlet the police dropped off," said Serge. "This neighborhood's getting hit by frogmen burglars. I saw something about it in the paper."

"Burglars?"

"And the perfect cover for attack. The most direct, undefended route to another Davenport home invasion." He crumpled the notice. "Since these divers have made the news, I'd bet anything it's given McGraw the idea."

"Why do you think that?"

"It's what I'd do."

THIRTY-FOUR

THAT NIGHT

*T*he house was dark.

A large-screen TV provided the only light. Dramatic, teletype theme music.

An anchorwoman filled the screen.

"Good evening and welcome to Eyewitness 7 Action News at eleven. We begin tonight's broadcast with the latest shocking developments in the near-fatal shooting of former Pittsburgh Steelers great——, who was wounded in a firefight with his wife earlier today and is currently listed in serious but stable condition at Tampa General. Meanwhile, police continue unraveling details of the bizarre shooting, which apparently was triggered when Mrs.——arrived unexpectedly at the Hall of Famer's winter home and intercepted mail containing photographs of a compromising nature with former cheerleader Mandy Steam, who was sunning herself on the back patio at the time and escaped gunfire by diving off the seawall, but fractured her skull on a kayak. Police theorized that the photos were part of an elaborate extortion plot masterminded by this man. . . ."

The TV switched to long-range footage of detectives questioning Jim Davenport just outside his front door.

". . . But after further interrogation, authorities dismissed him as just another obsessed fan. In Pittsburgh, however, regulars at one popular sports bar said not so fast on calling off the rush to judgment. From our sister station, News Action 4 . . ."

Screaming drunks in Steelers jackets and Afro wigs crammed their faces in the camera. " . . . *That [bleep]hole is [bleep]ing dead! . . . " "Yeah! [bleep]ing dead!" "He's [bleeped] . . . " "Steelers [bleeping] rule! . . . "*

The broadcast switched back to Tampa. "In other news, our Action 7 Investigative Eye on Florida Team has turned up additional developments on the controversial new series of Internet videos that make *Bum Fights* look like *Teletubbies*. As reported earlier, an anonymous individual has struck a chord across the entire nation, which experts attribute to a political backlash against the French. Meanwhile the tapes continued selling like wildfire on eBay before the popular auction site shut down all bidding just before noon. But not before our own Action 7 investigative reporter Bannister Truth was able to obtain a copy and track Web sales to a computer at the downtown Tampa library."

The TV switched to a newsman dramatically thrusting a video box toward the camera. CLOWNS VS. MIMES VOL. III, THIS TIME IT'S PERSONAL! "The tape is too disgusting to watch!" said the reporter. "Let's take a look. . . ."

The broadcast cut to a clown slamming a car door on a mime's head.

"Breaking news!" the anchorwoman interrupted. "Police are just now responding to the site of a grisly discovery in the bay . . ."—the screen showed a night view from the Channel 7 chopper—". . . where the disfigured body of a scuba diver was found banging against a seawall on Davis Islands . . ."

Serge finished watching the news from the couch in Gaylord Wainscotting's living room. The set clicked off. He walked to the back of the dark house and saw a helicopter spotlight sweep over the water.

Three houses up, a squad of detectives combed Jim Davenport's backyard.

"What kind of monster? . . ."

"I've never seen anything so horrible. . . ."

Police divers were in the water. They finished securing the corpse to a special litter. One gave the thumbs-up. Others began hoisting.

A uniformed officer approached the detectives in charge. "Just got an ID. McGraw, Lyle."

They watched the body come over the wall.

"Anyone who'd do such a thing is a complete psycho," said Sadler.

"I'm not even sure what I'm looking at," said Mayfield.

"A floater. They all bloat like that."

"Not like *that*," said the coroner, bending down for a closer look at the human puffer fish. "He hasn't been dead long enough for gases to build up from decomposition."

"Then what caused?—"

"I know what it looks like," said the coroner, "but there's no possible way."

Silence.

The coroner looked up. They were waiting.

"At least I *hope* it's not what I think." The coroner stood. "You heard rumors about terrorists planning to use scuba divers to attach magnetic bombs to the hulls of our ships?"

A few nods.

"Then you may also have heard those leaked reports about classified military programs training dolphins to patrol our ports, because their sonar is better than our most advanced hydrophones."

"But we don't have any dolphins around here like that," said Sadler. "Right?"

"That's where it gets tricky," said the coroner. "The Navy

denies it, but there's word of a special training facility in Key West."

"And?"

"They came up a couple dolphins short after Hurricane Wilma."

"Holy mother . . ."

"I don't understand," said Mayfield. "Even if a dolphin detects a scuba diver, how does it stop him, let alone cause this kind of mess?"

"The dolphins are fitted with a special weapon," said the coroner. "Believe me, it's one of the last ways you want to go."

"What kind of special weapon?"

EARLIER THAT NIGHT

"Serge," said Coleman, "my arms are getting tired."

"Just keep rowing."

"Why can't *you* row?"

Serge scanned the water off the starboard side with a night-vision monocular. "Because I'm on lookout—and I have to operate Serge's New Secret Weapon. It's a lot to deal with in a canoe."

Oars splashed in the moonlit bay. "I still don't understand how that thing works. All I know is you destroyed my laughing-gas dispenser."

"Your sacrifice for the community is duly noted."

"But it cost me ten bucks at a Bourbon Street head shop."

"It only made you fall down a lot."

"That's the whole point."

"Shhhhhhhhhhh!"

Coleman stopped rowing. "What is it?"

Serge peered over the side. "We have activity."

For the last hour, their canoe had slowly made its way

east from a boat launch across the harbor at Ballast Point, until they were now fifty yards off Davis Islands. In the green glow of Serge's nightscope, a figure in a black wet suit silently swam toward the seawall behind the Davenport residence.

The scope following a trail of bubbles. "Row to the right. . . . A little more . . . Okay, stop." Serge reached into the bottom of the canoe. "Almost over the diver. We'll drift the rest of the way with the tide."

"Can you see him?"

"Perfectly."

"What's he doing?"

"Stopping. He knows we're here."

"So your plan's ruined?"

"Naw, he just thinks it's a coincidence. Couple of health nuts out at night in a canoe. He's trying to remain undetected until we pass."

Serge grabbed his New Secret Weapon.

"What's he doing now?"

"Looking up at us. Good. Otherwise this thing might glance off the scuba tank. . . . Come on, just a little farther. . . . Almost over him . . . alllllllmost . . . Now!"

Serge quickly raised the harpoonlike device and thrust it down into the water with his right hand. His left grabbed a short, makeshift length of PVC pipe that rose three-quarters of the way up the spear's shaft, and gave it a fast twist.

Coleman cracked a Schlitz. "Where'd you get the idea for that thing?"

Serge maintained a firm two-handed grip as the pole jerked wildly. "Top-secret U.S. Navy program. Training dolphins in Key West to patrol ports for scuba-diving terrorists."

"But dolphins are so nice," said Coleman. "Would they actually attack a terrorist?"

"Not remotely," said Serge, still gripping the pole. "So they make a game of it by teaching dolphins to playfully tap their handlers in the chest with a small cylinder attached to their snouts." He jerked the weapon out of the water and laid it back in the bottom of the canoe. "The cylinders are empty during training. But during live patrol, they're loaded with a capsule of highly compressed gas and fitted with a spring-loaded needle. Very effective. And messy, one of the worst ways to go . . ."

The bloated diver bobbed to the surface like a cork, quivering next to the canoe.

". . . Chest cavity inflates with a massive amount of air, rupturing whatever internal organ took the needle and slowly crushing surrounding ones. . . ."

"I think he's trying to yell."

"Going to be hard with collapsed lungs."

Coleman finished his beer and watched the diver twitch with after-tremors. "But how did you make one of those secret Navy weapons from my nitrous dispenser?"

"You know how you stick the whip-it canisters inside the dispenser and twist it to puncture the seal, filling those balloons you suck to get high?"

"In my sleep."

"I just substituted one of those carbon-dioxide canisters they use in paint-ball guns. Same size. And where the balloon usually goes, I welded a glue syringe from The Home Depot. Then I mounted the whole thing on the end of a broomstick, and slipped a length of PVC plumbing pipe over it so I could twist the puncture mechanism from a safe distance. . . ."

The motionless diver began drifting away.

". . . And from there, the science of hydraulics takes over. Wait, not exactly hydraulics because fluids don't compress like gas. Hey, I just flashed on another installment of Great Moments in Florida Hydraulics History."

"Go for it."

"Remember when Disney World first opened Hall of the Presidents?"

"The robots only went up to Nixon then."

"Good one, Coleman. Impressed you retained that."

"I was on acid, and Nixon's cheeks turned into a killer octopus."

"True fact: The hydraulic fluid they originally used in the robots was red. But soon after the curtains went up on the exhibit, they switched to clear."

"Why?"

"During one of the first shows, Abraham Lincoln is in the middle of his speech, and a hydraulic line busts. All this red stuff starts spraying like a Monty Python skit. Audience is horrified. They thought Disney was doing the assassination."

Coleman resumed paddling as the tide banged the diver against the seawall. "Why do you remember stuff like that?"

Serge grabbed his own pair of oars. "It keeps me happy."

THIRTY-FIVE

COZUMEL

*A*nother perfect day in paradise. Local merchants began to drool. Ten minutes earlier, an arriving cruise ship had a massive bowel movement of tourists, who would soon clog the streets with American currency.

The G-Unit was on a roll. The night before, Edna hit two hundred bucks on a slot, and Eunice scored another eighty at blackjack. Time to throw around a little of that cash. They shopped and ate and lounged at a sidewalk café that served margaritas in glasses the size of goldfish bowls. Then more kiosks and haggling into the siesta hours, until it was time to head back. Which meant the duty-free shop.

Edith hunched over a park bench, jamming vodka deep into a jumbo straw tourist purse with Mexican flags and sun gods.

From behind: "Edith!"

"I'm not doing anything!"

Steve and the other ballroom guys walked toward them with those toothy smiles. "Love the T-shirt."

Edith looked down at her oversized tie-dye: 51% ANGEL, 49% BITCH. DON'T PUSH IT. She looked up. "Thanks for the champagne."

"Me?" Steve said coyly.

"What are you doing here?" asked Edna.

"Same thing as you. Shopping. Find anything good yet?"

Edith opened her straw bag. "Just booze."

"Have to fix that," said Steve. "We can't allow you to leave without a real piece of the Yucatán. I know these great little out-of-the-way shops. . . ."

An hour later, the women lugged bulky bags crammed with native gifts. A chicken ran by. They entered a deserted store at the end of an alley.

One shopping bag was lighter than the rest.

"Why aren't you getting stuff?" asked Eunice.

Edith picked up a knight from a hand-carved Aztec chess set. "Haven't seen anything I like yet."

"So what? Those guys are paying."

A grinning salesman appeared from nowhere. "You like chess set? Special price. Fifty dollars."

She put the knight down. "I don't play chess."

"Special price for new players. Ten dollars."

"You just said fifty."

"Five dollars."

"I don't know. . . ." She picked up a piece of onyx.

The salesman smiled. "You like hash pipe? Twenty dollars."

Edith set it down.

". . . Three dollars . . ."

She nearly crashed into Steve on the way out of the shop.

He smiled again, arms behind his back. "Pick a hand."

"What?"

"Just pick."

"Okay, the left."

Steve produced a gift-wrapped box the size of a toaster.

"For me?"

"Saw you were having trouble deciding, so I got a surprise. Something I know you'll love."

Edith raised it to her right ear.

"No!" Steve's arms flew out. "Don't shake it!"

"Fragile?"

"Very."

The other women gathered around.

"This is so exciting. . . ."

"Wonder what it could be. . . ."

Edith grabbed the tail of a ribbon and began to pull.

"Don't open it here," said Steve. "Wait till you're back on the ship. You'll have a special treat to look forward to."

She held it toward him. "I can't accept this."

Steve sternly pushed it back. "You must."

"But you've already spent too much on us."

"My feelings will be hurt."

"Okay," Edith said reluctantly. "Thanks."

Steve waved and headed off with his pals. "See you tonight in the ballroom."

"Wouldn't miss it." Edna put the box to her ear and shook it.

They took an open-air shuttle to the dock and headed up the gangway. A cheery ship's officer swiped their magnetic ID cards through the reader. Green lights. The women hoisted gift bags onto the X-ray belt.

"Wasn't that nice of them?" said Edna.

"Such gentlemen," said Eunice.

They retrieved their belongings from the other side of the belt, and started for their cabin.

"Excuse me? Ma'am? . . ."

They kept walking.

"Ma'am, stop!"

"What's that shouting about?" Edith turned around.

"Ma'am, would you please come back here?"

"What for?"

"Spot check. Place your bags on the table."

"It's okay," said Edith. "You've never checked us before."

"We need to check this time."

"But I don't fit the profile."

"That's why we have to check you," said the officer. "So the people who fit the profile don't get sore."

She haltingly placed her bag on the table. Hands reached inside. Vodka came out. "Ma'am, you were supposed to declare this."

"I was? I mean, how'd that get there? I'm confused. Are you my son?"

"It's all right, ma'am." He placed the bottle on another table behind him. "We'll just hold it for you until we get back to Tampa." He reached in the bag again. A gift box came out. "What's this?"

Edith shrugged.

"I'll have to open it." The ribbon and wrapping paper came off. He lifted the lid and peeled back packing tissue, revealing a dusty, clay Mayan figure.

Edith put on her glasses. "What's that?"

"Just a Chac-Mool."

"A what?"

"Common souvenir." He returned it to the bag and handed it back. "I've gotten all my relatives one."

TAMPA

Serge sat in the front of the support-group meeting room. Two minutes till the next session. The place was full. Nobody had bothered to change since the latest video shoot.

The moderator entered from the back door. He took one

step and stopped at the sight. Dozens of bruised clowns and mimes, costumes torn, makeup caked with dried blood, one of them flicking a switchblade open and closed. The moderator began walking again, but much slower. He reached the podium with a blank look. "Serge, what's going on?"

"We can't tell you."

"What?"

"It's like *Fight Club*."

"Fight Club?"

Ronald McDonald removed a toothpick. "The first rule of Clowns versus Mimes . . ."

The rest joined in: ". . . is you don't talk about Clowns versus Mimes."

The moderator stared helplessly at Serge. "I should have known you were behind this whole thing when I saw it on the news."

"Thank you."

"I wasn't saying that in a good way."

"Why not? I just gave America what it wanted before it knew it wanted it: clowns, mimes, bone-jarring violence, something for the entire family."

"But these people came here for help."

"And I cured them."

"Cured them? You've only made things worse! I'll have to double the meeting schedule just to repair your damage!"

"No offense," said Serge. "But they just dropped by out of politeness to say good-bye. They've outgrown your meetings."

"Wrong! They need to attend now more than ever!"

A white-faced man in a French cap placed two fingers on his forehead, like horns, then assumed a squatting position in the aisle next to his chair.

"What's that about?" asked the moderator.

A birthday-party clown held a magazine up sideways, letting the *Playboy* centerfold unfurl. "He says your meetings are bullshit."

"Please," begged the moderator. "Before it's too late. Stop listening to Serge!"

"Screw you!"

"Bite me!"

Mimes silently grabbed their crotches.

Ronald threw his toothpick aside and stood. "Fuck this lameness."

They got up and left en masse.

"Wait," said the moderator. "Come back! . . ."

SOUTHERN PENNSYLVANIA

Four A.M. Traffic was light as Interstate 79 wound through the hilly, dark countryside.

A Chevy van pulled away from a rest stop at the state line and headed south. The spare tire on the back had a Steelers wheel cover. The half dozen men inside discovered that their sixty-quart cooler was dangerously low on Miller.

All week long, TV reports from Tampa had been causing quite the stir inside a popular Pittsburgh sports bar. Then, on the seventh day of the news cycle, as the story began to fade and the clock edged toward closing time, people who had lives got back to them. Others ended up in the van.

One of the passengers talked into his cell and wrote something on the back of an envelope. "Thanks . . ." He hung up. "I got Davenport's address."

The driver looked over his shoulder. "Thought you said his phone was disconnected."

"Lucked out. I called this real estate friend of mine."

"At this hour?"

"I got him in trouble with his wife. There was screaming.

Anyway, he checked his computer for recent home sales in Tampa, and the guy just moved. . . ."—he refreshed his memory with the envelope—". . . to this place called Davis Islands."

The van's taillights faded into the West Virginia mountains.

THIRTY-SIX

GULF OF MEXICO

*T*he G-Unit stowed gifts around the cabin.

"Can't believe what those guys spent on us in that market."

"Just when you think all the best men are taken."

Edna held up a floral dress. "Isn't it beautiful?"

"And my turquoise earrings."

"And my . . . whatever this is . . ." Edith held up the dusty statue.

"I think they said it was Mayan," recalled Edna. "Chock-something."

"Seems really old," said Eunice.

"Just a replica." Edith held the statue closer and studied the odd, reclining figure with a bowl in its lap. "Kind of ugly."

"But you *are* going to keep it?"

"Have to." Edith set it on the TV. "Don't want to hurt Steve's feelings."

"Look at the time!" said Edna.

The women changed into their most fetching evening wear and headed up to the next deck. They entered the ballroom. "Where are those guys?"

"Around here somewhere," said Ethel. "They never miss a night."

The gals checked the usual spots, then canvassed the entire room, calling out names. Nothing. Edith grabbed the punch ladle. "That's funny."

But the women had such great moods, they took it in stride, instead hitting the slots, piano bar, galleria. They regrouped after midnight in the cabin. Edna pulled something from a shopping bag. "Look what I got!" She held up a clay Mayan figure.

"That's like mine," said Edith. She looked closer. "*Exactly* like mine."

"Thought yours was so exquisite I picked one up in the gift shop. They had whole rows on glass shelves. Apparently it's a very popular souvenir."

"You wasted your money," said Edith. "I would have given you mine."

"It was only ten bucks. Besides, you didn't want to hurt Steve's feelings. Remember?"

Edith stopped and looked at her own Chac-Mool atop the TV. "I can't believe you think that ogre is attractive."

"You have to get into the history," said Edna, untying a golden elastic string around the statue's neck and opening tiny pages. "Mine came with a little booklet. They used to drop the still-beating hearts of human sacrifices in the statue's lap. The original was much bigger."

"That's beautiful to you?"

"Fascinating's a better word. Plus it's a status symbol."

"How much did you drink tonight?"

"A lot. Listen: There's a warning here. Not really a warning. More like one of those info labels on cans of dolphin-safe tuna." Edna grabbed a pocket magnifying glass from her purse. "Says we hope you enjoy your purchase of this keepsake from Mexico's rich heritage, expertly hand-crafted blah, blah, blah, same as the original atop the pyramid in Chichén Itzá, as well as smaller ones approximately this size that individual Mayans worshipped in their homes, and we hope your appreciation will encourage you to join us in fighting the growing antiquities-smuggling trade that is robbing the Yucatán yada, yada, yada . . ."

"How's that a status symbol?"

"You know what this would be worth if it were real?"

"No."

"A lot."

"But it's *not* real."

Edna closed the magnifier. "I'm telling people it is. Like my cubic zirconia."

A Chevy van with Pennsylvania plates crossed the state line.

"Hank, aren't we going to Florida?"

"Mississippi's not on the way?"

"Not really."

"Shit."

The van slowed down at the next light for a U-turn. A giant foam index finger went out a window.

"Steelers number one!"

THIRTY-SEVEN

DAVIS ISLANDS

*M*artha heard a car come up the driveway and checked the front window. "It's them!" She ran out the door.

Mother and daughter hugged in the middle of the lawn. Then Martha turned to the dashing young man a few steps behind. "And you must be Trevor! I've heard so much. Pleasure to meet."

"I didn't know Debbie had a sister."

"Flattery will get you everywhere." She waved back at the house. "Jim, get over here. It's Trevor."

Jim trotted down the steps. He hugged his daughter, then: "Nice to meet you. I'm Jim."

"Trevor." Trevor Greenback, scion of one of the West Coast's most successful condo developers, bottom of his class at Yale. Handsome as they come, and he clearly took care of himself, the tight golf shirt advertising regular afternoons at the spa.

Jim looked at his watch. "We better get going. Reservations are for seven."

A short drive later, four tassled, leather-bound menus lay open around a table with fresh linen.

"Trevor," said Jim. "Debbie wasn't really clear. What exactly is it that you do?"

"Honey," said Martha. "He went to Yale."

"Taking time off right now," said Trevor. "Lining up some contacts."

"Debbie said you graduated three years ago."

"I was on the fencing team."

"And after that you? . . ."

"Took some time off."

"Doing what?"

"Jim," said Martha. "You're sounding like a police show."

"That's all right." Trevor leaned back and raised his chin toward Jim. "Been sailing."

"Daddy, he has a sailboat!"

"Should come with me sometime," said Trevor. "Ever sail?"

"No."

"That's okay. A lot of people haven't."

"What's that supposed to—"

"Trevor," said Martha. "Jim used to invest in real estate. Like your father. Bet you have a lot to talk about."

"Really?" Trevor turned to Jim. "Anything lately?"

"Picked up a piece of land near Fort Myers."

"Ooooh. Big mistake."

"Seemed like a great deal—"

Trevor shook his head. "Market's not right. You should have checked with me first."

"Jim, you should have checked with him first," said Martha.

"It's just a little investment," said Jim. "I was going to hold on to it long-term anyway."

Trevor shook his head.

"Not good?"

"There's still time," said Trevor. "Cut your losses and flip it to someone else who doesn't know what they're doing. I didn't mean the 'else' part."

"Maybe you did."

"Jim!" said Martha.

"What? We're just talking."

"Ever consider working out?" asked Trevor.

"Maybe I do."

"Then fire your trainer," said Trevor. "My spa's got a waiting list, but I'll get you in with Sven. He'll fix the upper body issues."

"What upper—"

Martha flapped her menu for distraction. "The roast duck looks irresistible."

A waiter waited. "Anything from our cellar?"

"You have a cellar in Florida?" asked Jim.

"No."

"I'd like a glass of white zinfandel," said Martha.

The waiter bowed out of the picture.

Martha closed her menu. "Jim, it's so sweet taking us here. Where'd you find out about this place?"

"Neighbor told me."

"Must be the nicest on the island."

It was. The Winery. Everything in the dining room said class. Paintings, statuary, little lamps on tables, a bubbling Roman fountain in the middle. The facade featured heavily tinted windows and squared-off shrubbery illuminated from beneath by unseen green and yellow spots. A lavender canvas awning arched over the entrance. The Davenports' table was near the door. Martha had a view out the front windows of sidewalk strollers and people eating Italian on a patio across the street. Jim was opposite her, looking into the room. It was an off night. Only a few other customers. He noticed a table in the rear corner.

Serge peeked over the top of a menu and waved.

Jim choked.

"What is it?" asked Martha. She glanced behind, then at Jim. "What's the matter?"

He hit himself in the chest. "Nothing."

Dinner was ordered. It came. They ate. Martha sat back and placed her napkin on the table. "That was wonderful."

In the back of the restaurant, Coleman tugged Serge's sleeve. "I have to go to the bathroom."

"So go."

Coleman got up and stumbled down a hallway on chardonnay legs. He bounced off one wall, overcorrected and caromed off the other. "Where *is* the men's room?" So many doors, so many choices. One said *Caballeros*. "That can't be it." Coleman kept going. He reached the end of the hallway and a final door. "This must be the place." He opened the door and stepped into an alley. "I don't think this is it." He turned back around and grabbed the handle. Locked. He clutched his legs together and looked both ways.

Back in the dining room, Martha glanced over her shoulder again. "Jim, what do you keep looking at?"

"Paintings."

Serge continued surveillance, scanning the room over the top of his menu. Just the Davenports and an underdressed man in jeans and a tractor-company baseball cap eating alone. Except he wasn't eating. Serge bent down for low-angle vantage. Beneath the table, the man screwed a suppression tube on the end of a .380 automatic. Serge placed his own pistol in his lap.

Out in the alley, Coleman stepped up to a Dumpster and assumed the position. He was about to unzip when a door opened. Two dishwashers stepped into the alley for a smoke break. "Hey! What do you think you're doing?"

"Nothing!" Coleman hobbled away and turned the corner into another, tighter alley between buildings. He stepped up to a wall. A door opened. Someone taking out garbage. "Hey!"

"I'm good!" Coleman staggered on. He squeezed between his legs. *Gotta go! Gotta go right now!* He turned another corner. "I'll just slide behind these bushes and nobody will be the wiser." He began hacking his way through the brush.

Back in the dining room, the dessert cart arrived.

"Everything looks so good!" said Martha.

Pie and cake were served.

A few tables away, the man in jeans stood and hid something inside his shirt.

Serge stood.

The man in jeans approached the Davenport party and began removing his hand from his shirt.

Serge was right behind, reaching inside his own shirt.

Jim looked up at Serge and gasped.

Martha saw something else and gasped. Everyone turned around. Coleman was inside the restaurant's front hedge, facing the window right behind their table, unable to see through the tinted glass. His eyes were closed, and he smiled with relief.

Martha dropped her dessert fork. "I may be sick."

The jeans man and Serge reached the table.

Coleman continued his business. Trevor angrily threw his napkin down. "I'm going to kill that jerk!" He jumped up. His chair flew out, hitting the man in jeans and knocking him off balance. A silenced bullet poofed through the ceiling. Cooter McGraw fell into Serge, who tumbled backward and conked his head.

Stars. Lights out.

Serge felt someone shaking his shoulder. "Mister, are you okay?"

He looked up in a daze at three waiters. "What happened?"

"You hit your head on the fountain."

Serge glanced around the room. "How long was I out?"

"Just a few minutes."

"Where'd that guy in the jeans go?"

"Took off right after you fell."

"Damn." Serge quickly pushed himself up; the staff jumped back when they saw the pistol he had been lying on. Serge grabbed the gun and ran out the door.

"Coleman!" Serge twirled around on the sidewalk. "Where are you?"

Coleman stepped out of the bushes at the end of the block, concealing a joint. "There you are. I've been looking all over."

"You idiot. Get in the car!"

The Comet sped off.

Cooter McGraw raced up Lobster Lane, past the Davenport residence, and parked two doors down. He jumped from his car and ran back, taking cover in shrubs next to a front door with shiny deco house numbers over the top: 888.

He waited.

Crickets.

Then, slowly, a sound at the end of the street. From around the corner, the reflection of headlights, and then headlights themselves, swinging south. Cooter ducked as the beams swept over the bushes. He checked his pistol's magazine and safety. The vehicle stopped at the curb.

Cooter tightened his fingers around the pistol's grip. The passenger door opened. He took aim and began squeezing the trigger. He stopped. What the—?

Empty beer cans flew onto the lawn. *"Wooooo! Steelers number one!"* Plump men in football jerseys piled out of the van. Someone in a black-and-yellow Afro wig threw a glass bottle against the side of the house. A security light came on.

"Dammit," Cooter muttered under his breath. "These boobs are going to ruin everything!"

"Woooo! Steelers!"

Cooter jumped from the bushes and rushed down to the sidewalk. "Can I help you?"

Someone in a Super Bowl T-shirt looked at a scrap of paper. "Is this 888 Lobster Lane?"

"Yes."

"You live here?"

"What do you want?"

"Your name Jim Davenport?"

"Look, fellas, it's kinda late."

Wham, wham, wham, wham. Kick, kick, kick. Wham, wham. They hopped back in the van and sped away from the man sprawled across the sidewalk. *"Steelers forever!"*

 **THIRTY-EIGHT**

DAVIS ISLANDS

*T*he Davenports' drive home was pressurized with domestic tension. Jim continued south on an empty island boulevard, just the distant red taillights up ahead from a Mercury.

"Martha—"

"That was revolting."

"Please don't let it ruin our evening."

"I haven't even gotten to the guy with the gun."

Jim chose the correct strategy of not talking. Five blocks ahead, the Comet's taillights turned onto Lobster Lane.

The Mercury raced up the street and skidded to a stop in front of 888. Serge got out as if an unconscious man on the sidewalk were perfectly normal. He popped the trunk. "Coleman, give me a hand!"

Jim turned onto their street.

"Why are you slowing down?" asked Martha.

"Who's that in front of our house?"

Serge slammed the trunk, jumped back in and sped off.

The marital chill continued as Jim parked in the driveway, and they went inside.

Numerous tires screeched in the street.

"What was that?" said Martha.

"I don't know."

The doorbell rang.

Jim looked through the peephole: a fisheye view of five men in black suits.

He opened the door. A silver badge. "Agent Boxer, FBI." They came inside without invitation.

Jim followed. "What's this about?"

"You remember the McGraw Brothers? . . ."

Jim and Martha flinched at the mention.

". . . The last one just got released from prison."

"Oh, I understand now," said Jim. "You're supposed to notify victims."

"It's a little more than that." The agent looked around the room. "Got a VCR?"

Jim opened an oak cabinet concealing the entertainment system. The agent pulled a video from his jacket and inserted it. He picked up four remote controls, studied the buttons, and handed the pile to Jim. "This is different from my system. Can you start the tape?"

"Sure . . ."

The show began. Tex McGraw stood alone in a dingy garage.

"We routinely get thousands of tapes," said Boxer. "Most are just garden-variety loons. Crazy threats, conspiracy theories, loners documenting empty lives, like public-access TV. Ninety-nine percent are just barking dogs that don't bite."

On screen, McGraw plugged an electrical cord into a socket, triggering a loud, buzzing sound.

"What are you trying to say?" asked Jim.

"This tape's different. We intercepted it on the way to the office of the prosecutor who put him in prison."

"He made some really bad threat?"

"No. He didn't make any threat at all," said Boxer. "In fact, he didn't even say a word. Those are the worst threats.

We've gotten a few of these in the past, mainly militia nuts upset about Waco and Ruby Ridge."

"I don't—"

"Just watch."

"What's he doing placing his own hand under that circular saw?"

"Turn it off," said Boxer. "You don't need to see any more. I think you get the picture."

Jim trembled. His fingers lost dexterity, hitting wrong buttons. The scene on TV only got worse.

"Turn it off!" yelled the agent.

"I'm trying." More wrong buttons. Video hideousness.

Martha screamed.

The agent grabbed the remote, but it was different from his system.

McGraw held his severed left hand in his right, and threw it. Boxer ran to the TV and reached for the power button. The bloody hand hit the screen. The television went black.

"Geez, I'm awfully sorry," said Boxer. "You weren't supposed to see that part."

Martha cried softly on the couch; Jim stood numb.

Boxer popped the tape out of the VCR. "We just wanted you to grasp the level of danger you're in."

"But how am I involved?" asked Jim. "You said the tape was sent to the prosecutor."

"Our best profiler worked around the clock to decipher his intentions. We theorize he's working his way down a revenge list."

"Why do you think that?"

"He also sent us a letter: 'I'm working my way down a revenge list.'"

"God," said Jim.

"Your name was on it. So was the defense attorney whose body we just found. Dental records."

"But why on earth would he cut off his own hand?"

"Psychological warfare," said Boxer. "He's on a suicide run. 'If I'll do this to myself, imagine what I'll do to you.' Trying to scare us."

Jim fell into a chair. "It's working."

"The Bureau can give you protection, but it would be better if you left town."

"Leave town?" said Martha.

"Maybe take a cruise," said Boxer. "We've seen these extreme, revenge-obsessed types before. They'll stop at absolutely nothing."

"Then we'll always be running," said Jim.

"We'll catch him," said Boxer. "Just foiled a plot against an arresting officer. Grabbed one of Tex's kin in a restaurant where McGraw told him to kidnap the officer and bring him to this empty piece of property where we discovered the lawyer's remains."

"Why is he making relatives take people into the woods instead of just killing them on the spot himself?"

"So he can have fun."

The doorbell again.

"I'll get that." Boxer turned the knob. More dark suits. Another badge.

"Agent Garfield, Secret Service."

"The Secret Service is interested in the McGraw case?" said Boxer.

"Who's McGraw?" Garfield reached in his jacket and pulled out a clear bag with two hundred-dollar bills. "Jim Davenport?"

"That's me."

"You passed counterfeit notes at a restaurant tonight."

Serge did his best work when it was dark and isolated. He slid his hands into rubber gloves, grabbed heavy-gauge cutters and began snipping wires. Unseen interstate traffic zipped by on the other side of a berm. Nobody around except Coleman and their surprise guest from the trunk, who was seated twenty yards away, trying to scream with a washcloth stuffed in his mouth.

Another snip. "Why do they always resist like that?"

A beer tab popped. "Serge, we don't have a key to turn this thing on."

"And that's when most people give up. But not Serge." He whittled the insulation off a pair of just-cut cable. "Notice how the activation key goes into the padlocked control box? That's their so-called security feature: You turn the key and, inside the box, it completes the electrical connection that starts everything up. But the wires whose circuit the key completes lead nakedly out the bottom of the box." Serge held a stripped wire in each gloved hand. He touched them together. Sparks. Then a flurry of mechanical movement in the background. Serge separated wires. Movement stopped. "Now for my final preparations." He grabbed his tote bag, opened the chain-link gate and stepped over a knee-high barrier.

Their guest's muted screams grew louder as Serge approached and set the bag on a concrete floor. Cooter McGraw squirmed furiously, but it was futile with all the ropes and knots and safety straps fastening him into the bucket seat. An impish smile spread across Serge's face as he narrated the emptying of his supply bag: "Steel-wool scouring pads, double-sided tape, nine-foot length of bare copper wire, big magnet, spare gas can. Your mind must be going in ten directions. What on earth can Professor Serge be up to? I love a good mystery, don't you? That's why I never just shoot a guy. Okay, I do, but only if I'm running late." Serge began taping steel-wool pads all over the man's shirt. "I like to be a proper host and entertain. And, just to be fair, I'll usually provide a slim way out of the jam I'm creating. In this case, it's that pedal by your feet. If you're really good, you could stave off disaster for hours, maybe even until someone arrives early for work in the morning and saves you." He lifted the gas can and soaked the hostage. "But don't give it full power from the natural panic that anyone would have in your situation." Serge tied one end of the copper wire to the magnet and heaved it straight up, where it stuck to the ceiling of metal mesh. A strand of copper trailed back down and hung next to Serge, ending a foot above the floor. "My advice? Finesse the throttle. Less is more." Serge clapped his hands together sharply. "What do you say we get started?"

More muffled screams.

"You're excited, too? Great!" Serge hopped back over the barrier and ran to the control box.

"I still don't get it," said Coleman.

"Observe, Kato." He grabbed a stripped wire in each gloved hand again. Coleman looked up at a darkened sign. FUN-O-RAMA. He looked back down at Cooter McGraw sitting in the middle of a fleet of silent bumper cars.

Serge twisted the wires together. The cars began moving randomly at idle speed, except for Cooter's, which zoomed by at top velocity.

"You're going too fast!" yelled Serge. "Finesse!"

"I don't think he's listening."

"And you try to help people."

Coleman turned away to light a joint against the wind. "So what's the deal here?"

"You still don't get it?"

Coleman shook his head.

"See how each car has a tall pole behind the driver's seat with a curved metal runner at the top, scraping the metal mesh ceiling?"

Coleman nodded.

"The mesh is electrified. It's how bumper cars get their power. If you find yourself soaked in gasoline with a bunch of steel wool taped to your chest—and in Florida that could happen at any time—the last thing you want to do is make a spark. Unfortunately, that's exactly what happens when you hit a live copper wire that some careless person left hanging from the ceiling by a magnet. Objective: Avoid the wire. Since he's tied up and can't steer, he's got to use the throttle and work with the other cars. . . ." Serge cupped his hands around his mouth. "Slow down! You're never going to last!"

The car headed straight for the wire at top speed.

"Ease off the juice," yelled Serge. "Synchronize it so that other car bumps you out of harm's way."

"He's slowing down," said Coleman. "The other car knocked him clear."

"Here he comes again," said Serge. "This time he'll have to speed up to bounce off the other car and miss the wire."

"Speed up!" yelled Coleman.

"He did it," said Serge. "Not bad."

Three more passes, three perfectly timed deflections.

"Nice work!" yelled Serge. "At this rate, he just might make it."

"Look," said Coleman. "He doesn't see that other car coming up in his blind spot."

"Watch out for that other—!"

The guys shielded their faces from the sudden light and heat.

Serge grabbed his car keys. "Let's go. Rachael's probably about to regain consciousness."

"But I want to watch."

"Don't be disgusting."

THIRTY-NINE

COZUMEL

traight-A college students bloodied themselves in falls, vomited and had indiscriminate sex, in that order, in the same hour.

Across the channel on the mainland lay the salsa flats of Cancún. Budget motels, even cheaper tequila. Farther inland, the town gave way to farmhouses and hot, dusty fields with a feverish yellow haze. Then even the farmhouses disappeared. Horned frogs and vultures. Eerily quiet, except for occasional gusts of spaghetti-western wind.

In the distance, a tiny '62 Chrysler station wagon sped down a bouncy dirt road at seventy miles an hour. Across the barren landscape, its kick-up cloud resembled a ground-level jet contrail. The left shock absorbers were history, and the station wagon listed like it had two wheels in a ditch.

A lone hacienda came into view. It appeared vacant. Not as much as a weed in the scorched, lifeless yard. Half the roof was gone; so was an interior wall. The windows had no glass, and, from the proper angle, you could see straight through the building to the maroon sun burning into the horizon.

The car parked. Three doors slammed and as many men in linen suits walked through an empty doorframe.

"Hello? Anybody here?" The Diaz Brothers split up. Tommy and Benito circled in opposite directions and bumped back into each other near the front. "Sure we have the right place?"

Rafael returned to the room with arms raised and a muzzle in his back, followed by five bearded men in tunics. They leveled Kalashnikovs.

Tommy and Benito racked their Uzis.

"Drop your weapons!" ordered the tallest tunic.

"You drop 'em!" answered Tommy.

Nobody did. They bore down on each other with empty eyes. It was a standoff. It was in Mexico.

"It doesn't have to be this way," said Tommy, sweaty finger slipping on the trigger. "Let's talk."

"No talk!" yelled the tunic. "We were never even supposed to meet!"

"Then why'd you set this up?"

"You lost the last package. You die."

"Not our fault. Someone killed the mule and took the shipment."

"Even worse. Your organization's fucked."

"You've obviously never been to that part of Florida," said Tommy. "Just another redneck rip-off."

"How'd you let someone else get to him? How'd he get out of your sight before you could retrieve the package?"

"We took a different ship back in case he got nailed at Customs. Just like you told us to."

The man ground his teeth and poked the air in front of Tommy with the Russian assault rifle. "That next package we gave you before we found out you couldn't be trusted. We want it back!"

"Too late. Already in the pipeline."

"Get it out of the pipeline!"

"We know what we're doing."

"You know how to lose a package."

"The mules are the problem. The type of person willing to take that kind of work isn't reliable," said Tommy. "That's why we're using a totally different method this time."

"A different method to lose a package?"

"Ever consider trying to be less annoying? You might think you're popular, but—"

"Shut up! What is this method?"

"Shut up or tell you the method?"

"The method, you fuck!"

"Okay, number one . . ." Tommy began and didn't stop until he'd laid out the plan to the final detail. ". . . and then we meet back in Tampa."

The man gritted his teeth harder.

"Come on," said Tommy. "We've already set it in motion. Weigh the risks of giving it a shot versus jumping in and mucking it up."

The teeth remained locked. Finally, the man released his trigger hand. "This is your last chance!" He left the room, and the others followed.

WAINSCOTTING RESIDENCE

The noise was deafening.

Party Day.

Serge stood in the open office door at the top of the stairs.

Below: A sea of derelicts filled the living room, laughing, shouting, stumbling, dancing to the driving stereo beat. Through the middle, Coleman pushed a rolling serving cart. *"Cocktails, pretzels, smoke . . . "* The mob was thickest on the far side of the room, Rachael stripteasing atop the bar. She captured a dollar with her tits. The serving cart rolled by. " *. . . Yellow jackets, psilocybin, Diet Coke . . . "*

Serge went back in the office. "This cannot end well."

An hour passed. Serge sat behind the office desk, deep in thought.

Knock-knock.

The door opened; music volume spiked.

" . . . *Rebel rebel, your face is a mess . . .* "

Coleman closed the door and walked over to the desk. "Serge . . ."

"Not now." Serge aimed his digital camera. Flash.

"Playing with your dirt again?"

"This isn't *playing.*"

"I thought you kept your dirt in tubes. What are all those flat things?"

"Bought a bunch of ant farms. Wanted to see how they behaved in different genius soil."

"How's it going?"

"Kerouac ants had another cave-in."

"Oh, yeah, just remembered," said Coleman. "I knew I came in here for a reason."

"To bother me?"

"No, someone's outside to see you."

"Who?"

"It's a surprise."

Another knock. The door opened. "Serge!"

"Lenny?"

"Long time!"

"What the hell are you doing here?"

"Heard you were having a party."

"You did? But . . . how? . . ."

"I called him," said Coleman. "Took the liberty of going through your address book. Except most of the entries were famous dead people and the names of cemeteries." He pointed at the open door. "Have to get back to my guests."

"The hostess with the mostest."

Lenny watched him leave, then turned to Serge. "You hang out with that dude?"

Serge took another photo. "Yeah, why?"

"He seems like, you know, a real loser."

"You're judging?"

"But I thought *I* was your best friend."

"You are."

"Then what's he?"

"My other best friend."

"You're seeing another best friend?"

PORT OF TAMPA

The SS *Serendipity* eased into its berth. Mooring lines secured. Gangway dropped.

The G-Unit stood near the front of a sweaty, impatient crush of people waiting for the hatch to open. It was important for them to be at the front because the ship had a short, ten-hour turnaround, and the ladies needed every second for their road rally around Tampa: prescriptions, banking, laundry, then back to their apartment to off-load acquisitions and grab whatnot.

The ship finally opened up. Edith grunted against the weight of her rolling suitcase. "Can't believe how heavy this is."

Edna struggled with her own. "How much did those guys buy us?"

"Too much."

Then down the ramp, and gravity reversed the problem, luggage threatening to steamroll the gals if it weren't for helpful crew members, who assisted them into the terminal. They reached Customs and another massive backup. There was a clock on the wall. Eunice looked up at it through the swinging, fringed balls of her sombrero. "Already behind schedule."

Edith was wiped when they reached the end of the luggage tables. "I need to lighten this." She began jettisoning ballast.

"You're getting rid of the statue?" said Ethel.

"Steve will never find out."

It took an eternity, but they finally cleared inspections and played the sympathy card to cut to the head of the cab line. They tipped the driver extra at the outset, and again when he completed their chore run in record time, dropping them at their apartment.

Police were swarming the place. The landlord stood in the background.

"What's going on?" asked Edna.

"Authorities uncovered a major counterfeiting operation."

"Are we in danger?"

The landlord shook his head. "Left in the middle of the night."

The women went inside their own unit, and Eunice bolted the door behind them. They fanned out, unpacking and repacking. Edith filled a dresser drawer. "I hope you're not actually going to leave that thing out in plain sight."

"What?" said Edna, carefully positioning her own Chac-Mool in a prominent spot on a bookshelf. "I think it looks great."

"It's hideous."

"Edith," said Eunice. "We're barely ever here. If she wants to display that stupid thing, what's the harm?"

They went back to their suitcases. ". . . still ugly."

A knock at the door.

"We expecting anyone?"

* * *

DAVENPORT RESIDENCE

Debbie and Trevor stood in the living room, filling a beach bag with swimsuits and towels.

Jim and Martha were out on the back porch for discussion privacy.

"What do you mean you don't like him?" asked Martha.

"I didn't say I don't like him. I'm just not sure he's right for Debbie."

"Jim, he's perfect. Comes from a great family."

"He doesn't even have a job."

"You just didn't like him disagreeing with you at dinner the other night."

"I didn't."

"See?"

"Martha, it's not about my feelings. If he's not deferential to parents on first meeting, how's he going to be treating *her* in a few years?"

"You read too much into nothing. It's good that he knows a lot about business."

"You're not picking up on this guy's act?"

"It's a natural fatherly instinct," said Martha. "He's competing for the attention of your daughter. Now, let's get back inside before they think we're talking about them."

"They won't think we're talking about him."

Trevor stuffed sunblock in the bag. "They're talking about us."

"Why do you say that?" asked Debbie.

"Your dad doesn't like me."

"Of course he likes you."

"It's perfectly natural for a father. Especially one whose dreams have passed him by."

Jim came in through the back door. "Oh, great. You're going to use our pool."

"No." Debbie continued stuffing her bag. "There's a big party down the block."

Across the room was a louvered closet door. Inside, a pair of eyes peeked through two of the top slats. The eyes belonged to an immense man with a self-amputated left hand.

"There's a party?" said Jim. "Where?"

"Three houses up. Big postmodern place," said Debbie. "You and Mom are invited, too."

"When?"

"Guy just came to the door."

"What guy?"

Debbie snapped the bag shut. "Stocky fellow."

"Mr. Wainscotting?"

"Didn't say. But he knew your name."

"I'm surprised he even remembered me."

Martha came in from the kitchen. "What's going on?"

"Wainscotting came by and invited us to a party."

"He did?"

Debbie hoisted a strap over her shoulder. "Me and Trevor are heading there now. You should join us."

Two jaundiced eyes kept watch from inside the closet. White knuckles quietly unholstered a .44 Magnum.

Jim walked over to his wife. "What do you think?"

"We do have to begin meeting the neighbors," said Martha. "And if he came by to personally invite us, it's only polite."

The Davenports continued talking in a part of the room out of sight from the closet, but they could still be heard. Tex McGraw held the pistol against his chest and slowly cocked the hammer so there would be no loss of accuracy from the rotation of the double-action mechanism.

"Okay," said Jim. "Let's go to the party. We need to get out of the house anyway."

One, two, three! . . .

The front door of the home closed; the closet door flew open. McGraw jumped out and spun around in the middle of an empty room. He ran to the windows and saw a couple strolling up the sidewalk.

 **FORTY**

OTHER SIDE OF DAVIS ISLANDS

*K*nock-knock-knock.

Edith checked the peephole. "I don't believe it." She undid the chain and opened the door. Tommy Diaz and his smiling brothers.

"Steve!" said Edith. "What the heck are you doing here?"

His hands were behind his back. "Is that how you welcome your old friends?" He whipped out a bouquet.

Edith sniffed the roses. "It's just such a surprise. Come on in."

"Lovely place you have here."

"Only for storage." She reached for a vase on the bookshelf.

"Edith!" said Tommy, looking at the shelf. "You already put out the present I gave you. That means so much to me!"

Edith glanced at Edna and telegraphed the conspiracy, then looked back at Tommy. "What did you think I was going to do, throw it out? I couldn't wait to find the perfect spot. First thing I did when we got in, isn't that right girls?"

"Absolutely." "First thing." "Hasn't stopped talking about it."

"That's great," said Tommy. "Some people think it's ugly and would have tossed it away, but I could tell you have sophisticated taste."

"It's the most beautiful thing I've ever seen."

Eunice looked at the men's hands. "What's in those bags?"

"More presents!" said Tommy. They unloaded designer clothes, handbags, chocolates.

"You have to stop spending money like this," said Edith.

Ethel sat to try new shoes. "She's talking crazy."

"It's nothing," said Tommy. "You're doing us a favor allowing the pleasure of treating such lovely ladies."

"Oh, stop it," said a blushing Eunice. The women became engrossed opening presents.

"How *can* I stop? . . ." Tommy turned with his back to the room, blocking the view of the bookcase. ". . . We're helpless in the presence of such lovely creatures. . . ." The Chac-Mool came off the shelf and went into Tommy's bag. A second, identical statue came out of the sack, replacing the first. "How about dinner tonight on the ship? Say, eight?"

"We're there." Edna pulled tissue from a Gucci purse. "By the way, how'd you find our apartment?"

The women looked up. The men were gone.

Serge recited poetry to the Jim Morrison ants. " . . . *Abyss, nothing, silent scream, eternal void, plus I'm just a fucking ant . . .* " He stopped and stretched. "I need a break. They're all starting to look like regular bugs."

He walked across the dark office and opened the door. "What?—" Four times as many people. Serge ran down the stairs.

"There you are!" said Coleman. "Check it out: This is the best party I've ever thrown!"

"Where'd all these people come from? I thought you said just a few of your closest friends."

"That's right. The rest are neighbors."

"What are neighbors doing here?"

"I invited them."

"Coleman!"

"Rule number one of power-partying: Avoid the police. Which means you invite all the neighbors. Some will come, but the real point is to make the ones who *don't* come feel included. Then they're less likely to call the cops when things get out of hand because, in a way, it's like reporting their own party. I went up and down the block knocking on doors."

"This is insane."

"Notice any police?"

"Yes!" Serge pointed out the front window. "Two in the driveway!"

"They're supposed to be there," said Coleman. "Rule number two: Rule number one doesn't work, and some assholes always call the cops. That's why I phoned the police department last week and hired a pair of off-duty officers for security. . . ."

"God help us."

". . . And when on-duty cops respond to the noise complaints, they see their buddies making overtime and don't want to screw up that sweet deal because next time it's their turn. Just keep bringing food to the curb."

Serge looked out the window. A squad car pulled up. The driveway officers smiled and waved with half-eaten hamburgers. The car left. Serge closed his eyes and massaged his temples.

"Serge . . ."

"Yes?"

"I don't mean to pry, but you know that friend of yours?"

"Lenny?"

"Did you really used to hang out with him?"

"Yeah, why?"

"He's kind of like . . . a total loser."

A long sigh.

"Serge?"

"What?"

"But I'm really your best friend, right?"

PORT OF TAMPA

"People are such slobs."

It was the quiet lull in the changeover between cruises. The ship took on fuel and food. Dockhands pressure-washed the hull. The afternoon Customs crew cleaned house in an inspection terminal that looked like the aftermath of a British soccer riot.

"Look at all this trash," said a short-sleeved inspector with an eagle patch on his shoulder. They swept up the small stuff and shoveled the rest: candy wrappers, Kleenex, soda cups, water bottles, newspapers, empty suitcases with broken zippers and handles. And the nontrash: wallets and cameras and cell phones forgotten in the rush. And stuff *remembered* at the last minute: pills and joints bought on the streets of Cozumel.

"Norton, look at this chess set."

"That's a nice one, Ralph. Too bad you can't keep it."

"I know." He set it in a styrene collection bin. "And here's another one of those ugly statues. I can't believe people actually buy this shit."

"I got one for my daughter's birthday last year."

"I mean the other statues."

"You wouldn't believe what those things are worth."

"What? This?" Ralph held out the clay Mayan figure. "It's just a cheap souvenir."

"No, I'm saying if it wasn't a replica. The genuine ones they've dug up go for like a hundred thousand dollars."

"How do you know?"

Norton looked back at a glassed-in break room at the end of the terminal. "Bulletin they posted last week."

"What bulletin?"

"You're supposed to read the board."

"Remind me."

"That State Department summit in Oaxtal. Armed guerrillas coming at night and looting archaeology sites. We're supposed to cooperate with the Mexican government to stop the smuggling of artifacts."

"While they publish guidebooks encouraging the smuggling of *people*?"

"I'm just telling you what's on the board."

Ralph went to toss the statue in the bin.

"Hold it!"

They turned. Another Customs officer. This one was exempt from trash detail because he had a "W.E.T." badge. Warrant Entry and Tactical Team. "What are you doing?"

"Throwing away trash."

The officer shook his head. "Have to tag and save anything that remotely looks like an artifact. Keep the diplomats happy."

"Since when?"

"Didn't you read the board?"

"Oh, *that*. I thought it started tomorrow."

"Just tag it."

"No problem." Ralph went to place it on the table. His right hand hit his left. He lost his grip. The statue bobbled. His hands shot out to make the grab, but it just tipped the figure higher into the air. He lunged and caught it . . . Nope, still loose. It bounced off his chest. The bumbling seemed like it would go on forever until Ralph finally trapped it against his thigh. "That was close!" He placed it on the table.

The W.E.T. officer shook his head again and walked away.

Norton came over. "Nice save. Can you imagine if that was real?"

"But it's not." He grabbed a tag from his pocket and turned around, knocking something off the table.

FORTY-ONE

WAINSCOTTING'S PAD

*J*im Davenport sprayed Cheez-Whiz on a Ritz. Someone came over. A peck on the cheek.

"Hi, Daddy."

"Hi, Debbie. Having fun?"

She nodded. "Great party. And your friend's real nice, although I think he's a little drunk. What did you call him? Wainscotting?"

"You talked to Wainscotting again? I haven't seen him."

"He's right over there." She pointed at Coleman.

"Oh, no."

"What's the matter?"

"Nothing." Jim looked around. "Where's Trevor?"

"Out by the pool."

Jim looked through sliding glass doors at his future son-in-law chatting up two bikini bunnies. "Debbie, I wanted to talk to you about Trevor. Are you sure—?"

"Isn't he wonderful?"

Jim smiled. "Yes, he is."

Another peck on the cheek. "Love you, Daddy."

"Love you, too."

She trotted off. Jim grabbed another Ritz. He stopped and stared at something on the counter. A round black-and-white

TV. He pressed the power button. Nothing. He slapped the side.

"Jim!" said Serge. "Great to see you!"

A cracker went into the ceiling fan.

"What's the matter?"

Jim's eyes shot around. "Martha can't see you!"

"She's still mad about the propeller?"

Davenport grabbed Serge by the arm and jerked him into a hallway.

"What is it?"

"Over here . . ." Jim darted into a bathroom with a five-hundred-dollar aqueduct faucet.

"You're shaking like a leaf."

"Serge, I'm begging! Please leave my family alone!"

"No can do. My code of friendship: I'll always be there for you."

Jim whined with pursed lips.

"Okay, spill it," said Serge.

"What?"

"Something else is bothering you. Serge can always tell."

Jim looked at the ground. Serge bent way over and turned his head so he was staring up at Jim. "You can trust me, buddy."

"It's . . . Debbie . . ."

"No!" yelled Serge, springing up and reaching under his shirt for the bulge in his waistband. "She in some kind of danger?"

"Getting married."

Serge's expression changed, and he shook Jim's hand vigorously. "Father of the bride! That's fabulous! Caterers, a big hall, DJs, florists, twenty grand just for openers unless you want dickheads to gossip. Plus Melvin's in college, and you got a new jumbo mortgage, so count on at least five years of skull-cracking financial pressure, which means even more tension with the wife. Congratulations!"

"That's not it," said Jim. "It's Trevor."

"Who's Trevor?"

"Big athletic type wearing the Yale bathing suit."

"You mean that guy out by the pool sticking dollars in Rachael's boobs? What about him?"

"It's probably just me. Martha thinks I'm overreacting. . . ." And Jim told him everything, blow by blow.

When he finished, Serge looked at him thoughtfully. "You aren't overreacting. Kid's got no respect. Luckily, you told me in time."

"Serge! No! Not this! *Especially* not this!"

"Exactly. I won't do a thing." He winked. "That way you can deny whatever happens with a clear conscience."

"Serge! . . ."

He ran off.

PORT OF TAMPA

A taxi screamed up to the cruise terminal. The driver jumped out and unloaded luggage. Edith opened her wallet. "And here's a little extra for your speeding."

Ethel extended the telescoping handle on her Samsonite. "Can't believe we got everything done and still made it back in time."

"Haven't made it yet," said Edith. "Need to see what kind of line at Customs."

They pushed through double doors. Luggage wheels squeaked across a largely vacant terminal. "In luck. Only a few deep at each station."

The woman joined a trickle of early-bird vacationers who wanted to avoid the last-second crush that always came with the Sunday evening departure for Cozumel. They placed suitcases on the table.

An inspector smiled at Edith. "Anything to declare?"

"You're a hottie."

While the terminal was quiet on the customer side, that couldn't be said for the administrative offices on the other. Agents from conflicting jurisdictions stepped on each other's toes. Overlapping cell phone conversations. Doors opened and slammed.

Edna started up the gangway. "Wonder what all that commotion's about."

"Someone must have gotten busted."

"Welcome aboard!"

Back in the terminal, the flurry of official activity centered on one highly secured room. Inside, armed guards and a long steel table. Forensic cameras flashed. Small, L-shaped rulers lay on the table to provide scale. At one end were carefully arranged pieces of a shattered Mayan statue. At the other, small plastic packages of white powder sealed with wax.

"Vasconia," said an agent sitting at a bank of surveillance monitors. "Check this out."

"Got something?"

The seated agent replayed an eight-hour-old security tape. "Take a look in the bottom corner at Customs line D." He slowed the video frame-by-frame. "See the statue in that person's hand?"

"But it's an old lady."

"Probably an unwitting mule. Check the ship's registry."

Deeper into the pathology of the party. Wilder and louder. Stereo on Three Dog Night. Public groping, wall damage. A surly group of clowns and mimes pushed their way to the patio. All the bedroom doors were locked, and all the bathrooms had blood trails. The garbage disposal ground to a calamitous halt from a dropped corkscrew. Sangria stains, cigarette butts, mashed food. The throw rugs would have to be thrown out. A GHB overdose was iced down in a bathtub; others applied pressure to a diving-board head wound sustained moments after someone yelled, "Hey everybody, watch this!"

Good times.

" . . . *Mama told me not to come!* . . . "

And the weather! Couldn't have dialed up a finer day. Not a cloud, the early-afternoon sun tanning the faithful on patio loungers, and filling the entire, open-layout house with warm energetic light.

Except one room.

Debbie and her fiancé followed Coleman up a futuristic set of free-floating Plexiglas stairs suspended from the ceiling by steel cables.

"What's this about?" asked Trevor.

"Someone wants to meet you."

"Who?"

"We're almost there."

They reached the top step. Coleman opened the door and gestured for them to enter.

The couple stepped inside the ultra-dark office. The door closed. Their eyes slowly adjusted, and they began making out a form sitting behind a large desk. The person turned on a dim, jade banker's lamp and nodded toward a pair of chairs in the middle of the room.

"What's this about?" Trevor asked as he slowly sat. "Who the hell are you?"

"A close personal friend of Jim."

"Friend of Jim's?" Trevor chuckled. "That figures."

"Excuse me?" said Serge. "I didn't quite catch that."

"Never mind." Trevor leaned back smugly. "What's Jim's *friend* want?"

Serge turned to the other chair. "Debbie, you are not to marry this man. I want you to come and live at home with the family. Tell him. He'll understand."

Debbie reached over and held Trevor's hand. "We're getting married."

"Debbie, you disappoint me."

"Honey," said Trevor. "Your father must be behind this joker. I told you he doesn't like me."

"Debbie, I'll ask you one more time. Please do not marry this man."

"But Serge," said Coleman. "He seems like a nice enough guy."

Serge slapped the top of the desk. "Coleman! Never take sides against the family!"

Trevor stood. "Enough of this stupidness. Debbie, let's go—"

"Sit back down."

"Screw you. We're out of here."

"I said, sit." Serge placed a shiny .45 automatic on top of the desk.

Debbie's eyes bulged. "What's the gun for?"

"It's not a real gun," said Trevor. "It's a starter pistol or some toy."

She gripped the arms of her chair. "How do you know?"

"Because any friend of your father is a wimp."

Serge ejected the magazine from the pistol's handle, adding unmistakably genuine bullets. He slammed the clip back home.

Trevor's behavior improved.

"What an incredible sense of humor!" Serge stood and casually waved the pistol. "Kidding like that about a dear friend whom you so clearly respect." He came out from behind the desk and placed a chummy arm around the young man's shoulders. "I was completely wrong: You're perfect for Debbie! Come with me, I want to show you something."

"What?"

"A gift for your special day." Serge led him to the back of the office. "It's right in there." He opened the door.

Trevor looked inside, then back at Serge. "It's just a closet."

Serge shoved him into a shoe rack. "Coleman, the stereo on that shelf. Crank it."

Coleman twisted a knob all the way to the right.

"*. . . Woke up this morning, got yourself a gun . . .* "

Serge went inside and shut the door.

A minute later, the door flew open. Trevor rushed past Debbie, hands clutching the center of his face. "He's fucking crazy!"

"But baby—"

"Wedding's off!" He ran down the stairs.

Debbie doubled over in her chair, crying louder than an ambulance.

"You'll get over him," said Serge. "Come look at my ants."

FORTY-TWO

SS SERENDIPITY

*T*hey're late," said Edna.

"Your watch must be slow." Edith flagged down a waiter. "What time is it?"

"Eight-fifteen."

"They're late."

Eunice looked out one of the portholes of the Jules Verne Dining Room. "That's funny. The ship's not going."

"Might as well order."

The women stretched it out as long as they could. Appetizers, salads, three courses and dessert. "Wonder what happened to them?"

"They stood us up is what happened," said Edith.

"I'm sure there's a good explanation," said Ethel. "You're not going to get mad at them after all they've done for us."

"But something's hinky. First, no-shows in the ballroom, then out of the blue they appear on our doorstep, now this."

Eunice pushed back an empty plate. "Let's not dwell."

The women wound their way down through the ship. Ethel fished in her purse for the magnetic room card.

The next cabin: A man in headphones tuned a small, odd-looking TV monitor. Two others stood behind him. "Camera working?"

"Almost there."

Diagonal interference lines cleared from the screen. Another adjustment, and a grainy black-and-white view of four old women came into focus.

Jim Davenport opened his mouth for a Triscuit with spinach dip.

Someone ran toward him.

"Debbie, you're crying! What's the matter?"

"Daddy! How could you?"

She ran out of the house, sobbing hysterically.

"Debbie, come back . . ."

From another direction: "Jim, how could you?"

"Martha, what's going on?"

"You know!"

"I don't."

"The wedding's off."

"Honey, come back . . ."

Martha stormed out the front door as Coleman and Lenny came in.

"Two-liter Pepsi bottle," said Coleman.

"Got you beat," said Lenny. "Gallon milk jug."

They walked past Jim and reached the bar. "Hey, Serge."

"Coleman. Lenny. But I thought you guys . . . I mean, you're actually getting along?"

"Oh, yeah," said Coleman. "At first I thought he was a real loser."

"Me too," said Lenny, making an L with a thumb and index finger.

"What changed your minds?"

"He's really ambitious," said Coleman.

"So is he," said Lenny.

"We were just comparing the biggest things we ever made bongs out of."

"And we're going to top it!"

"Maybe set a world record!"

"Let's go, Coleman!"

"Okay, Lenny!"

They disappeared into the crowd as Rachael emerged. Serge grabbed her as she went by.

"Let go of me!"

"Rachael, you can't keep walking around topless."

"Why not?"

"I don't need the heat. Look at the commotion you're creating." He pointed out the back windows at an armada of canoes and kayaks beyond the seawall.

"They're not here to watch me."

"What are they there for?"

"Souvenir footballs.——'s been throwing them around, but he's pretty fucked up."

"The ex-Steeler? I thought he was in the hospital."

"Just got out."

Serge checked the patio again. "I don't see him."

"He's inside now taking a free-basing break."

"Jesus, where?"

"The den."

Serge rushed over and jiggled a locked knob. He pounded the door. "Open up!"

Urgent whispers inside. He banged again. "Open this door!"

Pause. "Who is it?"

"Let me in right now!"

The door opened a slit. Fumes knocked Serge back. A single eyeball rotated in the one-inch gap. "You cool?"

"Open this door!"

Pause. "Who sent you?"

"Stop free-basing!"

The eyeball didn't blink. "I'm not free-basing."

"I'm practically passing out from ether!"

Pause. "I don't smell anything."

"Open the door or I'll knock it in!"

The eyeball stared. "Want an autograph?"

Rachael walked up from behind with a tall glass. "Hey,——."

"Rachael!" The door opened wide. "Come on in, baby!"

She handed——the glass. "Brought you something."

"Thanks." He guzzled.

"Rachael!" said Serge.

"Something the matter?"

"Look!"

Rachael peered through a thick haze of smoke. Spilled drinks, dumped pot, cigarette ashes, spent matches, bent spoons, stray lines of coke, broken vodka bottle, condoms, chewed squares of paper, eyedropper of hash oil, two-foot bong, six-stem hookah, glass pipes, scattered Oxy tabs, Edgar Winter at full volume, dozen people draped over furniture, more on the floor, moaning, hallucinating, spit stringing from lips, including two hot babes from a chicken-wing franchise kneeling in front of the hundred-gallon aquarium, where they'd been for the last hour, palms pressed to the glass, tripping their brains out on fish gills opening and closing.

Rachael looked back at Serge. "I don't see a problem."

"Your friend has to stop free-basing! . . ."

" . . . *Come on and take a free ride! . . .* "

". . . And we need to get this room aired out before a spark blows the whole—" Serge snatched a lighter out of Rachael's hand.

She pulled the Marlboro from her mouth. "Hey!"

Serge opened the sliding doors to the patio and began flapping a towel.

FORTY-THREE

PORT OF TAMPA

*B*y sundown, the cruise terminal had calmed. Feds had hoped to find more coke-filled statues, but no luck. They currently finished mopping up a drug shipment so small it wasn't worth the paper for a press release. The only remaining drama was the cruise-line official annoying everyone about when he could release the ship.

A phone rang. The agent in charge answered. "... Actually, just about done. ... What? ... Where'd you hear—Yes, sir. Immediately." He began yelling before the phone was hung up: "Clear the building! Now!"

Someone sealing an evidence box: "But—"

"Drop everything! Code Orange!"

The cruise exec stood stupid. "What's going on?" Agents grabbed him under the arms, feet barely skimming the ground as he was hustled outside.

A convoy of black sedans raced up to the cruise terminal. Doors flew open. Men and women in tourist attire fanned out with concealed submachine guns and circled the building. Then they casually sat on benches and read newspapers.

Next: three large vans, United Asbestos Removal. They hopped the curb and raced up a pedestrian walkway to the entrance. Back doors flew open. Hazmat teams rushed inside with airtight helmets and portable breathers.

Another speeding sedan arrived from the opposite direction. Two more feet hit the ground: the new case agent in charge, who'd just Lear-jetted down from Washington. She was on a satellite-encrypted phone to northern Virginia. "Affirmative. We have a hot zone. . . . Activate Foxtrot . . ."

Serge continued through the house on crisis-prevention patrol. He reached the den and inspected empty hinges. "Where the heck did the door go?" He moved on to the kitchen, sighed and hit a grease fire with an extinguisher. He opened a sliding glass door and stepped onto the patio.

Back in the living room, an unblinking ex-Steelers player slid plastered along one of the walls like he was at the edge of a cliff. His right arm was in a sling, a brown paper bag clutched to his chest. He felt behind him and found the doorknob to a closet. His eyes darted one last time, and he jumped inside. The closet door closed; the front door of the house opened. In walked someone missing his left hand.

Serge circled the pool out back—*"No running!"* But it looked like things were finally leveling off. He began to relax. *Wait. What's that noise?* Loud, destructive and continuous. Not good. He followed the sound across the backyard. Where *was* it coming from? He opened a gate on the side of the house and approached the smaller, stand-alone building beside it. The racket grew louder as Serge reached down for a handle and pulled up the garage door.

"Coleman! Cut that thing off!"

Too loud.

"Coleman!"

Futile.

Serge yanked an electric plug from a socket. The room went silent. Coleman and Lenny looked around in puzzlement.

"Over here!" yelled Serge.

Coleman raised the safety visor on his helmet. "Hey, Serge. What do you think?"

"I don't know. I'm still processing data."

The den's missing door lay flat across two lumber horses; Lenny at one end with a T-square, Coleman at the other with a power saw.

"Okay, I give up," said Serge. "What are you doing?"

"What's it look like? Making a bong."

"Why do you need to destroy a door to make a bong?"

Coleman and Lenny looked at each other and began giggling.

"What's so funny?"

"Sorry," said Lenny. "Didn't mean to laugh. You don't smoke pot, so there's no possible way you could understand."

Coleman flipped his visor down. "Lenny, plug that back in."

"You got it."

The noise resumed beneath a spray of sawdust. Serge stepped outside and lowered the garage door.

PORT OF TAMPA

The agent dispatched from Washington had worked her way up through the ranks, earning every promotion twice over because of gender. Denise Wicks. She'd begun straight out of college as a field operative. Europe was the traditional first step, where she quickly distinguished herself. The other agents were busy along the prime minister's motorcade route, while she made the best of girl-duty, patrolling surrounding blocks in a Fiat. That's when she caught a brief glint out of the corner of her eye. She circled back and slowed as she passed a street vendor's kiosk. There, among thick bundles of flowers: the gleaming tip of a rocket tube. She looked in the other direction across a typical European square, people tossing coins in a fountain. A hundred yards beyond, the motorcade's lead vehicle appeared at the far end of the pigeon-filled plaza. She looked at her walkie-talkie. No time. All up to her. She made a quick U-turn, hitting the Fiat's gas pedal for a short burst and diving out the driver's door at twenty miles an hour. The car and kiosk went up in a fireball.

Bruised and bleeding, she fled the scene and was picked up by an unmarked TV-repair truck before local police arrived. Never officially happened. After that, the spy world's hot spots were her oyster. Indonesia, Lebanon, Colombia. Wicks was so good they sent her back to Washington to be a supervisor. Didn't like it, but that was an order.

Hours after arriving in Tampa, she had the scene wired tight, "tourists" guarding the perimeter. People in moon suits swept the terminal; plastic sheets up everywhere to block view. Word inevitably leaked out. The media swarmed and drooled, then sulked at the press release about another ho-hum government asbestos removal. Wicks made another walk-through, triple-checking that everything stayed on the rails. A cruise executive buzzed around her like a mosquito.

"When are you going to let us release the ship?"

"Be patient."

"But we're losing a fortune. The passengers are driving us nuts!"

"Have to make the terminal safe," said Wicks.

"What's that got to do with my ship?"

"We're setting up a temporary Customs checkpoint under a tent on the dock. Shouldn't take long."

"But the ship's *leaving*."

"Regulations."

"This is bullshit. I want to talk to someone in charge."

"I'm in charge."

"Can't we work something out? What do you want?"

"I want you to be quiet."

The executive stewed. Wicks caught something muttered under his breath: " . . . *woman* . . . "

"On second thought," said the agent. "When was the last time you had a Coast Guard inspection?"

"Last month. We're not due again until January."

"New program. Additional random checks."

"You're making that up."

"I'm sure she'll pass with flying colors. Only takes three or four days, unless there are violations. Then who knows?"

"You can't do this!"

She opened her cell phone and hit a stored number. "Captain Greene, this is Wicks—"

"Okay, wait. Stop. I'm sorry. Anything you want."

"Have to call you back . . ." Wicks closed the phone. "Anything?"

"Name it."

"I'd like you not to say another word, go back in your office, close the door and don't come out until I say."

The executive vanished.

Another agent had waited respectfully in the background. He stepped up. "Ship's completely secured, just like you ordered. Won't be going anywhere."

"Yes, she will," said Wicks. "I want her sailing thirty-six hours max."

"But didn't I just hear you tell that guy?—"

"Everything needs to return to normal as soon as possible.

I want whoever's behind this to think nothing's out of the ordinary."

"What do you have planned?"

"We're going fishing."

A commotion rippled through the crowded living room of the Wainscotting residence.

"Heads up!" yelled Coleman, carrying one end of a trimmed-down door.

"Coming through!" shouted Lenny, holding the other.

They entered the den.

A local affiliate TV truck sat outside the port. The cameraman pressed his right eye to the rubber viewfinder. They were going live.

". . . So if you have cruise reservations out of Tampa, plan arriving early for long lines at the temporary Customs tent until the emergency asbestos removal is complete. At the Port of Tampa, this is Jessica Thompson for Action Eyewitness News 7." She lowered her microphone and her smile. "We good?"

The cameraman nodded.

Farther along the curb, more news trucks: ". . . Get here extra early for expected Customs delays . . ." "Officials advise arriving at the port at least two hours . . ."

Agent Wicks was in a surprising moment of contentment. Rarely had a campaign of media disinformation gone so smoothly.

A white Lincoln pulled to the curb. A woman in an equally white business suit got out with a briefcase. "Agent Wicks?"

"Yes?"

"Madeline Joiner, Caribbean Crown Line."

"How can I help you?"

"By letting me apologize for Stan. He can be a little rough around the edges."

"Stan?"

"The guy who's afraid to come out of his office."

"He's still in there?"

"Whatever you said scared him witless."

"I didn't mean to . . ."

"In Stanley's case it's a good thing. But he really needs to go to the bathroom."

FORTY-FOUR

WAINSCOTTING RESIDENCE

A fight broke out by the pool. A clown crashed through a sliding glass door. Two mimes jumped on him.

Serge sensed something was wrong.

The living room listed out of balance, the crowd's center of gravity near the doorless den. Partygoers were abuzz as Serge pushed his way through.

"It's absolutely incredible."

"I've never seen anything like it."

"Must be some kind of world record."

"Their names are Coleman and Lenny."

The disorganized mob tapered quickly into a single-file waiting line that ran along the living room's north wall and through the den's entrance. Serge went inside, the smoke haze even soupier than before. He reached the front of the line.

Coleman prepared to flick his lighter again. "Now serving number forty-three!"

The next person handed Coleman a ticket and bent over to suck a plastic pipe.

"Hey, Serge," said Lenny.

"Great news," said Coleman.

"Our bong . . ."

". . . It works!"

The line moved slowly but efficiently. People walked away holding full lungs; the next lucky contestant stepped up.

"*That's* a bong?" said Serge.

"Biggest I've ever made," said Coleman. "Lenny, take the lighter. . . ."

"Ten-four."

Coleman cut through the line and stood beside Serge, pointing out respective groundbreaking features. "We sawed the door for a perfect fit, then squeezed a continuous bead of silicone bathroom caulk around the edge and pressed it down on top of the hundred-gallon aquarium for the crucial airtight seal. We also predrilled two holes for the PVC inhale pipe and the three-quarter-inch galvanized shower stem. . . ."

"Shower stem?"

"That's the water you hear running in the other room. We'll put it back when we're finished. The stem holds the bowl, which is the bottom half of that beer can containing a full quarter ounce of radioactive Gainesville furry bud. Takes ten people to finish a single hit." Coleman folded his arms and glowed with pride. The line ticked forward to another person.

Serge leaned to look inside the tank. The aquarium's electric aerator bubbled at one end, the dope bowl at the other. "Those fish look awfully crowded."

"Lowered the water level to optimize smoke-chamber volume ratio."

"The angelfish are swimming sideways."

"They're getting fucked up, too, gills filtering tetrahydrocannabinol, or THC, from the pot bubbles. . . . Watch this. . . ." Coleman returned to the front of the line and held up the next person. "Just be a sec." He grabbed a cardboard tube of fish food and tapped it into the plastic inhale stem.

Then he put his mouth over the end and blew in the opposite direction. Food flakes shot into the tank. A frenzy.

"Like piranha," said Serge.

"Fish munchies," said Coleman. "Another revolutionary feature. Their thrashing changes the gas-distribution model and increases dope potency, like those new tornado-carburetors that super-charge V-8 engines."

"Coleman," said Serge. "How can you be like you are the rest of the time and yet so smart about this pointlessness?"

"What do you mean?"

On the opposite side of the living room, a lone person returned from the bathroom. He stood apart from the crowd, filling a paper plate with crackers and scooping the center of a cheese ball to avoid the nut coating. A Wheat Thin went in Jim Davenport's mouth. He looked out the glass doors at the pool, where a knot of sports fans by the keg blocked his view of an immense man with no left hand working his way through the property on search-and-destroy. Jim looked another way and became curious about the commotion on the other side of the living room. He popped a final cracker in his mouth, dusted his hands and walked over to the back of the line snaking along the wall. "What's going on?"

"Some dudes made a radical bong from an aquarium!"

"Really? Wow. What's a bong?"

A glass door to the pool slid open. Cowboy boots clomped onto glazed Mexican tiles. Tex had acquired the target. He moved in a wide circle around the edge of the living room for a flanking assault.

Jim was on tiptoes, straining to see into the den.

Tex McGraw silently eased along the north wall. He closed to within twenty feet. A .44 revolver came out from under his shirt. Fifteen feet, ten . . . The target was still oblivious, leaning against the same wall, just on the other side of a door. McGraw stepped in front of the door and extended his arm. The barrel of the pistol neared the back of Jim's head. Point-blank. McGraw grinned wickedly. He began pulling the trigger. He paused and sniffed the air. What's that funky smell? Memories of his meth-country roots. He turned toward the slats of the closet door next to him. It smells like . . . ether . . .

Ka-boom!

The house's foundation rocked. The shock wave knocked the closest people down like candlepins. Serge ran out of the den. "What the fuck was that?"

The ex-Steeler's free-basing explosion in the closet had blown the door to pieces. It just missed Jim, but sent McGraw tumbling across the room. Splattered chemicals triggered a flash fire. Smoke detectors chirped painfully. Flames licked the ceiling, and panicked guests ran screaming with singed eyebrows.

"Serge," said Coleman, picking up his spherical TV. "Does this mean the party's over?"

"You idiot! Come on!"

They joined the multidirectional stampede for any exit that wasn't blocked. People collapsed coughing on the front lawn. Sirens whooped up the street. Hoses unrolled. Firefighters raced in with axes. A side door flew open, banging against the house. Tex McGraw stumbled out and limped away in shredded clothes.

Joiner walked along the dock with Agent Wicks. "Mind if I ask something else?"

"You want to know when the ship can leave?"

"Actually that was my second question, if the first went well."

"Shoot."

"A bunch of passengers want to cancel their trip. Can we let them off?"

"They're almost finished with the temporary tents."

"But they just went through Customs yesterday to get on, and never left port."

"Doesn't matter. Remember the Chilean crew smuggling heroin paste? We clear everything that comes off the ship, but not the ship itself. Once passengers step back aboard, they're recontaminated. Might as well have walked into another country."

"Understandable . . ."

In the background, shouting from the promenade deck, breaking glass, shrill sobs.

". . . But we need to do something," said Joiner. "Delayed passengers don't have a good shelf life."

Crash. Bang. *Motherfucker!*

"I'm in a real jam here," she continued. "The home office will decide within the hour whether to cancel the whole cruise, not to mention the next incoming ship that's doing circles at sea."

"Cancel?" Wicks hid her concern at the possibility of the ship not sailing.

"It's almost a done deal," said Joiner. "If those disgruntled passengers get off, occupancy drops below the breakeven point for fuel."

"Wait," said Wicks. "I have an idea to turn this around and make everyone even happier than before all this started."

"How?"

"My department will subsidize your fares for the trouble we've caused. You offer fifty percent discounts to the passengers already on board and get back some of those cancellations. Then phone previous customers who live locally and offer vacated cabins at the same rate. Raffle whatever's left to the public."

"But that'll cost a fortune. How can you afford it?"

"We're the government. Remember after Katrina when

we booked an entire fleet of ships at full price to stay in the New Orleans port for temporary housing? Next to that, this is a drop in the bucket. Promise to have you sailing by tomorrow afternoon."

"I don't know what to say."

"It'd be a great publicity stunt. And you'll probably end up with even higher occupancy than you started with. Can't hurt casino and bar revenue."

"You know too much about our business." Joiner smiled. "Who do you have to clear this with?"

"I don't."

"Look at the career on you!"

"Then it's a deal?"

"Deal."

Wicks looked toward the end of the dock. "That last news crew hasn't packed up yet. Might get good play if you catch them."

"Want to go on camera together?"

"Can't. Go ahead and take credit."

"Sure?"

"I insist."

"I owe you." Joiner headed for the journalists.

Wicks watched the camera lights come back on. Excellent, she thought, the perfect cover to get Foxtrot onboard.

One hour later. Serge and Coleman stood among a hundred rubberneckers staring across Lobster Lane at a smoldering empty lot.

"Serge, look, the blast fixed my TV. What luck."

Serge bit his lip.

Coleman noticed something in the grass. "Cool." He reached down and picked up an unbroken Heineken thrown clean of the house.

"What the hell do you think you're doing?" said Serge.

"Releasing the pressure so it won't foam."

"No, I mean how can you drink at a time like this?"

The bottle hissed and shot suds. "Celebrating my crowning achievement."

"Coleman! The house we were supposed to protect burned to the ground!"

"I know," said Coleman. "When you throw a blowout and it ends with the whole place leveled, it means you left everything you had on the partying playing field! You had nothing more to give! Just wish Lenny were here to see it."

"Dear God! You don't mean he's . . ."

Coleman nodded. "In big trouble. Left the house without telling his mom. Had to rush back."

FORTY-FIVE

PORT OF TAMPA

*T*he cut-rate cruise promotion was a smashing success. Thousands had assembled in front of the terminal by the time officials began calling out winning raffle numbers. News helicopters swooped overhead. A series of joyous cries erupted at random points throughout the crowd. "Yippee! I won!"

A megaphone rose again. "Six-two-nine."

"Over here!" Another raffle stub flapped in the air. "That's me! . . ."

"Seven-four-eight."

"Me! . . ."

And so forth. Until the crowd realized it was getting near the end. An ugliness began to percolate. Profanity, shoving. Someone complained their winning ticket had been muscled away by thugs. Police moved in.

Meanwhile, a second front of robust activity. Dozens of winners who never intended to board the ship conducted a vigorous black-market trade in cruise tickets for premiums of a hundred dollars or more.

Serge walked out of a men's room, leaving behind a scalper in an Oakland Raiders jacket happily filling his wallet with counterfeit bills.

"Did you get 'em?" asked Rachael.

Serge fanned out three tickets.

"Yes!" Coleman signaled touchdown. "The party continues!"

Back in the men's room: The man in the Raiders jacket looked up at the sound of an opening door. "Need a ticket? . . ."

Moments later, an oversized man missing his left hand exited the men's room with a ticket, a wallet of counterfeit money and a sporty new Raiders jacket.

Outside: The mob became surly as the most-hated people arrived. Cruise officials ushered VIP customers through express check-in.

"Booooo!" "Unfair!"

"Ow!" said Jim Davenport. "Something just hit my arm."

"They're throwing trash," said Martha.

Extra security arrived. Jim pulled two rolling suitcases through the terminal entrance. "Martha, what exactly did the woman from the cruise say on the phone?"

"That they appreciated our previous business, and a special had opened up for local customers. Fifty percent off, plus a free upgrade."

"Something doesn't sound right."

"Jim, you should just be thankful Debbie and Trevor reconciled."

Jim looked back at his daughter and fiancé wheeling luggage behind him. "They're really getting married on the cruise?"

"That's what they said."

The Davenports reached the part of the line where the towering ship became visible out the terminal's windows. Up on the vessel's fifth deck, four women looked over their balcony at a mass of people funneling onto the gangway.

"Finally," said Edna. "I thought we'd never get going."

The Davenports reached the hatch and showed their credentials. In they went. Boarding continued two by two, a Noah's Ark cross-section of Tampa Bay: blue-collar, button-down, families, swingers, lawyers, defendants, Tex McGraw, Steelers fans, clowns and mimes.

Two kinds of people don't have insurance. Super poor and super rich. The reason for the former is obvious. The latter is a function of math. Probability and payoff. Some of the wealthiest Floridians don't insure their homes—especially in the era of skyrocketing hurricane rates—because they can get a hefty return investing the premiums instead.

Gaylord Wainscotting found himself on the wrong side of the gamble. His Jaguar was parked cockeyed across the curb. Gaylord lay, facedown, on his charred lawn, screaming and kicking his feet.

A fire inspector stood over him. "You must have some kind of insurance."

"None! I'm ruined! I might as well kill myself!"

"You don't need to talk like that."

"Easy for you." He looked up with welling eyes. "The only thing left standing is my mailbox."

"Please don't do anything foolish."

"What does it matter?" Gaylord got back in the Jaguar, ran over his mailbox and drove away.

Three people in a black Expedition pulled up. "Just about to come on the market," said Steph.

A deep blast of a ship's horn. The vessel inched away from the dock. Cheerful people lined balconies and waved. Others claimed coveted lounge chairs on the upper deck.

Coleman lay in his stateroom bed and pointed at the waving passengers on TV. "Serge, what DVD of yours are we watching?"

"Titanic."

A horn blew again, this one much louder. Coleman looked out their balcony. "Are we sailing yet?"

"Coleman, the land's moving."

"Sometimes it does that with me anyway."

Serge stood at their cabin's entertainment console, precisely arranging his personal collection of cruise DVDs. *Titanic, The Perfect Storm, PT-109, Das Boot, The Sinking of the Bismarck, The Sinking of the Andrea Doria, Poseidon, The Poseidon Adventure, Beyond the Poseidon Adventure.* Then he lovingly removed his latest guy-gadget from a luggage pocket.

"What's that?"

"Sixty-gig personal digital movie viewer," said Serge. "Five-inch LCD screen in the letterbox format. Big-time movie magic in the elegant simplicity of a compact, travel-friendly package. I downloaded all my flicks into it."

"Why?"

"It's a cruise. I don't want to stay cooped up in my cabin the whole time." He turned it on. People began screaming and drowning. "This way I can walk around the ship enjoying movies."

Serge began unpacking.

Coleman hung his beer bong from a mirror.

Rachael found the key to the mini-bar.

Serge ran by.

Coleman sat back on the bed with rolling papers.

Rachael came over with an armload of miniatures.

Serge ran the other way.

For Coleman and Rachael, any type of trip in straight condition was cause for panic. To be on the safe side, they began toking and pouring. Serge ran by. He probed every nook, switched every switch, set the electronic combination on the safe, tightened the roll-proof luggage restraints, turned the temperature all the way down in the micro-fridge, changed the safe's combination, tested the ship's internal phone system—*"Hello?" "This is Room Service." "Just checking"*—stowed all his gear, restowed it, reset the safe, grabbed a digital camera, stuck his personal movie viewer in a pocket, opened the door to the hall and called to Coleman and Rachael. "Let's not waste time in the room."

Sunset was a postcard.

It drew an overflow audience to the pool deck. A Calypso band set the mood. A dozen daiquiri bars had Disney World lines. Some passengers swam, others lounged and read paperbacks by the fading light. But most were at the western railing with drinks and cameras.

Serge and Coleman leaned against their own remote section of rail, apart from the others, toward the fantail with the lifeboats. Serge was busy with his camera, and Coleman stuck his head inside the neck hole of his T-shirt to light a joint under current wind conditions.

Click, click, click. Serge lowered his camera and turned to the headless man. "What a view! I'm in a fuckin' fantastic mood! How about you? Can you dig it?"

"Absolutely." Coleman's head popped out. "Big boats are perfect for smoking dope."

"That was in *Moby-Dick*, right?"

"No, really. Absolutely safe. Ocean breeze clears the smell, and you hold the joint over the side. That way, even if The Man spots you, just flick it in the water. What's he gonna do?"

Serge paused and lifted his chin toward the horizon. "This has to be the most majestic sunset I've seen in my entire life. Let's stop and take it in the way God meant it to be." He reached in his pocket and began watching his personal movie viewer.

Coleman looked over at the tiny screen. "Where do I know that theme song from?"

"This thing also downloads old TV shows. It's *The Love Boat*."

"I loved that show," said Coleman.

"American classic," said Serge. "Populated entirely by guest stars whose careers had been tagged 'do not resuscitate.'"

"Is that Charles Nelson Riley?"

"I'm still pissed they canceled *Lidsville*."

Rachael returned from one of the drink lines sipping a zombie. She wanted a hit of Coleman's weed and tapped him on the shoulder.

Coleman jumped. "The Man!" He flung the joint over the side. The wind brought it back. A small explosion of sparks in Coleman's face. "Ahhhhh! My eyes!"

Rachael chased the windblown roach across the deck and stomped on it.

"Don't ruin this for me," said Serge. "The Skyway bridge is coming up. I've always wanted to sail under the Skyway."

Coleman blinked a few times. "I'm not blind. Good." He looked over the railing. "Wow! We're way the hell up here!"

"People don't realize the incredible freeboard these things have," said Serge. "The swimming pool back there is like twenty stories high."

"Doesn't look like we'll be able to fit under the Skyway."

"We will," said Serge, "but just barely." Click, click, click. "Let's dig the approach."

Rachael arrived with a flat joint. "Got a light?"

"Here."

She stuck her head inside her shirt.

FORTY-SIX

MEANWHILE . . .

*T*he highway trooper was out of his patrol car, pleading desperately. Suicide counselors arrived. "It's not as bad as you think. Let's talk . . ."

"What's to talk about?" said Gaylord Wainscotting, hitching a leg over the railing for his death leap.

"Don't do it!"

"Life's not worth living." Wainscotting pushed off, diving from the highest point of the Sunshine Skyway bridge.

He fell a short distance and splashed into the swimming pool of the SS *Serendipity*. He bobbed to the surface and looked around. "Fuck." He got out and took a seat at a bar.

Three people walked behind his stool.

Coleman and Rachael tugged Serge's sleeves. "Stop!" "There's a bar!"

He kept walking. "There'll be another shortly."

"How do you know?" asked Coleman.

"The first law of cruise ships: Passengers must always be within thirty feet of booze."

The trio continued across the Lido Deck, passing the Poolview Bar, the Oceanview Bar, the Terrace Bar, the Vista Bar, Tradewinds, Windjammers, Rumrunners, Schooners, Barnacles, Harpoon Hank's, Crabby Bill's, the Rusty

Anchor, the Crow's Nest, the Captain's Table, and the Poop Deck.

"Coleman . . . *Coleman*?" Serge looked around. "Where are you?"

"Serge! Look!" Coleman stood with arms outstretched. "I can touch two different bars at the same time. Jesus loves me."

"Will you stop fooling around and come on?"

Rachael's turn to veer off. She headed up a staircase to the highest sundeck on the ship, wrapped around one of the smokestacks.

"Where's she going?" asked Coleman.

Serge directed his attention to a sign near the bottom of the stairs. CLOTHING OPTIONAL.

"What's that mean?"

Serge told him.

"Wait," said Coleman. "You mean all these years I've seen that sign, there were naked babes?"

"This is what I keep trying to tell you," said Serge. "If you're going to live in this country, you need to speak the language."

They continued toward the bow. A growing crowd had begun following Serge. They passed an elevator. The doors opened. The Davenports stepped out.

"I can't believe my baby's getting married," said Martha. "It's going to be the most beautiful wedding ever. They'll stand right there under the waterslide."

Debbie squeezed Trevor's arm. "It's going to be a sunset ceremony."

They walked by the restrooms and into the atrium.

A restroom door opened behind them. An immense figure with one hand stepped out and headed toward the stern, continuing a sweep of the ship for his prey. He passed a handsomely chiseled man in a white uniform walking the other direction. An Iowa State freshman clung to his arm.

"You're really the captain?" They climbed through a port hatch onto the forward deck and heard yelling.

A man stood precariously at the very point of the bow. Dolphins frolicked below as the ship knifed through the sea. Serge raised his head into the wind. *"I'm the king of the world!"*

He stepped down and turned to the crowd that had been following. "Okay, you guys try. Let's build that confidence!"

Someone with big, floppy shoes stepped up. *"I'm the king of the world!"* The next person with a rubber ball for a nose: *"I'm king . . . "* Again and again.

A retired couple from Walla Walla reclined on a pair of loungers facing the other way. The wife was trying to read. "What's all that noise?"

Her husband looked over his shoulder. "People yelling *'I'm the king of the world!'* Like in *Titanic*."

She turned a page. "Who's yelling?"

"Bunch of clowns."

"No kidding."

Four elderly women walked in front of the couple.

"Any sign of Steve and his friends?"

"No," said Edna. More yelling from the bow. "What are those clowns doing?"

"Titanic."

"That reminds me," said Ethel. "I saw this beautiful necklace in the galleria called the Heart of the Ocean, exact replica of the one Kate Winslet wore in the movie."

"Just a cheap fake."

"No, the duty-free lady told me it was one hundred percent genuine tanzanite. Very rare."

"A gem so rare it can only be found on cruise ships."

The women stepped through a hatch and onto the starboard passageway. "Where *are* those guys?"

They scooted over to make way for an oncoming line of six men in shorts and tropical shirts, the same ones who had formed the undercover perimeter around the cruise terminal the day before. Foxtrot's backup team.

Actually, they weren't a real backup team. The primary unit was unavailable, on stakeout at Orlando International for a major ecstasy shipment from Rotterdam. These were six desk agents who constantly filed requests for a field assignment because they'd never had one. This was their first case. They were the *Backup* Backup Team. They were jazzed.

"I can't wait to meet Foxtrot!"

"How will we know who he is?"

"We're not supposed to know."

"Why not?"

"We're just backup. Foxtrot will only reveal himself if something goes wrong. If not, we'll never know who he was."

"Darn, I was hoping to meet him." They all stepped through a hatch onto the forward deck. "The guy's a freakin' legend."

"Freakin' head case from what I hear."

"That's what makes him so good—"

"I'm the king of the world!"

The tropical shirts stopped. "What's that yelling?"

Serge was back up on the rail, showing the others how to project with more intensity. He climbed down. "Just keep repeating and you'll get the hang of it. I'll check back later." He headed toward the starboard hatch. Coleman followed. "I still don't understand how we got this cruise so cheap."

"There are even better deals," said Serge. "When you're older, you can be a ballroom dancer and take all the cruises you want for free."

"Free?"

"Rich widows need someone to dance with."

"What do you have to do?"

Serge nodded politely at the approaching line of tropical shirts. "Just don't step on their toes during the fox-trot."

"Fox-trot?" said Coleman.

The tropical shirts turned as the pair walked by.

"You hear what that guy just called him?"

Two floors below, Promenade Deck, Agent Foxtrot anonymously joined the thick foot traffic flowing down nightclub row. It was called Boulevard of Dreams. Everyone had life preservers.

An emergency bell clanged three times. Passengers streamed up stairwells to their muster stations for the Coast Guard–required safety drill at the beginning of every cruise that everyone hated.

"Hold up!" yelled Serge, running into a restaurant and waving a preserver over his head. "Did I miss anything?"

"Sir, you're on time," said the calming voice of the crew member in charge of the muster station. "Just relax."

"Relax?" said Serge. "On one of these boats? Not after that rogue wave hit your other ship. Didn't flip like in the movies, but all those ambulances at the dock probably weren't the photos you wanted to see in the papers."

"Sir," the crew member said in an urgent whisper. "Please lower your voice."

"Oh, right. Better not get them hysterical to the point where they start counting lifeboats, because there aren't enough. I counted."

Something crashed into Serge from behind. "Coleman, what are you doing with that life preserver around your face?"

"Can't . . . breathe . . ."

"Because you got the strap around your neck three times. Put down that drink and let me help you."

"Sir, is your friend okay?"

"Not even close."

Serge finished refitting Coleman's flotation device, and the crew member got everyone's attention. "The safety drill will now begin. . . ." More of a talk than a drill. All the brainless things you're not supposed to do. ". . . No open fires in staterooms, no hanging off the outside of balconies—"

A shrill, piercing sound. The safety leader covered his ears in pain.

Serge waved something in the air. "Look at this really cool whistle I found in my life preserver! Can I keep it?"

"Sir, please . . ."

"Sorry."

"As I was saying . . ." The safety leader resumed his seemingly endless list of instructions. He stopped and looked around. "Do I hear screaming?"

Serge held up his movie viewer. "*Poseidon Adventure.* The original, not the remake with Kurt Russell . . . Ouch, that guy just fell in burning oil."

"Sir, please turn that off for the remainder of the safety drill."

"Sorry, you're right. Undivided attention!" Serge pulled a signal mirror from his pocket and held it to his face at a forty-five-degree upward angle.

The safety leader forgot where he'd left off, and started his talk again from the beginning. Someone bumped into his back. He stumbled and turned. Serge stumbled the other way and caught his balance.

"Sir . . ."

Serge angled the mirror to his face again and began walking. "I'm listening. Go ahead." He passed in front of the safety leader and crashed into a table.

"What are you doing?"

"What's it look like?" Serge tripped over a chair. "Learning to walk on the ceiling."

"This is the safety drill!"

"Exactly. I'm doing extra credit for the capsize part."

"Sir!"

Serge passed in front of the safety leader again. "Can't be

too prepared for the capsize part, especially ceiling-walking. Make one wrong turn at a chandelier and you end up banging on the sealed bulkhead of a flooding compartment: 'Dear God, I'm sorry for not paying attention during the safety drill! *Glub, glub, glub, glub, glub.*' That's no way to take a cruise."

FORTY-SEVEN

THAT EVENING

*T*he sky grew dark over the Gulf of Mexico. Passengers began filling the Nautilus Dining Room for the first formal seating. Moonlight shafted through portholes.

Serge was already planted in the middle of a large corner booth, napkin tucked into the neck of his life preserver. He chugged his third cup of coffee. Coleman finished another glass of champagne and signaled for the waiter. Not pictured: Rachael, shoplifting in the boutiques.

Others arrived at the booth. A wide polyester couple. Serge stood smartly. He elbowed Coleman.

"What?"

"Up!"

They shook hands. "Serge A. Storms, Tampa."

"Vernon Haymaker, Muncie. This is my wife, Pearl."

They sat. Serge sparkled with caffeine interest. "So, Vern, what do you do?"

"Plastic injection molding."

"Really?" Serge leaned forward on his elbows. "That's utterly fascinating! Would I recognize any of your work?"

"You know those little plastic scoops in powdered drink cans?"

"Yeah?"

"That's us."

"I use those! Small world!"

"Been there twenty-three years."

"So you must own the company now."

"No, I work on the line."

His wife nudged him. "You don't *just* work on the line." She turned to Serge. "He watches the temperature gauges."

"Good for you!" said Serge. "Very important position! Don't listen to the talk behind your back. Remember that big plastic-scoop explosion in Thailand? Poor bastards blown out factory windows with scoops melted in their hair. Except the guy at the temperature gauges who was vaporized on the spot." Serge held up an empty cup. "Waiter, more coffee." He bent forward, lowering his voice. "Heard a few guys fell in the vat of molten plastic, but they didn't throw out the batch. Just hushed it up and shipped the scoops out anyway. That's why I stopped using scoops."

More synthetic fiber arrived. Serge jumped up. "Serge A. Storms, sunny Tampa! . . ."

"Earl Pope, Newport News. This is my wife, Opal."

"So, Earl Pope . . . Hey, I just realized we got an Opal and a Pearl at the same table! If the next couple has a Ruby, I'll absolutely shit myself! What's your line, Earl?"

"Post-sandblasting."

"Post?"

"You know how they sandblast dry docks at the shipyards?"

"Of course."

"Someone has to scoop up the sand."

"That's *you*?"

The next table: six eavesdropping men in tropical shirts.

"We're not supposed to be this close. Violates protocol."

"But it's a once-in-a-lifetime chance to study his technique. . . ."

Next table: Martha Davenport swelled with joy as she gazed out a dark porthole. "Just think, Debbie: That was the last sunset you'll see single." Trevor: *Just think, this is your last night a free man.*

Diagonally across the restaurant was another large corner booth. A single person ate a slab of meat with his hand. The waiters had tried seating five different couples at the table, but they all suddenly lost their appetites. That was just fine with the lone diner. Tex McGraw methodically scanned the room. His eyes came to rest on a lean man with a napkin tucked in his life preserver.

". . . Just a puddle by the time they finally got the sand-blaster turned off," said Serge. "Ooooh, here comes our food."

Waiters arrived. Lobster for Serge, rib eye for Coleman. Two plates were placed in front of the others at their table.

"Serge," Coleman whispered. "Everyone else got steak *and* lobster."

Serge sawed his meat. "That's right. They ordered two entrées."

"Must be rich."

"No, just seasoned passengers. It's free."

"Huh?"

"Coleman, this is a cruise." He stuck a bite in his mouth. "All food's included."

"I don't understand."

Serge cut another piece of seafood. "You can order six entrées if you want. They don't give a fuck."

Coleman fell back in the booth and put a hand over his chest. "What have I been doing with my life?"

OUTSKIRTS OF CANCÚN

A vintage station wagon with bad shocks pulled up beside a vacant building in the middle of the night. Tommy Diaz got out and sighed. "Here we go again. . . ."

A minute later, two sets of armed men had automatic weapons leveled at each other.

"Doesn't this ever get old?" asked Tommy.

"You lost the package!" said the tallest tunic.

"I didn't lose the package. It was empty. There's a difference."

"Calling me a liar?"

"No. I'm just saying when we broke it open, there was nothing inside. You must have given us the wrong one."

"There was no mistake." The leader turned to the gunman on his left. "Right, Franz?"

"Right." The gunman sneered at the Diaz Brothers, itching to waste them. "It wasn't empty when it left here. I personally sealed it myself!"

The leader faced Tommy Diaz again. "I don't believe you." Suddenly he swung his Kalashnikov toward Franz. Bang.

The Diaz Brothers jumped back. "Jesus!" Tommy picked pieces of brain off his face. "You think *he* stole it?"

"No, that was about something else. I never liked him."

"Look," said Tommy. "Why don't we refund your money and call it a day."

"You lost our package!" The leader poked toward Tommy with the gun. "We want it back!"

"But it's just a couple ounces of coke. I don't understand the big deal."

"That was our test run."

"I know, I know," Tommy said sarcastically. "First the test run, then if all goes well, major kilos follow and everyone gets rich. I've seen the movies."

"You want to live? We want our package."

"How about I just pay for the cocaine that's so-called missing?"

The leader shot Franz in the head again.

"What are you doing?" said Tommy. "He's already dead!"

"Can't spare any more guys. . . . The package!"

"Okay, we'll pay you *and* deliver another statue for free."

"You've already fucked up two shipments. First, the guy at the train tracks. And now someone switched statues on you."

"Not a chance. I followed it every step of the way. We recruited the unwitting mules just like I told you, then met the old ladies back at their apartment."

"And there's no way they could have bought a second?"

"I'm telling you—"

Rafael tapped his brother. "Tommy, I saw a bunch of the same statues in the ship's store."

Tommy jabbed him in the stomach.

"One last chance," said the top tunic. "No foul-up this time. No mules. You personally make the delivery." He signaled with a slight wave of his gun. A subordinate disappeared behind a crumbling stucco wall and returned with another wooden crate. He placed it at the Diaz Brothers' feet.

Tommy looked down, then up. "How do we know your guys didn't give us another empty one?"

The leader answered by placing a hand on a grenade hanging from his belt.

Tommy rolled his eyes.

A cell phone rang. The theme from *Bonanza*.

"That's mine," said a gunman on the end. He took it in another room.

"Well . . ." Tommy picked up the case and pretended to yawn. "Have to get up bright and early . . ."

The one with the cell phone rushed back into the room and spoke in an excited foreign dialect.

The Diaz Brothers looked at each other. What language was that? They faced the leader again and saw something for the first time: worry.

"What is it?" asked Tommy.

The leader composed himself. "Nothing that changes our plans." He motioned toward another subordinate, who ran out of the room. Tommy's head fell backward on his neck in openmouthed exasperation. The subordinate returned with a small leather bag and handed it to his leader.

"Shaving kit?"

"A bonus."

He tossed the bag to Tommy, who unzipped it. Bank-bound packs of crisp, U.S. hundred-dollar bills. Tommy looked up. "Must be forty thousand."

"Fifty," said the leader. "Down payment."

"For what?"

"Additional assignment. You complete it, there'll be another hundred waiting when you get back."

"But that's more than the main job."

"You're going to have company on the ship."

"Who?"

"Just received word from one of our informants. American agent. Foxtrot. Been a pest for far too long. Much trouble in Iraq during the first Gulf War. You eliminate him."

"Hold on," said Tommy. "I thought you were drug kingpins?"

"We are."

"What were you doing in Iraq?"

"Uh, we ran a home-theater outlet."

"Wait a second. You're terrorists, aren't you?"

"Want the money or not?"

"I guess." Tommy passed the leather pouch to Rafael. "What are the details?"

"Our informant's working on a name. We'll get it to you at sea."

"How?"

"The ship's got an Internet café?"

Tommy nodded.

"The informant will put it up on our website."

FORTY-EIGHT

MIDNIGHT

*T*he SS *Serendipity* sailed deeper into international waters. The cloudless sky sparkled with an uncommon number of stars. Gaylord Wainscotting sobbed and weaved toward the stern. He passed a tipsy young man on a stool who whispered to the woman sitting next to him.

Slap.

Trevor rubbed his stinging cheek. He turned to the woman on the other side.

Slap.

In a piano bar several floors down, six men in tropical shirts: "Could you believe him at dinner?"

"That's why he's the legend."

Serge walked behind their stools. "Let's take the elevator." They got out several decks up.

"What is this place?" asked Rachael.

"Why is everyone wrecked?" asked Coleman.

"Boulevard of Dreams," said Serge. "The ship's nightclub row."

Eight layers of dance beat pounded from as many doorways. Strobes flashed through smoky windows and ricocheted around the promenade off everything shiny and fake. People staggered out the entrances of Rumors, Scandals, Attitudes,

Teasers, Escapades, Seductions, and a sports bar with forty TVs, Champs. The air was charged with the electric, anti-judgment excitement of sexual alliances made and broken in the time it took the roving mop-and-sawdust brigade to sop up unpleasantness.

Serge stepped over a puddle and dodged a careening Radio Shack substitute assistant weekend manager. Rachael discarded an empty souvenir cup. "Let's stop in one of these places."

"Can't. Have to find Jim."

"Fuck Jim. I want to dance." She veered off into the throbbing magnetic beat of Club Nitro.

"Why do you have to find Jim?" asked Coleman.

"Tex McGraw's on board."

"How do you know that?"

"Saw him outside the cruise terminal." Serge peeked in the sports bar. "But lost him before I could terminate."

"Is Jim in there?"

"Just a bunch of guys in Pittsburgh jerseys . . . Where can he be?"

"Try his room?"

"By phone *and* I knocked in person, but the whole family's out." He started walking again. "Let's check up top."

They took the aft stairwell and emerged under a sky of brilliant constellations. "Wait up." Coleman fell against a wall for an oxygen break. "Why don't we look for Jim later. I want to go to a bar."

"It's a moral obligation."

"That sounds boring. You told me how fun a cruise was."

"Tell you what." Serge held up a tiny LCD screen. "While we search for Jim, we'll watch *Titanic*."

"That's even more boring. All those rich assholes in old clothes doing nothing."

"Gets more interesting when the ship sinks."

"Sinks? What are you talking about?"

"How about this? There's a fuck scene."

"Let me see that thing!"

Serge handed over the viewer. "Only if you understand that the sex is just a pretext to sneak history lessons in for people otherwise doomed to repeat it."

They wound their way through scattered deck chairs.

Coleman pressed buttons. "Where's the damn sex scene?"

"It all starts when Leonardo sees Kate Winslet about to commit suicide by jumping over the back—Oh my God! Coleman! Over there!"

"What?"

Serge took off in full sprint toward the end of the ship. "Don't do it! Life is stupendous! . . ."

Ahead, a man stood on the wrong side of the railings, arms hooked backward over the top bar. He stared emptily into the ship's foamy wake.

"Stop! . . ."

Without drama, the man let his arms go limp. He began tipping over for an inelegant dive into the black sea.

The man suddenly felt himself seized around the waist. "I got you!" yelled Serge. "Don't worry! I won't let go!"

Serge had to give it his all, but he finally managed to drag the depressed man back over the rails, where he flopped to the deck. Serge collapsed in exhaustion next to him. "They say suicide is a permanent solution to temporary problems—"

The man looked over. "You!"

"Gaylord?" said Serge. "What a coincidence! How are you liking the cruise?"

"My house!"

"I guess an apology's in order."

"I'll kill you!"

"Maybe this isn't the best time." Serge left quickly toward the bow.

In the shadows, six floral shirts. "See those reflexes? . . ." They watched the pair cross the deck and vanish through automatic doors into the air-conditioned atrium.

Coleman grabbed a banister and looked down. "Zowza! How high are we?"

"Eight floors. Right back to where we started." Serge looked over the edge at a tiny baby grand in the middle of the lobby. The piano was surrounded by a bar. Slap. Trevor moved a stool over. Serge inhaled deeply. "I *love* atriums!" He paused to appreciate, eyes staring up at the geodesic glass skylight, then moving down, floor by floor, each a perfect circle, railings illuminated with multicolored fluorescent tubes. On the far side, a pair of glassed-in elevators, one going up, the other down. "Coleman! Let's ride the elevators!"

"Where to?"

"Up and down a hundred times! It's free!" He pointed toward the descending lift. "We can catch that one if we—Wait, we're in luck!"

"What's the matter?"

"In the elevator! It's Jim! We found him! Excellent! . . . Oh, no!"

"Not excellent?"

"In that other elevator coming up. It's Tex McGraw! . . . He doesn't see Jim yet. . . . Come on, don't look at the other elevator. Don't look. Please don't look . . ." The elevators passed each other. "He looked! He saw Jim! He's frantically pressing buttons to stop the elevator and head back down. Coleman! We have to hurry!"

They dashed to the nearest stairwell, and Serge raced down three flights. He ran out to the atrium railing and looked up. McGraw's elevator was in descent, one floor above. Serge looked down. Jim's elevator neared the lobby. He ran back to the stairwell just as Coleman made his way out. "McGraw's got to be stopped!"

Serge flew down two more flights and ran out to the railing again. McGraw was below him now, two levels above the lobby, where the other elevator had stopped. The doors opened; Jim got out.

Serge bolted back to the landing. "Coleman, where are you?"

"Up here." His voice echoed down the stairwell. "Waiting for the elevator."

Serge ran down more flights, then vaulted the last set of steps and tumbled into the lobby. He sprang up and ran out from behind the piano. Where was Jim? He looked back at the elevators. What the heck? Jim had changed his mind and gotten back in. The doors closed. McGraw watched Davenport pass the other way as his own elevator reached the bottom. Tex angrily mashed buttons and began ascending again.

"Oh, no!" Serge ran back around the piano.

Slap.

Trevor's head swiveled. It came to a rest, looking in the direction of someone galloping up the stairwell. "I don't believe it. That's the fucker who attacked me in the closet at the party!"

Coleman stood at the elevators on the fourth deck. The doors opened. "Hey, Jim! It's me, Coleman!"

Jim's eyes widened and he quickly pressed the close button. "Jim! . . ." The doors shut. The elevator went up.

Coleman pressed his own button again.

The next elevator came. The door opened. Tex McGraw. Coleman stepped back. The door closed.

Serge ran up the stairs in the background. "Coleman! Come on! . . ."

"My elevator's almost here."

More footsteps. Trevor ran up the stairs. "I'll kill that son of a bitch!"

Serge bounded onto the sixth level. He looked up and saw the bottoms of two elevators stopped on the next floor.

McGraw was just getting out; Jim had already left the atrium and entered Boulevard of Dreams. Serge ran back to the stairs.

Moments later, a slow-motion four-way foot pursuit commenced past the nightclubs: McGraw advancing on Jim, and Serge advancing on McGraw, followed by Trevor, fueled with drink. The sound of the young man's approach was masked by the demolition beat of Club Nitro. *"That bastard's dead! . . . "*

Tex started with what seemed an insurmountable lead, but the gap quickly closed.

"Perfect," Serge said under his breath. "I can get to Jim in time, just as long as nothing crazy happens to slow me down. But I must remain completely focused like a laser. Not the slightest distraction. Easy now, eassssy . . ." He pulled his personal movie viewer from his pocket and turned on the *The Hunt for Red October.* "Oh my God, it's the cook! Behind you!"

Behind Serge, Trevor charged the last few steps and planted his right foot to pounce.

Out of nowhere, a line of six tropical shirts formed a wall in front of him.

"Who the fuck are you?"

The answer came in fists.

Just as quickly as the shirts had appeared, they were gone. The party crowd stepped over a bloody and dazed Trevor lying across the Boulevard. Two security guards grabbed him under the arms. "Another drunk . . ."

Jim Davenport neared the end of the promenade and turned in the last door. He walked past a long line of TVs and took a seat in the back of Champs.

McGraw reached the doorway of the sports bar and stopped. A wicked smile crept across his face. Jim was cornered. The ex-con headed inside, savoring each step. Someone spiked a football on one of the TVs; a roar went up.

Serge arrived at the entrance. McGraw was only a few steps ahead, walking extra slow, and Jim was at the far end of the bar. Plenty of time to make his move. . . . One, two, *three!* . . . Serge charged.

Someone jumped off a chair and onto Serge's back. He beat Serge upside the head with a plastic beer bottle and clawed his eyes.

"You bastard!" yelled Wainscotting.

"Get off me!" shouted Serge.

Gaylord bit Serge's ear.

"Ahhhhhh!" Serge swatted back over his shoulder. He began spinning, but his passenger held on. They went faster and faster. The centrifugal force pulled Gaylord's legs straight out behind him. A few more dizzying revolutions and they flew apart. Gaylord sailed into a wall, and Serge flipped backward over a table of beer pitchers. He struck his head violently on the floor, stared up at the ceiling and thought he was in Connecticut.

Six tropical shirts rushed over. They raised Serge into a sitting position. One of them held up three fingers. "How many?"

"Tuba."

McGraw turned around at the sound of the commotion. Whatever it was, it was over. He directed his menace back to Jim. Tex increasingly relished the idea of performing the task bare-handed. Snap his neck? Slam nose cartilage into his brain? Thumb through eye socket? His twisted grin grew larger with each sadistic image. He squared his feet on the fifty-yard line painted across the middle of the bar's floor and cupped his hand around his mouth:

"Jim Davenport!"

Jim turned. Immediate recognition. He jettisoned off his stool and began backing up on rubber legs. Tex savored how each slow step forward heightened the terror in his adversary.

Someone at the bar turned to a friend in a black-and-yellow Afro wig. "Did someone just call that guy Jim Davenport?"

"I heard it, too."

Tex stepped right up to Jim. Hot, rancid breath. "Ready to die?" Jim's knees began buckling.

The man in the wig spun his stool toward the man at the rear of the club. "Yo! Jim Davenport!"

Jim looked over at the bar.

The men in Pittsburgh jerseys gave each other a quick look. "Is it possible we attacked the wrong guy?"

"Let's find out. . . . Hey! Jim! You live on Lobster Lane?"

Jim was in such a state of terror, he didn't even realize he reflexively nodded yes.

"It's Jim Davenport!" the Afro yelled to the other football fans at the bar. "Get him!"

They jumped off stools and stampeded past Tex. Jim shielded his face as the first fan took him down with a flying tackle, and the rest formed a fumble pile on top of him. Tex was fit to be tied. He wanted to kill them all, but the bar's security staff poured in, dressed like referees and blowing whistles. One threw a yellow flag; the rest began pulling apart the drunken tangle.

McGraw's face was crimson with rage as he was forced to accept the inevitable: Retreat. He started walking backward, swearing he'd get Jim at the very next opportunity. He felt something pointy and cold in his back.

"Let's take a walk," said Serge.

"Do you have any idea who I am?"

"Someone who's hard of hearing." Serge jabbed the knife a half inch, piercing Tex's jacket and producing a trickle of blood.

They left.

Coleman entered Boulevard of Dreams. "Serge? Where are you?" He stuck his head in Club Nitro and saw Rachael at the bar. She'd spent the last two hours drinking, smoking and breaking balls. The man on the next stool whispered.

Slap.

Trevor climbed off the stool, and Coleman climbed on. "Hey, Rachael."

"Oh, fuck."

Coleman waved for the bartender. An umbrella cocktail arrived. He pulled a cherry off the stem with his teeth. "Rachael, can I ask you a personal question?"

"No, I will not suck your dick."

Coleman look down into his drink. "Okay, let me think of another one. . . . Wait, I got it. Do you think, like, any of your friends might consider, you know, going out with a guy like me?"

Rachael exhaled a deep Marlboro drag toward the ceiling. "I can say this with complete confidence. Every woman I know would rather drive burning spears through her own eyes."

"So I have a chance with a blind girl?"

FORTY-NINE

JUST OFF THE COAST OF COZUMEL

*H*igh tide. The flukes of a Danforth boat anchor grabbed the sandy bottom. Its chain rose thirty feet to a cabin cruiser bobbing in the light chop. It was like any other such boat, except fishing poles were replaced with arrays of high-gain antennas.

These were the same waters where cruise passengers took reef excursions: red-and-white dive flags in Styrofoam buoys marking novice snorkelers splashing in the warm, shallow surf. Parrot fish, stingrays, nurse sharks, moray eels.

This particular cabin cruiser, however, was in deeper water, farther north than the tourist boats ventured. And it was the middle of the night. Beneath the boat, high-candle-power halogen beams split the darkness as divers swept the ocean floor.

Special agent Denise Wicks had been flown in from Tampa, and now paced impatiently on the cruiser's back deck. She leaned over the stern, watching the spotlights' greenish-yellow glow wavering up through emerald water.

The radio crackled. A diver with a special underwater microphone: "We found it."

Everyone rushed into the cabin and gathered around a video monitor with a live feed from the bottom.

"There it is," said the boat's pilot. "Just like we thought."
Wicks bent toward the screen. "We're too late."

SS *SERENDIPITY*

"Just keep walking," said Serge. "And don't try anything.
I'm pretty quick with a knife."

McGraw was going to try something, just as soon as they
got in Serge's stateroom, where there wouldn't be any witnesses or interference. He'd use the moment when Serge had
to close the door, a fleeting distraction, but all the opportunity that someone Tex's size needed.

They reached the room. Serge swiped a magnetic card
with a free hand and turned the knob. "Inside."

The pair took two steps. McGraw made his move. But
Serge had bet in advance what Tex might try. He left the
door open and knocked Tex cold with the butt of his combat
knife.

The world slowly returned to McGraw with a pounding
skull. Fuzzy reality came into focus. He tried to move. No
luck. His legs, arms and chest were tied fast to a chair in the
back of the cabin. Duct tape across his mouth. He felt something round between his teeth: a clear, flexible tube that exited through a hole in the tape and ran up the wall. It was
tied to a closet rod and capped with a funnel.

"Coleman's beer bong," said Serge, walking out from
behind the chair. "And I thought it was a brainless purchase.
But you can learn from anyone. That's why I like people."
Serge uncapped a bottle of drinking water and took a refreshing swig. "Wait. Can you believe me? The impolite
host. I'll bet you're thirsty!" Serge poured the rest of the
bottle in the funnel. McGraw couldn't figure it out: If this
guy was trying to drown him, why was he pouring slowly
enough so Tex could swallow and prevent it from going
down his lungs?

"Like cruising?" said Serge. "Me too! Bet you're dying to learn some incredible trivia. Luckily you drew me as your guide! Just read a fascinating study on rogue waves. People used to think they were an ancient mariner's myth. But after a number of twentieth-century sightings and photographic evidence, their existence could no longer be doubted!" Serge opened another water bottle and poured. "A sheer, ninety-foot wave almost capsized the *Queen Mary* in 1942 before she slowly righted herself. Will you stop looking at the tube and listen?" He finished pouring and grabbed another bottle. "People naturally assume there has to be some kind of underwater seismic event. Not true! Rogues can happen anywhere, a freak statistical anomaly of wave mechanics, usually when conflicting flows collide far out at sea and start a harmonic rhythm like a kid on a swing set going higher and higher. Always wanted to see a rogue wave. The cruise people try to cover up the possibility, but for customers like me, it's a selling point, the whole movie-of-the-week 'who's going to survive' angle. Hey, I just got a great idea!" Serge slipped a disk in the DVD. "Let's watch *The Poseidon Adventure*!" He uncapped another bottle. "Shelley Winters's finest work."

Dry-ice fog seeped over the dance floor in Club Nitro.

Coleman tapped Rachael's shoulder.

She swatted him away and continued talking with the man on her other side.

He tapped her shoulder again.

"Fuck off."

"But I want someone to talk to."

"Can't you see I'm trying to hook up with this guy?"

"What's he got that I don't?"

Rachael leaned back on her stool and made an all-encompassing gesture at Johnny Vegas.

"Oh," said Coleman. "That."

"Now leave me alone!"

"Can't we all talk together?"

"No!" She got up from her stool and turned to Vegas. "Your cabin?"

Johnny sprang off his own stool. "Yessss!" He took her by the arm.

Coleman slouched in inebriation. "You are *so* like Sharon."

Rachael stopped and looked back. "Who's Sharon?"

"This chick we used to know in Tampa."

"I had a sister in Tampa named Sharon. Ten years older. That's how I stumbled into your apartment. She used to live there."

"That's how *we* found the apartment." Coleman's head sagged lower and lower. "Our Sharon used to live there, too. What a coincidence: two roommates both named Sharon."

Rachael patted Johnny's hand. "Just be a second." She sat down next to Coleman. "When was the last time you saw her?"

"Guess it was this trip we took to the World Series in Miami." His forehead now rested on the bar. "Where's your sister now?"

"She died," said Rachael. "In Miami."

Johnny cleared his throat.

"Sorry," said Rachael. "Something's come up. . . ."

Johnny's crest fell.

". . . But I'll meet you later. You know that secluded mid-section balcony near the lifeboats?"

He nodded.

"One hour, lifeboat five," said Rachael. "Don't be late."

Johnny brightened and left. Rachael grabbed Coleman's hair and pulled his head up. "Tell me more about the World Series. . . ."

"Not much to tell . . ."

And he spilled it all: How Sharon had been on a road trip

with them down the East Coast, coked out of her skull, getting on Serge's last nerve. Then the final motel room confrontation in Miami Beach when she tried to kill Coleman, but Serge got the drop on her.

"Then what?" said Rachael.

"Put her in the trunk and left the car outside the stadium—"

A tremendous crash. Coleman and Rachael turned toward the front of Club Nitro.

A table had been upended, drinks everywhere. Tex McGraw struggled to his feet, staggered a few more steps and pulled down another table. People screamed. Security swooped in. Tex grabbed one of them by the front of his shirt, trying to communicate, but his speech was hopelessly slurred. Then he crashed back to the floor with an ugly thud and lay motionless. A pool of urine began to spread.

The chief of security arrived. "What are you standing around for? Get this jackass out of here. And call a janitor."

Two brawny men in tight black T-shirts reached down and grabbed his wrists. One suddenly dropped an arm, jumped up and turned sheet white.

"What are you doing?" said the security chief.

"He's . . . dead."

FIFTY

JUST OFF THE COAST OF COZUMEL

*E*very agent aboard the cabin cruiser immediately recognized the image on the video monitor: A clear, three-foot rectangle of shatterproof safety glass bolted to a steel table and anchored on the ocean floor. Through the front of the rectangle were two holes, where thick rubber gloves extended inside. It was a "clean box," the kind they use for premature births or to handle virulent biological samples at the Centers for Disease Control in Atlanta.

At the bottom of the box were two empty vials caked with white-powder residue.

Agent Wicks had said they were "too late" because the box was flooded with seawater and clearly abandoned.

"Get me a recovery crew!" If she was right about the box, there was no way the boat was equipped to handle it.

The American intelligence community had been on alert for a dirty radioactive bomb when they'd received word of a far more viable threat. A dirty cocaine bomb.

Someone stepped up to Wicks. "You really think this is where they mixed anthrax with the cocaine and sealed it inside those statues?"

"Explains our eclectic list of nine victims back in Florida," said Wicks.

"But why mix it with cocaine?"

"That's the whole point," said Wicks. "The main hurdles of a homeland anthrax attack are smuggling and nasal exposure. Cocaine solves both problems with a vengeance. Florida already has an extensive drug distribution network. Just mix the batch in a second country, stand back and let human nature do the rest. It practically delivers itself."

"Let me get this straight," said the other agent. "First we thought this was a black market antiquities operation, which was really a cover for cocaine smuggling, which turns out to be a vehicle for anthrax?"

"They're getting sharper," said Wicks.

The agent pointed at the empty clean box on the video monitor. "So what do we do now about this latest statue we just missed?"

Wicks looked up the coast at the twinkling lights of a distant cruise ship. "It's all up to Foxtrot."

SS *SERENDIPITY*

Club Nitro had been cleared of passengers. Sheets covered the front windows. Music off; lights on.

"Must have had too much to drink," said one of the guards. "Acute poisoning."

The ship's doctor shook his head. "No alcohol smell of any kind. And his pupils aren't right."

"But he was falling all over the place, slurring his words."

"That would fit," said the doctor.

"Fit what?"

"He drowned."

"What do you mean 'drowned'? He was breathing and talking."

"Not your run-of-the-mill drowning. This required a lot of help. I'm afraid we have a murderer on the ship."

"Now just a minute!" The ship's spirit director stepped forward. "We can't throw around words like murder and needlessly panic passengers. What do you really have to go on?"

The doctor looked down. "Massive colon and bladder evacuation."

"That's revolting!"

"I put it as delicately as I could."

A junior officer entered the club. "One of the maids just found this sticking out of a trash can near the elevators." He held up a beer bong with frayed strands of duct tape.

"What the heck's that?" asked the spirit director.

"Murder weapon," said the doctor.

The spirit director took a deep breath. "Okay, tell me what you *think* happened. But this is all off the record."

"Hydro-saturation," said the doctor. "Someone forced him to drink massive amounts of water. Probably tied up with the tube taped in his mouth. The whole trick was to pour at a precise, constant rate. Too fast and the stomach can't hold it, gag reflex. Too slow, he just urinates."

"Still, it's just water. How can that kill you?"

"Easier than you'd think. The human body is mostly fluid, billions of cells acting like microscopic water balloons, suspending nuclei and other genetic matter. But too much water and those little balloons swell to bursting point." He pointed at the extremely late Tex McGraw. "Autopsy will find massive cellular rupture in major organs, including the brain. That was the staggering and slurred speech. Utterly excruciating way to go."

"You've heard of cases like this before?"

"Some colleges banned it from fraternity hazing after pledges ended up in emergency rooms. And two disk jockeys accidentally killed a woman in a water-drinking contest for some stupid prize. But this time we've got a complete psychopath."

"Why do you say that?"

"It required at least a couple of sick, methodical hours to pour the water, long enough to take in a movie."

FIFTY-ONE

THREE A.M.

*A*ll quiet on the SS *Serendipity*. Nothing to report except the usual late-night stumbling back to staterooms and a few TVs turned up too loud.

It was peaceful inside Serge's room. The curtains were open, bathing his cabin in the wavy grayscale light of a full moon.

Coleman often slept like the dead; other times he pitched and twisted into different positions for hours, mumbling through a dreamscape of monsters and candy canes. Tonight, all the covers had been kicked off. Coleman lay inverted with his head toward the foot of the bed. The evening's alcohol intake triggered the bathroom urge. His eyes fluttered open.

Someone stood over him.

"Rachael, what are you doing there?" The moonlight sparkled off something in her hand. "Why do you have that knife?"

The blade flashed out. Coleman lifted a forearm in defense. Skin tore across his elbow.

"I'm bleeding!" He looked up from his arm. "Have you lost your mind?"

Rachael clutched the weapon in both fists and raised it over her head. "You killed my sister!"

The knife plunged. Coleman rolled to his right. The blade sliced the mattress where his head had just been.

"Rachael, what the hell are you talking about?"

"Her name was Sharon!"

"Sharon?" The blade came down again. Coleman rolled to his left. Another slash through the sheets. "Wait! Stop! There must be some kind of mistake!"

"There's no mistake. You blabbed everything at the bar. Now you die!"

The knife kept coming down. Coleman kept rolling. "I can explain."

"There's nothing to explain!" Another stabbing attempt, another evasion. Rachael was wired out of her head, providing both strength and inaccuracy. More rolling and slashing.

"Hold still! I want to skull-fuck you with this knife!"

Stab, stab, stab. All misses. Stuffing began coming out of the mattress. Something had to be done about all his squirming. She leaped on top of Coleman and straddled his chest, pinning his shoulders with her knees.

"Time to die!"

With Coleman under control, the rapid flailing of the knife gave way to sadistic toying. "Can't move, eh?" She smiled with evil glee, stroking his cheeks and lips with the sharp steel tip.

"Please! Stop!"

"Where do you want it first? Cut your tongue out? Cram the blade through an eyeball? Slice your nuts off and stuff 'em in that fat disgusting face?"

"Keep going," said Coleman. "Nothing I like yet."

Serge was in the other bed, sleeping on his side facing the window. He stirred from the commotion. "Will you two keep it down? I'm trying to catch some winks."

"Serge!"

"Shut up."

"Help!"

"What now?"

"Rachael's trying to kill me. And I have to pee."

Serge, still groggy. "Why would she want to do that?"

"Her sister was Sharon. She knows we killed her."

Serge rolled over. "Holy Jesus!"

The knife was high above her head for the death thrust.

Serge grabbed the alarm clock off the nightstand. The plug snapped out of the wall. The knife came flying down. Serge whipped the clock. It smacked Rachael in the temple, and she tumbled to the floor. Coleman jumped out of bed, ran in the bathroom and locked the door.

Rachael was up in a heartbeat, turning the knife on Serge with incandescent rage. "Bastard!"

Serge dashed over to the balcony door and opened it. "Bet you can't catch me!" He ran outside.

Rachael gave chase. Just as she crossed the threshold, Serge nailed her in the nose with a brutal elbow. She stumbled backward into the room. Serge advanced and clipped her jaw with a flurry of rabbit punches until she splayed across the carpet. Then he ran back onto the balcony and yanked a Class C fire extinguisher off the bulkhead.

Anyone else would have been unconscious for hours, but Rachael was still zooming on crank. She jumped back to her feet as Serge reentered the cabin. He deflected the knife with the side of the extinguisher, and caught her under the chin with the butt.

She went down again, and Serge pounced. Now it was her turn to get straddled. She bucked like a colt. "Get off me!"

"Nag, nag, nag." He grabbed the extinguisher and forced the nozzle through her lips. She struggled and coughed as he threaded the rubber hose a solid foot down her trachea. Then he covered her entire mouth with his left hand, leaving only enough room between his third and fourth fingers for the hose. More thrashing. Serge made a stiff arm and pushed down on her face with all his strength.

A toilet flushed. Coleman came out of the bathroom. "That feels better." He moseyed over to Serge. "Whatcha doin'?"

"Something I should have a long time ago."

Serge reached with his free hand and pulled the extinguisher's safety pin. "Sweet dreams." He squeezed the lever.

Rachael's chest instantly inflated beneath Serge. Her lungs reached capacity, and the extinguisher's contents raced back up her airway. Twin sprays of foam shot out both nostrils like seltzer bottles.

Serge rolled off her. Rachael jumped up.

"Watch out!" yelled Coleman. "She's got her knife again!"

"Won't do much good now."

She swung the blade erratically at both of them, over and over. They didn't even have to move. Every violent swipe was several feet off the mark, sometimes in the wrong direction. She staggered and twirled, still swinging the knife, crashing into walls and furniture. It didn't seem possible, but her fury actually increased: Rachael couldn't believe she was being irreversibly killed by Serge, and she took out her frustration by attacking the room in general, smashing mirrors, flinging dresser drawers, tipping the mini-fridge.

"Up on the bed!" said Serge. They hopped atop the same mattress for safe viewing as the Tasmanian devil continued its destructive spin through the cabin.

"What's happening?" asked Coleman.

Rachael pirouetted into the bathroom. Crash. A toilet lid flew out the door.

"She's drowning."

"On dry land?"

"A rare treat."

"Rare? But you said that's how you whacked Tex McGraw earlier this evening."

"Different method. Plus you told me about those DJs who already did it. Just fuckin' great. I worked hard on that idea, but nobody will believe it was mine first. So now they make me kill someone else."

"It's not fair."

"But you can't dwell or you'll never be happy."

Rachael came out of the bathroom and began slamming herself against the side of the TV console.

Coleman pointed. "What's she doing now?"

"Trying to pump her own chest." Serge yelled across the room: "Won't work!"

"Why not?" asked Coleman.

"You can pump if it's water. But fire-retardant foam acts on the scientific principal of cohesion. That's why I chose it."

"Co-what?"

"As foam bubbles fizz out, their chemical residue clings to lung walls, clogging brachia, which deliver oxygen to the bloodstream." He nodded toward Rachael, flapping spastically against the entertainment center. "It's all over now except the credits."

She came twirling back through the room, breaking lamps, tearing down curtains. Her eyes rolled back in her head as she lurched out the open balcony door, hit the railing with her pelvis and jackknifed over the side.

Johnny Vegas waited next to lifeboat number five. He grabbed the starboard railing, gazed up at the moon and felt an invigorating wind in his hair.

Rachael flew by a few feet from his face and quickly disappeared beneath the black waves. Johnny bit his lip and went back inside.

PORT OF CALL

*P*assengers streamed out of the ship under a hot morning sun. They hit the dock and hailed cabs for an ambitious bout of tourism in downtown Cozumel.

"What a crazy cruise," said Coleman, wobbling down the gangway. "McGraw and Rachael are both dead."

"I know," said Serge. "That eliminates the two major obstacles to truly appreciating travel: mortal danger and bullshit. Now we can enjoy ourselves."

They reached the dock and headed north; the Diaz Brothers arrived from the south and headed up the gangway. They produced stolen ID at the hatch, and Tommy Diaz set a shopping bag on the X-ray belt.

"What do we do now?" asked Benito.

A screener handed Tommy his bag with a small statue. "Check our e-mail."

They took an elevator to the main lobby.

Three more men with stolen credentials came up the ramp.

"Why are we taking this cruise?"

"Because I don't trust those stinking Diaz Brothers," said the lead tunic.

"Seemed okay to me."

"They're either traitors or fools. Either way I'm not taking the chance."

"What are you going to do?"

"We let them take care of Foxtrot. If they don't, we let them lead us to Foxtrot, and then *we* take care of Foxtrot. Then we take care of the stinking Diaz Brothers. No loose ends."

"But they have the statue."

"I gave them an empty one." He set his own shopping bag on the X-ray belt.

Three floors up, Tommy Diaz tapped a keyboard in the Internet Café. "Here it is." He opened an e-mail and clicked a hot link to a rudimentary website. He scrolled down and stopped. He logged off the computer.

"You got the name?" asked Rafael.

Tommy nodded. He headed across the atrium lobby to the ship's information desk. A short conversation. The woman behind the desk cheerfully looked something up. Then Tommy dashed toward a flight of stairs, and the others followed.

"What cabin?" asked Benito.

Tommy checked door numbers. "U115." They reached the next corridor. "There it is."

"Someone's coming out," said Rafael.

"Act inconspicuous."

They pretended to be opening another cabin door. The person from U115 smiled as he went by. They watched him turn the corner.

"Let's go," said Tommy. They followed their target up to the pool deck.

"You sure he's the right person?" asked Benito.

"Positive. I checked the name from the website at the information desk. Only one Davenport registered on this ship."

"Wasn't that the name on the scrap of paper we found in Bodine's trailer?"

"The same," said Tommy. "Now it all fits together. It

wasn't some random rip-off. A government agent's been onto our operation the whole time."

They continued tailing Jim.

"But he doesn't look anything like some super-dangerous agent," said Rafael. "He looks like a wimp."

"Don't be fooled," said Tommy. "I've read about these guys. Anyone can possess physical strength, but it takes an ultra-rare psychological makeup. They're the people you'd least suspect."

"Look, he's being insulted by those bodybuilders at the pool. He's just taking it."

"Fits the stuff I read," said Tommy. "These guys thrive on intense pressure. That's when they're like ice. But back in the real world, many are understimulated and can't function. Some become hyper-irritable and blow their temper at the least thing. Others go the opposite way and withdraw into a passive shell."

"Those kids are hitting him with squirt guns."

"Just keep your eyes open," said Tommy. "He might have a backup team."

Over on the mainland, Serge strolled past a quaint row of Cozumel shops. He suddenly stopped and spun around on the sidewalk. Six men in tropical shirts scattered and looked at postcards.

He began walking again. "Who *are* those guys?"

Every ten feet, people standing in doorways: *"Like Cuban cigars? . . . " "Cuban cigars here . . . "*

"Coleman, hurry up. We need to get back to the ship."

"Wait a second."

"But you've stopped in every single pharmacy asking if they have 'the good stuff.' "

"I like to shop."

A satellite phone vibrated. Foxtrot read the encrypted text message. A pair of three-man teams had just come aboard:

the Diaz Brothers, who'd been under surveillance for the last week, and a previously undetected cell the brothers had been observed with outside Cancún. It wasn't known which had the statue. . . . Oh, and your cover might be blown.

Foxtrot deleted the message and headed for the Veranda Deck.

Serge and Coleman returned to their cabin. Now that Jim was safe from McGraw, Serge could relax on his bed with a Travis McGee novel about a cruise ship.

Coleman tried tuning his spherical TV but only got grainy Spanish stations. "I'm bored."

Serge turned a page. "Read a book."

"Then I'll be more bored."

"I'm trying to read."

"What are you reading?"

Serge closed *Darker Than Amber* in frustration and went over to his DVD player.

"What are you watching?" asked Coleman.

"Yellow Submarine."

The TV showed a series of strange creatures opening and closing doors, darting across a long hallway.

Coleman picked up his round television. "I think I'll go out."

"Good."

Coleman left the cabin and began walking down a long hallway, people opening and closing doors. He was still fiddling with his TV when he came to a cleaning cart and a half-open door. He took a step inside. "Helllooooo? Anyone home?" The maid wasn't there. Good. He'd done this a million times. The cleaning crew couldn't possibly know every person in every room. If the maid returned, he'd just act cool like it was his own cabin. Then, ever so nonchalantly, he'd leave with the valuables.

Coleman closed the door and went to the dresser. He quickly found a watch, some rings and loose currency.

The maid returned.

"This really is my room! I didn't take anything!" He ran out the door.

The Diaz Brothers continued surveillance of Jim Davenport, now beneath the waterslide.

"What's he doing?" asked Benito.

"Looks like they're setting up for a wedding."

"Wedding?"

"I don't like the feel of this," said Tommy.

"Think we have the wrong guy?"

"No, we have the right guy," said Tommy. "I'm just having strong second thoughts about our friends from Cancún. I don't think they're who they claim to be."

"Why's that?"

"Their website. MyJihadSpace.com."

"What are you going to do?"

Tommy walked to a railing with his shopping bag and removed the statue. It splashed into the sea. "Deal's off."

"Uh-oh," said Rafael. "We have visitors."

"Who?"

Rafael tilted his head toward the other side of the deck, where three men in tunics tried to conceal themselves behind a faux tiki hut.

"What are they doing here?" asked Benito.

"A double cross," said Tommy. "That's the last straw. We may be smugglers, but we're still Americans!"

"What are you going to do?"

"Warn Davenport."

"Look, he's leaving."

"Probably heading back to his cabin. This is our chance."

Three men behind a tiki hut watched the Diaz Brothers

follow Jim across the deck and into a stairwell. The leader smiled.

"Why are you so happy?"

"They just told us who Foxtrot is."

Coleman had found another cleaning cart outside an open door. He rummaged through luggage.

Across the hall, another person stepped up to a door. The magnetic room key was different. It had a pair of wires running to a handheld device that looked like a department store inventory scanner. Digital numbers tumbled in the device's display. They stopped. A red light turned green. The person darted inside. A swift, professional search promptly yielded a dusty Mayan statue wrapped in a bath towel.

A maid arrived at a cabin and swiped her magnetic key. She opened the door and found Coleman going through a handbag.

"It really is my purse!" He ran out the door.

Coleman safely made it to the next level. He walked up the hall, changing channels on his round TV. *"Buenos . . . "* Another cleaning cart. U115. He went inside.

Coleman set his TV on the dresser and began checking all the usual places. Slim pickin's. He scooped a handful of dimes and nickels off a counter. Someone began fumbling with the doorknob. "Uh-oh." He ran to a corner and covered himself with a discarded bedspread that lay in a bunch.

The blanket quaked as someone moved through the cabin. It sounded like they went in the bathroom. Coleman peeked from under the bedspread. They *were* in the bathroom. He threw the covers off and ran out the door without closing it.

He raced around the corner and crashed into three Latin men wearing white linen suits. He took off again.

"Watch where the fuck you're going!" Rafael shouted down the hall.

"Forget him," said Tommy. "We have to find Davenport."

"How'd we lose him?"

"Because he's good. Let's check his cabin."

They turned the corner. U115.

"The door's open," said Benito.

Rafael stuck his head inside. "Hellllooo? Jim Davenport?" He came back out. "Nobody's home."

Tommy thought a moment. "Okay, we can go running around the ship and risk missing Davenport if he comes back. Or we can wait here and risk him running into our friends from Cancún." He squinted in thought, then nodded. "We wait here."

They went inside and closed the door.

Benito sat on a bed. "But even if we take care of Davenport, what about Cancún?"

"I've got my own plans for them," said Tommy. "They messed with the wrong Diaz Brothers . . ."

An undetected person in the bathroom quietly hid a towel-wrapped statue beneath the sink. Then a discreet hand slipped out of the bathroom and reached for a switch on the wall.

"Hey!" yelled Rafael. "Who turned off the lights?"

The action was efficiently merciless. Blazing-fast hands and feet.

Minutes later, the Diaz Brothers awoke in a pile in the hall.

FIFTY-THREE

ONE HOUR BEFORE SUNSET

Cabin U115.

Martha straightened Debbie's veil for the twentieth time. "Jim, doesn't our daughter look beautiful?"

Jim looked curiously at something on the dresser. A spherical TV. He turned it on. *"Buenos . . . "*

"Jim!"

"What?"

"Our daughter!"

"Debbie, you look beautiful."

"I think I'm going to cry," said Martha.

Jim smoothed out his tux. "I'll check on the caterers."

"Debbie," said Martha. "Your veil's crooked."

"Mom!"

Jim arrived on the pool deck. Hundreds of chairs had already been set up. He walked over to someone unfolding more seats in the back row.

"Don't we already have enough chairs?"

"No." More unfolding. "We always do this for weddings."

"Do what?"

"Like when a restaurant gets the whole room to sing 'Happy Birthday' for a complete stranger. The ship made a special announcement inviting everyone to the wedding."

"But we already agreed on the price. I don't think I can afford—"

"Complimentary."

"Wow," said Jim. "That's awfully nice of you."

"No, it's not." Another chair unfolded. "We sell more drinks, make a fortune."

The preacher showed up, then Trevor.

"Holy smokes!" said Jim. "What happened to your face?"

"Don't want to talk about it."

They kept arriving: the best man, ring girl, ushers, DJ, florist with a $500 magnolia trellis-arch, two extra bartenders and a rolling ice chest of Bud and Bud Lite in the new unbreakable plastic bottles.

One floor below, Serge entered the dining hall. "Coleman, where are you? We're going to be late for the wedding!" He reached the back of the restaurant; Coleman was sitting alone in a corner booth with six entrées.

Getting close now. The sun was a half hour from the horizon. Chairs began to fill: Midwesterners, New Englanders, spring-breakers, radio station winners, retired machinists, budding salesmen, blackballed labor organizers, the G-Unit, Steelers fans, clowns, mimes, the Diaz Brothers, the Brimleys, the *Backup* Backup Team, Gaylord Wainscotting, Serge, Coleman, Agent Foxtrot, Johnny Vegas and three men from Cancún.

"I don't understand what could have happened to our statue," said one of the tunics. "We searched the entire room."

The leader groused. "Foxtrot is what happened."

Finally, everyone was in place, the deck bathed in that magnificent golden glow when the sun is at the perfect angle. All the guests hummed with anticipation of Debbie's entrance.

Almost all. The Diaz Brothers watched the tunics; the tunics glared at the Diaz Brothers; Trevor and Wainscotting sneered at Serge; six men in tropical shirts eyed Trevor and

Wainscotting; Steelers fans followed an important game on small pocket TVs; Johnny Vegas winked at the maid of honor.

Someone cued the DJ. He inserted a CD. *"Here comes the bride . . . "*

The audience turned around. Jim swelled with pride as he escorted his daughter under the waterslide.

They reached the front. Everyone hushed. Trevor stepped up next to Debbie.

The preacher began reading the usual. Blah, blah, blah. Mimes dabbed their eyes. They finally got to the part: ". . . speak now or forever hold your peace . . ."

Tunics jumped up. "Foxtrot!"

Diaz Brothers jumped up. "Jim, look out!"

Wainscotting jumped up. "Serge, you son of a bitch!"

Steelers fans jumped up. "Touchdown!"

Tropical shirts jumped up. "Nobody move!"

Serge jumped up, pointed over the starboard side and pumped a fist. "Rogue wave! Yessssss!"

No time to prepare. The rogue wave was only a sixty-footer but closing at a wicked ninety miles per hour. It hit the *Serendipity* broadside, flooding the bow and splashing over the gunwales. Screaming passengers slid fast across the deck, vainly clawing wood. Fuel and hydraulic lines ruptured. Explosions, fires. It looked like the wedding would have to be postponed.

The ship listed thirty degrees and slowly came back. The deck was level again. People lay in shock, surprised they were still alive with just bruises and the occasional broken arm. They began climbing out from under pool furniture. Alarms clanged everywhere. Thanks to carefully rehearsed safety drills, people ran the wrong way and fought over life preservers.

Amid the chaos, several pairs of eyes locked in polygonal matrix: Jim Davenport, the Diaz Brothers, three tunics, six tropical shirts, Gaylord Wainscotting, Trevor and Serge.

"Davenport!" yelled Tommy Diaz. "Come with us. You're in danger. . . ."

"Jim!" yelled Serge. "Don't listen to him. Come with me. . . ."

Jim took off running. Everyone scampered down a flight of stairs, then another, and another. The Riviera Deck was ankle deep in water that had gushed through shattered portholes. Jim splashed his way toward the bow, and the others followed. At midship, the lights flickered, then went out for good, plunging the passageway into darkness. Everyone caught up with one another, and the fists began to fly.

It was pathetic. Off-the-mark punches on the wrong people, hair-pulling, kicking.

Then: different-sounding pugilism. Deliberate, precise. A new person at the party? Or somebody already there?

Everything changed at once. Agent Foxtrot spun through the hall, a martial arts tornado. Loud snapping, desperate shouts. It was over in moments. Voices silenced. Emergency lights came on. The floor was littered with unconscious Diaz Brothers and three men from Cancún. Jim and Serge were left standing without a scratch, along with a half dozen men in tropical shirts.

One of them grabbed Serge by his arm. "You're not safe here. . . ."

"Who *are* you guys?"

Calm had been restored topside. The ship was in no danger of foundering, but all engines remained stopped as a precaution until the Coast Guard could arrive to inspect structural integrity. Everyone had to keep their life preservers on. The Florida coast sat tantalizingly close on the horizon. Crankiness replaced terror. Drinks on the house.

Four decks below, a man in a gleaming white uniform had a magnum of Dom Pérignon in one hand and a bridesmaid in the other.

"I'll save you," said Johnny.

"I think everything's okay now."

"They just said that to avoid panic."

"What's the champagne for?"

Johnny stopped and broke the seal on an orange fiberglass drum. He dragged out a large rubber bundle, pulled a lanyard and threw it over the side. A round, twelve-foot raft inflated. Johnny stepped over the rail. "Come on . . ."

"I don't know."

"Trust me. I have a captain's uniform."

With the bars open again, the mood turned festive. Someone started an impromptu limbo contest, which the G-Unit won by simply walking upright under the bar.

The Coast Guard arrived and gave the *Serendipity* a clean bill of health. Miraculously, only minor injuries were reported, with the notable exception of three passengers from Cancún discovered in a lower hallway with fatally snapped necks, which were attributed to freak falls when the wave hit. Engines restarted. Serge circled the pool. "Coleman? Coleman, where are you?"

He walked around the smokestacks to the afterdeck, where Coleman staggered toward the stern, juggling three drinks.

"Coleman!"

Coleman came in two distinct flavors: drunk, and free-liquor drunk.

He was weaving all over the deck, bouncing off bulkheads and lifeboats.

"Coleman!"

He turned around, stumbling backward. "Hey, Serge. They're giving away booze!"

"Watch out!"

"Wha—"

Coleman hit the railing with the small of his back and flipped overboard. Serge took off in a mad dash, executing a perfect swan as he dove in the water after him.

EPILOGUE

*A*gent Foxtrot received another unofficial commendation for a mission that never existed. The terror cell from Cancún had been singlehandedly eliminated, and the bioweapon statue recovered. Next mission: Find the other statue that had reached the mainland a month earlier and went missing following the death of Bodine Biffle in a grisly railroad incident.

During the boredom of waiting for the Coast Guard to give an all-clear, the G-Unit struck up conversations with the Brimleys and decided they weren't so bad after all. The women had since entered into long-term relationships, grew to like everything about the guys, and were currently in the process of trying to change them.

Gaylord Wainscotting was successfully treated for depression and took a job as a waiter with his former country club's catering division. —

He currently balanced a silver tray and circulated through an open-house gala on Lobster Lane organized by a local real estate company.

The Davenports were moving again. Too much excitement. The only reason to stay in Tampa had been Debbie moving in nearby with Trevor. But now the wedding was permanently off after Trevor had used Debbie as a human shield during the rogue wave against incoming chairs and tables tumbling across the deck.

"Jim! Martha!" Steph rushed across the room. "Congratulations! They accepted your counteroffer."

"That was fast," said Martha.

"So I guess you're going to be in the market for a new home," said Steph. "What do you think about this place?"

"We just sold it," said Jim.

"Great investment potential," said Steph. "You saw how quickly it moved."

"I—"

"Let me see if I can catch the buyers before they leave."

Martha turned slowly in the middle of the living room. "I think I'm actually going to miss it here."

"You aren't changing your mind?" said Jim.

"Absolutely not."

She stared idly at a statue on the mantel. She stopped. "Jim, remember that night you went out with your support group? What actually happened?"

"You didn't want me to break confidentiality."

"Now I do."

So Jim told her the whole story: Serge, Bodine Biffle's trailer, everything.

Martha looked back at the mantel with disbelief. She went in the bathroom, closed the door and punched a number into an encrypted satellite phone. "This is Foxtrot . . ."

Johnny Vegas survived.

He washed ashore with a maid of honor the morning after the rogue wave. They would have been rescued sooner, but Johnny had turned off the raft's emergency positioning transmitter and lied about it.

Shortly after drifting away from the ship, Johnny reclined in the raft like James Bond with the babe and bottle of champagne.

The maid of honor had warmed to Johnny's dashing features, and she nuzzled into his side.

Johnny grabbed the magnum. "So how are we going to occupy ourselves until they rescue us?"

"I can think of something," she said with mischief.

Johnny strained to pop the cork. Just before it flew, he heard splashing in the water behind him. Serge swam toward them, dragging Coleman by the neck of his shirt. He hooked an arm over the edge of the raft and pulled himself up with a smile. "Got room for two more?"

They bobbed along. The sun began to set. Rich, magenta hues. Couldn't have been more romantic.

Johnny lay staring up at the sky, his head sagging backward over the edge of the raft.

The maid of honor sat across from him, snuggling into Serge and stroking his chest. "You're really under contract with a movie studio?"

Coleman tapped Johnny's shoulder and pointed at the bottle. "You going to drink that?"

They drifted into the sunset.

"I got an idea," said Serge. "We should sing."

The raft slowly became a dot on the ever-darkening horizon.

"*. . . There's got to be a morning after . . .* Shula!"

The World Wide Web just got a lot wilder:
Serge goes on-line and discovers a world (almost)
as sordid as his own, in *New York Times* bestselling
author Tim Dorsey's latest…

Nuclear JELLYFISH

Available 2009

Somewhere in cyberspace

*F*irst off, fuck the word Blog. I hate it and all who use it. "Lol," "imo," "Today's mood: Introspective yet ambivalent." Just shut up. The Internet was supposed to become the ultimate democratic forum. It did: Now everyone can be a porn star. Then there are these retarded blogs. It's been said that inside every life is a fascinating book, or at least a chapter. Wrong. Some people don't have a freakin' semicolon, like that woman in Delray who blogs everything her cat does, and her cat even has a blog and every word is meow. But you have to play the hand you're dealt, and I can't exactly stand on street corners with a megaphone sharing my Big Answers on Everything. That was my first choice, but a monkey wrench hit the works: a few itsy-bitsy little incidents. *Murder* is such a charged word. You know how some people fixate and won't let things go? They're called cops.

So I guess I should be thankful for the Internet. Especially since my newly launched travel advisory service demands the latest cutting-edge communication technology! Who better to guide you around my fine state? Right, I know what you're thinking: "Serge, without delay, give me an example with more value than I could expect to find elsewhere!" Okay, if you're staying at a budget motel that has *mandatory* daily maid service, they have a meth lab problem. Or I can tell you how to extract yourself from the wrong bar with only a paper clip and a ballpoint pen. And if you've ever seen a motel room scanned with one of those ultraviolet semen cams, your head would never hit another pillow. Does William Shatner provide this kind of biting insight? I think we both know the answer. Before I debuted this blog, I applied to all the big established Internet travel sites, but they said they didn't think their clients were interested in how to pick hookers who wouldn't take all their credit cards. I said, "Look, you can spend the rest of your days scrapping it out in the web site ghetto, or you can make the roaming gnome your bitch." I think there's something wrong with my phone because the line kept going dead at that point. So until I get proper sponsorship, I'm forced to put up my own wildcat site. Did I mention it's totally free? What a bargain! Let's get to it!

Serge's definition of total happiness: Florida, a full tank of gas and no appointments.

Except all the jerks down here keep making appointments with me. What are you gonna do? Someone has to instruct them. But as I always say, if you love your work, it's not really work. My psychiatrist disagrees of course, because she wants me to take meds for my ADD and OCD. I said, but those are the most important selling points on a travel writer's resume. We notice *everything*: bridge weight limits, discarded rolls of carpet padding, beached livestock skulls, plywood signs for pond demolition, bus stop benches advertising discount vasectomies, billboards for laser hair removal with "before" pictures of chicks with mustaches, witty country church marquees where Jesus battles Satan with puns, dilapidated rural homes with a baffling number of disabled school buses in the backyard, and malfunctioning brake lights on the car up ahead where the hostage in the trunk ripped out wiring. Then my shrink asks about the manic-depression. I say I'm never depressed. She says, what about when you beat up jerks? I say I'm happy then, too.

I decided to start this service because everyone is always coming up to me and saying, "Serge, you should start a travel service." They actually say, "What the fuck's your problem?" But I can read between the lines. I'm constantly seeing clueless Europeans with pasty legs stumbling around the wrong motels, and I shake my head. Yep, they're going to get robbed. So I run up to them and say they're going to get robbed. Then I say, not me, put your hands down. Now they're not thinking straight and don't listen when I explain that tanning those legs would cut their homicide target rate in half. But they'd already know that if they subscribed to Serge's Florida Experience! (Free!)

From the Mailbag: "Hey Serge, how did Florida become Dirtbag Central"? Because if you pass out in the snow, you die.

Hold the phone. Speaking of passing out, Coleman wants to give a travel tip. "Don't buy any coke from Rico. It's stomped on." Coleman, that's not a travel tip . . . . No, it's not . . . No, I'm won't help you get your money back . . . . Anyhoo, where was I? Weirdness. Florida has such a rarefied per capita concentration that CNN might as well be the local news. Some guy shot a Wendy's manager over the restaurant's three sauce-packet limit; alligator attacks naked guy on crack doing backstrokes in retention culvert; driver falls out of car at forty-five miles an hour opening door to spit, smuggler makes it through airport security with monkey under his hat. And if something *does* happen in another state, it's just a matter of time for the Florida shoe to drop. You say some criminal Rhodes scholar stole Crystal Gayle's tour bus in Tennessee? Gee, where on earth might he head next?

Today's Tip: A three sauce-packet limit is wrong. But pulling a gun is just as wrong. Go to Arby's instead. They understand packet dynamics.

To the Mailbag! . . . Uh-oh. It's Agent Mahoney. "I'm going to get you." What a broken record. Mahoney blames me for *everything*, especially the stuff I've done. To compound it, there's been a recent spike in businessmen mugged at hotels by highly organized crews. And now someone's going after the robbers. So Mahoney naturally thinks it's me, just because I happened to be at all the same places at the same time. I wish it was me (lol).

Mahoney, Mahoney, Mahoney . . . maybe that explains this nagging sensation I've been having lately, like something really bad's about to happen. Can't quite put my finger on it. And I'm not the superstitious type, which is why I don't like superstitious people. They're bad luck. But everyone's number eventually comes up, and I've already skated through more than my share of tough jams. So just block it out. Enough negative thoughts! I hate them. They suck. They piss me off. I'm so angry at negative thoughts! If they were people, I'd get a chainsaw and . . . You're still doing it. Have to bear down. Concentrate: Appreciate God's gift of this beautiful day where the Florida sun is shining and my gas tank's full. Now I'm so happy I could burst! Off we go!

Comic tales of Florida murder and mayhem

by TIM DORSEY

THE STINGRAY SHUFFLE
978-0-06-055693-8

When serial-killing local Florida historian Serge A. Storms is off his meds, no one is safe—especially when $5 million in cash is involved.

TRIGGERFISH TWIST
978-0-06-103155-7

Ensconced in a lovely tropical villa, Jim Davenport anticipates the good life to come—but the neighborhood is not quite what it seems.

ORANGE CRUSH
978-0-06-103154-0

Unthreatening Florida governor-by-default Marlon Conrad is a shoo-in for re-election, until he undergoes a radical personality shift during military action in the Balkans.

HAMMERHEAD RANCH MOTEL
978-0-380-73234-0

Visitors come well armed to the Hammerhead Ranch Motel, because there's a different schemer or slimeball lurking behind every door.

FLORIDA ROADKILL
978-0-380-73233-3

A handful of people are about to cross paths with a suitcase filled with five million dollars in stolen insurance money, and all of them want it.